'Lena Rivers

Mary J. Holmes

Contents

'LENA RIVERS

BY

Mary J. Holmes

PREFACE.

If it be true, as some have said, that a secret *is safer in a* preface *than else-where, it would be worse than folly for me to waste the "midnight oil," in the manufacture of an article which no one would read, and which would serve no purpose, save the adding of a page or so to a volume perhaps al-ready too large. But I do not think so.* I *wot of a few who, with a horror of anything savoring of* humbug, wade industriously through a preface, be it never so lengthy, hoping therein to find the moral, without which the story would, of course, be valueless. To such I would say, seek no further, for though I claim for "'Lena Rivers," a moral--yes, half a dozen morals, if you please--I shall not put them in the preface, as I prefer having them sought after, for what I have written I wish to have read.

Reared among the rugged hills of the Bay State, and for a time constantly associated with a class of people known the wide world over as Yankees, it is no more than natural that I should often write of the places and scenes with which I have been the most familiar. In my delineations of New England character I have aimed to copy from memory, and in no one instance, I believe, have I overdrawn the pictures; for among the New England mountains there lives many a "Grandma Nichols," a "Joel Slocum," or a "Nancy Scovandyke," while the wide world holds more than one 'Lena, with her high temper, extreme beauty, and rare combination of those qualities which make the female character so lovely.

Nearly the same remarks will also apply to my portraitures of Kentucky life and character, for it has been my good fortune to spend a year and a half in that state, and in my descriptions of country lanes and country life, I have with a few exceptions copied from what I saw. Mrs. Livingstone *and* Mrs. Graham *are characters found everywhere, while the impulsive* John Jr., and the generous-hearted Durward, represent a class of individuals who belong more exclusively to the "sunny south."

I have endeavored to make this book both a good and an interesting one, and if I have failed in my attempt, it is too late to remedy it now; and, such as it is, I give it to the world, trusting that the same favor and forbearance which have been awarded to my other works, will also be extended to this.

M. J. H.

BROCKPORT, N. Y., October, 1856.

CHAPTER I.
'LENA.

For many days the storm continued. Highways were blocked up, while roads less frequented were rendered wholly impassable. The oldest inhabitants of Oakland had "never seen the like before," and they shook their gray heads ominously as over and adown the New England mountains the howling wind swept furiously, now shrieking exultingly as one by one the huge forest trees bent before its power, and again dying away in a low, sad wail, as it shook the casement of some low-roofed cottage, where the blazing fire, "high piled upon the hearth," danced merrily to the sound of the storm-wind, and then, whirling in fantastic circles, disappeared up the broad-mouthed chimney.

For nearly a week there was scarcely a sign of life in the streets of Oakland, but at the end of that time the storm abated, and the December sun, emerging from its dark hiding-place, once more looked smilingly down upon the white, untrodden snow, which covered the earth for miles and miles around. Rapidly the roads were broken; paths were made on the narrow sidewalk, and then the villagers bethought themselves of their mountain neighbors, who might perchance have suffered from the severity of the storm. Far up the mountain side in an old yellow farmhouse, which had withstood the blasts of many a winter, lived Grandfather and Grandmother Nichols, as they were familiarly called, and ere the sun-setting, arrangements were made for paying them a visit.

Oakland was a small rural village, nestled among rocky hills, where the word fashion was seldom heard, and where many of the primitive customs of our forefathers still prevailed. Consequently, neither the buxom maidens, nor the hale old matrons, felt in the least disgraced as they piled promiscuously upon the four-ox sled, which erelong was moving slowly through the mammoth drifts which lay upon the mountain road. As they drew near the farmhouse, they noticed that the blue paper curtains which shaded the windows of Grandma Nichols' "spare room," were rolled up, while the faint glimmer of a tallow candle within, indicated that the room possessed an occupant. Who could it be? Possibly it was John, the proud man, who lived in Kentucky, and who, to please his wealthy bride exchanged the plebeian name of Nichols, for that of Livingstone, which his high-born lady fancied was more aristocratic in its sounding!

"And if it be John," said the passengers of the ox sled, with whom that gentleman was no great favorite, "if it be John, we'll take ourselves home as fast as ever we can."

Satisfied with this resolution, they kept on their way until they reached the wide gateway, where they were met by Mr. Nichols, whose greeting they fancied was less cordial than usual. With a simple "how d'ye do," he led the way into the spacious kitchen, which answered the treble purpose of dining-room, sitting-room, and cook-room. Grandma Nichols, too, appeared somewhat disturbed, but she met her visitors with an air which seemed to say, she was determined to make the best of her trouble, whatever it might be.

The door of the "spare room" was slightly ajar, and while the visitors were disrobing, one young girl, more curious than the rest, peered cautiously in, exclaiming as she did so, "Mother! mother! Helena is in there on the bed, pale as a ghost."

"Yes, Heleny is in there," interrupted Grandma Nichols, who overheard the girl's remark. "She got hum the fust night of the storm, and what's queerer than all, she's been married better than a year."

"Married! Married! Helena married! Who to? Where's her husband?" asked a dozen voices in the same breath.

Grandfather Nichols groaned as if in pain, and his wife, glancing anxiously toward the door of her daughter's room, said in reply to the last question, "That's the worst on't. He was some grand rascal, who lived at the suthard, and come up here to see what he could do. He thought Heleny was handsome, I s'pose, and married her, making her keep it still because his folks in Car'lina wouldn't like it. Of course he got sick of her, and jest afore the baby was born he gin her five hundred dollars and left her."

A murmur of surprise ran round the room, accompanied with a look of incredulity, which Grandma Nichols quickly divined, and while her withered cheek crimsoned at the implied disgrace, she added in an elevated tone of voice, "It's true as the Bible. Old Father Blanchard's son, that used to preach here, married them, and Heleny brought us a letter from him, saying it was true. Here 'tis,--read it yourselves, if you don't b'lieve me;" and she drew from a side drawer a letter, on the back of which, the villagers recognized the well remembered handwriting of their former pastor.

This proof of Helena's innocence was hardly relished by the clever gossips of Oakland, for the young girl, though kind-hearted and gentle, was far too beautiful to be a general favorite. Mothers saw in her a rival for their daughters, while the daughters looked enviously upon her clear white brow, and shining chestnut hair; which fell in wavy curls about her neck and shoulders. Two years before our story opens, she had left her mountain home to try the mysteries of millinery in the city, where a distant relative of her mother was living. Here her uncommon beauty attracted much attention, drawing erelong to her side a wealthy young southerner, who, just freed from the restraints of college life, found it vastly agreeable making love to the fair Helena. Simple-minded, and wholly unused to the ways of the world, she believed each word he said, and when at last he proposed marriage, she not only consented, but also promised to keep it a secret for a time, until he could in a measure reconcile his father, who he feared might disinherit him for wedding a penniless bride.

"Wait, darling, until he knows you," said he, "and then he will gladly welcome you as his daughter."

Accordingly, one dark, wintry night, when neither moon nor stars were visible, Helena stole softly from her quiet room at Mrs. Warren's, and in less than an hour was the lawful bride of Harry Rivers, the wife of the clergyman alone witnessing the ceremony.

"I wish I could take you home at once," said young Rivers, who was less a rascal than a coward; "I wish I could take you home at once, but it cannot be. We must wait awhile."

So Helena went back to Mrs. Warren's, where for a few weeks she stayed, and then saying she was going home, she left and became the mistress of a neat little cottage which stood a mile or two from the city. Here for several months young

Rivers devoted himself entirely to her happiness, seeming to forget that there was aught else in the world save his "beautiful 'Lena," as he was wont to call her. But at last there came a change. Harry seemed sad, and absent-minded, though ever kind to Helena, who strove in vain to learn the cause of his uneasiness.

One morning when, later than usual, she awoke, she missed him from her side; and on the table near her lay a letter containing the following:--

"Forgive me, darling, that I leave you so abruptly. Circumstances render it neccessary, but be assured, I shall come back again. In the mean time, you had better return to your parents, where I will seek you. Enclosed are five hundred dollars, enough for your present need. Farewell.

"H. RIVERS."

There was one bitter cry of hopeless anguish, and when Helena Rivers again awoke to perfect consciousness, she lay in a darkened room, soft footsteps passed in and out, kind faces, in which were mingled pity and reproach, bent anxiously over her, while at her side lay a little tender thing, her infant daughter, three weeks old. And now there arose within her a strong desire to see once more her childhood's home, to lay her aching head upon her mother's lap, and pour out the tale of grief which was crushing the life from out her young heart.

As soon, therefore, as her health would permit, she started for Oakland, taking the precaution to procure from the clergyman, who had married her, a letter confirming the fact. Wretched and weary she reached her home at the dusk of evening, and with a bitter cry fell fainting in the arms of her mother, who having heard regularly from her, never dreamed that she was elsewhere than in the employ of Mrs. Warren. With streaming eyes and trembling hands the old man and his wife made ready the spare room for the wanderer more than once blessing the fearful storm which for a time, at least, would keep away the prying eyes of those who, they feared, would hardly credit their daughter's story.

And their fears were right, for many of those who visited them on the night of which we have spoken, disbelieved the tale, mentally pronouncing the clergyman's letter a forgery, got up by Helena to deceive her parents. Consequently, of the few who from time to time came to the old farmhouse, nearly all were actuated by motives of curiosity, rather than by feelings of pity for the young girl-mother, who, though feeling their neglect, scarcely heeded it. Strong in the knowledge of her own innocence, she lay day after day, watching and waiting for one who never came. But at last, as days glided into weeks, and weeks into months, hope died away, and turning wearily upon her pillow, she prayed that she might die; and when the days grew bright and gladsome in the warm spring sun, when the snow was melted from off the mountain tops, and the first robin's note was heard by the farmhouse door, Helena laid her baby on her mother's bosom, and without a murmur glided down the dark, broad river, whose deep waters move onward and onward, but never return.

When it was known in Oakland that Helena was dead, there came a reaction, and those who had been loudest in their condemnation, were now the first to hasten forward with offers of kindness and words of sympathy. But neither tears nor regrets could recall to life the fair young girl, who, wondrously beautiful even in death, slept calmly in her narrow coffin, a smile of sadness wreathing her lips, as if her last prayer had been for one who had robbed her thus early of happiness and life. In the bright green valley at the foot of the mountain, they buried her, and the old father, as he saw the damp earth fall upon her grave, asked that he too might die. But his wife, younger by several years, prayed to live--live that she might protect and care for the little orphan, who first by its young mother's tears, and again by the waters of the baptismal fountain, was christened HELENA RIVERS;--the 'Lena of our story.

CHAPTER II.
JOHN.

Ten years of sunlight and shadow have passed away, and the little grave at the foot of the mountain is now grass-grown and sunken. Ten times have the snows of winter fallen upon the hoary head of Grandfather Nichols, bleaching his thin locks to their own whiteness and bending his sturdy frame, until now, the old man lay dying--dying in the same blue-curtained room, where years agone his only daughter was born, and where ten years before she had died. Carefully did Mrs. Nichols nurse him, watching, weeping, and praying that he might live, while little 'Lena gladly shared her grandmother's vigils, hovering ever by the bedside of her grandfather, who seemed more quiet when her soft hand smoothed his tangled hair or wiped the cold moisture from his brow. The villagers, too, remembering their neglect, when once before death had brooded over the mountain farmhouse, now daily came with offers of assistance.

But one thing still was wanting. John, their only remaining child, was absent, and the sick man's heart grew sad and his eyes dim with tears, as day by day went by, and still he did not come. Several times had 'Lena written to her uncle, apprising him of his father's danger, and once only had he answered. It was a brief, formal letter, written, evidently, under some constraint, but it said that he was coming, and with childish joy the old man had placed it beneath his pillow, withdrawing it occasionally for 'Lena to read again, particularly the passage, "Dear father, I am sorry you are sick."

"Heaven bless him! I know he's sorry," Mr. Nichols would say. "He was always a good boy--is a good boy now. Ain't he, Martha?"

And mother-like, Mrs. Nichols would answer, "Yes," forcing back the while the tears which would start when she thought how long the "good boy" had ne-

glected them, eighteen years having elapsed since he had crossed the threshold of
his home.

With his hand plighted to one of the village maidens, he had left Oakland to
seek his fortune, going first to New York, then to Ohio, and finally wending his
way southward, to Kentucky. Here he remained, readily falling into the luxurious
habits of those around him, and gradually forgetting the low-roofed farmhouse far
away to the northward, where dwelt a gray-haired pair and a beautiful young girl,
his parents and his sister. She to whom his vows were plighted was neither graceful
nor cultivated, and when, occasionally, her tall, spare figure and uncouth manners
arose before him, in contrast with the fair forms around him, he smiled derisively
at the thoughts of making her his wife.

About this time there came from New Orleans a wealthy invalid, with his only
daughter Matilda. She was a proud haughty girl, whose disposition, naturally una-
miable, was rendered still worse by a disappointment from which she was suffering.
Accidentally Mr. Richards, her father, made the acquaintance of John Nichols, conceiving for him a violent fancy, and finally securing him as a constant companion.
For several weeks John appeared utterly oblivious to the presence of Matilda who,
accustomed to adulation, began at last to feel piqued at his neglect, and to strive in
many ways to attract his attention.

John, who was ambitious, met her advances more than half way, and finally,
encouraged by her father, offered her his heart and hand. Under other circumstances, Matilda would undoubtedly have spurned him with contempt; but having
heard that her recreant lover was about taking to himself a bride, she felt a desire,
as she expressed it, "to let him know she could marry too." Accordingly, John was
accepted, on condition that he changed the name of Nichols, which Miss Richards
particularly disliked, to that of Livingstone. This was easily done, and the next
letter which went to Oakland carried the news of John's marriage with the proud
Matilda.

A few months later and Mr. Richards died, leaving his entire property to his
daughter and her husband. John was now richer far than even in his wildest dreams
he had ever hoped to be, and yet like many others, he found that riches alone could
not insure happiness. And, indeed, to be happy with Matilda Richards, seemed
impossible. Proud, avaricious, and overbearing, she continually taunted her hus-

band with his entire dependence upon her, carefully watching him, lest any of her hoarded wealth should find its way to the scanty purse of his parents, of whom she always spoke with contempt.

Never but once had they asked for aid, and that to help them rear the little 'Lena. Influenced by his wife, John replied sneeringly, scouting the idea of Helena's marriage, denouncing her as his sister, and saying of her child, that the poor-house stood ready for such as she! This letter 'Lena had accidentally found among her grandfather's papers, and though its contents gave her no definite impression concerning her mother, it inspired her with a dislike for her uncle, whose coming she greatly dreaded, for it was confidently expected that she, together with her grandmother, would return with him to Kentucky.

"You'll be better off there than here," said her grandfather one day, when speaking of the subject. "Your Uncle John is rich, and you'll grow up a fine lady."

"I don't want to be a lady--I won't be a lady," said 'Lena passionately. "I don't like Uncle John. He called my mother a bad woman and me a little brat! I hate him!" and the beautiful brown eyes glittering with tears flashed forth their anger quite as eloquently as language could express it.

The next moment 'Lena was bending over her grandfather, asking to be forgiven for the hasty words which she knew had caused him pain. "I'll try to like him," said she, as the palsied hand stroked her disordered curls in token of forgiveness, "I'll try to like him," adding mentally, "but I do hope he won't come."

It would seem that 'Lena's wish was to be granted, for weeks glided by and there came no tidings of the absent one. Daily Mr. Nichols grew weaker, and when there was no longer hope of life, his heart yearned more and more to once more behold his son; to hear again, ere he died, the blessed name of father.

"'Lena," said Mrs. Nichols one afternoon when her husband seemed worse, "'Lena, it's time for the stage, and do you run down to the 'turn' and see if your uncle's come; something tells me he'll be here to-night."

'Lena obeyed, and throwing on her faded calico sunbonnet, she was soon at the "turn," a point in the road from which the village hotel was plainly discernible. The stage had just arrived, and 'Lena saw that one of the passengers evidently intended stopping, for he seemed to be giving directions concerning his baggage.

"That's Uncle John, I most know," thought she, and seating herself on a rock beneath some white birches, so common in New England, she awaited his approach. She was right in her conjecture, for the stranger was John Livingstone, returned after many years, but so changed that the jolly landlord, who had known him when a boy, and with whom he had cracked many a joke, now hardly dared to address him, he seemed so cold and haughty.

"I will leave my trunk here for a few days," said John, "and perhaps I shall wish for a room. Got any decent accommodations?"

"Wonder if he don't calculate to sleep to hum," thought the landlord, replying at the same instant, "Yes, sir, tip-top accommodations. Hain't more'n tew beds in any room, and nowadays we allers has a wash-bowl and pitcher; don't go to the sink as we used to when you lived round here."

With a gesture of impatience Mr. Livingstone left the house and started up the mountain road, where 'Lena still kept her watch. Oh, how that walk recalled to him the memories of other days, which came thronging about him as one by one familiar way-marks appeared, reminding him of his childhood, when he roamed over that mountain-side with those who were now scattered far and wide, some on the deep, blue sea, some at the distant west, and others far away across the dark river of death. He had mingled much with the world since last he had traversed that road, and his heart had grown callous and indifferent, but he was not entirely hardened, and when at the "turn" in the road, he came suddenly upon the tall walnut tree, on whose shaggy bark his name was carved, together with that of another--a maiden--he started as if smitten with a heavy blow, and dashing a tear from his eye he exclaimed "Oh that I were a boy again!"

From her seat on the mossy rock 'Lena had been watching him. She was very ardent and impulsive, strong in her likes and dislikes, but quite ready to change the latter if she saw any indications of improvement in the person disliked. For her uncle she had conceived a great aversion, and when she saw him approaching, thrusting aside the thistles and dandelions with his gold-headed cane, she mimicked his motions, wondering "if he didn't feel big because he wore a large gold chain dangling from his jacket pocket."

But when she saw his emotions beneath the walnut tree, her opinion suddenly changed. "A very bad man wouldn't cry," she thought, and springing to his side, she grasped his hand, exclaiming, "I know you are my Uncle John, and I'm real glad you've come. Granny thought you never would, and grandpa asks for you all the time."

Had his buried sister arisen before him, Mr. Livingstone would hardly have been more startled, for in form and feature 'Lena was exactly what her mother had been at her age. The same clear complexion, large brown eyes, and wavy hair; and the tones of her voice, too, how they thrilled the heart of the strong man, making him a boy again, guiding the steps of his baby sister, or bearing her gently in his arms when the path was steep and stony. It was but a moment, however, and then the vision faded. His sister was dead, and the little girl before him was her child--the child of shame he believed, or rather, his wife had said it so often that he began to believe it. Glancing at the old-womanish garb in which Mrs. Nichols always arrayed her, a smile of mingled scorn and pity curled his lips, as he thought of presenting her to his fastidious wife and elegant daughters; then withdrawing the hand which she had taken, he said, "And you are 'Lena--'Lena Nichols they call you, I suppose."

'Lena's old dislike began to return, and placing both hands upon her hips in imitation of her grandmother she replied, "No 'tain't 'Lena Nichols, neither. It's 'Lena Rivers. Granny says so, and the town clark has got it so on his book. How are my cousins? Are they pretty well? And how is Ant?"

Mr. Livingstone winced, at the same time feeling amused at this little specimen of Yankeeism, in which he saw so much of his mother. Poor little 'Lena! how should she know any better, living as she always had with two old people, whose language savored so much of the days before the flood! Some such thought passed through Mr. Livingstone's mind, and very civilly he answered her concerning the health of her cousins and aunt; proceeding next to question her of his father, who, she said, "had never seen a well day since her mother died."

"Is there any one with him except your grandmother?" asked Mr. Livingstone; and Lena replied, "Aunt Nancy Scovandyke has been with us a few days, and is there now."

At the sound of that name John started, coloring so deeply that 'Lena observed it, and asked "if he knew Miss Scovandyke?"

"I used to," said he, while 'Lena continued: "She's a nice woman, and though she ain't any connection, I call her aunt. Granny thinks a sight of her."

Miss Scovandyke was evidently an unpleasant topic for Mr. Livingstone, and changing the subject, he said, "What makes you say Granny, child?"

'Lena blushed painfully. 'Twas the first word she had ever uttered, her grandmother having taught it to her, and encouraged her in its use. Besides that, 'Lena had a great horror of anything which she fancied was at all "stuck up," and thinking an entire change from Granny *to* Grandmother would be altogether too much, she still persisted in occasionally using her favorite word, in spite of the ridicule it frequently called forth from her school companions. Thinking to herself that it was none of her uncle's business what she called her grandmother, she made no reply, and in a few moments they came in sight of the yellow farmhouse, which looked to Mr. Livingstone just as it did when he left it, eighteen years before. There was the tall poplar, with its green leaves rustling in the breeze, just as they had done years ago, when from a distant hill-top he looked back to catch the last glimpse of his home. The well in the rear was the same--the lilac bushes in front--the tansy patch on the right and the gable-roofed barn on the left; all were there; nothing was changed but himself.

Mechanically he followed 'Lena into the yard, half expecting to see bleaching upon the grass the same web of home-made cloth, which he remembered had lain there when he went away. One thing alone seemed strange. The blue paper curtains were rolled away from the "spare room" windows, which were open as if to admit as much air as possible.

"I shouldn't wonder if grandpa was worse," said 'Lena, hurrying him along and ushering him at once into the sick-room.

At first Mrs. Nichols did not observe him, for she was bending tenderly over the white, wrinkled face, which lay upon the small, scanty pillow. John thought "how small and scanty they were," while he almost shuddered at the sound of his footsteps upon the uncarpeted floor. Everything was dreary and comfortless, and his conscience reproached him that his old father should die so poor, when he counted his money by thousands.

As he passed the window his tall figure obscured the fading daylight, causing his mother to raise her head, and in a moment her long, bony arms were twined around his neck. The cruel letter, his long neglect, were all forgotten in the joy of once more beholding her "darling boy," whose bearded cheek she kissed again and again. John was unused to such demonstrations of affection, except, indeed, from his little golden-haired Anna, who was refined *and* polished, and all that, which made a vast difference, as he thought. Still, he returned his mother's greeting with a tolerably good grace, managing, however, to tear himself from her as soon as possible.

"How is my father?" he asked; and his mother replied, "He grew worse right away after 'Leny went out, and he seemed so put to't for breath, that Nancy went for the doctor----"

Here a movement from the invalid arrested her attention and going to the bedside she saw that he was awake. Bending over him she whispered softly, "John has come. Would you like to see him?"

Quickly the feeble arms were outstretched, as if to feel what could not be seen, for the old man's eyesight was dim with the shadows of death.

Taking both his father's hands in his, John said, "Here I am, father; can't you see me?"

"No, John, no; I can't see you." And the poor man wept like a little child. Soon growing more calm, he continued: "Your voice is the same that it was years ago, when you lived with us at home. That hasn't changed, though they say your name has. Oh, John, my boy, how could you do so? 'Twas a good name--my name--and you the only one left to bear it. What made you do so, oh John, John?"

Mr. Livingstone did not reply, and after a moment his father again spoke; "John, lay your hand on my forehead. It's cold as ice. I am dying, and your mother will be left alone. We are poor, my son; poorer than you think. The homestead is mortgaged for all it's worth and there are only a few dollars in the purse. Oh, I worked so hard to earn them for her and the girl--Helena's child. Now, John, promise me that when I am gone they shall go with you to your home in the west. Promise, and I shall die happy."

This was a new idea to John, and for a time he hesitated. He glanced at his mother; she was ignorant and peculiar, but she was his mother still. He looked at 'Lena, she was beautiful--he knew that, but she was odd and old-fashioned. He thought of his haughty wife, his headstrong son and his imperious daughter. What would they say if he made that promise, for if he made it he would keep it.

A long time his father awaited his answer, and then he spoke again: "Won't you give your old mother a home?"

The voice was weaker than when it spoke before, and John knew that life was fast ebbing away, for the brow on which his hand was resting was cold and damp with the moisture of death. He could no longer refuse, and the promise was given.

The next morning, the deep-toned bell of Oakland told that another soul was gone, and the villagers as they counted the three score strokes and ten knew that Grandfather Nichols was numbered with the dead.

CHAPTER III.
PACKING UP.

The funeral was over, and in the quiet valley by the side of his only daughter, Grandfather Nichols was laid to rest. As far as possible his father's business was settled, and then John began to speak of his returning. More than once had he repented of the promise made to his father, and as the time passed on he shrank more and more from introducing his "plebeian" mother to his "lady" wife, who, he knew, was meditating an open rebellion.

Immediately after his father's death he had written to his wife, telling her all, and trying as far as he was able to smooth matters over, so that his mother might at least have a decent reception. In a violent passion, his wife had answered, that "she never would submit to it--never. When I married you," said she, "I didn't suppose I was marrying the 'old woman,' young one, and all; and as for my having them to maintain, I will not, so Mr. John Nichols, you understand it."

When Mrs. Livingstone was particularly angry, she called her husband Mr. John Nichols, and when Mr. John Nichols was particularly angry, he did as he pleased, so in this case he replied that "he should bring home as many 'old women' and 'young ones' as he liked, and she might help herself if she could!"

This state of things was hardly favorable to the future happiness of Grandma Nichols, who, wholly unsuspecting and deeming herself as good as anybody, never dreamed that her presence would be unwelcome to her daughter-in-law, whom she thought to assist in various ways, "taking perhaps the whole heft of the housework upon herself--though," she added, "I mean to begin just as I can hold out. I've hearn of such things as son's wives shirkin' the whole on to their old mothers, and the minit 'Tilda shows any signs of that, I shall back out, I tell you."

John, who overheard this remark, bit his lip with vexation, and then burst into a laugh as he fancied the elegant Mrs. Livingstone's dismay at hearing herself called 'Tilda. Had John chosen, he could have given his mother a few useful hints with regard to her treatment of his wife, but such an idea never entered his brain. He was a man of few words, and generally allowed himself to be controlled by circumstances, thinking that the easiest way of getting through the world. He was very proud, and keenly felt how mortifying it would be to present his mother to his fashionable acquaintances; but that was in the future--many miles away--he wouldn't trouble himself about it now; so he passed his time mostly in rambling through the woods and over the hills, while his mother, good soul, busied herself with the preparations for her journey, inviting each and every one of her neighbors to "be sure and visit her if they ever came that way," and urging some of them to come on purpose and "spend the winter."

Among those who promised compliance with this last request, was Miss Nancy Scovandyke, whom we have once before mentioned, and who, as the reader will have inferred, was the first love of John Livingstone. On the night of his arrival, she had been sent in quest of the physician, and when on her return she learned from 'Lena that he had come, she kept out of sight, thinking she would wait awhile before she met him. "Not that she cared the snap of her finger for him," the said, "only it was natural that she should hate to see him."

But when the time did come, she met it bravely, shaking his hand and speaking to him as if nothing had ever happened, and while he was wondering how he ever could have fancied her, she, too, was mentally styling herself "a fool," for having liked "such a pussy, overgrown thing!" Dearly did Miss Nancy love excitement, and during the days that Mrs. Nichols was packing up, she was busy helping her to stow away the "crockery," which the old lady declared should go, particularly the "blue set, which she'd had ever since the day but one before John was born, and which she intended as a part of 'Leny's settin' out. Then, too, John's wife could use 'em when she had a good deal of company; 'twould save buyin' new, and every little helped!"

"I wonder, now, if 'Tilda takes snuff," said Mrs. Nichols, one day, seating herself upon an empty drygoods box which stood in the middle of the floor, and helping herself to an enormous pinch of her favorite Maccaboy; "I wonder if she takes snuff, 'cause if she does, we shall take a sight of comfort together."

"I don't much b'lieve she does," answered Miss Nancy, whose face was very red with trying to cram a pair of cracked bellows into the already crowded top of John's leathern trunk, "I don't b'lieve she does, for somehow it seems to me she's a mighty nipped-up thing, not an atom like you nor me."

"Like enough," returned Mrs. Nichols, finishing her snuff, and wiping her fingers upon the corner of her checked apron; "but, Nancy, can you tell me how in the world I'm ever going to carry this mop? It's bran new, never been used above a dozen times, and I can't afford to give it away."

At this point, John, who was sitting in the adjoining room, came forward. Hitherto he had not interfered in the least in his mother's arrangements, but had looked silently on while she packed away article after article which she would never need, and which undoubtedly would be consigned to the flames the moment her back was turned. The mop business, however, was too much for him, and before Miss Nancy had time to reply, he said, "For heaven's sake, mother, how many traps do you propose taking, and what do you imagine we can do with a mop? Why, I dare say not one of my servants would know how to use it, and it's a wonder if some of the little chaps didn't take it for a horse before night."

"A nigger *ride my mop!* my new mop!" exclaimed Mrs. Nichols, rolling up her eyes in astonishment, while Miss Nancy, turning to John, said, "In the name of the people, how do you live without mops? I should s'pose you'd rot alive!"

"I am not much versed in the mysteries of housekeeping," returned John, with a smile; "but it's my impression that what little cleaning our floors get is done with a cloth."

"Wall, if I won't give it up now," said Miss Nancy. "As good an abolutionist as you used to be, make the poor colored folks wash the floor with a rag, on their hands and knees! It can't be that you indulge a hope, if you'll do such things!"

John made Miss Nancy no answer, but turning to his mother, he said, "I'm in earnest, mother, about your carrying so many useless things. We don't want them. Our house is full now, and besides that, Mrs. Livingstone is very particular about the style of her furniture, and I am afraid yours would hardly come up to her ideas of elegance."

"That chist of drawers," said Mrs. Nichols, pointing to an old-fashioned, high-topped bureau, "cost an ocean of money when 'twas new, and if the brasses on it was rubbed up, 'Tilda couldn't tell 'em from gold, unless she's seen more on't than I have, which ain't much likely, bein' I'm double her age."

"The chest does very well for you, I admit," said John; "but we have neither use nor room for it, so if you can't sell it, why, give it away, or burn it, one or the other."

Mrs. Nichols saw he was decided, and forthwith 'Lena was dispatched to Widow Fisher's, to see if she would take it at half price. The widow had no fancy for second-hand articles, consequently Miss Nancy was told "to keep it, and maybe she'd sometime have a chance to send it to Kentucky. It won't come amiss, I know, s'posin' they be well on't. I b'lieve in lookin' out for a rainy day. I can teach 'Tilda economy yet," whispered Mrs. Nichols, glancing toward the room where John sat, whistling, whittling, and pondering in his own mind the best way if reconciling his wife to what could not well be helped.

'Lena, who was naturally quick-sighted, had partially divined the cause of her uncle's moodiness. The more she saw of him the better she liked him, and she began to think that she would willingly try to cure herself of the peculiarities which evidently annoyed him, if he would only notice her a little, which he was not likely to do. He seldom noticed any child, much less little 'Lena, who he fancied was ignorant as well as awkward; but he did not know her.

One day when, as usual, he sat whittling and thinking, 'Lena approached him softly, and laying her hand upon his knee, said rather timidly, "Uncle, I wish you'd tell me something about my cousins."

"What about them," he asked, somewhat gruffly, for it grated upon his feelings to hear his daughters called cousin by her.

"I want to know how they look, and which one I shall like the best," continued 'Lena.

"You'll like Anna the best," said her uncle, and 'Lena asked, "Why! What sort of a girl is she? Does she love to go to school and study?"

"None too well, I reckon," returned her uncle, adding that "there were not many little girls who did."

"Why I ***do," said 'Lena, and her uncle, stopping for a moment his whittling, replied rather scornfully,*** "You! I should like to know what you ever studied besides the spelling-book!"

'Lena reddened, for she knew that, whether deservedly or not, she bore the reputation of being an excellent scholar, for one of her age, and now she rather tartly answered, "I study geography, arithmetic, grammar, and----" history, she was going to add, but her uncle stopped her, saying, "That'll do, that'll do. You study all these? Now I don't suppose you know what one of 'em is."

"Yes, I do," said 'Lena, with a good deal of spirit. "Olney's geography is a description of the earth; Colburn's arithmetic is the science of numbers: Smith's grammar teaches us how to speak correctly."

"Why don't you do it then," asked her uncle.

"Do what?" said 'Lena, and her uncle continued, "Why don't you make some use of your boasted knowledge of grammar? Why, my Anna has never seen the inside of a grammar, as I know of, but she don't talk like you do."

"Don't what, sir?" said 'Lena,

"Don't talk like you do," repeated her uncle, while 'Lena's eyes fairly danced with mischief as she asked, "if that were good grammar."

Mr. Livingstone colored, thinking it just possible that he himself might sometimes be guilty of the same things for which he had so harshly chided 'Lena, of whom from this time he began to think more favorably. It could hardly be said that he treated her with any more attention, and still there was a difference which she felt, and which made her very happy.

CHAPTER IV.
ON THE ROAD.

At last the packing-up process came to an end, everything too poor to sell, and too good to give away, had found a place--some here, some there, and some in John's trunk, among his ruffled bosoms, collars, dickeys, and so forth. Miss Nancy, who stood by until the last, was made the receiver of sundry cracked teacups, noseless pitchers, and iron spoons, which could not be disposed of elsewhere.

And now every box and trunk was ready. Farmer Truesdale's red wagon stood at the door, waiting to convey them to the depot, and nothing remained for Grandma Nichols, but to bid adieu to the old spot, endeared to her by so many associations. Again and again she went from room to room, weeping always, and lingering longest in the one where her children were born, and where her husband and daughter had died. In the corner stood the old low-post bedstead, the first she had ever owned, and now how vividly she recalled the time long years before, when she, a happy maiden, ordered that bedstead, blushing deeply at the sly allusion which the cabinet maker made to her approaching marriage. He, too, was with her, strong and healthy. Now, he was gone from her side forever. His couch was a narrow coffin, and the old bedstead stood there, naked--empty. Seating herself upon it, the poor old lady rocked to and fro, moaning in her grief, and wishing that she were not going to Kentucky, or that it were possible now to remain at her mountain home. Summoning all her courage, she gave one glance at the familiar objects around her, at the flowers she had planted, and then taking 'Lena's hand, went down to the gate, where her son waited.

He saw she had been weeping, and though he could not appreciate the cause of her tears, in his heart he pitied her, and his voice and manner were unusually kind as he helped her to the best seat in the wagon, and asked if she were comfortable. Then his eye fell upon her dress, and his pity changed to anger as he wondered if she was wholly devoid of taste. At the time of his father's death, he purchased decent mourning for both his mother and 'Lena; but these Mrs. Nichols pronounced "altogether too good for the nasty cars; nobody'd think any better of them for being rigged out in their best meetin' gowns."

So the bombazine was packed away, and in its place she wore a dark blue and white spotted calico, which John could have sworn she had twenty years before, and which was not unlikely, as she never wore out a garment. She was an enemy to long skirts, hence hers came just to her ankles, and as her black stockings had been footed with white, there was visible a dark rim. Altogether she presented a rather grotesque appearance, with her oblong work-bag, in which were her snuff-box, brass spectacles and half a dozen "nutcakes," which would "save John's buying dinner."

Unlike her grandmother's, 'Lena's dress was a great deal too long, and as she never wore pantalets, she had the look of a premature old woman, instead of a child ten summers old, as she was. Still the uncommon beauty of her face, and the natural gracefulness of her form, atoned in a measure for the singularity of her appearance.

In the doorway stood Miss Nancy, and by her side her nephew, Joel Slocum, a freckle-faced boy, who had frequently shown a preference for 'Lena, by going with her for her grandmother's cow, bringing her harvest apples, and letting her ride on his sled oftener than the other girls at school. Strange to say, his affection was not returned, and now, notwithstanding he several times wiped both eyes and nose, on the end of which there was an enormous freck, 'Lena did not relent at all, but with a simple "Good-bye, Jo," she sprang into the wagon, which moved rapidly away.

It was about five miles from the farmhouse to the depot, and when half that distance had been gone over, Mrs. Nichols suddenly seized the reins, ordering the driver to stop, and saying, "she must go straight back, for on the shelf of the north room cupboard she had left a whole paper of tea, which she couldn't afford to lose!"

"Drive on," said Johny rather angrily, at the same time telling his mother that he could buy her a ton of tea if she wanted it.

"But that was already bought, and 'twould have saved so much," said she, softly wiping away a tear, which was occasioned partly by her son's manner, and partly by the great loss she felt she sustained in leaving behind her favorite "old hyson."

This saving *was a matter of which Grandma Nichols said so much, that John, who was himself slightly avaricious, began to regret that he ever knew the definition of the word* save. Lest our readers get a wrong impression of Mrs. Nichols, we must say that she possessed very many sterling qualities, and her habits of extreme economy resulted more from the manner in which she had been compelled to live, than from natural stinginess. For this John hardly made allowance enough, and his mother's remarks, instead of restraining him, only made him more lavish of his money than he would otherwise have been.

When Mrs. Nichols and 'Lena entered the cars, they of course attracted universal attention, which annoyed John excessively. In Oakland, where his mother was known and appreciated, he could bear it, but among strangers, and with those of his own caste, it was different, so motioning them into the first unoccupied seat, he sauntered on with an air which seemed to say, "they were nothing to him," and finding a vacant seat at the other end of the car, he took possession of it. Scarcely, however, had he entered into conversation with a gentleman near him, when some one grasped his arm, and looking up, he saw his mother, her box in one hand; and an enormous pinch of snuff in the other.

"John," said she, elevating her voice so as to drown the noise of the cars, "I never thought on't till this minit, but I'd just as lief ride in the second-class cars as not, and it only costs half as much!"

Mr. Livingstone colored crimson, and bade her go back, saying that if he paid the fare she needn't feel troubled about the cost. Just as she was turning to leave, the loud ring and whistle, as the train neared a crossing, startled her, and in great alarm she asked if "somethin' hadn't bust!"

John made no answer, but the gentleman near him very politely explained to her the cause of the disturbance, after which, she returned to her seat. When the conductor appeared, he fortunately came in at the door nearest John, who pointed out the two, for whom he had tickets, and then turned again to converse with the gentleman, who, though a stranger, was from Louisville, Kentucky, and whose acquaintance was easily made. The sight of the conductor awoke in Mrs. Nichols's brain a new idea, and after peering out upon the platform, she went rushing up to her son, telling him that: "the trunks, box, feather bed, and all, were every one on 'em left!"

"No, they are not," said John; "I saw them aboard myself."

"Wall, then, they're lost off, for as sure as you're born, there ain't one on 'em in here; and there's as much as twenty weight of new feathers, besides all the crockery! Holler to 'em to stop quick!"

The stranger, pitying Mr. Livingstone's chagrin, kindly explained to her that there was a baggage car on purpose for trunks and the like, and that her feather bed was undoubtedly safe. This quieted her, and mentally styling him "a proper nice man," she again returned to her seat.

"A rare specimen of the raw Yankee," said the stranger to John, never dreaming in what relation she stood to him.

"Yes," answered John, not thinking it at all necessary to make any further explanations.

By this time Mrs. Nichols had attracted the attention of all the passengers, who watched her movements with great interest. Among these was a fine-looking youth, fifteen or sixteen years of age, who sat directly in front of 'Lena. He had a remarkably open, pleasing countenance, while there was that in his eyes which showed him to be a lover of fun. Thinking he had now found it in a rich form, he turned partly round, and would undoubtedly have quizzed Mrs. Nichols unmercifully, had not something in the appearance of 'Lena prevented him. This was also her first ride in the cars, but she possessed a tact of concealing the fact, and if she sometimes felt frightened, she looked in the faces of those around her, gathering from them that there was no danger. She knew that her grandmother was making herself ridiculous, and her eyes filled with tears as she whispered, "Do sit still, granny; everybody is looking at you."

The young lad noticed this, and while it quelled in him the spirit of ridicule, it awoke a strange interest in 'Lena, who he saw was beautiful, spite of her unseemly guise. She was a dear lover of nature, and as the cars sped on through the wild mountain scenery, between Pittsfield and Albany, she stood at the open window, her hands closely locked together, her lips slightly parted, and her eyes wide with wonder at the country through which they were passing. At her grandmother's suggestion she had removed her bonnet, and the brown curls which clustered around her white forehead and neck were moved up and down by the fresh breeze which was blowing. The youth was a passionate admirer of beauty, come in what garb it might, and now as he watched, he felt a strong desire to touch one of the glossy ringlets which floated within his reach. There would be no harm in it, he thought--"she was only a little girl, and he was almost a man--had tried to shave, and was going to enter college in the fall." Still he felt some doubts as to the propriety of the act, and was about making up his mind that he had better not, when the train shot into the "tunnel," and for an instant they were in total darkness. Quick as thought his hand sought the brown curls, but they were gone, and when the cars again emerged into daylight, 'Lena's arms were around her grandmother's neck, trying to hold her down, for the old lady, sure of a smash-up *this time, had attempted to rise, screaming loudly for* "John!"

The boy laughed aloud--he could not help it; but when 'Lena's eyes turned re-provingly upon him, he felt sorry; and anxious to make amends, addressed himself very politely to Mrs. Nichols, explaining to her that it was a "tunnel" through which they had passed, and assuring her there was no danger whatever. Then turning to 'Lena, he said, "I reckon your grandmother is not much accustomed to traveling."

"No, sir," answered 'Lena, the rich blood dyeing her cheek at being addressed by a stranger.

It was the first time any one had ever said "sir" to the boy, and now feeling quite like patronizing the little girl, he continued: "I believe old people generally are timid when they enter the cars for the first time."

Nothing from 'Lena except a slight straightening up of her body, and a smooth-ing down of her dress, but the ice was broken, and erelong she and her companion were conversing as familiarly as if they had known each other for years. Still the boy was not inquisitive--he did not ask her name, or where she was going, though he told her that his home was in Louisville, and that at Albany he was to take the boat for New York, where his mother was stopping with some friends. He also told her that the gentleman near the door, with dark eyes and whiskers, was his father.

Glancing toward the person indicated, 'Lena saw that it was the same gentle-man who, all the afternoon, had been talking with her uncle. He was noble look-ing, and she felt glad that he was the father of the boy--he was just such a man, she fancied, as ought to be his father--just such a man as she could wish her father to be--and then 'Lena felt glad that the youth had asked her nothing concerning her parentage, for, though her grandmother had seldom mentioned her father in her presence, there were others ready and willing to inform her that he was a villain, who broke her mother's heart.

When they reached Albany, the boy rose, and offering his hand to 'Lena, said "I suppose I must bid you good-bye, but I'd like right well to go farther with you."

At this moment the stranger gentleman came up, and on seeing how his son was occupied, said smilingly, "So-ho! Durward, you always manage to make some lady acquaintance."

"Yes, father," returned the boy called Durward, "but not always one like this. Isn't she pretty," he added in a whisper.

The stranger's eyes fell upon 'Lena's face, and for a moment, as if by some strange fascination, seemed riveted there; but the crowd pressed him forward, and 'Lena only heard him reply to his son, "Yes, Durward, very pretty; but hurry, or we shall lose the boat."

The next moment they were gone. Leaning from the window, 'Lena tried to catch another glimpse of him, but in vain. He was gone--she would never see him again, she thought; and then she fell into a reverie concerning his home, his mother, his sisters, if he had any, and finally ended by wishing that she were his sister, and the daughter of his father. While she was thus pondering, her grandmother, also, was busy, and when 'Lena looked round for her she was gone. Stepping from the car, 'Lena espied her in the distance, standing by her uncle and anxiously watching for the appearance of her "great trunk, little trunk, band-box, and bag." Each of these articles was forthcoming, and in a few moments they were on the ferry-boat crossing the blue waters of the Hudson, Mrs. Nichols declaring that "if she'd known it wasn't a bridge she was steppin' onto, she'd be bound they wouldn't have got her on in one while."

"Do sit down," said 'Lena; "the other people don't seem to be afraid, and I'm sure we needn't."

This Mrs. Nichols was more willing to do, as directly at her side was another old lady, traveling for the first time, frightened and anxious. To her Mrs. Nichols addressed herself, announcing her firm belief that "she should be blew sky high before she reached Kentucky, where she was going to live with her son John, who she supposed was well off, worth twenty negroes or more; but," she added, lowering her voice, "I don't b'lieve in no such, and I mean he shall set 'em free--poor critters, duddin' from mornin' till night without a cent of pay. He says they call him 'master,' but I'll warrant he'll never catch me a'callin' him so to one on 'em. I promised Nancy Scovandyke that I wouldn't, and I won't!"

Here a little popcorn boy came 'round, which reminded Mrs. Nichols of her money, and that she hadn't once looked after it since she started. Thinking this as favorable a time as she would have, she drew from her capacious pocket an old knit purse, and commenced counting out its contents, piece by piece.

"Beware of pickpockets!" said some one in her ear, and with the exclamation of "Oh the Lord!" the purse disappeared in her pocket, on which she kept her hand until the boat touched the opposite shore. Then in the confusion and excitement it was withdrawn, the purse was forgotten, and when on board the night express for Buffalo it was again looked for, it was gone!

With a wild outcry the horror-stricken matron sprang up, calling for John, who in some alarm came to her side, asking what she wanted.

"I've lost my purse. Somebody's stole it. Lock the door quick, and search every man, woman, and child in the car!"

The conductor, who chanced to be present, now came up, demanding an explanation, and trying to convince Mrs. Nichols how improbable it was that any one present had her money.

"Stop the train then, and let me get off."

"Had you a large amount?" asked the conductor.

"Every cent I had in the world. Ain't you going to let me get off?" was the answer.

The conductor looked inquiringly at John, who shook his head, at the same time whispering to his mother not to feel so badly, as he would give her all the money she wanted. Then placing a ten dollar bill in her hand, he took a seat behind her. We doubt whether this would have quieted the old lady, had not a happy idea that moment entered her mind, causing her to exclaim loudly, "There, now, I've just this minute thought. I hadn't but five dollars in my purse; t'other fifty I sewed up in an old night-gown sleeve, and tucked it away in that satchel up there," pointing to 'Lena's traveling bag, which hung over her head. She would undoubtedly have designated the very corner of said satchel in which her money could be found, had not her son touched her shoulder, bidding her be silent and not tell everybody where her money was, if she didn't want it stolen.

Mrs. Nichols made no reply, but when she thought she was not observed, she arose, and slyly taking down the satchel, placed it under her. Then seating herself upon it, she gave a sigh of relief as she thought, "they'd have to work hard to get it now, without her knowing it!" Dear old soul, when arrived at her journey's end, how much comfort she took in recounting over and over again the incidents of the robbery, wondering if it was, as John said, the very man who had so kindly cautioned her to beware of pickpockets, and who thus ascertained where she kept her purse. Nancy Scovandyke, too, was duly informed of her loss, and charged when she came to Kentucky, "to look out on the ferry-boat for a youngish, good-looking man, with brown frock coat, blue cravat, and mouth full of white teeth."

At Buffalo Mr. Livingstone had hard work to coax his mother on board the steamboat, but he finally succeeded, and as the weather chanced to be fine, she declared that ride on the lake to be the pleasantest part of her journey. At Cleveland they took the cars for Cincinnati, going thence to Lexington by stage. On ordinary occasions Mr. Livingstone would have preferred the river, but knowing that in all probability he should meet with some of his friends upon the boat, he chose the route via Lexington, where he stopped at the Phoenix, as was his usual custom.

After seeing his mother and niece into the public parlor he left them for a time, saying he had some business to transact in the city. Scarcely was he gone when the sound of shuffling footsteps in the hall announced an arrival, and a moment after, a boy, apparently fifteen years of age, appeared in the door. He was richly though carelessly dressed, and notwithstanding the good-humored expression of his rather handsome face, there was in his whole appearance an indescribable something which at once pronounced him to be a "fast" boy. A rowdy hat was set on one side of his head, after the most approved fashion, while in his hand he held a lighted cigar, which he applied to his mouth when he saw the parlor was unoccupied, save by an "old woman" and a "little girl."

Instinctively 'Lena shrank from him, and withdrawing herself as far as possible within the recess of the window, pretended to be busily watching the passers-by.

But she did not escape his notice, and after coolly surveying her for a moment, he walked up to her, saying, "How d'ye, polywog? I'll be hanged if I know to what gender you belong--woman or gal--which is it, hey?"

"None of your business," was 'Lena's ready answer.

"Spunky, ain't you," said he, unceremoniously pulling one of the brown curls which Durward had so longed to touch. "Seems to me your hair don't match the rest of you; wonder if 'tisn't somebody else's head set on your shoulders."

"No, it ain't. It's my own head, and you just let it alone," returned 'Lena, growing more and more indignant, and wondering if this were a specimen of Kentucky boys.

"Don't be saucy," continued her tormentor; "I only want to see what sort of stuff you are made of."

"Made of dirt" muttered 'Lena.

"I reckon you are," returned the boy; "but say, where did *you come from and who* do you live with?"

"I came from Massachusetts, and I live with granny," said 'Lena, thinking that if she answered him civilly, he would perhaps let her alone. But she was mistaken.

Glancing at "granny," he burst into a loud laugh, and then placing his hat a little more on one side, and assuming a nasal twang, he said, "Neow dew tell, if you're from Massachusetts. How dew you dew, little Yankee, and how are all the folks to hum?"

Feeling sure that not only herself but all her relations were included in this insult, 'Lena darted forward hitting him a blow in the face, which he returned by puffing smoke into hers, whereupon she snatched the cigar from his mouth and hurled it into the street, bidding him "touch her again if he dared." All this transpired so rapidly that Mrs. Nichols had hardly time to understand its meaning, but fully comprehending it now, she was about coming to the rescue, when her son reappeared, exclaiming, "John, John Livingstone, Jr., how came you here?"

Had a cannon exploded at the feet of John Jr., as he was called, he could not have been more startled. He was not expecting his father for two or three days, and was making the most of his absence by having what he called a regular "spree." Taking him altogether, he was, without being naturally bad, a spoiled child, whom no one could manage except his father, and as his father seldom tried, he was of course seldom managed. Never yet had he remained at any school more than two quarters, for if he were not sent away, he generally ran away, sure of finding a champion in his mother, who had always petted him, calling him, "Johnny darling," until he one day very coolly informed her that she was "a silly old fool," and that "he'd thank her not to 'Johnny darling' him any longer."

It would be difficult to describe the amazement of John Jr. when 'Lena was presented to him as his cousin, and Mrs. Nichols as his grandmother. Something which sounded very much like an oath escaped his lips, as turning to his father he muttered, "Won't mother go into fits?" Then, as he began to realize the ludicrousness of the whole affair, he exclaimed, "Rich, good, by gracious!" and laughing loudly, he walked away to regale himself with another cigar.

Lena began to tremble for her future happiness, if this boy was to live in the same house with her. She did not know that she had already more than half won his good opinion, for he was far better pleased with her antagonistical demonstrations, than he would have been had she cried or ran from him, as his sister Anna generally did when he teased her. After a few moments here turned to the parlor, and walking up to Mrs. Nichols, commenced talking very sociably with her, calling her "Granny," and winking slyly at 'Lena as he did so. Mr. Livingstone had too much good sense to sit quietly by and hear his mother ridiculed by his son, and in a loud, stern voice he bade the young gentleman "behave himself."

"Law, now," said Mrs. Nichols, "let him talk if he wants to. I like to hear him. He's the only grandson I've got."

This speech had the effect of silencing John Jr. quite as much as his father's command. If he could tease his grandmother by talking to her, he would take delight in doing so, but if she wanted *him to talk--that was quite another thing. So moving away from her, he took a seat near 'Lena, telling her her dress was "a heap too short," and occasionally pinching her, just to vary the sport! This last, however, 'Lena returned with so much force that he grew weary of the fun, and informing her that he was going to a* circus which was in town that evening, he arose to leave the room.

Mr. Livingstone, who partially overheard what he had said, stopped him and asked "where he was going?"

Feigning a yawn and rubbing his eyes, John Jr. replied that "he was confounded sleepy and was going to bed."

"'Lena, where did he say he was going?" asked her uncle.

'Lena trembled, for John Jr. had clinched his fist, and was shaking it threateningly at her.

"Where did he say he was going?" repeated her uncle.

Poor 'Lena had never told a lie in her life, and now braving her cousin's anger, she said, "To the circus, sir. Oh, I wish you had not asked me."

"You'll get your pay for that," muttered John Jr. sullenly reseating himself by his father, who kept an eye on him until he saw him safely in his room.

Much as John Jr. frightened 'Lena with his threats, in his heart he respected her for telling the truth, and if the next morning on their way home in the stage, in which his father compelled him to take a seat, he frequently found it convenient to step on her feet, it was more from a natural propensity to torment than from any lurking feeling of revenge. 'Lena was nowise backward in returning his cousinly attentions, and so between an interchange of kicks, wry faces, and so forth, they proceeded toward "Maple Grove," a description of which will be given in another chapter.

CHAPTER V.
MAPLE GROVE.

The residence of Mr. Livingstone, or rather of Mr. Livingstone's wife, was a large, handsome building, such as one often finds in Kentucky, particularly in the country. Like most planters' houses, it stood at some little distance from the street, from which its massive walls, wreathed with evergreen, were just discernible. The carriage road which led to it passed first through a heavy iron gate guarded by huge bronze lions, so natural and life-like, that Mrs. Nichols, when first she saw them, uttered a cry of fear. Next came a beautiful maple grove, followed by a long, green lawn, dotted here and there with forest trees and having on its right a deep running brook, whose waters, farther on at the rear of the garden, were formed into a miniature fish-pond.

The house itself was of brick--two storied, and surrounded on three sides with a double piazza, whose pillars were entwined with climbing roses, honey-suckle, and running vines, so closely interwoven as to give it the appearance of an immense summer-house. In the spacious yard in front, tall shade trees and bright green grass were growing, while in the well-kept garden at the left, bloomed an endless variety of roses and flowering shrubs, which in their season filled the air with perfume, and made the spot brilliant with beauty. Directly through the center of this garden ran the stream of which we have spoken, and as its mossy banks were never disturbed, they presented the appearance of a soft, velvety ridge, where each spring the starry dandelion and the blue-eyed violet grew.

Across the brook two small foot-bridges had been built, both of which were latticed and overgrown by luxuriant grape-vines, whose dark, green foliage was now intermingled with clusters of the rich purple fruit. At the right, and somewhat in the rear of the building, was a group of linden trees, overshadowing the whitewashed houses of the negroes, who, imitating as far as possible the taste of their master, beautified their dwellings with hop-vines, creepers, hollyhocks and the like. Altogether, it was as 'Lena said, "just the kind of place which one reads of in stories," and which is often found at the "sunny south." The interior of the building corresponded with the exterior, for with one exception, the residence of a wealthy Englishman, Mrs. Livingstone prided herself upon having the best furnished house in the county; consequently neither pains nor money had been spared in the selection of the furniture, which was of the most costly kind.

Carrie, the eldest of the daughters, was now about thirteen years of age. Proud, imperious, deceitful, and self-willed, she was hated by the servants, and disliked by her equals. Some thought her pretty. She felt sure of it, and many an hour she spent before the mirror, admiring herself and anticipating the time when she would be a grown-up lady, and as a matter of course, a belle. Her mother unfortunately belonged to that class who seem to think that the chief aim in life is to secure a "brilliant match," and thinking she could not commence too soon, she had early instilled into her favorite daughter's mind the necessity of appearing to the best possible advantage, when in the presence of wealth and distinction, pointing out her own marriage as a proof of the unhappiness resulting from unequal matches. In this way Carrie had early learned that her father owed his present position to her mother's condescension in marrying him--that he was once a poor boy living among the northern hills--that his parents were poor, ignorant and vulgar--and that there was with them a little girl, their daughter's child, who never had a father, and whom she must never on any occasion call her cousin.

All this had likewise been told to Anna, the youngest daughter, who was about 'Lena's age, but upon her it made no impression. If her father was once poor, he was in her opinion none the worse for that--and if he liked his parents, that was a sufficient reason why she should like them too, and if little 'Lena was an orphan, she pitied her, and hoped she might sometime see her and tell her so! Thus Anna reasoned, while her mother, terribly shocked at her low-bred taste, strove to instill into her mind some of her own more aristocratic notions. But all in vain, for Anna was purely democratic, loving everybody and beloved by everybody in return. It is true she had no particular liking for books or study of any kind, but she was gentle and affectionate in her manner, and kindly considerate of other people's feelings.

With her father she was a favorite, and to her he always looked for sympathy, which she seldom failed to give--not in words, it is true, but whenever he seemed to be in trouble, she would climb into his lap, wind her arms around his neck, and laying her golden head upon his shoulder, would sit thus until his brow and heart grew lighter as he felt there was yet something in the wide world which loved and cared for him.

For Carrie Mrs. Livingstone had great expectations, but Anna she feared would never make a "brilliant match." For a long time Anna meditated upon this, wondering what a "brilliant match" could mean, and at last she determined to seek an explanation from Captain Atherton, a bachelor and a millionaire, who was in the habit of visiting them, and who always noticed and petted her more than he did Carrie. Accordingly, the next time he came, and they were alone in the parlor, she broached the subject, asking him what it meant.

Laughing loudly, the Captain drew her toward him, saying, "Why, marrying rich, you little novice. For instance, if one of these days you should be my little wife, I dare say your mother would think you had made a brilliant match!" and the well-preserved gentleman of forty glanced complacently at himself in the mirror thinking how probable it was that his youthfulness would be unimpaired for at least ten years to come!

Anna laughed, for to her his words then conveyed no serious meaning, but with more than her usual quickness she replied, that "she would as soon marry her grandfather."

With Mrs. Livingstone the reader is partially acquainted. In her youth she had been pretty, and now at thirty-eight she was not without pretensions to beauty, notwithstanding her sallow complexion and sunken eyes, Her hair, which was very abundant, was bright and glossy, and her mouth, in which the dentist had done his best, would have been handsome, had it not been for a certain draw at the corners, which gave it a scornful and rather disagreeable expression. In her disposition she was overbearing and tyrannical, fond of ruling, and deeming her husband a monster of ingratitude if ever in any way he manifested a spirit of rebellion. Didn't she marry him? and now they were married, didn't her money support him? And wasn't it exceedingly amiable in her always to speak of their children as ours! But as for the rest, 'twas my ***house,*** my ***servants,*** my ***carriage, and*** my ***horses.***

All mine --"Mrs. John Livingstone's--Miss Matilda Richards that was!"

Occasionally, however, her husband's spirit was roused, and then, after a series of tears, sick-headaches, and then spasms, "Miss Matilda Richards that Was" was compelled to yield her face for many days wearing the look of a much-injured, heart-broken woman. Still her influence over him was great, else she had never so effectually weakened every tie which bound him to his native home, making him ashamed of his parents and of everything pertaining to them. When her husband first wrote, to her that his father was dead and that he had promised to take charge of his mother and 'Lena, she new into a violent rage, which was increased ten-fold when she received his second letter, wherein he announced his intention of bringing them home in spite of her. Bursting into tears she declared "she'd leave the house before she'd have it filled up with a lot of paupers. Who did John Nichols think he was, and who did he think she was! Besides that, where was he going to put them? for there wasn't a place for them that she knew of!"

"Why, mother," said Anna who was pleased with the prospect of a new grandmother and cousin, "Why, mother, what a story. There's the two big chambers and bedrooms, besides the one next to Carrie's and mine. Oh, do put them in there. It'll be so nice to have grandma and cousin 'Lena so near me."

"Anna Livingstone!" returned the indignant lady, "Never let me hear you say grandma and cousin again."

"But they be grandma and cousin," persisted Anna, while her mother commenced lamenting the circumstance which had made them so, wishing, as she had often done before, that she had never married John Nichols.

"I reckon you are not the only one that wishes so," slyly whispered John Jr., who was a witness to her emotion.

Anna was naturally of an inquiring mind, and her mother's last remark awoke within her a new and strange train of thought, causing her to wonder whose little girl she would have been, her father's or mother's, in case they had each married some one else! As there was no one whose opinion Anna dared to ask, the question is undoubtedly to this day, with her, unsolved.

The next morning when Mrs. Livingstone arose, her anger of the day before was somewhat abated, and knowing from past experience that it was useless to resist her husband when once he was determined, she wisely concluded that as they were now probably on the road, it was best to try to endure, for a time, at least, what could not well be helped. And now arose the perplexing question, "What should she do with them? where should she put them that they would be the most out of the way? for she could never suffer them to be round when she had company." The chamber of which Anna had spoken was out of the question, for it was too nice, and besides that, it was reserved for the children of her New Orleans friends, who nearly every summer came up to visit her.

At the rear of the building was a long, low room, containing a fireplace and two windows, which looked out upon the negro quarters and the hemp fields beyond. This room, which in the summer was used for storing feather-beds, blankets, and so forth, was plastered, but minus either paper or paint. Still it was quite comfortable, "better than they were accustomed to at home," Mrs. Livingstone said, and this she decided to give them. Accordingly the negroes were set at work scrubbing the floor, washing the windows, and scouring the sills, until the room at least possessed the virtue of being clean. A faded carpet, discarded as good for nothing, and over which the rats had long held their nightly revels, was brought to light, shaken, mended, and nailed down--then came a bedstead, which Mrs. Livingstone had designed as a Christmas gift to one of the negroes, but which of course would do well enough for her mother-in-law. Next followed an old wooden rocking-chair, whose ancestry Anna had tried in vain to trace, and which Carrie had often proposed burning. This, with two or three more chairs of a later date, a small wardrobe, and a square table, completed the furniture of the room, if we except the plain muslin curtains which shaded the windows, destitute of blinds. Taking it by itself, the room looked tolerably well, but when compared with the richly furnished apartments around it, it seemed meager and poor indeed; "but if they wanted anything better, they could get it themselves. They were welcome to make any alterations they chose."

This mode of reasoning hardly satisfied Anna, and unknown to her mother she took from her own chamber a handsome hearth-rug, and carrying it to her grandmother's room, laid it before the fireplace. Coming accidentally upon a roll of green paper, she, with the help of Corinda, a black girl, made some shades for the windows, which faced the west, rendering the room intolerably hot during the summer season. Then, at the suggestion of Corinda, she looped back the muslin curtains with some green ribbons, which she had intended using for her "dolly's dress." The bare appearance of the table troubled her, but by rummaging, she brought to light a cast-off spread, which, though soiled and worn, was on one side quite handsome.

"Now, if we only had something for the mantel," said she; "it seems so empty."

Corinda thought a moment, then rolling up the whites of her eyes, replied, "Don't you mind them little pitchers" (meaning vases) "which Master Atherton done gin you? They'd look mighty fine up thar, full of sprigs and posies."

Without hesitating a moment Anna brought the vases, and as she did not know the exact time when her grandmother would arrive, she determined to fill them with fresh flowers every morning.

"There, it looks a heap better, don't it, Carrie?" said she to her sister, who chanced to be passing the door and looked in.

"You must be smart," answered Carrie, "taking so much pains just for them; and as I live, if you haven't got those elegant vases that Captain Atherton gave you for a birthday present! I know mother won't like it. I mean to tell her;" and away she ran with the important news.

"There, I told you so," said she, quickly returning. "She says you carry them straight back and let the room alone."

Anna began to cry, saying "the vases were hers, and she should think she might do what she pleased with them."

"What did you go and blab for, you great for shame, you?" exclaimed John Jr., suddenly appearing in the doorway, at the same time giving Carrie a push, which set her to crying, and brought Mrs. Livingstone to the scene of action,

"Can't my vases stay in here? Nobody'll hurt 'em, and they'll look so pretty," said Anna.

"Can't that hateful John behave, and let me alone?" said Carrie.

"And can't Carrie quit sticking her nose in other folks' business?" chimed in John Jr.

"Oh Lordy, what a fuss," said Corinda, while poor Mrs. Livingstone, half distracted, took refuge under one of her dreadful headaches, and telling her children "to fight their own battles and let her alone," returned to her room.

"A body'd s'pose marster's kin warn't of no kind of count," said Aunt Milly, the head cook, to a group of sables, who, in the kitchen, were discussing the furniture of the "trump'ry room," as they were in the habit of calling the chamber set apart for Mrs. Nichols. "Yes, they would s'pose they warn't of no kind o' count, the way miss goes on, ravin' and tarin' and puttin' 'em off with low-lived truck that we black folks wouldn't begin to tache with the tongs. Massy knows ef my ole mother warn't dead and gone to kingdom come, I should never think o' sarvin' her so, and I don't set myself up to be nothin' but an old nigger, and a black one at that. But Lor' that's the way with more'n half the white folks. They jine the church, and then they think they done got a title deed to one of them houses up in heaven (that nobody ever built) sure enough. Goin' straight thar, as fast as a span of race-horses can carry 'em. Ki! Won't they be disappointed, some on 'em, and Miss Matilda 'long the rest, when she drives up, hosses all a reekin' sweat, and spects to walk straight into the best room, but is told to go to the kitchen and turn hoe-cakes for us niggers, who are eatin' at the fust table, with silver forks and napkins----?"

Here old Milly stopped to breathe, and her daughter Vine, who had listened breathlessly to her mother's description of the "good time coming," asked "when these things come to pass, if Miss Carrie wouldn't have to swing the feathers over the table to keep off the flies, instead of herself?"

"Yes, that she will, child," returned her mother; "Things is all gwine to be changed in the wink of your eye. Miss Anna read that very tex' to me last Sunday and I knew in a minit what it meant. Now thar's Miss Anna, blessed lamb. She's one of 'em that'll wear her white gowns and stay in t'other room, with her face shinin' like an ile lamp!"

While this interesting conversation was going on in the kitchen, John Jr., in the parlor was teasing his mother for money, with which to go up to Lexington the next day. "You may just as well give it to me without any fuss," said he, "for if you don't, I'll get my bills at the Phoenix charged. The old man is good, and they'll trust. But then a feller feels more independent when he can pay down, and treat a friend, if he likes; so hand over four or five Vs."

At first Mrs. Livingstone refused, but her head ached so hard and her "nerves trembled so," that she did not feel equal to the task of contending with John Jr., who was always sure in the end to have his own way. Yielding at last to his importunities, she gave him fifteen dollars, charging him to "keep out of bad company and be a good boy."

"Trust me for that," said he, and pulling the tail of Anna's pet kitten, upsetting Carrie's work-box, poking a black baby's ribs with his walking cane, and knocking down a cob-house, which "Thomas Jefferson" had been all day building, he mounted his favorite "Firelock," and together with a young negro, rode off.

"The Lord send us a little peace now," said Aunt Milly, tossing her squalling baby up in the air, and telling Thomas Jefferson not to cry, "for his young master was done gone off."

"And I hope to goodness he'll stay off a spell," she added, "for thar's ole Sam to pay the whole time he's at home, and if ever thar was a tickled critter in this world it's me, when he clar's out."

"I'm glad, too," said Anna, who had been sent to the kitchen to stop the screaming, "and I wish he'd stay ever so long, for I don't take a bit of comfort when he's at home."

"Great hateful! I wish he didn't live here," said Carrie, gathering up her spools, thimble and scissors, while Mrs. Livingstone, feeling that his absence had taken a load from her shoulders, settled herself upon her silken lounge and tried to sleep.

Amid all this rejoicing at his departure, John Jr. put spurs to the fleet Firelock, who soon carried him to Lexington, where, as we have seen, he came unexpectedly upon his father, who, not daring to trust him on horseback, lest he should play the truant, took him into the stage with himself, leaving Firelock to the care of the negro.

CHAPTER VI.
THE ARRIVAL.

O h, mother, get up quick--the stage has driven up at the gate, and I reckon pa has come," said Anna, bursting into the room where her mother, who was suffering from a headache, was still in bed.

Raising herself upon her elbow, and pushing aside the rich, heavy curtains, Mrs. Livingstone looked out upon the mud-bespattered vehicle, from which a leg, encased in a black and white stocking, was just making its egress. "Oh, heavens!" said she, burying her face again in the downy pillows. Woman's curiosity, however, soon prevailed over all other feelings, and again looking out she obtained a full view of her mother-in-law, who, having emerged from the coach, was picking out her boxes, trunks, and so forth. When they were all found, Mr. Livingstone ordered two negroes to carry them to the side piazza, where they were soon mounted by three or four little darkies, Thomas Jefferson among the rest.

"John, John" said Mrs. Nichols, "them niggers won't scent my things, will they?"

"Don't talk, granny," whispered 'Lena, painfully conscious of the curious eyes fixed upon them by the bevy of blacks, who had come out to greet their master, and who with sidelong glances at each other, were inspecting the new comers.

"Don't talk! why not?" said Mrs. Nichols, rather sharply. "This is a free country I suppose." Then bethinking herself, she added quickly, "Oh, I forgot, 'taint free here!"

After examining the satchel and finding that the night gown sleeve was safe, Mrs. Nichols took up her line of march for the house, herself carrying her umbrella and band-box, which she would not intrust to the care of the negroes, "as like enough they'd break the umberell, or squash her caps."

"The trumpery room is plenty good enough for 'em," thought Corinda, retreating into the kitchen and cutting sundry flourishes in token of her contempt.

The moment 'Lena came in sight, Mrs. Livingstone exclaimed, "Oh, mercy, which is the oldest?" and truly, poor 'Lena did present a sorry figure,

Her bonnet, never very handsome or fashionable, had received an ugly crook in front, which neither her grandmother or uncle had noticed, and of which John Jr. would not tell her, thinking that the worse she looked the more fun he would have! Her skirts were not very full, and her dress hung straight around her, making her of the same bigness from her head to her feet. Her shoes, which had been given to her by one of the neighbors, were altogether too large, and it was with considerable difficulty that she could keep them on, but then as they were a present, Mrs. Nichols said "it was a pity not to get all the good out of them she could."

In front of herself and grandmother, walked Mr. Livingstone, moody, silent, and cross. Behind them was John Jr., mimicking first 'Lena's gait and then his grandmother's. The negroes, convulsed with laughter, darted hither and thither, running against and over each other, and finally disappearing, some behind the house and some into the kitchen, and all retaining a position from which they could have a full view of the proceedings. On the piazza stood Anna and Carrie, the one with her handkerchief stuffed in her mouth, and the other with her mouth open, astounded at the unlooked-for spectacle.

"Oh, what shall I do, what shall I do?" groaned Mrs. Livingstone.

"Do? Get up and dress yourself, and come and see your new relations: that's what I should do," answered John Jr., who, tired of mimicking, had run forward, and now rushed unceremoniously into his mother's sleeping-room, leaving the door open behind him.

"John Livingstone, what do you mean?" said she, "shut that door this minute."

Feigning not to hear her, John Jr. ran back to the piazza, which he reached just in time to hear the presentation of his sisters.

"This is Carrie, and this is Anna," said Mr. Livingstone, pointing to each one as he pronounced her name.

Marching straight up to Carrie and extending her hand, Mrs. Nichols exclaimed, "Now I want to know if this is Car'line. I'd no idee she was so big. You pretty well, Car'line?"

Very haughtily Carrie touched the ends of her grandmother's fingers, and with stately gravity replied that she was well.

Turning next to Anna, Mrs. Nichols continued, "And this is Anny. Looks weakly 'pears to me, kind of blue around the eyes as though she was fitty. Never have fits, do you, dear?"

"No, ma'am," answered Anna, struggling hard to keep from laughing outright.

Here Mr. Livingstone inquired for his wife, and on being told that she was sick, started for her room.

"Sick? Is your marm sick?" asked Mrs. Nichols of John Jr. "Wall, I guess I'll go right in and sea if I can't do somethin' for her. I'm tolerable good at nussin'."

Following her son, who did not observe her, she entered unannounced into the presence of her elegant daughter-in-law, who, with a little shriek, covered her head with the bed-clothes. Knowing that she meant well, and never dreaming that she was intruding, Mrs. Nichols walked up to the bedside, saying, "How de do, 'Tilda? I suppose you know I'm your mother--come all the way from Massachusetts to live with you. What is the matter? Do you take anything for your sickness?"

A groan was Mrs. Livingstone's only answer.

"Little hystericky, I guess," suggested Mrs. Nichols, adding that "settin' her feet in middlin' hot water is good for that."

"She is nervous, and the sight of strangers makes her worse. So I reckon you'd better go out for the present," said Mr. Livingstone, who really pitied his wife. Then calling Corinda, he bade her show his mother to her room.

Corinda obeyed, and Mrs. Nichols followed her, asking her on the way "what her surname was, how old she was, if she knew how to read, and if she hadn't a good deal rather be free than to be a slave!" to which Corinda replied, that "she didn't know what a surname meant, that she didn't know how old she was, that she didn't know how to read, and that she didn't know whether she'd like to be free or not, but reckoned she shouldn't."

"A half-witted gal that," thought Mrs. Nichols, "and I guess 'Tilda don't set much store by her." Then dropping into the wooden rocking-chair and laying aside her bonnet, she for the first time noticed that 'Lena was not with her, and asked Corinda to go for her.

Corinda complied, leaving the room just in time to stifle a laugh, as she saw

Mrs. Nichols stoop down to examine the hearth-rug, wondering "how much it cost when 'twas new."

We left 'Lena standing on the steps of the piazza.

At a glance she had taken in the whole--had comprehended that there was no affinity whatever between herself and the objects around her, and a wild, intense longing filled her heart to be once more among her native hills. She had witnessed the merriment of the blacks, the scornful curl of Carrie's lip, the half-suppressed ridicule of Anna, when they met her grandmother, and now uncertain of her own reception, she stood before her cousins not knowing whether to advance or run away. For a moment there was an awkward silence, and then John Jr., bent on mischief, whispered to Carrie, "Look at that pinch in her bonnet, and just see her shoes! Big as little sailboats!"

This was too much for Lena. She already disliked John Jr., and now, flying into a violent passion, she drew off her shoes, and hurling them at the young gentle-man's head fled away, away, she knew not, cared not whither, so that she got out of sight and hearing. Coming at last to the arbor bridge across the brook in the garden, she paused for breath, and throwing herself upon a seat, burst into a flood of tears. For several minutes she sobbed so loudly that she did not hear the sound of foot-steps upon the graveled walk. Anna had followed her, partly out of curiosity, and partly out of pity, the latter of which preponderated when she saw how bitterly her cousin was weeping. Going up to her she said, "Don t cry so, 'Lena. Look up and talk. It's Anna, your cousin."

'Lena had not yet recovered from her angry fit, and thinking Anna only came to tease her, and perhaps again ridicule her bonnet, she tore the article, from her head, and bending it up double, threw it into the stream, which carried it down to the fish-pond, where for two or three hours it furnished amusement for some little negroes, who, calling it a crab, fished for it with hook and line! For a moment Anna stood watching the bonnet as it sailed along down the stream, thinking it looked better there than on its owner's head, but wondering why 'Lena had thrown it away. Then again addressing her cousin, she asked why she had done so?

"It's a homely old thing, and I hate it," answered 'Lena, again bursting into tears. "I hate everybody, and I wish I was dead, or back in Massachusetts, I don't care which!"

With her impressions of the "Bay State," where her mother said folks lived on "cold beans and codfish," Anna thought she should prefer the first alternative, but she did not say so; and after a little she tried again to comfort 'Lena, telling her "she liked her, or at least she was going to like her a heap."

"No, you ain't," returned 'Lena. "You laughed at me and granny both. I saw you do it, and you think I don't know anything, but I do. I've been through Olney's geography, and Colburn's arithmetic twice!"

This was more than Anna could say. She had no scholarship of which to boast; but she had a heart brimful of love, and in reply to 'Lena's accusation of having laughed at her, she replied, "I know I laughed, for grandma looked so funny I couldn't help it. But I won't any more. I pity you because your mother is dead, and you never had any father, ma says."

This made 'Lena cry again, while Anna continued, "Pa'll buy you some new clothes I reckon, and if he don't, I'll give you some of mine, for I've got heaps, and they'll fit you I most know. Here's my mark--" pointing to a cut upon the door-post. "Here's mine, and Carrie's and brother's. Stand up and see if you don't measure like I do,"

'Lena complied, and to Anna's great joy they were just of a height.

"I'm so glad," said she. "Now, come to my room and Corinda will fix you up mighty nice before mother sees you."

Hand-in-hand the two girls started for the house, but had not gone far when they heard some one calling, "Ho, Miss 'Lena, whar is you? Ole miss done want you." At the same time Corinda made her appearance round the corner of the piazza.

"Here, Cora," said Anna. "Come with me to my room; I want you."

With a broad grin Corinda followed her young mistress, while 'Lena, never having been accustomed to any negro save the one with whom many New England children are threatened when they cry, clung closer to Anna's side, occasionally casting a timid glance toward the dark-browed girl who followed them. In the upper hall they met with Carrie, who in passing 'Lena held back her dress, as if fearing contamination from a contact with her cousin's plainer garments. Painfully alive to the slightest insult, 'Lena reddened, while Anna said, "Never mind--that's just like Cad, but nobody cares for her ."

Thus reassured 'Lena followed on, until they reached Anna's room, which they were about to enter, when the shrill voice of Mrs. Nichols fell upon their ears, calling, "'Leny, 'Leny, where upon airth is she?"

"Let's go to her first," said 'Lena, and leading the way Anna soon ushered her into her grandmother's room which, child as she was, 'Lena readily saw was far different from the handsome apartments of which she had obtained a passing glance.

But Mrs. Nichols had not thought of this--and was doubtless better satisfied with her present quarters than she would have been with the best furnished chamber in the house. The moment her granddaughter appeared, she exclaimed, "'Leny Rivers, where have you been? I was worried to death, for fear you might be runnin' after some of them paltry niggers. And now whilst I think on't, I charge you never to go a nigh 'em; I'd no idee they were such half-naked, nasty critters."

This prohibition was a novelty to Anna, who spent many happy hours with her sable-hued companions, never deeming herself the worse for it. Her grandmother's first remark, however, struck her still more forcibly, and she immediately asked, "Grandma, what did you call 'Lena, just now? 'Lena what?"

"I called her by her name, 'Lena Rivers. What should I call her?" returned Mrs. Nichols.

"Why, I thought her name was 'Lena Nichols; ma said 'twas," answered Anna.

Mrs. Nichols was very sensitive to any slight cast upon 'Lena's birth, and she rather tartly informed Anna, that "her mother didn't know everything," adding that "'Lena's father was Mr. Rivers, and there wasn't half so much reason why she should be called Nichols as there was why Anna should, for that was her father's name, the one by which he was baptized, the same day with Nancy Scovandyke, who's jest his age, only he was born about a quarter past four in the morning, and she not till some time in the afternoon!"

"But where is Mr. Rivers?" asked Anna more interested in him than in the exact minute of her father's birth.

"The Lord only knows," returned Mrs. Nichols. "Little girls shouldn't ask too many questions."

This silenced Anna, and satisfied her that there was some mystery connected with 'Lena. The mention of Nancy Scovandyke reminded Mrs. Nichols of the dishes which that lady had packed away, and anxious to see if they were safe, she turned to

'Lena saying, "I guess we'll have time before dinner to unpack my trunks, for I want to know how the crockery stood the racket. Anny, you run down and tell your pa to fetch 'em up here, that's a good girl."

In her eagerness to know what those weather-beaten boxes contained, Anna forgot her scheme of dressing 'Lena, and ran down, not to call her father, but the black boy, Adam. It took her a long time to find him, and Mrs. Nichols, growing impatient, determined to go herself, spite of 'Lena's entreaties that she would stay where she was. Passing down the long stairway, and out upon the piazza, she espied a negro girl on her hands and knees engaged in cleaning the steps with a cloth. Instantly remembering her mop, she greatly lamented that she had left it behind--"'twould come so handy now," thought she, but there was no help for it.

Walking up to the girl, whose name she did not know, she said, "Sissy, can you tell me where John is?"

Quickly "Sissy's" ivories became visible, as she replied, "We hain't got any such nigger as John."

With a silent invective upon negroes in general, and this one in particular, Mrs. Nichols choked, stammered, and finally said, "I didn't ask for a nigger ; I want your master, John !"

Had the old lady been a Catholic, she would have crossed herself for thus early breaking her promise to Nancy Scovandyke. As it was, she mentally asked forgiveness, and as the colored girl "didn't know where marster was," but "reckoned he had gone somewhar," she turned aside, and seeking her son's room, again entered unannounced. Mrs. Livingstone, who was up and dressed, frowned darkly upon her visitor. But Mrs. Nichols did not heed it, and advancing forward, she said, "Do you feel any better, 'Tilda? I'd keep kinder still to-day, and not try to do much, for if you feel any consarned about the housework, I'd just as lief see to't a little after dinner as not."

"I have all confidence in Milly's management, and seldom trouble myself about the affairs of the kitchen," answered Mrs. Livingstone.

"Wall, then," returned her mother-in-law, nothing daunted, "Wall, then, mebby you'd like to have me come in and set with you a while."

It would be impossible for us to depict Mrs. Livingstone's look of surprise and anger at this proposition. Her face alternately flushed and then grew pale, until at last she found voice to say, "I greatly prefer being alone, madam. It annoys me excessively to have any one round."

"Considerable kind o' touchy," thought Mrs. Nichols, "but then the poor critter is sick, and I shan't lay it up agin her."

Taking out her snuff-box, she offered it to her daughter, telling her that "like enough 'twould cure her headache." Mrs. Livingstone's first impulse was to strike it from her mother's hand, but knowing how unladylike that would be, she restrained herself, and turning away her head, replied, "Ugh! no! The very sight of it makes me sick."

"How you do talk! Wall, I've seen folks that it sarved jest so; but you'll get over it. Now there was Nancy Scovandyke--did John ever say anything about her? Wall, she couldn't bear snuff till after her disappointment--John told you, I suppose?"

"No, madam, my husband has never told me anything concerning his eastern friends, neither do I wish to hear anything of them," returned Mrs. Livingstone, her patience on the point of giving out.

"Never told you nothin' about Nancy Scovandyke! If that don't beat all! Why, he was----"

She was prevented from finishing the sentence, which would undoubtedly have raised a domestic breeze, when Anna came to tell her that the trunks were carried to her room.

"I'll come right up then," said she, adding, more to herself than any one else, "If I ain't mistaken, I've got a little paper of saffron somewhere, which I mean to steep for 'Tilda. Her skin looks desput jandissy!"

When Mr. Livingstone again entered his wife's room, he found her in a collapsed state of anger and mortification.

"John ***Nichols," said she, with a strong emphasis on the first word, which sounded very much like*** Jarn, "do you mean to kill me by bringing that vulgar, ignorant thing here, walking into my room without knocking--calling me 'Tilda, and prating about Nancy somebody----"

John started. His wife knew nothing of his affaire du coeur with Miss Nancy, and for his own peace of mind 't was desirable that she should not. Mentally resolving to give her a few hints, he endeavored to conciliate his wife, by saying that he knew "his mother was troublesome, but she must try not to notice her oddities."

"I wonder how I can help it, when she forces herself upon me continually," returned his wife. "I must either deep the doors locked, or live in constant terror."

"It's bad, I know," said he, smoothing her glossy hair, "but then, she's old, you know. Have you seen 'Lena?"

"No, neither do I wish to, if she's at all like her grandmother," answered Mrs. Livingstone.

"She's handsome," suggested Mr. Livingstone.

"Pshaw! handsome!" repeated his wife, scornfully, while he replied, "Yes, handsomer than either of our daughters, and with the same advantages, I've no doubt she'd surpass them both."

"Those advantages, then, she shall never have," returned Mrs. Livingstone, already jealous of a child she had only seen at a distance.

Mr. Livingstone made no reply, but felt that he'd made a mistake in praising 'Lena, in whom he began to feel a degree of interest for which he could not account. He did not know that way down in the depths of his heart, calloused over as it was by worldly selfishness, there was yet a tender spot, a lingering memory of his only sister whom 'Lena so strongly resembled. If left to himself, he would undoubtedly have taken pride in seeing his niece improve, and as it was, he determined that she should at home receive the same instruction that his daughters did. Perhaps he might not send her away to school. He didn't know how that would be--his wife held the purse, and taking refuge behind that excuse, he for the present dismissed the subject. (So much for marrying a rich wife and nothing else. This we throw in gratis!)

Meantime grandma had returned to her room, at the door of which she found John Jr. and Carrie, both curious to know what was in those boxes, one of which had burst open and been tied up with a rope.

"Come, children," said she, "don't stay out there--come in."

"We prefer remaining here," said Carrie, in a tone and manner so nearly resembling her mother, that Mrs. Nichols could not refrain from saying, "chip of the old block!"

"That's so, by cracky. You've hit her this time, granny," exclaimed John Jr., snapping his fingers under Carrie's nose, which being rather long, was frequently a subject of his ridicule.

"Let me be, John Livingstone," said Carrie, while 'Lena resolved never again to use the word "granny," which she knew her cousin had taken up on purpose to tease her.

"Come, 'Lena, catch hold and help me untie this rope, I b'lieve the crockery's in here," said Mrs. Nichols to 'Lena, who soon opened the chest, disclosing to view as motley a variety of articles as is often seen.

Among the rest was the "blue set," a part of her "setting out," as his grandmother told John Jr., at the same time dwelling at length upon their great value. Mistaking Carrie's look of contempt for envy, Mrs. Nichols chucked her under the chin, telling her "May be there was something for her, if she was a good girl."

"Now, Cad, turn your nose up clear to the top of your head," said John Jr., vastly enjoying his sister's vexation.

"Where does your marm keep her china? I want to put this with it," said Mrs. Nichols to Anna, who, uncertain what reply to make, looked at Carrie to answer for her.

"I reckon mother don't want that old stuff stuck into her china-closet," said Carrie, elevating her nose to a height wholly satisfactory to John Jr., who unbuttoned one of his waistband buttons to give himself room to laugh.

"Mortal sakes alive! I wonder if she don't," returned Mrs. Nichols, beginning to get an inkling of Carrie's character, and the estimation in which her valuables were held.

"Here's a nice little cupboard over the fireplace; I'd put them here," said 'Lena.

"Yes," chimed in John Jr., imitating both his grandmother and cousin; "yes, granny, put 'em there; the niggers are awful critters to steal, and like enough you'd 'lose 'em if they sot in with marm's!"

This argument prevailed. The dishes were put away in the cupboard, 'Lena thinking that with all his badness John Jr., was of some use after all. At last, tired of looking on, Anna suggested to 'Lena, who did not seem to be helping matters forward much, that the should go and be dressed up as had been first proposed. Readily divining her sister's intention, Carrie ran with it to her mother, who sent back word that "'Lena must mind her own affairs, and let Anna's dresses alone!"

This undeserved thrust made 'Lena cry, while Anna declared "her mother never said any such thing," which Carrie understood as an insinuation that she had told a falsehood. Accordingly a quarrel of words ensued between the two sisters, which was finally quelled by John Jr., who called to Carrie "to come down, as she'd got a letter from Durward Bellmont."

Durward! How that name made 'Lena's heart leap! Was it her Durward--the boy in the cars? She almost hoped not, for somehow the idea of his writing to Carrie was not a pleasant one. At last summoning courage, she asked Anna who he was, and was told that he lived in Louisville with his stepfather, Mr. Graham, and that Carrie about two months before had met him in Frankfort at Colonel Douglass's, where she was in the habit of visiting. "Colonel Douglass," continued Anna, "has got a right nice little girl whose name is Nellie. Then there's Mabel Ross, a sort of cousin, who lives with them part of the time. She's an orphan and a great heiress. You mustn't tell anybody for the world, but I overheard ma say that she wanted John to marry Mabel, she's so rich--but pshaw! he won't for she's awful babyish and ugly looking. Captain Atherton is related to Nellie, and during the holidays she and Mabel are coming up to spend a week, and I'll bet Durward is coming too. Cad teased him, and he said may be he would if he didn't go to college this fall. I'll run down and see."

Soon returning, she brought the news that it was as she had conjectured. Durward, who was now travelling, was not going to college until the next fall and at Christmas he was coming to the country with his cousin.

"Oh, I'm so glad," said Anna. "We'll have a time, for ma'll invite them here, of course. Cad thinks a heap of Durward, and I want so bad to see him. Don't you?"

'Lena made no direct reply, for much as she would like to see her compagnon du voyage, she felt an unwillingness to meet him in the presence of Carrie, who she knew would spare no pains to mortify her. Soon forgetting Durward, Anna again alluded to her plan of dressing 'Lena, wishing "Cad would mind her own business." Then, as a new idea entered her head, she brightened up, exclaiming, "I know what I can do. I'll have Corinda curl your hair real pretty. You've got beautiful hair. A heap nicer than my yellow flax."

'Lena offered no remonstrance, and Corinda, who came at the call of her young mistress, immediately commenced brushing and curling the bright, wavy hair which Anna had rightly called beautiful. While this was going on, Grandma

Nichols, who had always adhered to the good old puritanical custom of dining exactly at twelve o'clock, began to wonder why dinner was not forthcoming. She had breakfasted in Versailles, but like many travelers, could not eat much at a hotel, and now her stomach clamored loudly for food. Three times had she walked back and forth before what she supposed was the kitchen, and from which a savory smell of something was issuing, and at last determining to stop and reconnoiter, she started for the door.

The northern reader at all acquainted with southern life, knows well that a kitchen there and a kitchen here are two widely different things--ours, particularly in the country, being frequently used as a dining-room, while a southern lady would almost as soon think of eating in the barn as in her cook-room. Like most other planters, Mr. Livingstone's kitchen was separate and at some little distance from the main building, causing grandma to wonder "how the poor critters managed to carry victuals back and to when it was cold and slippery."

When Aunt Milly, who was up to her elbows in dough, saw her visitor approaching, she exclaimed, "Lor'-a-mighty, if thar ain't ole miss coming straight into this lookin' hole! Jeff, you quit that ar' pokin' in dem ashes, and knock Lion out that kittle; does you har? And you, Polly," speaking to a superannuated negress who was sitting near the table, "you just shove that ar' piece of dough, I done save to bake for you and me, under your char, whar she won't see it."

Polly complied, and by this time Mrs. Nichols was at the door, surveying the premises, and thinking how differently she'd make things look after a little.

"Does missus want anything?" asked Aunt Milly, and grandma replied, "Yes, I want to know if 'tain't nigh about noon."

This is a term never used among the blacks, and rolling up her white eyes, Aunt Milly answered, "You done got me now, sartin, for this chile know nothin' what you mean more'n the deadest critter livin'."

As well as she could, Mrs. Nichols explained her meaning, and Aunt Milly replied, "Oh, yes, yes, I know now. 'Is it most dinner time?' Yes--dinner'll be done ready in an hour. We never has it till two no day, and when we has company not till three."

Confident that she should starve, Mrs. Nichols advanced a step or two into the kitchen, whereupon Aunt Milly commenced making excuses, saying, "she was gwine to clar up one of these days, and then if Thomas Jefferson and Marquis De Lafayette didn't quit that litterin' they'd cotch it"

Attracted by the clean appearance of Aunt Polly, who, not having to work, prided herself upon always being neatly dressed, Mrs. Nichols walked up to her, and, to use a vulgar expression, the two old ladies were soon "hand-in-glove," Mrs. Nichols informing her of her loss, and how sorry Nancy Scovandyke would feel when she heard of it, and ending by giving her the full particulars of her husband's sickness and death. In return Aunt Polly said that "she was born and bred along with ole Marster Richards, Miss Matilda's father, and that she, too, had buried a husband."

With a deep sigh, Mrs. Nichols was about, to commiserate her, when Aunt Polly cut her short by saying, "'Twant of no kind o' count, as she never relished him much."

"Some drunken critter, I warrant," thought Mrs. Nichols, at the same time asking what his name was.

"Jeems," said Aunt Polly.

This was not definite enough for Mrs. Nichols, who asked for the surname, "Jeems what?"

"Jeems Atherton, I reckon, bein' he 'longed to ole Marster Atherton," said Polly.

For a time Mrs. Nichols had forgotten her hunger but the habit of sixty years was not so easily broken and she now hinted so strongly of the emptiness of her stomach that Aunt Polly, emboldened by her familiarity, said, "I never wait for the rest, but have my cup of tea or coffee just when I feel like it, and if missus wouldn't mind takin' a bite with a nigger, she's welcome."

"Say nothin' about it. We shall all be white in heaven."

"Dat am de trufe," muttered Milly, mentally assigning Mrs. Nichols a more exalted occupation than that of turning hoe-cakes!

Two cups and saucers were forthwith produced, Milly acting as a waiter for fear Aunt Polly would leave her seat and so disclose to view the loaf of bread which had been hidden under the chair! Some coffee was poured from the pot, which still stood on the stove, and then the little negroes, amused with the novelty of the thing, ran shouting and yelling that, "ole miss was eatin' in the kitchen 'long with

Lion, Aunt Polly and the other dogs!"

The coffee being drank, Mrs. Nichols returned to the house, thinking "what sights of comfort she should take with Mrs. Atherton," whom she pronounced to be "a likely, clever woman as ever was."

Scarcely had she reached her room when the dinner-bell rang, every note falling like an ice-bolt on the heart of 'Lena, who, though hungry like her grandmother, still greatly dreaded the dinner, fearing her inability to acquit herself creditably. Corinda had finished her hair, and Anna, looking over her wardrobe and coming upon the black dress which her father had purchased for her, had insisted upon 'Lena's wearing it. It was of rather more modern make than any of her other dresses, and when her toilet was completed, she looked uncommonly well. Still she trembled violently as Anna led her to the dining-room.

Neither Mrs. Nichols nor Mrs. Livingstone had yet made their appearance, but the latter soon came languidly in, wrapped in a rose-colored shawl, which John Jr., said "she wore to give a delicate tint to her yellow complexion." She was in the worst of humors, having just been opening her husband's trunk, where she found the numerous articles which had been stowed away by Nancy Scovandyke. Very angrily she had ordered them removed from her sight, and at this very moment the little negroes in the yard were playing with the cracked bellows, calling them a "blubber," and filling them with water to see it run out!

Except through the window, Mrs. Livingstone had not yet seen 'Lena, and now dropping into her chair, she never raised her eyes until Anna said, "Mother, mother, this is 'Lena. Look at her."

Thus importuned, Mrs. Livingstone looked up, and the frown with which she was prepared to greet her niece softened somewhat, for 'Lena was not a child to be looked upon and despised. Plain and humble as was her dress, there was something in her fine, open face, which at once interested and commanded respect, John Jr., had felt it; his father had felt it; and his mother felt it too, but it awoke in her a feeling of bitterness as she thought how the fair young girl before her might in time rival her daughters. At a glance, she saw that 'Lena was beautiful, and that it was quite as much a beauty of intellect as of feature and form.

"Yes," thought she, "husband was right when he said that, with the same advantages, she'd soon outstrip her cousins--but it shall never be--never," and the white teeth shut firmly together, as the cold, proud woman bowed a welcome.

At this moment Mrs. Nichols appeared. Stimulated by the example of 'Lena, she, too, had changed her dress, and now in black bombazine, white muslin cap, and shining silk apron, she presented so respectable an appearance that her son's face instantly brightened.

"Come, mother, we are waiting for you," said he, as she stopped on her way to ask Vine, the fly girl, "how she did, and if it wasn't hard work to swing them feathers."

Not being very bright, Vine replied with a grim, "Dun know, miss."

Taking her seat next to her son, Mrs. Nichols said when offered a plate of soup, "I don't often eat broth, besides that, I ain't much hungry, as I've just been takin' a bite with Miss Atherton?"

"With whom?" asked Mr. Livingstone, John Jr., Carrie, and Anna, in the same breath.

"With Miss Polly Atherton, that nice old colored lady in the kitchen," said Mrs. Nichols.

The scowl on Mrs. Livingstone's face darkened visibly, while her husband, thinking it time to speak, said, "It is my wish, mother, that you keep away from the kitchen. It does the negroes no good to be meddled with, and besides that, when you are hungry the servants will take you something."

"Accustomed to eat in the kitchen, probably," muttered Carrie, with all the air of a young lady of twenty.

"Hold on to your nose, Cad," whispered John Jr., thereby attracting his sister's attention to himself.

By this time the soup was removed, and a fine large turkey appeared.

"What a noble great feller. Gobbler, ain't it?" asked Mrs. Nichols, touching the turkey with the knife.

John Jr., roared, and was ordered from the table by his father, while 'Lena, who stepped on her grandmother's toes to keep her from talking, was told by that lady "to keep her feet still." Along with the desert came ice-cream, which Mrs. Nichols had never before tasted, and now fancying that she was dreadfully burned, she quickly deposited her first mouthful upon her plate.

"What's the matter, grandma? Can't you eat it?" asked Anna.

"Yes, I kin eat it, but I don't hanker arter it," answered her grandmother, pushing the plate aside.

Dinner being over, Mrs. Nichols returned to her room, but soon growing weary, she started out to view the premises. Coming suddenly upon a group of young negroes, she discovered her bellows, the water dripping from the nose, while a little farther on she espied 'Lena's bonnet, which the negroes had at last succeeded in catching, and which, wet as it was, now adorned the head of Thomas Jefferson! In a trice the old lady's principles were forgotten, and she cuffed the negroes with a right good will, hitting Jeff, the hardest, and, as a matter of course, making him yell the loudest. Out came Aunt Milly, scolding and muttering about "white folks tendin' to thar own business," and reversing her decision with regard to Mrs. Nichols' position in the next world. Cuff, the watch-dog, whose kennell was close by, set up a tremendous howling, while John Jr., always on hand, danced a jig to the sound of the direful music.

"For heaven's sake, husband, go out and see what's the matter," said Mrs. Livingstone, slightly alarmed at the unusual noise.

John complied, and reached the spot just in time to catch a glimpse of John Jr.'s heels as he gave the finishing touch to his exploit, while Mrs. Nichols, highly incensed, marched from the field of battle with the bonnet and bellows, thinking "if them niggers was only her'n they'd catch it!"

CHAPTER VII.
MALCOLM EVERETT.

It would be tiresome both to ourselves and our readers, were we to enumerate the many mortifications which both Mr. and Mrs. Livingstone were compelled to endure from their mother, who gradually came to understand her true position in the family. One by one her ideas of teaching them economy were given up, as was also all hopes of ever being at all familiar with her daughter, whom, at her son's request, she had ceased to call "'Tilda."

"Mebby you want me to say Miss Livingstone," said she, "but I shan't. I'll call her Miss Nichols, or Matilda, just which she chooses."

Of course Mrs. Livingstone chose the latter, wincing, though, every time she heard it. Dreading a scene which he knew was sure to follow a disclosure of his engagement with Miss Nancy, Mr. Livingstone had requested his mother to keep it from his wife, and she, appreciating his motive, promised secrecy, lamenting the while the ill-fortune which had prevented Nancy from being her daughter-in-law, and dwelling frequently upon the comfort she should take were Nancy there in Matilda's place. On the whole, however, she was tolerably contented; the novelty of Kentucky life pleased her, and at last, like most northern people, she fell in with the habits of those around her. Still her Massachusetts friends were not forgotten, and many a letter, wonderful for its composition and orthography, found its way to Nancy Scovandyke, who wrote in return that "some time or other she should surely visit Kentucky," asking further if the "big bugs" didn't prefer eastern teachers for their children, and hinting at her desire to engage in that capacity when she came south!

"Now, that's the very thing," exclaimed Mrs. Nichols, folding the letter (directed wrong side up) and resuming her knitting. "Nancy's larnin' is plenty good enough to teach Caroline and Anny, and I mean to speak to John about it right away."

"I wouldn't do any such thing," said 'Lena, seeing at a glance how such a proposal would be received.

"Why not?" asked Mrs. Nichols, and 'Lena replied, "I don't think Nancy would suit Aunt Livingstone at all, and besides that, they've engaged a teacher, a Mr. Everett, and expect him next week."

"You don't say so?" returned Mrs. Nichols. "I never hearn a word on't. Where 'bouts is he from, and how much do they give him a week?"

The latter 'Lena knew nothing about, but she replied that "she believed he was from Rockford, a village near Rochester, New York."

"Why, Nancy Scovandyke's sister lives there. I wouldn't wonder if he knew her."

"Very likely," returned Lena, catching her bonnet and hurrying off to ride with Captain Atherton and Anna.

As we have once before observed, Anna was a great favorite with the captain, who had petted her until John Jr. teased her unmercifully, calling him her gray-haired lover, and the like. This made Anna exceedingly sensitive, and now when the captain called for her to ride, as he frequently did, she refused to go unless the invitation was also extended to 'Lena, who in this way got many a pleasant ride around the country. She was fast learning to like Kentucky, and would have been very happy had her aunt and Carrie been a little more gracious. But the former seldom spoke to her, and the latter only to ridicule something which she said or did.

Many and amusing were the disputes between the two girls concerning their peculiarities of speech, Carrie bidding 'Lena "quit her Yankee habit of eternally guessing," and 'Lena retorting that "she would when Carrie stopped her everlasting reckoning." To avoid the remarks of the neighbors, who she knew were watching her narrowly, Mrs. Livingstone had purchased 'Lena two or three dresses, which, though greatly inferior to those worn by Carrie and Anna, were still fashionably made, and so much improved 'Lena's looks, that her manners improved, also, for what child does not appear to better advantage when conscious of looking well? More than once had her uncle's hand rested for a moment on her brown curls, while his thoughts were traversing the past, and in fancy his fingers were again straying among the silken locks now resting in the grave. It would seem as if the mother from her coffin was pleading for her child, for all the better nature of Mr. Livingstone was aroused; and when he secured the services of Mr. Everett, who was highly recommended both as a scholar and gentleman, he determined that 'Lena should share the same advantages with his daughters. To this Mrs. Livingstone made no serious objection, for as Mr. Everett would teach in the house, it would not do to debar 'Lena from the privilege of attending his school; and as the highest position to which she could aspire was to be governess in some private family, she felt willing, she said, that she should have a chance of acquiring the common branches.

And now Mr. Everett was daily expected. Anna, who had no fondness for books, greatly dreaded his arrival, thinking within herself how many pranks she'd play off upon him, provided 'Lena would lend a helping hand, which she much doubted. John Jr., too, who for a time, at least, was to be placed under Mr. Everett's instruction, felt in no wise eager for his arrival, fearing, as he told 'Lena that "between the 'old man' and the tutor, he would be kept a little too straight for a gentleman of his habits;" and it was with no particular emotions of pleasure that he and Anna saw the stage stop before the gate one pleasant morning toward the middle of November. Running to one of the front windows, Carrie, 'Lena, and Anna watched their new teacher, each after her own fashion commenting upon his appearance.

"Ugh," exclaimed Anna, "what a green, boyish looking thing! I reckon nobody's going to be afraid of him."

"I say he's real handsome," said Carrie, who being thirteen years of age, had already, in her own mind, practiced many a little coquetry upon the stranger.

"I like him," was 'Lena's brief remark.

Mr. Everett was a pale, intellectual looking man, scarcely twenty years of age, and appearing still younger so that Anna was not wholly wrong when she called him boyish. Still there was in his large black eye a firmness and decision which bespoke the man strong within him, and which put to flight all of Anna's preconceived notions of rebellion. With the utmost composure he returned Mrs. Livingstone's greeting, and the proud lady half bit her lip with vexation as she saw how little he seemed awed by her presence.

Malcolm Everett was not one to acknowledge superiority where there was none, and though ever polite toward Mrs. Livingstone, there was something in his manner which forbade her treating him as aught save an equal. He was not to be trampled down, and for once in her life Mrs. Livingstone had found a person who would neither cringe to her nor flatter. The children were not presented to him until dinner time, when, with the air of a young desperado, John Jr. marched into the dining-room, eying, his teacher askance, calculating his strength, and returning his greeting with a simple nod. Mr. Everett scanned him from head to foot, and then turned to Carrie half smiling at the great dignity which she assumed. With 'Lena and Anna he seemed better pleased, holding their hands and smiling down upon them through rows of teeth which Anna pronounced the whitest she had ever seen.

Mr. Livingstone was not at home, and when his mother appeared, Mrs. Livingstone did not think proper to introduce her. But if by this omission she thought to keep the old lady silent, she was mistaken, for the moment Mrs. Nichols was seated, she commenced with, "Your name is Everett, I b'lieve?"

"Yes, ma'am," said he, bowing very gracefully toward her.

"Any kin to the governor that was?"

"No, ma'am, none whatever," and the white teeth became slightly visible for a moment, but soon disappeared.

"You are from Rockford, 'Lena tells me?"

"Yes, ma'am. Have you friends there?"

"Yes--or that is, Nancy Scovandyke's sister, Betsy Scovandyke that used to be, lives there. May be you know her. Her name is Bacon--Betsy Bacon. She's a widder and keeps boarders."

"Ah," said he, the teeth this time becoming wholly visible, "I've heard of Mrs. Bacon, but have not the honor of her acquaintance. You are from the east, I perceive."

"Law, now! how did you know that!" asked Mrs. Nichols, while Mr. Everett answered, "I guessed at it," with a peculiar emphasis on the word guessed, which led 'Lena to think he had used it purposely and not from habit.

Mr. Everett possessed in a remarkable degree the faculty of making those around him both respect and like him, and ere six weeks had passed, he had won the love of all his pupils. Even John Jr. was greatly improved, and Carrie seemed suddenly reawakened into a thirst for knowledge, deeming no task too long, and no amount of study too hard, if it won the commendation of her teacher. 'Lena, who committed to memory with great ease, and who consequently did not deserve so much credit for her always perfect lessons, seldom received a word of praise, while poor Anna, notoriously lazy when books were concerned, cried almost every day, because as she said, "Mr. Everett didn't like her as he did the rest, else why did he look at her so much, watching her all the while, and keeping her after school to get her lessons over, when he knew how she hated them."

Once Mrs. Livingstone ventured to remonstrate, telling him that Anna was very sensitive, and required altogether different treatment from Carrie. "She thinks you dislike her," said she, "and while she retains this impression, she will do nothing as far as learning is concerned; so if you do not like her, try and make her think you do!"

There was a peculiar look in Mr. Everett's dark eyes as he answered, "You may think it strange, Mrs. Livingstone, but of all my pupils I love Anna the best! I know I find more fault with her, and am perhaps more severe with her than with the rest, but it's because I would make her what I wish her to be. Pardon me, madam, but Anna does not possess the same amount of intellect with her cousin or sister, but by proper culture she will make a fine, intelligent woman."

Mrs. Livingstone hardly relished being told that one child was inferior to the other, but she could not well help herself--Mr. Everett would say what he pleased--and thus the conference ended. From that time Mr. Everett was exceedingly kind to Anna, wiping away the tears which invariably came when told that she must stay with him in the school-room after the rest were gone; then, instead of seating himself in rigid silence at a distance until her task was learned, he would sit by her side, occasionally smoothing her long curls and speaking encouragingly to her as she pored over some hard rule of grammar, or puzzled her brains with some difficult problem in Colburn. Erelong the result of all this became manifest. Anna grew fonder of her books, more ready to learn, and--more willing to be kept after school!

Ah, little did Mrs. Livingstone think what she was doing when she bade young Malcolm Everett make her warm-hearted, impulsive daughter think he liked her!

CHAPTER VIII.
SCHEMING.

"Mother, where's 'Lena's dress? Hasn't she got any?" asked Anna, one morning, about two weeks before Christmas, as she bent over a promiscuous pile of merinoes, delaines, and plaid silks, her own and Carrie's dresses for the coming holidays. "Say, mother, didn't you buy 'Lena any?"

Thus interrogated, Mrs. Livingstone replied, "I wonder if you think I'm made of money! 'Lena is indebted to me now for more than she can ever pay. As long as I give her a home and am at so much expense in educating her, she of course can't expect me to dress her as I do you. There's Carrie's brown delaine and your blue one, which I intend to have made over for her, and she ought to be satisfied with that, for they are much better than anything she had when she came here."

And the lady glanced toward the spot where 'Lena sat, admiring the new things, in which she had no share, and longing to ask the question which Anna had asked for her, and which had now been answered. John Jr., who was present, and who knew that Mr. Everett had been engaged to teach in the family long before it was known that 'Lena was coming, now said to his cousin, who arose to leave, "Yes, 'Lena, mother's a model of generosity, and you'll never be able to repay her for her kindness in allowing you to wear the girls' old duds, which would otherwise be given to the blacks, and in permitting you to recite to Mr. Everett, who, of course, was hired on your account."

The slamming together of the door as 'Lena left the room brought the young gentleman's remarks to a close, and wishing to escape the lecture which he saw was preparing for him, he, too, made his exit.

Christmas was coming, and with it Durward Bellmont, and about his coming

Mrs. Livingstone felt some little anxiety. Always scheming, and always looking ahead, she was expecting great results from this visit. Durward was not only immensely wealthy, but was also descended on his father's side from one of England's noblemen. Altogether he was, she thought, a "decided catch," and though he was now only sixteen, while Carrie was but thirteen, lifelong impressions had been made at even an earlier period, and Mrs. Livingstone resolved that her pretty daughter should at least have all the advantages of dress with which to set off her charms. Concerning Anna's appearance she cared less, for she had but little hope of her, unless, indeed--but 'twas too soon to think of that--she would wait, and perhaps in good time 't would all come round naturally and as a matter of course. So she encouraged her daughter's intimacy with Captain Atherton, who, until Malcolm Everett appeared, was in Anna's estimation the best man living. Now, however, she made an exception in favor of her teacher, "who," as she told the captain, "neither wore false teeth, nor kept in his pocket a pair of specks, to be slyly used when he fancied no one saw him."

Captain Atherton coughed, colored, laughed, and saying that "Mr. Everett was a mash kind of a boy," swore eternal enmity toward him, and under the mask of friendship--watched! Eleven years before, when Anna was a baby, Mrs. Livingstone had playfully told the captain, who was one day deploring his want of a wife, that if he would wait he should have her daughter. To this he agreed, and the circumstance, trivial as it was, made a more than ordinary impression upon his mind; and though he as yet had no definite idea that the promise would ever be fulfilled, the little girl was to him an object of uncommon interest. Mrs. Livingstone knew this, and whenever Anna's future prospects were the subject of her meditations, she generally fell back upon that fact as an item not to be despised.

Now, however, her thoughts were turned into another and widely different channel. Christmas week was to be spent by Durward Bellmont partly at Captain Atherton's and partly at her own house, and as Mrs. Livingstone was not ignorant of the effect a becoming dress has upon a pretty face, she determined that Carrie should, at least, have that advantage. Anna, too, was to fare like her sister, while no thought was bestowed upon poor 'Lena's wardrobe, until her husband, who accompanied her to Frankfort, suggested that a certain pattern, which he fancied would be becoming to 'Lena should be purchased.

With an angry scowl, Mrs. Livingstone muttered something about "spending so much money for other folks' young ones." Then remembering the old delaines, and knowing by the tone of her husband's voice that he was in earnest, she quickly rejoined, "Why, 'Lena's got two new dresses at home."

Never doubting his wife's word, Mr. Livingstone was satisfied, and nothing more was said upon the subject. Business of importance made it necessary for him to go for a few weeks to New Orleans, and he was now on his way thither, his wife having accompanied him as far as Frankfort, where he took the boat, while she returned home. When 'Lena left the room after learning that she had no part in the mass of Christmas finery, she repaired to the arbor bridge, where she had wept so bitterly on the first day of her arrival, and which was now her favorite resort. For a time she sat watching the leaping waters, swollen by the winter rains, and wondering if it were not possible that they started at first from the pebbly spring which gushed so cool and clear from the mountain-side near her old New England home. This reminded her of where and what she was now--a dependent on the bounty of those who wished her away, and who almost every day of her life made her feel it so keenly, too. Not one among them loved her except Anna, and would not her affection change as they grew older? Then her thoughts took another direction.

Durward Bellmont was coming--but did she wish to see him? Could she bear the sneering remarks which she knew Carrie would make concerning herself? And how would he be affected by them? Would he ask her of her father? and if so, what had she to say?

Many a time had she tried to penetrate the dark mystery of her birth, but her grandmother was wholly non-committal. Once, too, when her uncle seemed kinder than usual, she had ventured to ask him of her father, and with a frown he had replied, that "the least she knew of him the better!" Still 'Lena felt sure that he was a good man, and that some time or other she would find him.

All day long the clouds had been threatening rain, which began to fall soon after 'Lena entered the arbor, but so absorbed was she in her own thoughts, that she did not observe it until her clothes were perfectly dampened; then starting up, she repaired to the house. For several days she had not been well, and this exposure brought on a severe cold, which confined her to her room for nearly two weeks. Meantime the dress-making process went on, Anna keeping 'Lena constantly apprised of its progress, and occasionally wearing in some article for her inspection. This reminded 'Lena of her own wardrobe, and knowing that it would not be attended to while she was sick, she made such haste to be well, that on Thursday at tea-time she took her accustomed seat at the table. After supper she lingered awhile in the parlor, hoping something would be said, but she waited in vain, and was about leaving, when a few words spoken by Carrie in an adjoining room caught her ear and arrested her attention.

They were--"And so 'Lena came down to-night. I dare say she thinks you'll set Miss Simpson at work upon my old delaine."

"Perhaps so," returned Mrs. Livingstone, "but I don't see how Miss Simpson can do it, unless you put off having that silk apron embroidered."

"I shan't do any such thing," said Carrie, glad of an excuse to keep 'Lena out of the way. "What matter is it if she don't come down when the company are here? I'd rather she wouldn't, for she's so green and awkward, and Durward is so fastidious in such matters, that I'd rather he wouldn't know she's a relative of ours! I know he'd tell his mother, and they say she is very particular about his associates."

'Lena's first impulse was to defy her cousin to her face--to tell her she had seen Durward Bellmont, and that he didn't laugh at her either. But her next thought was calmer and more rational. Possibly under Carrie's influence he might make fun of her, and resolving on no condition whatever to make herself visible while he was in the house, she returned to her room, and throwing herself upon the bed, wept until she fell asleep.

"When is Miss Simpson going to fix 'Lena's dress?" asked Anna, as day after day passed, and nothing was said of the brown delaine.

For an instant Miss Simpson's nimble fingers were still, as she awaited the answer to a question which had occurred to her several times. She was a kind-hearted, intelligent girl, find at a glance had seen how matters stood. She, too, was an orphan, and her sympathies were all enlisted in behalf of the neglected 'Lena. She had heard from Anna of the brown delaine, and in her own mind she had determined that it should be fitted with the utmost taste of which she was capable.

Her speculations, however, were brought to a close by Mrs. Livingstone's saying in reply to Anna, that "'Lena seemed so wholly uninterested, and cared so little about seeing the company, she had decided not to have the dress fixed until after

Christmas week."

The fiery expression of two large, glittering eyes, which at that moment peered in at the door, convinced Miss Simpson that her employer had hardly told the truth, and she secretly determined that 'Lena should have the dress whether she would or not. Accordingly, the next time she and Anna were alone, she asked for the delaine, entrusting her secret to Anna, who, thinking no harm, promised to keep it from her mother. But to get 'Lena fitted was a more difficult matter. Her spirit was roused, and for a time she resisted their combined efforts. At last, however, she yielded, and by working late at night in her own room, Miss Simpson managed to finished the dress, in which 'Lena really looked better than did either of her cousins in their garments of far richer materials. Still she was resolved not to go down, and Anna, fearing what her mother might say, dared not urge her very strongly hoping, though, that "something would turn up."

*   *   *   *   *   *

Durward Bellmont, Nellie Douglass, and Mabel Ross had arrived at Captain Atherton's. Mrs. Livingstone and her daughters had called upon them, inviting them to spend a few days at Maple Grove, where they were to meet some other young people "selected from the wealthiest families in the neighborhood," Mrs. Livingstone said, at the same time patting the sallow cheek of Mabel, whose reputed hundred thousand she intended should one day increase the importance of her own family.

The invitation was accepted--the day had arrived, the guests were momentarily expected, and Carrie, before the long mirror, was admiring herself, alternately frowning upon John Jr., who was mimicking her "airs," and scolding Anna for fretting because 'Lena could not be induced to join them. Finding that her niece was resolved not to appear, Mrs. Livingstone, for looks' sake, had changed her tactics, saying, "'Lena could come down if she chose--she was sure there was nothing to prevent."

Knowing this, Anna had exhausted all her powers of eloquence upon her cousin. But she still remained inexorable, greatly to the astonishment of her grandmother who for several days had been suffering from a rheumatic affection, notwithstanding which she "meant to hobble down if possible, for" said she, "I want to see this Durward Bellmont. Matilda says he's got Noble blood in him. I used to know a family of Nobles in Massachusetts, and I think like as not he's some kin!"

Carrie, to whom this remark was made, communicated it to her mother, who forthwith repaired to Mrs. Nichols' room, telling her "that 'twas a child's party," and hinting pretty strongly that she was neither wanted nor expected in the parlor, and would confer a great favor by keeping aloof.

"Wall, wall," said Mrs. Nichols, who had learned to dread her daughter's displeasure, "I'd as lief stay up here as not, but I do want 'Lena to jine 'em. She's young and would enjoy it."

Without a word of answer Mrs. Livingstone walked away, leaving 'Lena more determined than ever not to go down. When the evening at last arrived, Anna insisted so strongly upon her wearing the delaine, for fear of what might happen, that 'Lena consented, curling her hair with great care, and feeling a momentary thrill of pride as she saw how well she looked.

"When we get nicely to enjoying ourselves," said Anna, "you come down and look through the glass door, for I do want you to see Durward, he's so handsome--but there's the carriage--I must go;" and away ran Anna down the stairs, while 'Lena flew to one of the front windows to see the company as they rode up.

First came Captain Atherton's carriage, and in it the captain and his maiden sister, together with a pale, sickly-looking girl, whom 'Lena knew to be Mabel Ross. Behind them rode Durward Bellmont, and at his side, on a spirited little pony was another girl, thirteen or fourteen years of age, but in her long riding-dress looking older, because taller. 'Lena readily guessed that this was Nellie Douglass, and at a glance she recognized the Durward of the cars--grown handsomer and taller since then, she thought. With a nimble bound he leaped from his saddle, kissing his hand to Carrie, who with her sunniest smile ran past him to welcome Nellie. A pang, not of jealousy, but of an undefined something, shot through 'Lena's heart, and dropping the heavy curtain, she turned away, while the tears gathered thickly in her large brown eyes.

"Where's 'Lena?" asked Captain Atherton, of Anna, warming his red fingers before the blazing grate, and looking round upon the group of girls gathered near.

Glancing at her mother, Anna replied, "She says she don't want to come down."

"Bashful," returned the captain, while Nellie Douglass asked, "who 'Lena was," at the same time returning the pinch *which John Jr. had slyly given her as a mode of showing his preference, for Nellie* was his favorite.

Fearful of Anna's reply, Mrs. Livingstone answered, carelessly, "She's the child of one of Mr. Livingstone's poor relations, and we've taken her awhile out of charity."

At any other time John Jr. would doubtless have questioned his mother's word, but now so engrossed was he with the merry, hoydenish Nellie, that he scarcely heard her remark, or noticed the absence of 'Lena. With the exception of his cousin, Nellie was the only girl whom John Jr. could endure--"the rest," he said, "were so stuck up and affected."

For Mabel Ross, he seemed to have a particular aversion. Not because she was so very disagreeable, but because his mother continually reminded him of what she hoped would one day be, "and this," he said, "was enough to make a 'feller' hate a girl." So without considering that Mabel was not to blame, he ridiculed her unmercifully, calling her "a bundle of medicine," and making fun of her thin, sallow face, which really appeared to great disadvantage when contrasted with Nellie's bright eyes and round, rosy cheeks.

When the guests were all assembled, Carrie, not knowing whether Durward Bellmont would relish plays, seated herself demurely upon the sofa, prepared to act the dignified young lady, or any other character she might think necessary.

"Get up, Cad," said John Jr. "Nobody's going to act like they were at a funeral; get up, and let's play something."

As the rest seemed to be similarly inclined, Carrie arose, and erelong the joyous shouts reached 'Lena, making her half wish that she, too, was there. Remembering Anna's suggestion of looking through the glass door she stole softly down the stairs, and stationing herself behind the door, looked in on the scene. Mr. Everett, usually so dignified, had joined in the game, claiming "forfeits" from Anna more frequently than was considered at all necessary by the captain, who for a time looked jealously on, and then declaring himself as young as any of them, joined them with a right good will.

"Blind man's buff," was next proposed, and 'Lena's heart leaped up, for that was her favorite game. John Jr. was first blinded, but he caught them so easily that all declared he could see, and loud were the calls for Durward to take his place. This he willingly did, and whether he could see or not, he suffered them to pass directly under his hands, thus giving entire satisfaction. On account of the heat of the rooms, Anna, on passing the glass door, threw it open, and the next time Durward came round he marched directly into the hall, seizing 'Lena, who was trying to hide.

Feeling her long curls, he exclaimed, "Anna, you are caught."

"No, I ain't Anna; let me go," said 'Lena, struggling to escape.

This brought all the girls to the spot, while Durward, snatching the muffler from his eyes, looked down with astonishment upon the trembling 'Lena, who would have escaped had she not been so securely hemmed in.

"Ain't you ashamed, 'Lena, to be peeking?" asked Carrie, while Durward repeated--"'Lena! 'Lena! I've seen her before in the cars between Springfield and Albany; but how came she here?"

"She lives here--she's our cousin," said Anna, notwithstanding the twitch given to her sleeve by Carrie, who did not care to have the relationship exposed.

"Your cousin," said Durward, "and where's the old lady who was with her?"

"The one she called granny?" asked John Jr., on purpose to rouse up his fiery little cousin.

"No, I don't call her granny, neither--I've quit it," said 'Lena, angrily, adding, as a sly hit at Kentucky talk, "she's up stars, sick with the rheumatism."

"Good," said Durward, "but why are you not down here with us?"

"I didn't want to come," was her reply; and Durward, leading her into the parlor, continued, "but now that you are here, you must stay."

"Pretty, isn't she," said Nellie, as the full blaze of the chandelier fell upon 'Lena.

"Rath-er," was Carrie's hesitating reply.

She felt annoyed that 'Lena should be in the parlor, and provoked that Durward should notice her in any way, and at the first opportunity she told him "how much she both troubled and mortified them, by her vulgarity and obstinacy," adding that "she had a most violent temper." From Nellie she had learned that Durward particularly disliked passionate girls, and for this reason she strove to give him the impression that 'Lena was such an one. Once or twice she fancied him half inclined to disbelieve her, as he saw how readily 'Lena joined in their amusements, and how good-humoredly she bore John Jr.'s teasing, and then she hoped something would occur to prove her words true. Her wish was gratified.

The next day was dark and stormy, confining the young people to the house. About ten o'clock the negro who had been to the post-office returned, bringing letters for the family, among which was one for 'Lena, so curious in its shape and superscription, that even the negro grinned as he handed it out. 'Lena was not then present, and Carrie, taking the letter, exclaimed, "Now if this isn't the last specimen from Yankeedom. Just listen,--" and she spelled out the direction--" To Mis HELL-ENY RIVERS, state of kentucky, county of woodford, Dorsey post offis, care of Mis nichals ."

Unobserved by any one, 'Lena had entered the parlor in time to hear every word, and when Carrie, chancing to espy her, held out the letter, saying, "Here, Helleny, I guess this came from down east," she darted forward, and striking the letter from Carrie's hands stamped upon it with her foot, declaring "she'd never open it in the world," and saying "they might do what they pleased with it for all of her."

"Read it--may we read it?" eagerly asked Carrie, delighted to see 'Lena doing such justice to her reputation.

"Yes, read it!" almost screamed 'Lena, and before any one could interpose a word, Carrie had broken the seal and commenced reading, announcing, first, that it came from "Joel Slocum!" It was as follows:

"Dear Helleny, mebby you'll wonder when you see a letter from me, but I'll be hanged if I can help 'ritin', I am so confounded lonesome now you are gone, that I dun know nothing what to do with myself. So I set on the great rock where the saxefax grows; and think, and think till it seems 's ef my head would bust open. Wall, how do you git along down amongst them heathenish Kentucks & niggers? I s'pose there ain't no great difference between 'em, is there? When I git a little more larnin', I b'lieve I'll come down there to keep school. O, I forgot to tell you that our old line back cow has got a calf--the prettiest little critter--Dad has gin her to me, and I call her Helleny, I do, I swow! And when she capers round she makes me think of the way you danced 'High putty Martin' the time you stuck a sliver in your heel--"

Up to this point 'Lena had stood immovable, amid the loud shouts of her companions, but the fire of a hundred volcanoes burned within and flashed from her eyes. And now springing forward, she caught the letter from Carrie's hand, and inflicting a long scratch upon her forehead, fled from the room. Had not Durward Bellmont been present, Carrie would have flown after her cousin, to avenge the insult, and even now she was for a moment thrown off her guard, and starting forward, exclaimed, "the tigress!"

Drawing his fine cambric handkerchief from his pocket, Durward gently wiped the blood from her white brow, saying "Never mind. It is not a deep scratch."

"I wish 'twas deeper," muttered John Jr. "You'd no business to serve her so mean."

An angry retort rose to Carrie's lips, but, just in time to prevent its utterance, Durward also spoke, saying, "It was too bad to tease her so, but we were all more or less to blame, and I'm not sure but we ought to apologize."

Carrie felt that she would die, almost, before she'd apologize to such as 'Lena, and still she thought it might be well enough to give Durward the impression that she was doing, her best to make amends for her fault. Accordingly, the next time her cousin appeared in the parlor she was all smiles and affability, talking a great deal to 'Lena, who returned very short but civil answers, while her face wore a look which Durward construed into defiance and hatred of everybody and everything.

"Too passionate," thought he, turning from her to Carrie, whose voice, modulated to its softest tones, rang out clear and musical, as she sported and laughed with her moody cousin, appearing the very essence of sweetness and amiability!

Pity he could not have known how bitterly 'Lena had wept over her hasty action--not because he witnessed it, but because she knew it was wrong! Pity he could not have read the tear-blotted note, which she laid on Carrie's work-box, and in which was written, "I am sorry, Carrie, that I hurt you so. I didn't know what I was about, but I will try and not get so angry again."

Pity, too, that he did not see the look of contempt with which Carrie perused this note; and when the two girls accidentally met in the upper hall, and 'Lena laid her hand gently on Carrie's arm, it is a thousand pities he was not present to see how fiercely she was repulsed, Carrie exclaiming, "Get out of my sight! I hate you, and so do all of them downstairs, Durward in particular."

Had he known all this he would have thought differently of 'Lena, who, feeling that she was not wanted in the parlor, kept herself entirely aloof, never again appearing during the remainder of his stay. Once Durward asked for her, and half laughingly Carrie replied, that "she had not yet recovered from her pouting fit." Could he have known her real occupation, he might have changed his mind again. The stormy weather had so increased Mrs. Nichols' rheumatic complaint, that now, perfectly crippled, she lay as helpless as a child, carefully nursed by 'Lena and old Aunt Polly, who, spite of her own infirmities, had hobbled in to wait upon her friend. Never but once did Mrs. Livingstone go near her mother's sick-room--"the smell of herbs made her faint," she said! But to do her justice, we must say that she gave Polly unqualified permission to order anything she pleased for the invalid.

Toward the close of the third day, the company left. Nellie Douglass, who really liked 'Lena, and wished to bid her good-bye, whispered to John Jr., asking him to show her the way to his cousin's room. No one except members of the family had ever been in Mrs. Nichols' apartment, and for a moment John Jr. hesitated, knowing well that Nellie could not fail to observe the contrast it presented to the other richly-furnished chambers.

"They ought to be mortified--it'll serve 'em right," he thought, at last, and motioning Nellie to fallow him, he silently led the way to his grandmother's room, where their knock was answered by Aunt Polly's gruff voice, which bade them "come in."

They obeyed, but Nellie started back when she saw how greatly inferior was this room to the others around it. In an instant her eye took in everything, and she readily comprehended the whole.

"It isn't my doings, by a jug-full!" whispered John Jr., himself reddening as he noted the different articles of furniture which had never before seemed so meager and poor.

On the humble bed, in a half-upright position, lay Mrs. Nichols, white as the snowy cap-border which shaded her face. Behind her sat 'Lena, supporting her head, and when Nellie entered, she was carefully pushing back the few gray locks which had fallen over the invalid's forehead, her own bright curls mingling with them, and resting, some on her neck, and some on her grandmother's shoulder. A deep flush dyed her cheeks when she saw Nellie, who thought she had never looked upon a sight more beautiful.

"I did not know your grandmother was ill," said she, coming forward and gently touching the swollen hand which lay outside the counterpane.

Mrs. Nichols was not too ill to talk, and forthwith she commenced a history of her malady, beginning at the time she first had it when 'Lena's mother was a year and a day old, frequently quoting Nancy Scovandyke, and highly entertaining Nellie, who listened until warned by the sound of the carriage, as it came round to the door, that she must go.

"We are going back to Uncle Atherton's," said she, "but I wanted to bid you good-bye, and ask you to visit me in Frankfort with your cousins. Will you do so?"

This was wholly unexpected to 'Lena, who, without replying, burst info tears. Nellie hardly knew what to do. She seldom cried herself--she did not like to see others cry--and still she did not blame 'Lena, for she felt that she could not help it. At last, taking her hand, she bade her farewell, asking if she should not carry a good-bye to the others.

"Yes, to Mabel," said 'Lena.

"And not Durward?" asked Nellie.

With something of her old spirit 'Lena answered, "No, he hates me--Carrie says so."

"Cad's a fool," muttered John Jr., while Nellie rejoined, "Durward never hated anybody, and even if he did, he would not say so--I mean to tell him;" and with another good-bye she was gone.

On the stairs she met Durward, who was looking for her, and asked where she had been.

"To bid 'Lena good-bye; don't you want to go too?" said Nellie.

"Why, yes, if you are sure she won't scratch my eyes out," he returned, gayly, following his cousin.

"I reckon I'd better tell 'Lena to come out into the hall--she may not want you in there," said John Jr., and hastening forward he told his cousin what was wanted.

Oh, how 'Lena longed to go, but pride, and the remembrance of Carrie's words, prevented her, and coldly answering, "No, I don't wish to see him," she turned away to hide the tears and pain which those words had cost her.

This visit to Grandma Nichols' room was productive of some good, for John Jr., did not fail of repeating to his mother the impression which he saw was made on Nellie's mind, adding, that "though Durward did not venture in, Nellie would of course tell him all about it. And then," said he, "I wouldn't give much for his opinion of your treatment of your mother."

Angry, because she felt the truth of what her son said, Mrs. Livingstone demanded "what he'd have her do."

"Do?" he repeated, "give grandmother a decent room, or else fix that one up, so it won't look like the old scratch had been having a cotillon there. Paper and paint it, and make it look decent."

Upon this last piece of advice Mrs. Livingstone resolved to act, for recently several vague rumors had reached her ear, touching her neglect of her mother-in-law, and she began herself to think it just possible that a little of her money would be well expended in adding to the comfort of her husband's mother. Accordingly, as soon as Mrs. Nichols was able to sit up, her room underwent a thorough renovation, and though no great amount of money was expended upon it, it was fitted up with so much taste that the poor old lady, whom John Jr., 'Lena and Anna, had adroitly kept out of the way until her room was finished, actually burst into tears when first ushered into her light, airy apartment, in which everything looked so cheerful and pleasant.

"'Tilda has now and then a good streak," said she, while Aunt Milly, who had taken a great deal of interest in the repairing of the room, felt inclined to change her favorite theory with regard to her mistress' future condition.

CHAPTER IX.
FIVE YEARS LATER.

A nd in the fair city of elms we again open the scene. It was commencement at Yale, and the crowd which filled the old Center church were listening breathlessly to the tide of eloquence poured forth by the young valedictorian.

Durward Bellmont, first in his studies, first in his class, and first in the esteem of his fellow-students, had been unanimously chosen to that post of honor, and as the gathered multitude hung upon his words and gazed upon his manly beauty, they felt mat a better choice could not well have been made. At the right of the platform sat a group of ladies, friends, it would seem, of the speaker, for ever and anon his eyes turned in that direction, and as if each glance incited him to fresh efforts, his eloquence increased, until at last no sound save that of his deep-toned voice was heard, so rapt was every one in the words of the young orator. But when his speech was ended, there arose deafening shouts of applause, while bouquets fell in perfect showers at his feet. Among them was one smaller and more elegant than the rest, and as if it were more precious, too, it was the first which Durward took from the floor.

"See, Carrie, he gives you the preference," whispered one of the young ladies on the right, and Carrie Livingstone for she it was, felt a thrill of gratified pride, when she saw how carefully he guarded the bouquet, which during all the exercises she had made her especial care, calling attention to it in so many different ways that hardly any one who saw it in Durward's possession, could fail of knowing from what source it same.

But then everybody said they were engaged--so what did it matter? Everybody but John Jr., who was John Jr. still, and who while openly denying the engagement, teasingly hinted "that 'twas no fault of Cad's."

For the last three years, Carrie, Nellie, Mabel, and Anna had been inmates of the seminary in New Haven, and as they were now considered sufficiently accomplished to enter at once upon all the gayeties of fashionable life, John Jr. had come on "to see the elephant," as he said, and to accompany them home. Carrie had fulfilled the promise of her girlhood, and even her brother acknowledged that she was handsome in spite of her nose, which like everybody's else, still continued to be the most prominent feature of her face. She was proud, too, as well as beautiful, and throughout the city she was known as the "haughty southern belle," admired by some and disliked by many. Among the students she was not half so popular as her unpretending sister, whose laughing blue eyes and sunny brown hair were often toasted, together with the classical brow and dignified bearing of Nellie Douglass, who had lost some of the hoydenish propensities of her girlhood, and who was now a graceful, elegant creature just merging into nineteen--the pride of her widowed father, and the idol still of John Jr., whose boyish preference had ripened into a kind of love such as only he could feel.

With poor Mabel Ross it had fared worse, her plain face and dumpy little figure never receiving the least attention except from Durward Bellmont, who pitying her lonely condition, frequently left more congenial society for the sake of entertaining her. Of any one else Carrie would have been jealous, but feeling sure that Mabel had no attraction save her wealth, and knowing that Durward did not care for that, she occasionally suffered him to leave her side, always feeling amply repaid by the evident reluctance with which he left her society for that of Mabel's.

When ill-naturedly rallied by his companions upon his preference for Carrie, Durward would sometimes laughingly refer them to the old worn-out story of the fox and the grapes, for to scarcely any one save himself did Carrie think it worth her while to be even gracious. This conduct was entirely at variance with her natural disposition, for she was fond of admiration, come from what source it might, and she would never have been so cold and distant to all save Durward, had she not once heard him say that "he heartily despised a flirt; and that no young lady could at all interest him if he suspected her of being a coquette."

This, then, was the secret of her reserve. She was resolved upon winning Durward Bellmont, deeming no sacrifice too great if in the end it secured the prize. It is true there was one sophomore, a perfumed, brainless fop, from Rockford, N. Y., who, next to Durward, was apparently most in favor, but the idea of her entertaining even a shadow of a liking for Tom Lakin, was too ludicrous to be harbored for a moment, so his attentions went for naught, public opinion uniting in giving her to Mr. Bellmont.

With the lapse of years, Anna, too, had greatly improved. The extreme delicacy of her figure was gone, and though her complexion was as white and pure as marble, it denoted perfect health. With John Jr. she was still the favorite sister, the one whom he loved the best. "Carrie was too stiff and proud," he said, and though when he met her in New Haven, after a year's absence, his greeting was kind and brotherly, he soon turned from her to Anna and Nellie, utterly neglecting Mabel, who turned away to her chamber to cry, because no one cared for her.

Frequently had his mother reminded him of the importance of securing a wealthy bride, always finishing her discourse by speaking of Mr. Douglass' small income, and enlarging upon the immense wealth of Mabel Ross, whose very name had become disagreeable to John Jr. At one time his father had hoped he, too, would enter college, but the young man derided the idea of his ever making a scholar, saying, however, more in sport than in earnest, that "he was willing to enter a store, or learn a trade, so that in case he was ever obliged to earn his own living, he would have some means of doing it;" but to this his mother would not listen. He was her "darling boy," and "his hands, soft and white as those of a girl, should never become hardened and embrowned by labor!" So, while his sisters were away at school, he was at home, hunting, fishing, riding, teasing his grandmother, tormenting the servants, and shocking his mother by threatening to make love to his cousin 'Lena, to whom he was at once a pest and a comfort, and who now claims a share of our attention.

When it was decided to send Carrie and Anna to New Haven, Mr. Livingstone proposed that 'Lena should also accompany them, but this plan Mrs. Livingstone opposed with all her force, declaring that her money should never be spent in educating the "beggarly relatives" of her husband, who in this, as in numerous other matters, was forced to yield the point. As Mr. Everett's services were now no longer needed, he accepted the offer of a situation in the family of General Fontaine, a high-bred, southern gentleman, whose plantation was distant but half a mile from

"Maple Grove;" and as he there taught a regular school, having under his charge several of the daughters of the neighboring planters, it was decided that 'Lena also should continue under his instruction.

Thus while Carrie and Anna were going through the daily routine of a fashionable boarding-school, 'Lena was storing her mind with useful knowledge, and though her accomplishments were not quite so showy as those of her cousins, they had in them the ring of the pure metal. Although her charms were as yet but partially developed, she was a creature of rare loveliness, and many who saw her for the first time, marveled that aught so beautiful could be real. She had never seen Durward Bellmont since that remarkable Christmas week, but many a time had her cheeks flushed with a feeling which she could not define, as she read Anna's accounts of the flattering attentions which he paid to Carrie, who, when at home, still treated her with haughty contempt or cool indifference.

But for this she did not care. She knew she was loved by Anna, and liked by John Jr., and she hoped--nay, half believed--that she was not wholly indifferent to her uncle, who, while he seldom made any show of his affection, still in his heart admired and felt proud of her. With his wife it was different. She hated 'Lena-- hated her because she was beautiful and talented, and because in her presence Carrie and Anna were ever in the shade. Still her niece was too general a favorite in the neighborhood to allow of open hostility at home, and so the proud woman ground together her glittering teeth-- and waited!

Among the many who admired 'Lena, there was no one who gave her such full and unbounded homage as did her grandmother, whose life at Maple Grove had been one of shadow, seldom mingled with sunshine. Gradually had she learned the estimation in which she was held by her son's wife, and she felt how bitter it was to eat the bread of dependence. As far as she was able, 'Lena shielded her from the sneers of her aunt, who thinking she had done all that was required of her when she fixed their room, would for days and even weeks appear utterly oblivious of their presence, or frown darkly whenever chance threw them in her way. She had raised no objection to 'Lena's continuing a pupil of Mr. Everett, who, she hoped, would not prove indifferent to her charms, fancying that in this way she would sooner be rid of one whom she feared as a rival of her daughters.

But she was mistaken; for much as Malcolm Everett might admire 'Lena, another image than hers was enshrined in his heart, and most carefully guarded was the little golden curl, cut in seeming sport from the head it once adorned, and, now treasured as a sacred memento of the past. Believing that it would be so because she wished it to be so, Mrs. Livingstone had more than once whispered to her female friends her surmises that Malcolm Everett would marry 'Lena, and at the time of which we are speaking, it was pretty generally understood that a strong liking, at least, if not an engagement, existed between them.

Old Captain Atherton, grown more smooth and portly, rubbed his fat hands complacently, and while applying Twigg's Preparation to his hair, congratulated himself that the only rival he had ever feared was now out of his way. Thinking, too, that 'Lena had conferred a great favor upon himself by taking Mr. Everett from off his mind, became exceedingly polite to her, making her little presents and frequently asking her to ride. Whenever these invitations were accepted, they were sure to be followed by a ludicrous description to Anna, who laughed merrily over her cousin's letters, declaring herself half jealous of her "gray-haired lover," as she termed the captain.

All such communications were eagerly seized by Carrie, and fully discussed in the presence of Durward, who gradually received the impression that 'Lena was a flirt, a species of womankind which he held in great abhorrence. Just before he left New Haven, he received a letter from his stepfather, requesting him to stop for a day or two at Captain Atherton's, where he would join him, as he wished to look at a country-seat near Mr. Livingstone's, which was now for sale. This plan gave immense satisfaction to Carrie, and when her brother proposed that Durward should stop at their father's instead of the captain's, she seconded the invitation so warmly, that Durward finally consented, and word was immediately sent to Mrs. Livingstone to hold herself in readiness to receive Mr. Bellmont.

"Oh, I do hope your father will secure Woodlawn," said Carrie, as in the parlor of the Burnett House, Cincinnati, they were discussing the projected purchase.

The other young ladies had gone out shopping, and John Jr., who was present, and who felt just like teasing his sister, replied, "What do you care? Mrs. Graham has no daughters, and she won't fancy such a chit as you, so it must be Durward's society that you so much desire, bit I can assure you that your nose will be broken when once he sees our 'Lena."

Carrie turned toward the window to hide her wrath at this speech, while Durward asked if "Miss Rivers were so very handsome?"

"Handsome!" repeated John. "That don't begin to express it. Cad *is what I call* handsome, but 'Lena is beautiful, more beautiful, most beautiful--now you have it superlatively. Such complexion--such eyes--such hair--I'll be hanged if I haven't been more than half in love with her myself."

"I really begin to tremble," said Durward, laughingly while Carrie rejoined, "You've only to make the slightest advance, and your love will be returned ten-fold, for 'Lena is very susceptible, and already encourages several admirers."

"There, my fair sister, you are slightly mistaken," interrupted John Jr., who was going on farther in his remarks, when Durward asked if "she ever left any marks *of her affection," referring to the scratch she had given Carrie; who, before her brother had time to speak, replied that "the* will *and the* claws remained the same, though common decency kept them hidden when it was necessary."

"That's downright slander," said John Jr., determined now upon defending his cousin, "'Lena has a high temper, I acknowledge, but she tries hard to govern it, and for nearly two years I've not seen her angry once, though she's had every provocation under heaven."

"She knows when *and* where to be amiable," retorted Carrie. "Any one of her admirers would tell the same story with yourself."

At this juncture John Jr. was called for a moment from the room, and Carrie, fearing she had said too much, immediately apologized to Durward, saying, "it was not often that she allowed herself to speak against her cousin, and that she should not have done so now, were not John so much blinded, that her mother, knowing Lena's ambitious nature, sometimes seriously feared the consequence. I know," said she, "that John fancies Nellie, but 'Lena's influence over him is very great."

Durward made no reply, and Carrie continued: "I'm always sorry when I speak against 'Lena; she is my cousin, and I wouldn't prejudice any one against her; so you must forget my unkind remarks, which would never have been uttered in the presence of a stranger. She is handsome and agreeable, and you must like her in spite of what I said."

"I cannot refuse when so fair a lady pleads her cause," was Durward's gallant answer, and as the other young ladies then entered the room, the conversation ceased.

Meanwhile 'Lena was very differently employed. Nearly a year had elapsed since she had seen her cousins, and her heart bounded with joy at the thought of meeting Anna, whom she dearly loved. Carrie was to her an object of indifference, rather than dislike, and ofttimes had she thought, "If she would only let me love her." But it could not be, for there was no affinity between them. Carrie was proud and overbearing--jealous of her high-spirited cousin, who, as John Jr. had said, strove hard to subdue her temper, and who now seldom resented Carrie's insults, except when they were leveled at her aged grandmother.

As we have before stated, news' had been received at Maple Grove that Durward would accompany her cousins home. Mr. Graham would, of course, join him there, and accordingly, extensive preparations were immediately commenced. An unusual degree of sickness was prevailing among the female portion of Mrs. Livingstone's servants, and the very day before the company was expected, Aunt Milly, the head cook was taken suddenly ill. Coaxing, scolding, and threatening were alike ineffectual. The old negress would not say she was well when she wasn't, and as Hagar, the next in command, was also sick (lazy, as her mistress called it,) Mrs. Livingstone was herself obliged to superintend the cookery.

"Crosser than a bar," as the little darkies said, she flew back and forth, from kitchen to pantry, her bunch of keys rattling, the corners of her mouth drawn back, and her hands raised ready to strike at anything that came in her way. As if there were a fatality attending her movements, she was unfortunate in whatever she undertook. The cake was burned black, the custard curdled, the preserves were found to be working, the big preserve dish got broken, a thunder shower soured the cream, and taking it all in all, she really had trouble enough to disconcert the most experienced housekeeper. Still, the few negroes able to assist, thought "she needn't be so fetch-ed cross."

But cross she was, feeling more than once inclined to lay witchcraft to the charge of old Milly, who comfortably ensconced in bed, listened in dismay to the disastrous accounts brought her from time to time from the kitchen, mentally congratulating herself the while upon not being within hearing of her mistress' tongue. Once Mrs. Nichols attempted to help, but she was repulsed so angrily that 'Lena did not presume to offer her services until the day of their arrival, when, without a word, she repaired to the chambers, which she swept and dusted, arranging the furniture, and making everything ready for the comfort of the travelers. Then descending to the parlors, she went through the same process there, filled the vases with fresh flowers, looped back the curtains, opened the piano, wheeled the sofa a little to the right, the large chair a little to the left, and then going to the dining-room, she set the table in the most perfect order, doing all so quietly that her aunt knew nothing of it until it was done. Jake the coachman, had gone down to Frankfort after them, and as he was not expected to return until between three and four, dinner was deferred until that hour.

From sunrise Mrs. Livingstone had worked industriously, until her face and temper were at a boiling heat. The clock was on the point of striking three, and she was bending over a roasting turkey, when 'Lena ventured to approach her, saying, "I have seen Aunt Milly baste a turkey many a time, and I am sure I can do it as well as she."

"Well, what of it?" was the uncivil answer.

'Lena's temper choked her, but forcing it down, she replied: "Why, it is almost three, and I thought perhaps you would want to cool and dress yourself before they came. I can see to the dinner, I know I can. Please let me try."

Somewhat mollified by her niece's kind manner, Mrs. Livingstone resigned her post and repaired to her own room, while 'Lena, confining her long curls to the top of her head and donning the wide check-apron which her aunt had thrown aside, set herself at work with a right good will.

"What dat ar you say?" exclaimed Aunt Milly, lifting her woolly head from her pillow, and looking at the little colored girl, who had brought to her the news that "young miss was in de kitchen." "What dat ar you tellin'? Miss 'Leny pokin' 'mong de pots and kittles, and dis ole nigger lazin' in bed jes like white folks. Long as 'twas ole miss, I didn't seer. Good 'nough for her to roast, blister, and bile; done get used to it, case she's got to in kingdom come, no mistake--he!--he! But little Miss 'Leny, it's too bad to bake her lamb's-wool hands and face, and all de quality comin': I'll hobble up thar, if I can stand."

Suiting the action to the word she got out of bed, and crawling up to the kitchen, insisted upon taking 'Lena's place, saying, "she could sit in her chair and tell the rest what to do."

For a time 'Lena hesitated, the old woman seemed so faint and weak, but the sound of wheels decided her. Springing to the sideboard in the dining-room, she brought Aunt Milly a glass of wine, which revived her so much that she now felt willing to leave her. By this time the carriage was at the door, and to escape unobserved was now her great object. But this she could not do, for as she was crossing the hall, Anna espied her, and darting forward, seized her around the neck, at the same time dragging her toward Carrie, who, with Durward's eye upon her, kissed her twice; then turning to him, she said, "I suppose you do not need an introduction to Miss Rivers?"

Durward was almost guilty of the rudeness of staring at the strangeness of 'Lena's appearance, for as nearly as she could, she looked like a fright. Bending over hot stoves and boiling gravies is not very beneficial to one's complexion, and 'Lena's cheeks, neck, forehead, and nose were of a purplish red--her hair was tucked back in a manner exceedingly unbecoming, while the broad check-apron, which came nearly to her feet, tended in nowise to improve her appearance. She felt it keenly, and after returning Durward's salutation, she broke away before Anna or John, Jr., who were both surprised at her looks, had time to ask a question.

Running up to her room, her first impulse was to cry, but knowing that would disfigure her still more, she bathed her burning face and neck, brushed out her curls, threw on a simple muslin dress, and started for the parlor, of which Durward and Carrie were at that moment the only occupants. As she was passing the outer door, she observed upon one of the piazza pillars a half-blown rose, and for a moment stopped to admire it. Durward, who sat in a corner, did not see her, but Carrie did, and a malicious feeling prompted her to draw out her companion, who she felt sure was disappointed in 'Lena's face. They were speaking of a lady whom they saw at Frankfort, and whom Carrie pronounced "perfectly beautiful," while Durward would hardly admit that she was even good-looking.

"I am surprised at your taste," said Carrie, adding, as she noticed the proximity of her cousin, "I think she resembles 'Lena, and of course you'll acknowledge she is beautiful."

"She was beautiful five years ago, but she's greatly changed since then," answered Durward, never suspecting the exquisite satisfaction his words afforded Carrie, who replied, "You had better keep that opinion to yourself, and not express it before Captain Atherton or brother John."

"Who takes my name in vain?" asked John Jr., himself appearing at a side door.

"Oh, John," said Carrie, "we were just disputing about 'Lena. Durward does not think her handsome."

"Durward be hanged!" answered John, making a feint of drawing from his pocket a pistol which was not there. "What fault has he to find with 'Lena?"

"A little too rosy, that's all," said Durward, laughingly, while John continued, "She did look confounded red and dowdyish, for her. I don't understand it myself."

Here the hem of the muslin dress on which Carrie's eye had all the while been resting, disappeared, and as there was no longer an incentive for ill-natured remarks, the amiable young lady adroitly changed the conversation.

John Jr. also caught a glimpse of the retreating figure, and started in pursuit, in the course of his search passing the kitchen, where he was instantly hailed by Aunt Milly, who, while bemoaning her own aches and pains, did not fail to tell him how "Miss 'Lena, like aborned angel dropped right out of 'tarnity, had been in thar, burning her skin to a fiery red, a-tryin' to get up a tip-top dinner."

"So ho!" thought the young man, "that explains it;" and turning on his heel, he walked back to the house just as the last bell was ringing for dinner.

On entering the dining-room, he found all the family assembled, except 'Lena. She had excused herself on the plea of a severe headache, and now in her own room was chiding herself for being so much affected by a remark accidentally overheard. What did she care if Durward did think her plain? He was nothing to her, and never would be--and again she bathed her head, which really was aching sadly.

"And so 'Lena's got the headache," said John Jr. "Well, I don't wonder, cooking all the dinner as she did."

"What do you mean?" asked Anna, while Mrs. Livingstone's angry frown bade her son keep silence,

Filial obedience, however, was not one of John Jr.'s cardinal virtues, and in a few words, he repeated what Aunt Milly had told him, adding aside to Durward, "This explains the extreme rosiness which so much offended your lordship. When next you see her, you'll change your mind."

Suddenly remembering that his grandmother had not been introduced, he now presented her to Durward. The Noble's blood had long been forgotten, but grandma was never at a loss for a subject, and she commenced talking notwithstanding Carrie's efforts to keep her still.

"Now I think on't, Car'line," said she at last, turning to her granddaughter, "now I think on't, what made you propose to have my dinner sent up to my room. I hain't et there but once this great while, and that was the day General Fontaine's folks were here, and Matilda thought I warn't able to come down."

Durward's half-concealed smile showed that he understood it all, while John Jr., in his element when his grandmother was talking, managed, to lead her on, until she reached her favorite theme--Nancy Scovandyke. Here a look from her son silenced her, and as dinner was just then over, Durward missed of hearing that remarkable lady's history.

Late in the afternoon, as the family were sitting upon the piazza, 'Lena joined them. Her headache had passed away, leaving her face a shade whiter than usual. The flush was gone from her forehead and nose, but mindful of Durward's remark, the roses deepened on her cheek, which only increased her loveliness.

"I acknowledge that I was wrong--your cousin is beautiful," whispered Durward to Carrie, who, mentally hating the beauty which had never before struck her so forcibly, replied in her softest tones, "I knew you would, and I hope you'll be equally ready to forgive her for winning hearts only to break them, for with that face how can she help it?"

"A handsome face is no excuse for coquetry," answered Durward; "neither can I think Miss Rivers guilty of it. At all events, I mean to venture a little nearer," and before Carrie could frame a reasonable excuse for keeping him at her side, he had crossed ever and taken a seat by 'Lena, with whom he was soon in the midst of an animated conversation, his surprise each moment increasing at the depth of intellect she displayed, for the beauty of her mind was equal to that of her person. Had it not been for the remembrance of Carrie's insinuations, his admiration would have been complete. But anything like coquetry he heartily despised, and one great secret of his liking for Carrie, was her evident freedom from that fault. As yet he had seen nothing to condemn in 'Lena's conduct. Wholly unaffected, she talked with him as she would have talked with any stranger, and still there was in her manner a certain coldness for which he could not account.

"Perhaps she thinks me not worth the winning," thought he, and in spite of his principles, he erelong found himself exerting all his powers to please and interest her.

About tea-time, Captain Atherton rode into the yard, and simultaneously with his arrival, Mr. Everett came also. Immediately remembering what he had heard, Durward, in his eagerness to watch 'Lena, failed to note the crimson flush on Anna's usually pale cheek, as Malcolm bent over her with his low-spoken, tender words of welcome, and when the phthisicky captain, claiming the privilege of an old friend, kissed the blushing Anna, Durward in his blindness attributed the scornful expression of 'Lena's face to a feeling of unwillingness that any save herself should share the attentions even of the captain! And in this impression he was erelong confirmed.

Drawing his chair up to Anna, Captain Atherton managed to keep Malcolm at a distance, while he himself wholly monopolized the young girl, who cast imploring glances toward her cousin, as if asking for relief. Many a time, on similar occasions, had 'Lena claimed the attention of the captain, for the sake of leaving Anna free to converse with Malcolm, and now understanding what was wanted of her, she nodded in token that she would come to the rescue. Just then, Mrs. Livingstone, who had kept an eye upon her niece, drew near, and as she seemed to want a seat; 'Lena instantly arose and offered hers, going herself to the place where the captain was sitting. Erelong, her lively sallies and the captain's loud laugh began to attract Mrs. Livingstone's attention, and observing that Durward's eyes were frequently drawn that way, she thought proper to make some remarks concerning the impropriety of her niece's conduct.

"I do wish," said she, apparently speaking more to herself than to Durward, "I do wish 'Lena would learn discretion, and let Captain Atherton alone, when she knows how much her behavior annoys Mr. Everett."

"Is Mr. Everett anything to her!" asked Durward, half hoping that she would not confirm what Carrie had before hinted.

"If he isn't he ought to be," answered Mrs. Livingstone, with an ominous shake of the head. "Rumor says they are engaged, and though when questioned she denies it, she gives people abundant reason to think so, and yet every chance she gets, she flirts with Captain Atherton, as you see her doing now."

"What can she or any other young girl possibly want of that old man?" asked Durward, laughing at the very idea.

"He is rich. 'Lena is poor, proud, and ambitious--there lies the secret," was Mrs. Livingstone's reply, and thinking she had said enough for the present, she excused herself, while she went to give orders concerning supper.

John Jr., and Carrie, too, had disappeared, and thus left to himself, Durward had nothing to do but to watch 'Lena, who, as she saw symptoms of desertion in the anxious glances which the captain cast toward Anna, redoubled her exertions to keep him at her side, thus confirming Durward in the belief that she really was what her aunt and Carrie had represented her to be. "Poor, proud, and ambitious," rang in his ears, and as he mistook the mischievous look which 'Lena frequently sent toward Anna and Malcolm, for a desire to see how the latter was affected by her conduct, he thought "Fickle as fair," at the same time congratulating himself that he had obtained an insight into her real character, ere her exceeding beauty and agreeable manners had made any particular impression upon him.

Knowing she had done nothing to offend him, and feeling piqued at his indifference, 'Lena in turn treated him so coldly, that even Carrie was satisfied with the phase which affairs had assumed, and that night, in the privacy of her mother's dressing-room, expressed her pleasure that matters were progressing so finely.

"You've no idea, mother," said she, "how much he detests anything like coquetry. Nellie Douglass thinks it's a kind of monomania with him, and I am inclined to believe it is so."

"In that case," answered Mrs. Livingstone, "it behooves you, in his presence, to be very careful how you demean yourself toward other gentlemen."

"I haven't lived nineteen years for nothing," said Carrie, folding her soft white hands complacently one over the other.

"Speaking of Nellie Douglass," continued Mrs. Livingstone, who had long desired this interview with her daughter, "speaking of Nellie, reminds me of your brother, who seems perfectly crazy about her."

"And what if he does ?" asked Carrie, her thoughts far more intent upon Durward Bellmont than her brother. "Isn't Nellie good enough for him?"

"Yes, good enough, I admit," returned her mother, "but I think I can find a far more suitable match--Mabel Ross, for instance. Her fortune is said to be immense, while Mr. Douglass is worth little or nothing."

"When you bring about a union between John Livingstone Jr. and Mabel Ross, I shall have full confidence in your powers to do anything, even to the marrying of Anna and Grandfather Atherton," answered Carrie, to whom her mother's schemes were no secret.

"And that, too, I'll effect, rather than see her thrown away upon a low bred northerner, who shall never wed her--never;" and the haughty woman paced up and down her room, devising numerous ways by which her long cherished three-fold plan should be effected.

The next morning, Durward arose much earlier than was his usual custom, and going out into the garden he came suddenly upon 'Lena. "This," said he, "is a pleasure which I did not expect when I rather unwillingly tore myself from my pillow."

All the coldness of the night before was gone, but 'Lena could not so soon forget, and quite indifferently she answered, that "she learned to rise early among the New England hills."

"An excellent practice, and one which more of our young ladies would do well to imitate," returned Durward, at the same time speaking of the beautifying effect which the morning air had upon her complexion.

'Lena reddened, for she recalled his words of yesterday concerning her plainness, and somewhat sharply she replied, that "any information regarding her personal appearance was wholly unnecessary, as she knew very well how she looked."

Durward bit his lip, and resolving never to compliment her again, walked on in silence at her side, while 'Lena, repenting of her hasty words, and desirous of making amends, exerted herself to be agreeable; and by the time the breakfast-bell rang, Durward mentally pronounced her "a perfect mystery," which he would take delight in unraveling!

CHAPTER X.
MR. AND MRS. GRAHAM.

Breakfast had been some time over, when the roll of carriage wheels and a loud ring at the door, announced the arrival of Mr. Graham, who, true to his appointment with Durward, had come up to meet him, accompanied by Mrs. Graham. This lady, who could boast of having once been the bride of an English lord, to say nothing of belonging to the "very first family of Virginia," was a sort of bugbear to Mrs. Livingstone, who, haughty and overbearing to her equals, was nevertheless cringing and cowardly in the presence of those whom she considered her superiors. Never having seen Mrs. Graham, her ideas concerning her were quite elevated, and now when she came unexpectedly, it quite overcame her. Unfortunately, too, she was this morning suffering from a nervous headache, the result of the excitement and late hours of the night before, and on learning that Mrs. Graham was in the parlor, she fell back in her rocking-chair, and between a groan and a sigh, declared her utter inability to see her at present, saying that Carrie must play the part of hostess until such time as she felt composed enough to undertake it.

"Oh, I can't--I shan't--that ends it!" said Carrie, who, though a good deal dressed on Durward's account, still felt anxious to give a few more finishing touches to her toilet, and to see if her hair and complexion were all right, ere she ventured into the august presence ef her "mother-in-law elect," as she confidently considered Mrs. Graham.

"Anna must go, then," persisted Mrs. Livingstone, who knew full well how useless it would be to press Carrie farther. "Anna must go--where is she? Call her, 'Lena."

But Anna was away over the fields, enjoying with Mr. Everett a walk which had been planned the night previous, and when 'Lena returned with the intelligence that she was nowhere to be found, her aunt in great distress exclaimed, "Mercy me! what will Mrs. Graham think--and Mr. Livingstone, too, keeps running back and forth for somebody to entertain her. What shall I do! I can't go in looking so yellow and jaded as I now do!"

'Lena's first thought was to bring her aunt's powderball, as the surest way of remedying the yellow skin, but knowing that such an act would be deeply resented, she quickly repressed the idea, offering instead to go herself to the parlor.

"You! What could you say to her?" returned Mrs. Livingstone, to whom the proposition was not altogether displeasing.

"I can at least answer her questions," returned 'Lena and after a moment her aunt consented, wondering the while how 'Lena, in her plain gingham wrapper and linen collar, could be willing to meet the fashionable Mrs. Graham.

"But then," thought she, "she has so little sensibility, I don't s'pose she cares! and why should she? Mrs. Graham will of course look upon her as only a little above a servant"--and with this complimentary reflection upon her niece, Mrs. Livingstone retired to her dressing-room, while 'Lena, with a beating heart and slightly heightened color, repaired to the parlor.

On a sofa by the window sat Mrs. Graham, and the moment 'Lena's eye fell upon her, her fears vanished, while she could hardly repress a smile at the idea of being afraid of her. She was a short, dumpy, florid looking woman, showily, and as 'Lena thought, overdressed for morning, as her person was covered with jewelry, which flashed and sparkled with every movement. Her forehead was very low, and marked by a scowl of discontent which was habitual, for with everything to make her happy, Mrs. Graham was far from being so. Exceedingly nervous and fidgety, she was apt to see only the darker side, and when her husband and son, who were of exactly opposite temperaments, strove to laugh her into good spirits, they generally made the matter worse, as she usually reproached them with having no feeling or sympathy for her.

Accustomed to a great deal of attention, she had fretted herself into quite a fever at Mrs. Livingstone's apparent lack of courtesy in not hastening to receive her, and when 'Lena's light step was heard in the hall, she turned toward the door with a frown which seemed to ask why she had not come sooner. Durward, who

was present immediately introduced his mother, at the same time admiring the extreme dignity of 'Lena's manner as she received the lady's greeting, apologizing for
her aunt's non-appearance, saying "she was suffering from a severe headache, and
begged to be excused for an hour or so."

"Quite excusable," returned Mrs. Graham, at the same time saying something
in a low tone about it's not being her wish to stop there so early, as she knew she
was not expected.

"But perfectly welcome, nevertheless," 'Lena hastened to say, thinking that for
the time being the reputation of her uncle's house was resting upon her shoulders.

"I dare say," was Mrs. Graham's ungracious answer, and then her little gray,
deep-set eyes rested upon 'Lena, wondering if she were "a governess or what?" and
thinking it strange that she should seem so perfectly self-possessed.

Insensibly, too, 'Lena's manner won upon her, for spite of her fretfulness, Mrs.
Graham at heart was a kindly disposed woman. Ill health and long years of dissipation had helped to make her what she was. Besides this, she was not quite happy
in her domestic relations, for though Mr. Graham possessed all the requisites of a
kind and affectionate husband, he could not remove from her mind the belief that
he liked others better then he did herself! 'Twas in vain that he alternately laughed
at and reasoned with her on the subject. She was not to be convinced, and so poor
Mr. Graham, who was really exceedingly polite and affable to the ladies, was almost
constantly provoking the green-eyed monster by his attentions to some one of the
fair sex. In spite of his nightly "Caudle" lectures, he would transgress again and
again, until his wife's patience was exhausted, and now she affected to have given
him up, turning for comfort and affection toward Durward, who was her special
delight, "the very apple of her eye--he was so much like his father, Sir Arthur, who
during the whole year that she lived with him had never once given her cause for
jealousy."

Just before 'Lena entered the parlor Mr. Graham, had for a moment stepped
out with Mr. Livingstone, but soon returning, he, too, was introduced to the young
lady. It was strange, considering 'Lena's uncommon beauty, that Mrs. Graham did
not watch her husband's manner, but for once in her life she felt no fears, and looking from the window, she failed to note the sudden pallor which overspread his face
when Mr. Livingstone presented to him "Miss Rivers--my niece."

Mr. Graham was a tall, finely-formed man, with a broad, good-humored face, whose expression instantly demanded respect from strangers, while his pleasant, affable deportment universally won the friendship of ail who knew him. And 'Lena was not an exception to the general rule, for the moment his warm hand grasped hers and his kindly beaming eye rested upon her, her heart went toward him as a friend, while she wondered why he looked at her so long and earnestly, twice repeating her name--"Miss Rivers-- Rivers ."

From the first, 'Lena had recognized him as the same gentleman whom Durward had called father in the cars years ago, and when, as if to apologize for his singular conduct, he asked if they had never met before, she referred him to that time, saying "she thought it strange that he should remember her."

"Old acquaintances--ah--indeed !" and little Mrs. Graham nodded and fanned, while her round, florid face grew more florid, and her linen cambric went up to her forehead as if trying to smooth out the scowl which was of too long standing to be smoothed.

"Yes, my dear," said Mr. Graham, turning toward his wife, "I had entirely forgotten the circumstance, but it seems I saw her in the cars when we took our eastern tour six or seven years ago. You were quite a little girl then"--turning to 'Lena.

"Only ten," was the reply, and Mrs. Graham, ashamed of herself and anxious to make amends, softened considerable toward 'Lena, asking "how long she had lived in Kentucky--where she used to live--and where her mother was."

At this question, Mr. Graham, who was talking with Mr. Livingstone, suddenly stopped.

"My mother is dead," answered 'Lena.

"And your father?"

"Gone to Canada!" interrupted Durward, who had heard vague rumors of 'Lena's parentage, and who did not quite like his mother's being so inquisitive.

Mrs. Graham laughed; she always did at whatever Durward said; while Mr. Graham replied to a remark made by Mr. Livingstone some time before. Here John Jr. appeared, and after being formally introduced, he seated himself by his cousin, addressing to her some trivial remark, and calling her 'Lena . It was well for Mr. Graham's after peace that his wife was just then too much engrossed with Durward to observe the effect which that name produced upon him.

Abruptly rising he turned toward Mr. Livingstone, saying, "You were telling me about a fine species of cactus which you have in your yard--suppose we go and see it."

The cactus having been duly examined, praised, and commented upon, Mr. Graham casually remarked, "Your niece is a fine-looking girl--'Lena, I think your son called her?"

"Yes, or Helena, which was her mother's name."

"And her mother was your sister, Helena Livingstone?"

"No, sir, Nichols. I changed my name to gratify a fancy of my wife," returned Mr. Livingstone, thinking it better to tell the truth at once.

Again Mr. Graham bent over the cactus, inspecting it minutely, and keeping his face for a long time concealed from his friend, whose thoughts, as was usually the case when his sister was mentioned, were far back in the past. When at last Mr. Graham lifted his head there were no traces of the stormy emotions which had shaken his very heart-strings, and with a firm, composed step he walked back to the parlor, where he found both Mrs. Livingstone and Carrie just paying their respects to his lady.

Nothing could be more marked than the difference between Carrie's and 'Lena's manner toward Mrs. Graham. Even Durward noticed it, and while he could not sufficiently admire the quiet self-possession of the latter, who in her simple morning wrapper and linen collar had met his mother on perfectly equal terms, he for the first time in his life felt a kind of contempt (pity he called it,) for Carrie, who, in an elegantly embroidered double-gown confined by a rich cord and tassels, which almost swept the floor, treated his mother with a fawning servility as disgusting to him as it was pleasing to the lady in question. Accustomed to the utmost deference on account of her wealth and her husband's station, Mrs. Graham had felt as if something were withheld from her, when neither Mrs. Livingstone nor her daughters rushed to receive and welcome her; but now all was forgotten, for nothing could be more flattering than their attentions. Both mother and daughter having the son in view, did their best, and when at last Mrs. Graham asked to be shown to her room, Carrie, instead of ringing for a servant, offered to conduct her thither herself; whereupon Mrs. Graham laid her hand caressingly upon her shoulders, calling her a "dear little pet," and asking "where she stole those bright, naughty eyes!"

A smothered laugh from John Jr. and a certain low soft sound which he was in the habit of producing when desirous of reminding his sister of her nose, made the "bright, naughty eyes" flash so angrily, that even Durward noticed it, and wondered if 'Lena's temper had not been transferred to her cousin.

"That young girl--'Lena, I think you call her--is a relative of yours," said Mrs. Graham to Carrie, as they were ascending the stairs.

"Ye-es, our cousin, I suppose," answered Carrie.

"She bears a very aristocratic name, that of Rivers--does she belong to a Virginia family?"

Carrie looked mysterious and answered, "I never knew anything of her father, and indeed, I reckon no one does"--then after a moment she added, "Almost every family has some objectionable relative, with which they could willingly dispense."

"Very true," returned Mrs. Graham, "What a pity we couldn't all have been born in England. There, dear, you can leave me now."

Accordingly Carrie started for the parlor, meeting in the hall her mother, who was in a sea of trouble concerning the dinner. "Old Milly," she said, "had gone to bed out of pure hatefulness, pretending she had got a collapse, as she called it."

"Can't Hagar do," asked Carrie, anxious that Mrs. Graham's first dinner with them should be in style.

"Yes, but she can't do everything--somebody must superintend her, and as for burning myself brown over the dishes and then coming to the table, I won't."

"Why not make 'Lena go into the kitchen--it won't hurt her to-day more than it did yesterday," suggested Carrie.

"A good idea," returned her mother, and stepping to the parlor door she called 'Lena from a most interesting conversation with Mr. Graham, who, the moment his wife was gone, had taken a seat by her side, and now seemed oblivious to all else save her.

There was a strange tenderness in the tones of his voice and in the expression of his eyes as they rested upon her, and Durward, who well knew his mother's peculiarities, felt glad that she was not present, while at the same time he wondered that his father should appear so deeply interested in an entire stranger.

"'Lena, I wish to speak with you," said Mrs. Livingstone, appearing at the door, and 'Lena, gracefully excusing herself, left the room, while Mr. Graham commenced pacing the floor in a slow, abstracted manner, ever and anon wiping away the beaded drops which stood thickly on his forehead.

Meantime, 'Lena, having learned for what she was wanted, went without a word to the kitchen, though her proud nature rebelled, and it was with difficulty she could force down the bitter spirit which she felt rising within her. Had her aunt or Carrie shared her labors, or had the former asked instead of commanded her to go, she would have done it willingly. But now in quite a perturbed state of mind she bent over pastry and pudding, scarcely knowing which was which, until a pleasant voice at her side made her start, and looking up she saw Anna, who had just returned from her walk, and who on learning how matters stood, declared her intention of helping too.

"If there's anything I like, it's being in a muss," said she, and throwing aside her leghorn flat, pinning up her sleeves, and fastening back her curls in imitation of 'Lena, she was soon up to her elbows in cooking--her dress literally covered with flour, eggs, and cream, and her face as red as the currant jelly which Hagar brought from the china closet. "There's a pie fit for a queen or Lady Graham either," said she, depositing in the huge oven her first attempt in the pie line.

But alas! Malcolm Everett's words of love spoken beneath the wide-spreading sycamore were still ringing in Anna's ears, so it was no wonder she salted the custard instead of sweetening it. But no one noticed the mistake, and when the pie was done, both 'Lena and Hagar praised its white, uncurdled appearance.

"Now we shall just have time to change our dresses," said Anna, when everything pertaining to the dinner was in readiness, but 'Lena, knowing how flushed and heated she was, and remembering Durward's distaste of high colors, announced her determination of not appearing at the table.

"I shall see that grandma is nicely dressed," said she, "and you must look after her a little, for I shall not come down."

So saying she ran up to her room, where she found Mrs. Nichols in a great state of fermentation to know "who was below, and what the doin's was, I should of gone down," said she, "but I know'd 'Tilda would be madder'n a hornet."

'Lena commended her discretion in remaining where she was, and then informing her that Mr. Bellmont's father and mother were there, she proceeded to make some alterations in her dress. The handsome black silk and neat lace cap, both the Christmas gift of John Jr., were donned, and then, staff in hand, the old lady started for the dining-room, 'Lena giving her numerous charges not to talk much, and on no account to mention her favorite topic--Nancy Scovandyke!

"Nancy's as good any day as Miss Graham, if she did marry a live lord," was grandma's mental comment, as the last-mentioned lady, rustling in a heavy brocade and loaded down with jewelry, took her place at the table.

Purposely, Mrs. Livingstone omitted an introduction which her husband, through fear of her, perhaps, failed to give. But not so with John Jr. To be sure, he cared not a fig, on his grandmother's account, whether she were introduced or not, for he well knew she would not hesitate to make their acquaintance; but knowing how it would annoy his mother and Carrie, he called out, in a loud tone, "My grandmother, Mrs. Nichols--Mr. and Mrs. Graham."

Mr. Graham started so quickly that his wife asked "if anything stung him."

"Yes--no," said he, at the same time indicating that it was not worth while to mind it.

"Got stung, have you?" said Mrs. Nichols. "Mebby 'twas a bumble-bee--seems 'sef I smelt one; but like enough it's the scent on Car'line's handkercher."

Mrs. Graham frowned majestically, but it was entirely lost on grandma, who, after a time, forgetful of 'Lena's caution, said, "I b'lieve they say you're from Virginny!"

"Yes, madam, Virginia is my native state,'" returned Mrs. Graham, clipping off each word as if it were burning her tongue.

"Anywheres near Richmond?" continued Mrs. Nichols.

"I was born in Richmond, madam."

"Law, now I who knows but you're well acquainted with Nancy Scovandyke's kin."

Mrs. Graham turned as red as the cranberry sauce upon her plate, as she replied, "I've not the honor of knowing either Miss Scovandyke or any of her relatives."

"Wall, she's a smart, likely gal, or woman I s'pose you'd call her, bein' she's just the age of my son."

Here Mrs. Nichols, suddenly remembering 'Lena's charge, stopped, but John Jr., who loved to see the fun go on, started her again, by asking what relatives Miss

Scovandyke had in Virginia.

"'Leny told me not to mention Nancy, but bein' you've asked a civil question, 'tain't more'n fair for me to answer it. Better'n forty year ago Nancy's mother's aunt----"

"Which would be Miss Nancy's great-aunt," interrupted John Jr.

"Bless the boy," returned the old lady, "he's got the Nichols' head for figgerin'. Yes, Nancy's great-aunt though she was six years and two months younger'n Nancy's mother. Wall, as I was sayin', she went off to Virginny to teach music. She was prouder'n Lucifer, and after a spell she married a southerner, rich as a Jew, and then she never took no more notice of her folks to hum, than's ef they hadn't been. But the poor critter didn't live long to enjoy it, for when her first baby was born, she died. 'Twas a little girl, but her folks in Massachusetts have never heard a word whether she's dead or alive. Joel Slocum, that's Nancy's nephew, says he means to go down there some day, and look her up, but I wouldn't bother with 'em, for that side of the house always did feel big, and above Nancy's folks, thinkin' Nancy's mother married beneath her."

Mrs. Graham must have enjoyed her dinner very much, for during grandma's recital she applied herself assiduously to her plate, never once looking up, while her face and neck were literally spotted, either with heat, excitement or anger. These spots at last attracted Mrs. Nichols' attention, causing her to ask the lady "if she warn't pestered with erysipelas."

"I am not aware of it, madam," answered Mrs. Graham, and grandma replied, "It looks mighty like it to me, and I've seen a good deal on't, for Nancy Scovandyke has allers had it more or less. Now I think on't," she continued, as if bent on tormenting her companion, "now I think on't, you look quite a considerable like Nancy--the same forehead and complexion--only she's a head taller. Hain't you noticed it, John?"

"No, I have not," answered John, at the same time proposing a change in the conversation, as he presumed "they had all heard enough of Nancy Scovandyke."

At this moment the dessert appeared, and with it Anna's pie. John Jr. was the first to taste it, and with an expression of disgust he exclaimed, "Horror, mother, who made this pie?"

Mrs. Livingstone needed but one glance at her guests to know that something was wrong, and darting an angry frown at Hagar, who was busy at a side-table, she wondered "if there ever was any one who had so much trouble with servants as herself."

Anna saw the gathering storm, and knowing full well that it would burst on poor Hagar's head, spoke out, "Hagar is not in the fault, mother--no one but myself is to blame. I made the pie, and must have put in salt instead of sugar."

"You made the pie!" repeated Mrs. Livingstone angrily, "What business had you in the kitchen? Pity we hadn't a few more servants, for then we should all be obliged to turn drudges."

Anna was about to reply, when John Jr. prevented her, by asking, "if it hurt his sister to be in the kitchen any more than it did 'Lena, who," he said, "worked there both yesterday and to-day, burning herself until she is ashamed to appear at the table."

Mortified beyond measure at what had occurred, Mrs. Livingstone hastened to explain that her servants were nearly all sick, and that in her dilemma, 'Lena had volunteered her services, adding by way of compliment, undoubtedly, that "her niece seemed peculiarly adapted to such work--indeed, that her forte lay among pots and kettles."

An expression of scorn, unusual to Mr. Graham, passed over his face, and in a sarcastic tone he asked Mrs. Livingstone, "if she thought it detracted from a young lady's worth, to be skilled in whatever pertained to the domestic affairs of a family."

Ready to turn whichever way the wind did, Mrs. Livingstone replied, "Not at all--not at all. I mean that my daughters shall learn everything, so that their husbands will find in them every necessary qualification."

"Then you confidently expect them to catch husbands some time or other," said John Jr., whereupon Carrie blushed, and looked very interesting, while Anna retorted, "Of course we shall. I wouldn't be an old maid for the world--I'd run away first!"

And amidst the laughter which this speech called forth the company retired from the table. For some time past Mrs. Nichols had walked with a cane, limping even then. Observing this, Mr. Graham, with his usual gallantry, offered her his arm, which she willingly accepted, casting a look of triumph upon her daughter-in-law, who apparently was not so well pleased. So thorough had been grandma's training, that she did not often venture into the parlor without a special invitation from its mistress, but on this occasion, Mr. Graham led her in there as a matter of course, and placing her upon the sofa, seated himself by her side, and commenced questioning her concerning her former home and history. Never in her life had Mrs. Nichols felt more communicative, and never before had she so attentive a listener. Particularly did he hang upon every word, when she told him of her Helena, of her exceeding beauty, her untimely death, and rascally husband.

"Rivers--Rivers," said he, "what kind of a looking man was he?"

"The Lord only knows--I never see him," returned Mrs. Nichols. "But this much I do know, he was one scandalous villain, and if an old woman's curses can do him any harm, he's had mine a plenty of times."

"You do wrong to talk so," said Mr. Graham, "for who knows how bitterly he may have repented of the great wrong done to your daughter."

"Then why in the name of common sense don't he hunt up her child, and own her--he needn't be ashamed of 'Leny."

"Very true," answered Mr. Graham. "No one need be ashamed of her. I should be proud to call her my daughter. But as I was saying, perhaps this Rivers has married a second time, keeping his first marriage a secret from his wife, who is so proud and high-spirited that now, after the lapse of years, he dares not tell her for fear of what might follow."

"Then she's a good-for-nothing, stuck-up thing, and he's a cowardly puppy! That's my opinion on 'em, and I'll tell 'em so, if ever I see 'em!" exclaimed Mrs. Nichols, her wrath waxing warmer and warmer toward the destroyer of her daughter.

Pausing for breath, she helped herself to a pinch of her favorite Maccaboy, and then passed it to Mr. Graham, who, to her astonishment, took some, slyly casting it aside when she did not see him. This emboldened the old lady to offer it to Mrs. Graham, who, languidly reclining upon the end of the sofa, sat talking to Carrie, who, on a low stool at her feet, was looking up into her face as if in perfect admiration. Without deigning other reply than a haughty shake of the head, Mrs. Graham cast a deprecating glance toward Carrie, who muttered, "How disgusting! But for pa's sake we tolerate it."

Here 'Lena entered the parlor, very neatly dressed, and looking fresh and blooming as a rose. There was no vacant seat near except one between Durward and John Jr., which, at the invitation of the latter, she accepted. A peculiar smile flitted over Carrie's face, which was noticed by Mrs. Graham, and attributed to the right cause. Ere long Durward, John Jr., 'Lena and Anna, who had joined them, left the house, and from the window Carrie saw that they were amusing themselves by playing "Graces." Gradually the sound of their voices increased, and as 'Lena's clear, musical laugh rang out above the rest, Mrs. Graham and Carrie looked out just in time to see Durward holding the struggling girl, while John Jr., claimed the reward of his having thrown the "grace hoop" upon her head.

Inexpressibly shocked, the precise Mrs. Graham asked, "What kind of a girl is your cousin?" to which Carrie replied, "You have a fair sample of her," at the same time nodding toward 'Lena, who was unmercifully pulling John Jr.'s ears as a reward for his presumption.

"Rather hoydenish, I should think," returned Mrs. Graham, secretly hoping Durward would not become enamored of her.

At length the party left the yard, and repairing to the garden, sat down in one of the arbor bridges, where they were joined by Malcolm Everett, who naturally, and as a matter of course, appropriated Anna to himself, Durward observed this, and when he saw them walk away together, while 'Lena appeared wholly unconcerned, he began to think that possibly Mrs. Livingstone was mistaken when she hinted of an engagement between her niece and Mr. Everett. Knowing John Jr.'s straightforward way of speaking, he determined to sound him, so he said, "Your sister and Mr. Everett evidently prefer each other's society to ours."

"Oh, yes," answered John. "I saw that years ago, when Anna wasn't knee-high; and I'm glad of it, for Everett is a mighty fine fellow."

'Lena, too, united in praising her teacher, until Durward felt certain that she had never entertained for him any feeling stronger than that of friendship; and as to her flirting seriously with Captain Atherton, the idea was too preposterous to be harbored for a single moment. Once exonerated from these charges, it was strange how fast 'Lena rose in his estimation, and when John Jr., with a loud yawn, asked if they did not wish he would leave them alone, more in earnest than in fun Durward replied, "Yes, yes, do."

"I reckon I will," said John, shaking down his tight pants, and pulling at his long coat sleeves. "I never want anybody round when I'm with Nellie Douglass."

So saying, he walked off, leaving Durward and 'Lena alone. That neither of them felt at all sorry, was proved by the length of time which they remained together, for when more than an hour afterward Mrs. Graham proposed to Carrie to take a turn in the garden, she found the young couple still in the arbor, so wholly engrossed that they neither saw nor heard her until she stood before them.

'Lena was an excellent horsewoman, and Durward had just proposed a ride early the next morning, when his mother, forcing down her wrath, laid her hand on his shoulder, and as if the proposition had come from 'Lena instead of her son, she said, "No, no, Miss Rivers, Durward can't go--he has got to drive me over to Woodlawn, together with Carrie and Anna, whom I have asked to accompany me; so you see 'twill be impossible for him to ride with you."

"Unless she goes with us," interrupted Durward. "You would like to visit Woodlawn, would you not, Miss Rivers?"

"Oh, very much," was 'Lena's reply, while Mrs. Graham continued, "I am sorry I cannot extend my invitation to Miss Rivers, but our carriage will be full, and I cannot endure to be crowded."

"It has carried six many a time," said Durward, "and if she will go, I will take you on my lap, or anywhere."

Of course 'Lena declined--he knew she would--and determined not to be outwitted by his mother, whose aim he saw, he continued, "I shan't release you from your engagement to ride with me. We will start early and get back before mother is up, so our excursion will in no way interfere with my driving her to Woodlawn after breakfast."

Mrs. Graham was too polite to raise any further objection, but resolving not to leave them to finish their tete-a-tete, she threw herself upon one of the seats, and commenced talking to her son, while Carrie, burning with jealousy and vexation, started for the house, where she laid her grievances before her mother, who, equally enraged, declared her intention of "hereafter watching the vixen pretty closely."

"And she's going to ride with him to-morrow morning, you say. Well, I fancy I can prevent that."

"How?" asked Carrie, eagerly, and her mother replied, "You know she always rides Fleetfoot, which now, with the other horses, is in the Grattan woods, two miles away. Of course she'll order Caesar to bring him up to the stable, but I shall countermand that order, bidding him say nothing to her about it. He dare not disobey me, and when in the morning she asks for the pony, he can tell her just how it is."

"Capital! capital!" exclaimed Carrie, never suspecting that there had been a listener, even John Jr., who all the while was sitting in the back parlor.

"Whew!" thought the young man. "Plotting, are they? Well, I'll see how good I am at counterplotting."

So, slipping quietly out of the house, he went in quest of his servant, Bill, telling him to go after Fleetfoot, whom he was to put in the lower stable instead of the one where she was usually kept; "and then in the morning, long before the sun is up," said he, "do you have her at the door for one of the young ladies to ride."

"Yes, marster," answered Bill, looking around for his old straw hat.

"Now, see how quick you can go," John Jr. continued, adding as an incentive to haste, that if Bill would get the pony stabled before old Caesar, who had gone to Versailles, should return, he would give him ten cents.

Bill needed no other inducement than the promise of money, and without stopping to find his hat, he started off bare-headed, upon the run, returning in the course of an hour and claiming his reward, as Caesar had not yet got home.

"All right," said John Jr., tossing him the silver. "And now remember to keep your tongue between your teeth."

Bill had kept too many secrets for his young master to think of tattling about something which to him seemed of no consequence whatever, and he walked off, eying his dime, and wishing he could earn one so easily every day.

Meantime John Jr. sought out 'Lena, to whom he said, "And so you are going to ride to-morrow morning?"

"How did you know?" she asked, and John, looking very wise, replied, that "little girls should not ask too many questions," adding, that as he supposed she would of course want Fleetfoot, he had ordered Bill to have her at the door early in the morning.

"Much obliged," answered 'Lena. "I was about giving it up when I heard the pony was in the Grattan woods, for Caesar is so cross I hated to ask him to go for her; but now I'll say nothing to him about it."

That night when Caesar was eating his supper in the kitchen, his mistress suddenly appeared, asking, "if he had received any orders to go for Fleetfoot."

The old negro, who was naturally cross, began to scowl, "No, miss, and Lord knows I don't want to tote clar off to the Grattan woods to-night."

"You needn't, either, and if any one tells you to go don't you do it," returned Mrs. Livingstone.

"Somebody's playin' possum, that's sartin," thought Bill, who was present, and began putting things together. "Somebody's playin' possum, but they don't catch this child leakin'."

"Have you told him?" whispered Carrie, meeting her mother in the hall.

Mrs. Livingstone nodded, adding in an undertone, that "she presumed the ride was given up, as Lena had said nothing to Caesar about the pony."

With her mind thus at ease, Carrie returned to the parlor, where she commenced talking to Mrs. Graham of their projected visit to Woodlawn, dwelling upon it as if it had been a tour to Europe, and evidently exulting that 'Lena was to be left behind.

CHAPTER XI.
WOODLAWN.

Next morning, long before the sun appeared above the eastern horizon, Fleetfoot, attended by Bill, stood before the door saddled and waiting for its young rider, while near by it was Firelock, which Durward had borrowed of John Jr. At last 'Lena appeared, and if Durward had admired her beauty before, his admiration was now greatly increased when he saw how well she looked in her neatly fitting riding dress and tasteful straw hat. After bidding her good morning, he advanced to assist her in mounting, but declining his offer, she with one bound sprang into the saddle,

"Jumps like a toad," said Bill. "Ain't stiff and clumsy like Miss Carrie, who allus has to be done sot on."

At a word from Durward they galloped briskly away, the clatter of their horses' hoofs arousing and bringing to the window Mrs. Graham, who had a suspicion of what was going on. Pushing aside the silken curtain, she looked uneasily after them, wondering if in reality her son cared aught for the graceful creature at his side, and thinking if he did, how hard she would labor to overcome his liking. Mrs. Graham was not the only one who watched them, for fearing lest Bill should not awake, John Jr. had foregone his morning nap, himself calling up the negro, and now from his window he, too, looked after them until they entered upon the turnpike and were lost to view. Then, with some very complimentary reflections upon Lena's riding, he returned to his pillow, thinking to himself, "There's a girl worth having. By Jove, if I'd never seen Nellie Douglass, and 'Lena wasn't my cousin, wouldn't I keep mother in the hysterics most of the time!"

On reaching the turnpike, Durward halted, while he asked 'Lena "where she wished to go."

"Anywhere you please," said she, when, for reasons of his own, he proposed that they should ride over to Woodlawn.

'Lena was certainly excusable if she felt a secret feeling of satisfaction in thinking she was after all the first of the family to visit Woodlawn, of which she had heard so much, that it seemed like a perfect Eldorado. It was a grand old building, standing on a cross road about three miles from the turnpike, and commanding quite an extensive view of the country around. It was formerly owned by a wealthy Englishman, who spent his winters in New Orleans and his summers in the country. The year before he had died insolvent, Woodlawn falling into the hands of his creditors, who now offered it for sale, together with the gorgeous furniture which still remained just as the family had left it. To the left of the building was a large, handsome park, in which the former owner had kept a number of deer, and now as Durward and 'Lena rode up and down the shaded avenues, these graceful creatures would occasionally spring up and bound away with the fleetness of the wind.

The garden and yard in front were laid out with perfect taste, the former combining both the useful and the agreeable. A luxurious grape-vine wreathed itself over the arched entrance, while the wide, graveled walks were bordered, some with box, and others with choice flowers, now choked and overgrown with weeds, but showing marks of great beauty, when properly tended and cared for. At the extremity of the principal walk, which extended the entire length of the garden, was a summer house, fitted up with everything which could make it attractive, during the sultry heat of summer, while farther on through the little gate was a handsome grove or continuation of the park, with many well-beaten paths winding through it and terminating finally at the side of a tiny sheet of water, which within a few years had forced itself through the limestone soil natural to Kentucky.

Owing to some old feud, the English family had not been on visiting terms with the Livingstones; consequently, 'Lena had never before been at Woodlawn, and her admiration increased with every step, and when at last they entered the house and stood within the elegant drawing-rooms, it knew no bounds. She remembered the time when she had thought her uncle's furniture splendid beyond anything in the world, but it could not compare with the magnificence around her, and for a few moments she stood as if transfixed with astonishment. Durward had been highly amused at her enthusiastic remarks concerning the grounds, and now noticing her silence, he asked "what was the matter?"

"Oh, I am half-afraid to speak, lest this beautiful room should prove an illusion and fade away," said she.

"Is it then so much more beautiful than anything you ever saw before?" he asked; and she replied, "Oh, yes, far more so," at the same time giving him a laughable description of her amazement when she first saw the inside of her uncle's house, and ending by saying, "But you can imagine it all, for you saw me in the cars, and can judge pretty well what were my ideas of the world."

Wishing to see if 'Lena would attempt to conceal her former humble mode of living Durward said, "I have never heard anything concerning your eastern home and how you lived there--will you please to tell me?"

"There's nothing to tell which will interest you," answered 'Lena; but Durward thought there was, and leading her to a sofa, he bade her commence.

Durward had a peculiar way of making people do what he pleased, and now at his bidding 'Lena told him of her mountain-home, with its low-roof, bare walls, and oaken floors--of herself, when, a bare-footed little girl, she picked huckleberries *with* Joel Slocum! And then, in lower and more subdued tones, she spoke of her mother's grave in the valley, near which her beloved grandfather--the only father she had ever known--was now sleeping. 'Lena never spoke of her grandfather without weeping. She could not help it. Her tears came naturally, as they did when first they told her he was dead, and now laying her head upon the arm of the sofa, she sobbed like a child.

Durward's sympathies were all enlisted, and without stopping to consider the propriety or impropriety of the act, he drew her gently toward him, trying to soothe her grief, calling her 'Lena, and smoothing back the curls which had fallen over her face. As soon as possible 'Lena released herself from him, and drying her tears, proposed that they should go over the house, as it was nearly time for them to return home. Accordingly, they passed on through room after room, 'Lena's quick eye taking in and appreciating everything which she saw, while Durward was no less lost in admiration of her, for speaking of herself so frankly as she had done. Many young ladies, he well knew, would shrink from acknowledging that their home was once in a brown, old-fashioned house among wild and rugged mountains, and 'Lena's truthfulness in speaking not only of this, but many similar things connected with her early history, inspired him with a respect of her which he had never before felt for any young lady of his acquaintance.

But little was said by either of them as they went over the house, until Durward, prompted by something, he could not resist suddenly asked his companion "how she would like to be mistress of Woodlawn?"

Had it been Carrie to whom this question was put, she would have blushed and simpered, expecting nothing short of an immediate offer, but 'Lena quickly replied, "Not at all," laughingly giving as an insuperable objection, "the size of the house and the number of windows she would have to wash!"

With a loud laugh Durward proposed that they should now return home, and again mounting their horses, they started for Maple Grove, which they reached just after the family had finished breakfast. With the first ring of the bell, John Jr., eager not to lose an iota of what might occur, was at the table, and when his mother and Carrie, anxious at the non-appearance of Durward and 'Lena, cast wistful glances toward each other, he very indifferently asked Mrs. Graham "if her son had returned from his ride."

"I've not seen him," answered the lady, her scowl deepening and her lower jaw dropping slightly, as it usually did when she was ill at ease.

"Who's gone to ride?" asked Mr. Graham; and John Jr. replied that Durward and 'Lena had been riding nearly two hours, adding, that "they must find each other exceedingly interesting to be gone so long."

This last was for the express benefit of his mother, whose frown kept company with Mrs. Graham's scowl. Chopping her steak into mince-meat, and almost biting a piece from her cup as she sipped her coffee, she at last found voice to ask, "what horse 'Lena rode!"

"Fleetfoot, of course," said John Jr., at the same time telling his father he thought "he ought to give 'Lena a pony of her own, for she was accounted the best rider in the county, and Fleetfoot was getting old and clumsy."

The moment breakfast was over, Mrs. Livingstone went in quest of Caesar, whom she abused for disobeying her orders, threatening him with the calaboose, and anything else which came to her mind. Old Caesar was taken by surprise, and being rather slow of speech, was trying to think of something to say, when John Jr., who had followed his mother, came to his aid, saying that "he himself had sent Bill for Fleetfoot," and adding aside to his mother, that "the next time she and Cad were plotting mischief he'd advise them to see who was in the back parlor!"

Always ready to suspect 'Lena of evil, Mrs. Livingstone immediately supposed it was she who had listened; but before she could frame a reply, John Jr. walked off, leaving her undecided whether to cowhide Caesar, 'Lena, or her son, the first of whom, taking advantage of the pause followed the example of his young master and stole away. The tramp of horses' feet was now heard, and Mrs. Livingstone, mentally resolving that Fleetfoot should be sold, repaired to the door in time to see Durward carefully lift 'Lena from her pony and place her upon the ground. Mrs. Graham, Carrie, and Annie were all standing upon the piazza, and as 'Lena came up the walk, her eyes sparkling and her bright face glowing with exercise, Anna exclaimed, "Isn't she beautiful?" at the same time asking her "where she had been."

"To Woodlawn," answered 'Lena.

"To Woodlawn!" repeated Mrs. Graham.

"To Woodlawn!" echoed Mrs. Livingstone, while Carrie brought up the rear by exclaiming, "To Woodlawn! pray what took you there?"

"The pony," answered 'Lena, as she passed into the house.

Thinking it best to put Mrs. Graham on her guard, Mrs. Livingstone said to her, in a low tone, "I would advise you to keep an eye upon your son, if he is at all susceptible, for there is no bound to 'Lena's ambition."

Mrs. Graham made no direct reply, but the flashing of her little gray eye was a sufficient answer, and satisfied with the result of her caution, Mrs. Livingstone reentered the house. Two hours afterward, the carriage stood at the door waiting to convey the party to Woodlawn. It had been arranged that Mrs. Graham, Carrie, Anna, and Durward should ride in the carriage, while Mr. Graham went on horseback. Purposely, Carrie loitered behind her companions, who being first, of course took the back seat, leaving her the privilege of riding by the side of Durward. This was exactly what she wanted, and leaning back on her elbow, she complacently awaited his coming. But how was she chagrined, when, in his stead, appeared Mr. Graham, who sprang into the carriage and took a seat beside her; saying to his wife's look of inquiry, that as John Jr. had concluded to go, Durward preferred riding on horseback with him, adding, in his usually polite way, "And I, you know, would always rather go with the ladies. But where is Miss Rivers?" he continued. "Why isn't she here?"

"Simply because she wasn't invited, I suppose," returned his wife, detecting the disappointment in his face.

"Not invited!" he repeated; "I didn't know as this trip was of sufficient consequence to need a special invitation. I thought, of course, she was here----"

"Or you would have gone on horseback," said his wife, ever ready to catch at straws.

Mr. Graham saw the rising jealousy in time to repress the truthful: answer--"Yes"--while he compromised the matter by saying that "the presence of three fair ladies ought to satisfy him."

Carrie was too much disappointed even to smile, and during all the ride she was extremely taciturn, hardly replying at all to Mr. Graham's lively sallies, and winning golden laurels in the opinion of Mrs. Graham, who secretly thought her husband altogether too agreeable. As they turned into the long avenue which led to Woodlawn, and Carrie thought of the ride which 'Lena had enjoyed alone with its owner--for such was Durward reported to be--her heart swelled with bitterness toward her cousin, in whom she saw a dreaded rival. But when they reached the house, and Durward assisted her to alight, keeping at her side while they walked over the grounds, her jealousy vanished, and with her sweetest smile she looked up into his face, affecting a world of childish simplicity, and making, as she believed, a very favorable impression.

"I wonder if you are as much pleased with Woodlawn as your cousin," said Durward, noticing that her mind seemed to be more intent on foreign subjects than the scenery around her.

"Oh, no, I dare say not," returned Carrie. "'Lena was never accustomed to anything until she came to Kentucky, and now I suppose she thinks she must go into ecstacies over everything, though I sometimes wish she wouldn't betray her ignorance quite so often."

"According to her description, her home in Massachusetts was widely different from her present one," said Durward, and Carrie quickly replied, "I wonder now if she bored you with an account of her former home! You must have been edified, and had a delightful ride, I declare."

"And I assure you I never had a pleasanter one, for Miss Rivers is, I think, an exceedingly agreeable companion," returned Durward, beginning to see the drift of her remarks.

Here Mr. Graham called to his son, and excusing himself from Carrie, he did not again return to her until it was time to go home. Meantime, at Maple Grove, Mrs. Livingstone, in the worst possible humor, was finding fault with poor 'Lena, accusing her of eavesdropping, and asking her if she did not begin to believe the old adage, that listeners never heard any good of themselves. In perfect astonishment 'Lena demanded what she meant, saying she had never, to her knowledge, been guilty of listening.

Without any explanation, whatever, Mrs. Livingstone declared herself "satisfied now, for a person who would listen and then deny it, was capable of almost anything."

"What do you mean, madam?" said 'Lena, her temper getting the ascendency. "Explain yourself, for no one shall accuse me of lying without an attempt to prove it."

With a sneer Mrs. Livingstone replied, "I wonder what you can do! Will you bring to your assistance some one of your numerous admirers?"

"Admirers! What admirers?" asked 'Lena, and her aunt replied, "I'll give you credit for feigning the best of any one I ever saw, but you can't deceive me. I know very well of your intrigues to entrap Mr. Bellmont. But it is not strange that you should inherit something of your mother's nature; and you know what she was!"

This was too much, and with eyes flashing fire through the glittering tears, which shone like diamonds, 'Lena sprang to her feet, exclaiming, "Yes, I do know what she was. She was a far more worthy woman than you, and if in my presence you dare again breathe aught against her name, you shall rue it----"

"That she shall, so help me heaven," murmured a voice near, which neither Mrs. Livingstone nor 'Lena heard, nor were they aware of any one's presence until Mr. Graham suddenly appeared in the doorway.

At his wife's request he had exchanged places with his son, and riding on before the rest, had reached home first, being just in time to overhear the last part of the conversation between Mrs. Livingstone and 'Lena. Instantly changing her manner, Mrs. Livingstone motioned her niece from the room, heaving a deep sigh as the door closed after her, and saying that "none but those who had tried it knew what a thankless job it was to rear the offspring of others."

There was a peculiar look in Mr. Graham's eyes, as he answered, "In your case I will gladly relieve you, if my wife is willing. I have taken a great fancy to Miss Rivers, and would like to adopt her as my daughter. I will speak to Mrs. Graham to-night."

Much as she disliked 'Lena, Mrs. Livingstone would not for the world have her become an inmate of Mr. Graham's family, where she would be constantly thrown in Durward's way; and immediately changing her tactics, she replied, "I thank you for your kind offer, but I know my husband would not think of such a thing; neither should I be quite willing for her to leave us, much as she troubles me."

Mr. Graham bowed stiffly, and left the house. That night, after he had retired to his room, he seemed unusually distracted, pacing up and down the apartment, occasionally pausing to gaze out into the moonlit sky, and then resuming his measured tread. At last nerving himself to brave the difficulty, he stopped before his wife, to whom he made known his plan of adopting 'Lena.

"It seems hasty, I know," said he, "but she is just the kind of person I would like to have round--just such a one as I would wish my daughter to be if I had one. In short, I like her, and with your consent I will adopt her as my own, and take her from this place where I know she's not wanted. What say you, Lucy?"

"Will you adopt the old woman too?" asked Mrs. Graham, whose face was turned away so as to hide its expression.

"That is an after consideration," returned her husband, "but if you are willing, I will either take her to our home, or provide for her elsewhere--but come, what do you say?"

All this time Mrs. Graham had sat bolt upright, her little dumpling hands folded one within the other, the long transparent nails making deep indentures in the soft flesh, and her gray eyes emitting green gleams of scorn. The answer her husband sought came at length, and was characteristic of the woman. Hissing out the words from between her teeth, she replied, "When I take 'Lena Rivers into my family for my husband and son to make love to, alternately, I shall be ready for the lunatic asylum at Lexington."

"And what objection have you to her?" asked Mr. Graham; to which his wife replied, "The very fact, sir, that you wish it, is a sufficient reason why I will not have her; besides that, you must misjudge me strangely if you think I'd be willing for my son to come daily in contact with a girl of her doubtful parentage."

"What know you of her parentage?" said Mr. Graham, his lips turning slightly pale.

"Yes, what do I know?" answered his wife. "Her father, if she has any, is a rascal, a villain----"

"Yes, yes, all of that," muttered Mr. Graham, while his wife continued, "And her mother a poor, low, mean, ignorant----"

"Hold!" thundered Mr. Graham. "You shall not speak so of any woman of whom you know nothing, much less of 'Lena Rivers' mother."

"And pray what do you know of her--is she an old acquaintance?" asked Mrs. Graham, throwing into her manner as much of insolence as possible.

"I know," returned Mr. Graham, "that 'Lena's mother could be nothing else than respectable."

"Undoubtedly; but of this be assured--the daughter shall never, by my permission, darken my doors," said Mrs. Graham, growing more and more excited, and continuing--"I know you of old, Harry Graham; and I know now that your great desire to secure Woodlawn was so as to be near her, but it shan't be."

In her excitement, Mrs. Graham forgot that it was herself who had first suggested Woodlawn as a residence, and that until within a day or two her husband and 'Lena were entire strangers. But this made no difference. She was bent upon being unreasonable, and for nearly an hour she fretted and cried, declaring herself the most abused of her sex, and wishing she had never seen her husband, who, in his heart, warmly seconded that wish, wisely resolving not to mention the offending 'Lena again in the presence of his wife.

The next day the bargain for Woodlawn was completed; after which, Mr. and Mrs. Graham, together with Durward, returned to Louisville, intending to take possession of their new home about the first of October.

CHAPTER XII.
MRS. GRAHAM AT HOME.

As the summer advanced, extensive preparations were commenced for repairing Woodlawn, which was to be fitted up in a style suited to the luxurious taste of its rightful owner, which, as report said, was in reality Durward. He had conceived a fancy for the place five years before, when visiting in the neighborhood, and on learning that it was for sale, he had purchased it, at the suggestion of his mother, proposing to his father that for a time, at least, he should be its nominal possessor. What reason he had for this he hardly knew himself, unless it was that he disliked being flattered as a man of great wealth, choosing rather to be esteemed for what he really was.

And, indeed, few of his age were more generally beloved than was he. Courteous, kind-hearted, and generous almost to a fault, he gained friends wherever he went, and it was with some reason that Mrs. Graham thought herself blessed above mothers, in the possession of such a son. "He is so like me," she would say, in speaking of his many virtues, when, in fact, there was scarcely anything in common between them, for nearly all of Durward's sterling qualities were either inherited from his own father, or the result of many years' companionship with his stepfather. Possessed of the most exquisite taste, he exercised it in the arrangement of Woodlawn, which, under his skillful management, began in a few weeks to assume a more beautiful appearance than it had ever before worn.

Once in two weeks either Mr. Graham or Durward came out to see how matters were progressing, the latter usually accepting Mrs. Livingstone's pressing invitation to make her house his home. This he was the more willing to do, as it threw him into the society of 'Lena, who was fast becoming an object of absorbing interest to him. The more he saw of her, the more was his admiration increased, and oftentimes, when joked concerning his preference for Carrie, he smiled to think how people were deceived, determining, however, to keep his own secret until such time as he should be convinced that 'Lena was all he could desire in a wife. For her poverty and humble birth he cared nothing. If she were poor, he was rich, and he possessed too much good sense to deem himself better than she, because the blood of a nobleman flowed in his veins. He knew that she was highly gifted and beautiful, and could he be assured that she was equally true-hearted, he would not hesitate a moment.

But Mrs. Livingstone's insinuation that she was a heartless coquette, troubled him, and though he could not believe it without more proof than he had yet received, he determined to wait and watch, studying her character, the while, to see if there was in her aught of evil. In this state of affairs, it was hardly more than natural that his manner toward her should be rather more reserved than that which he assumed toward Carrie, for whom he cared nothing, and with whom he talked laughed, and rode, forgetting her the moment she was out of his sight, and never suspecting how much importance she attached to his every word and look, construing into tokens of admiration the most casual remark, such as he would utter to any one. This was of advantage to 'Lena, for, secure of their prize, both Mrs. Livingstone and Carrie, for a time, at least, ceased to persecute her, seldom speaking of her in Durward's presence, and, as a general thing, acting as though she were not in existence.

John Jr., too, who had imposed upon himself the duty of watching his mother and sister, seeing no signs of hostility, now withdrew his espionage, amusing himself, instead, by galloping three times a week over to Frankfort, the home of Nellie Douglass, and by keeping an eye upon Captain Atherton, who, as a spider would watch a fly, was lying in wait for the unsuspecting Anna.

At last all was in readiness at Woodlawn for the reception of Mrs. Graham, who came up early in October, bringing with her a larger train of house servants than was often seen in Woodford county. About three weeks after her arrival, invitations were issued for a party or "house warming," as the negroes termed it. Nero, Durward's valet, brought the tiny notes to Mr. Livingstone's, giving them into the care of Carrie, who took them immediately to her mother's room.

"It's Durward's handwriting," said she, glancing at the superscriptions, and reading as she did so--"Mr. and Mrs. Livingstone"--"Mr. John Livingstone, Jr."--"Miss Carrie Livingstone"--"Miss Anna Livingstone"--" Miss 'Lena Rivers;" and here she stopped, in utter dismay, continuing, as her mother looked up inquiringly--"And as I live, one for grandma--'MRS. MARTHA NICHOLS!'"

"Impossible!" exclaimed Mrs. Livingstone, reaching out her hand for the billet. "Yes, 'tis Mrs. Martha Nichols!--what can it mean?"

A peep behind the scenes would have told her what it meant. For once in his life Mr. Graham had exercised the right of being master in his own house, declaring that if Mrs. Nichols were not invited with the family, there should be no party at all. Mrs. Graham saw that he was in earnest, and yielded the point, knowing that in all probability the old lady would not be permitted to attend. Her husband had expected a like opposition with regard to 'Lena, but he was disappointed, for his wife, forgetting her declaration that 'Lena should never darken her doors and thinking it would not do to slight her, consented that, on her uncle's account, she should be invited. Accordingly, the notes were despatched, producing the effect we have seen.

"How perfectly ridiculous to invite grandma!" said Carrie. "It's bad enough to have 'Lena stuck in with us, for of course she'll go."

"Why of course?" asked Mrs. Livingstone. "The invitations are at my disposal now; and if I choose to withhold two of them, no one will be blamed but Nero, who was careless and dropped them! 'Lena has nothing decent to wear, and I don't feel like expending much more for a person so ungrateful as she is. You ought to have heard how impudent she was that time you all went to Woodlawn."

Then followed a one-sided description of that morning's occurrence, Mrs. Livingstone working herself up to such a pitch of excitement, that before her recital was finished, she had determined at all events to keep back 'Lena's invitation, as a method of punishing her for her "insolence," as she termed it.

"Mrs. Graham will thank me for it, I know," said she, "for she cannot endure her; and besides that, I don't think 'Lena expects to be invited, so there's no harm done."

Carrie was not yet quite so hardened as her mother, and for a moment her better nature shrank from so mean a transaction, which might, after all, be found out, involving them in a still worse difficulty; but as the thought flashed upon her that possibly 'Lena might again attract Durward toward her, she assented, and they were about putting the notes aside, when John Jr. came in, catching up his grandmother's note the first thing, and exclaiming, "Oh, rich!-- capital! I hope she'll go!" Then, before his mother could interpose a word, he darted away in quest of Mrs. Nichols, whose surprise was fully equal to that of Mrs. Livingstone and Carrie.

"Now, you don't say I've got an invite," said she, leaving the darning-needle in the stocking-heel which she was mending, and wiping her steel-bowed spectacles. "Come, 'Leny, you read it, that's a good girl."

'Lena complied, and taking the note from her cousin's hand, read that Mrs. Graham would be at home Thursday evening, etc.

"But where's the invite? That don't say anything about me!" said Mrs. Nichols, beginning to fear that it was a humbug after all.

As well as they could, 'Lena and John Jr. explained it to her, and then, fully convinced that she was really invited, Mrs. Nichols began to wonder what she should wear, and how she should go, asking John "if he couldn't tackle up and carry her in the shay," as she called the single buggy.

"Certainly," answered John Jr. willing to do anything for the sake of the fun which he knew would ensue from his grandmother's attendance.

'Lena thought otherwise, for much as she desired to gratify her grandmother, she would not for the world expose her to the ridicule which her appearance at a fashionable party would call forth. Glancing reprovingly at her cousin, she said, "I wouldn't think of going, grandma, for you are lame and old, and there'll be so many people there, all strangers, too, that you won't enjoy it at all. Besides that, we'll have a nice time at home together---I'll read to you all the evening."

"We," repeated John Jr. "Pray, are you not going?"

"Not without an invitation," said 'Lena smilingly.

"True, true," returned her cousin. "It's downstairs, I dare say. I only stopped to look at this. I'll go and get yours now."

Suiting the action to the word, he descended to his mother's room, asking for "'Lena's card."

"'Lena's card! What do you mean?" said Mrs. Livingstone, looking up from the book she was reading, while Carrie for a moment suspended her needle-work.

"'Lena's invitation; you know well enough what I mean," returned John Jr., tumbling over the notes which lay upon the table, and failing to find the one for which he was seeking.

"You'll have to ask Mrs. Graham for it, I presume, as it's not here," was Mrs. Livingstone's quiet answer.

"Thunder!" roared John Jr., "'Lena not invited! That's a smart caper. But there's some mistake about it, I know. Who brought them?"

"Nero brought them," said Carrie, "and I think it is strange that grandmother should be invited and 'Lena left out. But I suppose Mrs. Graham has her reasons. She don't seem to fancy 'Lena much."

"Mrs. Graham go to grass," muttered John Jr., leaving the room and slamming the door after him with great violence.

'Twas a pity he did not look in one of the drawers of his mother's work-box, for there, safe and sound, lay the missing note! But he did not think of that. He only knew that 'Lena was slighted, and for the next two hours he raved and fretted, sometimes declaring he would not go, and again wishing Mrs. Graham in a temperature but little suited to her round, fat proportions.

"Wall, if they feel too big to invite 'Leny, they needn't expect to see me there, that's just all there is about it," said grandma, settling herself in her rocking-chair, and telling 'Lena "she wouldn't care an atom if she's in her place."

But 'Lena did care. No one likes to be slighted, and she was not an exception to the general rule. Owing to her aunt's skillful management she had never yet attended a large party, and it was but natural that she should now wish to go. But it could not be, and she was obliged to content herself with the hopes of a minute description from Anna; Carrie she would not trust, for she well knew that whatever she told would be greatly exaggerated.

Mrs. Graham undoubtedly wished to give her friends ample time to prepare, for her invitations were issued nearly a week in advance. This suited Carrie, who had a longer time to decide upon what would be becoming, and when at last a decision was made, she could do nothing but talk about her dress, which really was beautiful, consisting of a pink and white silk, with an over-skirt of soft, rich lace. This, after it was completed, was tried on at least half a dozen times, and the effect carefully studied before the long mirror. Anna, who cared much less for dress than her sister, decided upon a black flounced skirt and velvet basque. This was Mr. Everett's taste, and whatever suited him suited her.

"I do think it's too bad that 'Lena is not invited," said she one day, when Carrie, as usual, was discussing the party. "She would enjoy it so much. I don't understand, either, why she is omitted, for Mr. Graham seemed to like her, and Durward too----"

"A great ways off, you mean," interrupted Carrie. "For my part, I see nothing strange in the omission. It is no worse to leave her out than scores of others who will not be invited."

"But to come into the house and ask all but her," said Anna. "It does not seem right. She is as good as we are."

"That's as people think," returned Carrie, while John Jr., who was just going out to ride, and had stopped a moment at the door, exclaimed, "Zounds, Cad, I wonder if you fancy yourself better than 'Lena Rivers. If you do, you are the only one that thinks so. Why, you can't begin to compare with her, and it's a confounded shame that she isn't invited, and so I shall tell them if I have a good chance."

"You'll look smart fishing for an invitation, won't you?" said Carrie, her fears instantly aroused, but John Jr. was out of her hearing almost before the words were uttered.

Mounting Firelock, he started off for Versailles, falling in with Durward, who was bound for the same place. After the usual greetings were exchanged, Durward said, "I suppose you are all coming on Thursday night?"

"Yes," returned John Jr., "I believe the old folks, Cad, and Anna intend doing so."

"But where's Miss Rivers? Doesn't she honor us with her presence?" asked Durward, in some concern.

John Jr.'s first impulse, as he afterwards said, was "to knock him off from his horse," but a second thought convinced him there might be some mistake; so he replied that "it was hardly to be supposed Miss Rivers would attend without an invitation--she wasn't quite so verdant as that!"

"Without an invitation!" repeated Durward, stopping short in the road. "'Lena not invited! It isn't so! I directed one to her myself, and gave it to Nero, together with the rest which were designed for your family. He must have lost it. I'll ask him the moment I get home, and see that it is all made right. She must come, any way, for I wouldn't give----"

Here he stopped, as if he had said too much, but John Jr. finished the sentence for him.

"Wouldn't give a picayune for the whole affair without her--that's what you mean, and why not say so? I speak right out about Nellie, and she isn't one half as handsome as 'Lena."

"It isn't 'Lena's beauty that I admire altogether," returned Durward. "I like her for her frankness, and because I think her conduct is actuated by the best of principles; perhaps I am mistaken----"

"No, you are not," again interrupted John Jr., "'Lena is just what she seems to be. There's no deception in her. She isn't one thing to-day and another to-morrow. Spunky as the old Nick, you know, but still she governs her temper admirably, and between you and me, I know I'm a better man than I should have been had she never come to live with us. How well I remember the first time I saw her," he continued, repeating to Durward the particulars of their interview in Lexington, and describing her introduction to his sisters. "From the moment she refused to tell that lie for me, I liked her," said he, "and when she dealt me that blow in my face, my admiration was complete."

Durward thought he could dispense with the blow, but he laughed heartily at John's description of his spirited cousin, thinking, too, how different was his opinion of her from that which his mother evidently entertained. Still, if Mrs. Livingstone was prejudiced, John Jr. might also be somewhat biased, so he would not yet make up his mind; but on one thing he was resolved--she should be invited, and for fear of contingencies, he would carry the card himself.

Accordingly, on his return home, Nero was closely questioned, and negro-like, called down all manner of evil upon himself "if he done drapped the note any whar. 'Strue as I live and breathe, Mas'r Bellmont," said he, "I done carried Miss 'Leny's invite with the rest, and guv 'em all to the young lady with the big nose!"

Had Durward understood Mrs. Livingstone a little better, he might have believed him; but now it was but natural for him to suppose that Nero had accidentally dropped it. So he wrote another, taking it himself, and asking for "Miss Rivers." Carrie, who was in the parlor and saw him coming up to the house, instantly flew to the glass, smoothing her collar, puffing out her hair a little more, pinching her cheek, which was not quite so red as usual, and wishing that she was alone. But unfortunately, both Anna and 'Lena were present, and as there was no means of being rid of them, she retained her seat at the piano, carelessly turning over the leaves of her music book, when the door opened and Corinda, not Durward, appeared.

"If you please, Miss 'Lena," said the girl, "Marster Bellmont want to speak with you in the hall."

"With 'Lena! How funny!" exclaimed Carrie. "Are you sure it was 'Lena?"

"Yes, sure--he done ask for Miss Rivers."

"Ask him in, why don't you?" said Carrie, suspecting his errand, and thinking to keep herself from all suspicion by appearing "wonderfully pleased" that 'Lena was not intentionally neglected. Before Corinda could reply, 'Lena had stepped into the hall, and was standing face to face with Durward, who retained her hand, while he asked if "she really believed they, intended to slight her," at the same time explaining how it came to his knowledge, and saying "he hoped she would not fail to attend."

'Lena hesitated, but he pressed her so hard, saying he should surely think she distrusted them if she refused, that she finally consented, and he took his leave, playfully threatening to come for her himself if she were not there with the rest.

"You feel better, now, don't you ?" said Carrie with a sneer, as 'Lena re-entered the parlor.

"Yes, a great deal," was 'Lena's truthful answer.

"Oh, I'm real glad!" exclaimed Anna. "I most knew 'twas a mistake all the time, and I did so want you to go. What will you wear? Let me see. Why, you haven't got anything suitable, have you?"

This was true, for 'Lena had nothing fit for the occasion, and she was beginning to wish she had not been invited, when her uncle came in, and to him Anna forthwith stated the case, saying 'Lena must have a new dress, and suggesting embroidered muslin.

"How ridiculous!" muttered Carrie, thrumming away at the piano. "There's no time to make dresses now. They should have invited her earlier."

"Isn't Miss Simpson still here?" asked her father.

Anna replied that she was, and then turning to 'Lena, Mr. Livingstone asked if "she wanted to go very much."

The tears which shone in her eyes were a sufficient answer, and when at supper that night, inquiry was made for Mr. Livingstone, it was said that he had gone to Frankfort.

"To Frankfort!" repeated his wife. "What has he gone there for?"

No one knew until late in the evening, when he returned home, bringing with him 'Lena's dress, which Anna pronounced "the sweetest thing she ever saw," at the same time running with it to her cousin. There was company in the parlor, which for a time kept down the gathering storm in Mrs. Livingstone's face, but the moment they were gone, and she was alone with her husband in their room, it burst forth, and in angry tones she demanded "what he meant by spending her money in that way, and without her consent?"

Before making any reply, Mr. Livingstone stepped to her work-box, and opening the little drawer, held to view the missing note. Then turning to his wife, whose face was very pale, he said, "This morning I made a discovery which exonerates Nero from all blame. I understand it fully, and while I knew you were capable of almost anything, I must say I did not think you would be guilty of quite so mean an act. Stay," he continued, as he saw her about to speak, "you are my wife, and as 'Lena is at last invited, your secret is safe, but remember, it must not be repeated. You understand me, do you?"

Mrs. Livingstone was struck dumb with mortification and astonishment--the first, that she was detected, and the last, that her husband dare assume such language toward her. But he had her in his power--she knew that--and for a time it rendered her very docile, causing her to consult with Miss Simpson concerning the fitting of 'Lena's dress, herself standing by when it was done, and suggesting one or two improvements, until 'Lena, perfectly bewildered, wondered what had come over her aunt, that she should be so unusually kind. Carrie, too, learning from her mother how matters stood, thought proper to change her manner, and while in her heart she hoped something would occur to keep 'Lena at home, she loudly expressed her pleasure that she was going, offering to lend her several little ornaments, and doing many things which puzzled 'Lena, who readily saw that she was feigning what she did not feel.

Meanwhile, grandma, learning that 'Lena was invited, declared her intention of going. "I shouldn't of gin up in the first on't," said she, "only I wanted to show 'em proper resentment; but now it's different, and I'll go, anyway--'Tilda may say what she's a mind to."

It was in vain that 'Lena reasoned the case. Grandma was decided, and it was not until both her son and daughter interfered, the one advising and the other commanding her to stay at home, that she yielded with a burst of tears, for grandma was now in her second childhood, and easily moved. It was terrible to 'Lena to see her grandmother weep, and twining her arms around her neck, she tried to soothe her, saying, "she would willingly stay at home with her if she wished it."

Mrs. Nichols was not selfish enough to suffer this. "No, 'Leny," said she, "I want you to go and enjoy yourself while you are young, for you'll sometime be old and in the way;" and the old creature covered her face with her shriveled hands and wept.

But she was of too cheerful a nature long to remember grief, and drying her tears, she soon forgot her trouble in the pride and satisfaction which she felt when she saw how well the white muslin became 'Lena, who, John Jr., said, never looked so beautifully as she did when arrayed for the party. Mr. Livingstone had not been sparing of his money when he purchased the party dress, which was a richly embroidered muslin, and fell in soft folds around 'Lena's graceful figure. Her long flowing curls were intertwined with a few natural flowers, her only attempt at ornament of any kind, and, indeed, ornaments would have been sadly out of place on 'Lena'.

It was between nine and ten when the party from Maple Grove reached Woodlawn, where they found a large company assembled, some in the drawing-rooms below, and others still lingering at the toilet in the dressing chamber. Among these last were Nellie Douglass and Mabel Ross, the latter of whom Mrs. Livingstone was perfectly delighted to see, overwhelming her with caresses, and urging her to stop for awhile at Maple Grove.

"I shall be so glad to have you with us, and the country air will do you so much good, that you must not refuse," said she, pinching Mabel's sallow cheek, and stroking her straight, glossy hair, which, in contrast with the bandeau of pearls that she wore, looked dark as midnight.

Spite of her wealth, Mabel had long been accustomed to neglect, and there was something so kind in Mrs. Livingstone's motherly demeanor, that the heart of the young orphan warmed toward her, and tears glittered in her large, mournful eyes, the only beauty, save her hair, of which she could boast. Very few had ever cared for poor Mabel, who, though warm-hearted and affectionate, required to be known in order to be appreciated, and as she was naturally shy and retiring, there were not many who felt at all acquainted with her. Left alone in the world at a very early age, she had never known what it was to possess a real, disinterested friend, unless we except Nellie Douglass, who, while there was nothing congenial between them, had always tried to treat Mabel as she herself would wish to be treated, were she in like circumstances.

Many had professed friendship for the sake of the gain which they knew would accrue, for she was generous to a fault, bestowing with a lavish hand upon those whom she loved, and who had too often proved false, denouncing her as utterly spiritless and insipid. So often had she been deceived, that now, at the age of eighteen, she had learned to distrust her fellow creatures, and oftentimes in secret would she weep bitterly over her lonely condition, lamenting the plain face and unattractive manners, which she fancied rendered her an object of dislike. Still there was about her a depth of feeling of which none had ever dreamed, and it only required a skillful hand to mold her into an altogether different being. She was, perhaps, too easily influenced, for in spite of her distrust, a pleasant word or kind look would win her to almost anything.

Of this weakness Mrs. Livingstone seemed well aware, and for the better accomplishment of her plan, she deemed it necessary that Mabel should believe her to be the best friend she had in the world. Accordingly, she now flattered and petted her, calling her "darling," and "dearest," and urging her to stop at Maple Grove, until she consented, "provided Nellie Douglas were willing."

"Oh, I don't care," answered Nellie, whose gay, dashing disposition poorly accorded with the listless, sickly Mabel, and who felt it rather a relief than otherwise to be rid of her.

So it was decided that she should stay at Maple Grove, and then Mrs. Livingstone, passing her arm around her waist, whispered, "Go down with me," at the same time starting for the parlor, followed by her daughters, Nellie, and 'Lena. In the hall they met with John Jr. He had heard Nellie's voice, and stationing himself at the head of the stairs, was waiting her appearance.

"Miss Ross," said Mrs. Livingstone to her son, at the same time indicating her willingness to give her into his care.

But John Jr. would not take the hint. Bowing stiffly to Mabel, he passed on toward Nellie, in his eagerness stepping on Carrie's train and drawing from her an exclamation of anger at his awkwardness. Mrs. Livingstone glanced backward just in time to see the look of affection with which her son regarded Nellie, as she placed her soft hand confidingly upon his arm, and gazed upward smilingly into his face. She dared not slight Miss Douglass in public, but with a mental invective against her, she drew Mabel closer to her side, and smoothing down the heavy folds of her moire antique, entered the drawing-room, which was brilliantly lighted, and filled with the beauty and fashion of Lexington, Frankfort, and Versailles.

At the door they met Durward, who, as he took 'Lena's hand, said, "It is well you remembered your promise, for I was about starting after you." This observation did not escape Mrs. Livingstone, who, besides having her son and Nellie under her special cognizance, had also an eye upon her niece and Anna. Her espionage of the latter, however, was not needed immediately, owing to her being straightway appropriated by Captain Atherton, who, in dainty white kids, and vest to match (the color not the material), strutted back and forth with Anna tucked under his arm, until the poor girl was ready to cry with vexation.

When the guests had nearly all arrived, both Mr. Graham and Durward started for 'Lena, the latter reaching her first, and paying her so many little attentions, that the curiosity of others was aroused, and frequently was the question asked, "Who is she, the beautiful young lady in white muslin and curls?"

Nothing of all this escaped Mrs. Livingstone, and once, in passing near her niece, she managed to whisper, "For heaven's sake don't show your ignorance of etiquette by taxing Mr. Bellmont's good nature any longer. It's very improper to claim any one's attention so long, and you are calling forth remarks."

Then quickly changing the whisper into her softest tones, she said to Durward, "How can you resist such beseeching glances as those ladies send toward you?" nodding to a group of girls of which Carrie was one.

'Lena colored scarlet, and gazed wistfully around the room in quest of some other shelter when Durward should relinquish her, as she felt he would surely do, but none presented itself. Her uncle was playing the agreeable to Miss Atherton,

Mr. Graham to some other lady, while John Jr. kept closely at Nellie's side, forgetful of all else.

"What shall I do?" said 'Lena, unconsciously and half aloud.

"Stay with me," answered Durward, drawing her hand further within his arm, and bending upon her a look of admiration which she could not mistake.

Several times they passed and repassed Mrs. Graham, who was highly incensed at her son's proceedings, and at last actually asked him "if he did not intend noticing anyone except Miss Rivers," adding, as an apology for her rudeness (for Mrs. Graham prided herself upon being very polite in her own house), "she has charms enough to win a dozen gallants, but there are others here who need attention from you. There's Miss Livingstone, you've hardly spoken with her to-night."

Thus importuned, Durward released 'Lena and walked away, attaching himself to Carrie, who clung to him closer, if possible, than did the old captain to Anna. About this time Mr. Everett came. He had been necessarily detained, and now, after paying his respects to the host and hostess, he started in quest of Anna, who was still held "in durance vile" by the captain. But the moment she saw Malcolm, she uttered a low exclamation of joy, and without a single apology, broke abruptly away from her ancient cavalier, whose little watery eyes looked daggers after her for an instant; then consoling himself with the reflection that he was tolerably sure of her, do what she would, he walked up to her mother, kindly relieving her for a time of her charge, who was becoming rather tiresome. Frequently, by nods, winks, and frowns, had Mrs. Livingstone tried to bring her son to a sense of his improper conduct in devoting himself exclusively to one individual, and neglecting all others.

But her efforts were all in vain. John Jr. was incorrigible, slyly whispering to Nellie, that "he had no idea of beauing a medicine chest." This he said, referring to Mabel's ill health, for among his other oddities, John Jr. had a particular aversion to sickly ladies. Of course Nellie reproved him for his unkind remarks, at the same time warmly defending Mabel, "who," she said, "had been delicate from infancy, and suffered far more than was generally suspected."

"Let her stay at home, then," was John Jr.'s answer, as he led Nellie toward the supper-room, which the company were just then entering.

About an hour after supper the guests began to leave, Mrs. Livingstone being the first to propose going. As she was ascending the stairs, John Jr. observed that

Mabel was with her, and turning to 'Lena, who now leaned on his arm, he said, "There goes the future Mrs. John Jr.--so mother thinks!"

"Where?" asked 'Lena, looking around.

"Why, there," continued John, pointing toward Mabel. "Haven't you noticed with what parental solicitude mother watches over her?"

"I saw them together," answered 'Lena, "and I thought it very kind in my aunt, for no one else seemed to notice her, and I felt sorry for her. She is going home with us, I believe.",

"Going home with us!" repeated John Jr. "In the name of the people, what is she going home with us for?"

"Why," returned 'Lena, "your mother thinks the country air will do her good."

"Un-doubtedly," said John, with a sneer. "Mother's motives are usually very disinterested. I wonder she don't propose to the old captain to take up his quarters with us, so she can nurse him!"

With this state of feeling, it was hardly natural that John Jr. should be very polite toward Mabel, and when his mother asked him to help her into the carriage, he complied so ungraciously, that Mabel observed it, and looked wonderingly at her patroness for an explanation.

"Only one of his freaks, love--he'll get over it," said Mrs. Livingstone, while poor Mabel, sinking back among the cushions, wept silently, thinking that everybody hated her.

When 'Lena came down to bid her host and hostess good-night, the former retained her hand, while he expressed his sorrow at her leaving so soon. "I meant to have seen more of you," said he, "but you must visit us often--will you not?"

Neither the action nor the words escaped Mrs. Graham's observation, and the lecture which she that night read her offending spouse, had the effect to keep him awake until the morning was growing gray in the east. Then, when he was asleep, he so far forgot himself and the wide-open ears beside him as actually to breathe the name of 'Lena in his dreams!

Mrs. Graham needed no farther confirmation of her suspicions, and at the breakfast-table next morning, she gave her son a lengthened account of her husband's great sin in dreaming of a young girl, and that girl 'Lena Rivers. Durward laughed heartily and then, either to tease his mother, or to make his father's guilt less heinous in her eyes, he replied, "It is a little singular that our minds should run in the same channel, for, I, too, dreamed of 'Lena Rivers!"

Poor Mrs. Graham. A double task was now imposed upon her--that of watching both husband and son; but she was accustomed to it, for her life, since her second marriage, had been one continued series of watching for evil where there was none. And now, with a growing hatred toward 'Lena, she determined to increase her vigilance, feeling sure she should discover something if she only continued faithful to the end.

CHAPTER XIII.
MABEL.

The morning following the party, Mr. Livingstone's family were assembled in the parlor, discussing the various events of the previous night. John Jr., 'Lena, and Anna declared themselves to have been highly pleased with everything, while Carrie in the worst of humors, pronounced it "a perfect bore," saying she never had so disagreeable a time in all her life, and ending her ill-natured remarks by a malicious thrust at 'Lena, for having so long kept Mr. Bellmont at her side.

"I suppose you fancy he would have looked better with you, but I think he showed his good taste by preferring 'Lena," said John Jr.; then turning toward the large easy-chair, where Mabel sat, pale, weary, and spiritless, he asked "how she had enjoyed herself."

With the exception of his accustomed "good-morning," this was the first time he had that day addressed her, and it was so unexpected, that it brought a bright glow to her cheek, making John Jr. think she was "not so horribly ugly after all."

But she was very unfortunate in her answer, which was, "that on account of her ill health, she seldom enjoyed anything of the kind." Then pressing her hand upon her forehead, she continued, "My head is aching dreadfully, as a punishment for last night's dissipation."

Three times before, he had heard her speak of her aching head, and now, with an impatient gesture, he was turning away, when his mother said, "Poor girl, she really looks miserable. I think a ride would do her good. Suppose you take her with you--I heard you say you were going to Versailles."

If there was anything in which Mabel excelled, it was horsemanship, she being a better rider, if possible; than 'Lena, and now, at Mrs. Livingstone's proposition, she looked up eagerly at John Jr., who replied,

"Oh, hang it all! mother, I can't always be bothered with a girl;" then as he saw how Mabel's countenance fell, he continued, "Let 'Lena ride with her--she wants to, I know."

"Certainly," said 'Lena, whose heart warmed toward the orphan girl, partly because she was an orphan, and partly because she saw that she was neglected and unloved.

As yet Mabel cared nothing for John Jr., nor even suspected his mother's object in detaining her as a guest. So when 'Lena was proposed as a substitute she seemed equally well pleased, and the young man, as he walked off to order the ponies, mentally termed himself a bear for his rudeness; "for after all," thought he, "it's mother who has designs upon me, not Mabel. She isn't to blame."

This opinion once satisfactorily settled, it was strange how soon John Jr. began to be sociable with Mabel, finding her much more agreeable than he had at first supposed, and even acknowledging to 'Lena that "she was a good deal of a girl, after all, were it not for her everlasting headaches and the smell of medicine," which he declared she always carried about with her.

"Hush-sh," said 'Lena--"you shan't talk so, for she is sick a great deal, and she does not feign it, either."

"Perhaps not," returned John Jr., "but she can at least keep her miserable feelings to herself. Nobody wants to know how many times she's been blistered and bled!"

Still John Jr. acknowledged that there were somethings in Mabel which he liked, for no one could live long with her and not admire her gentleness and uncommon sweetness of disposition, which manifested itself in numerous little acts of kindness to those around her. Never before in her life had she been so constantly associated with a young gentleman, and as she was quite susceptible, it is hardly more than natural that erelong thoughts of John Jr. mingled in both her sleeping and waking dreams. She could not understand him, but the more his changeful moods puzzled her, the more she felt interested in him, and her eyes would alternately sparkle at a kind word from him, or fill with tears at the abruptness of his speeches; while he seemed to take special delight in seeing how easily he could move her from one extreme to the other.

Silently Mrs. Livingstone looked on, carefully noting each change, and warily calculating its result. Not once since Mabel became an inmate of her family had she mentioned her to her son, for she deemed it best to wait, and let matters take their course. But at last, anxious to know his real opinion, she determined to sound him. Accordingly, one day when they were alone, she spoke of Mabel, asking him if he did not think she improved upon acquaintance, at the same time enumerating her many excellent qualities, and saying that whoever married her would get a prize, to say nothing of a fortune.

Quickly comprehending the drift of her remarks, John Jr. replied, "I dare say, and whoever wishes for both prize and fortune, is welcome to them for all me."

"I thought you liked Mabel," said his mother; and John answered, "So I do like her, but for pity's sake, is a man obliged to marry every girl he likes? Mabel does very well to tease and amuse one, but when you come to the marrying part, why, that's another thing."

"And what objection have you to her," continued his mother, growing very fidgety and red.

"Several," returned John, "She has altogether too many aches and pains to suit me; then she has no spirit whatever; and last, but not least, I like somebody else. So, mother mine, you may as well give up all hopes of that hundred thousand down in Alabama, for I shall never marry Mabel Ross, never."

Mrs. Livingstone was now not only red and fidgety but very angry, and, in an elevated tone of voice, she said, "I s'pose it's Nellie Douglass you mean, but if you knew all of her that I do, I reckon----"

Here she paused, insinuating that she could tell something dreadful, if she would! But John Jr. took no notice of her hints, and when he got a chance, he replied, "You are quite a Yankee at guessing, for if Nellie will have me, I surely will have her."

"Marry her, then," retorted his mother--"marry her with all her poverty, but for heaven's sake, don't give so much encouragement to a poor defenseless girl."

Wishing Mabel in Guinea, and declaring he'd neither speak to nor look at her again, if common civilities were construed into encouragement, John Jr. strode out of the room, determining, as the surest method of ending the trouble, to go forthwith to Nellie, and in a plain, straight-forward way make her an offer of himself.

With him, to will was to do, and in about an hour he was descending the long hill which leads into Frankfort. Unfortunately, Nellie had gone for a few weeks to Madison, and again mounting Firelock, the young man galloped back, reaching home just as the family were sitting down to supper. Not feeling hungry, and wishing to avoid, as long as possible, the sight of his mother and Mabel, whom he believed were leagued against him, he repaired to the parlor, whistling loudly, and making much more noise than was at all necessary.

"If you please, Mr. Livingstone, won't you be a little more quiet, for my head aches so hard to-night," said a languid voice, from the depths of the huge easy-chair which stood before the glowing grate.

Glancing toward what he had at first supposed to be a bundle of shawls, John Jr. saw Mabel Ross, her forehead bandaged up and her lips white as ashes, while the purple rings about her heavy eyes, told of the pain she was enduring.

"Thunder!" was John's exclamation, as he strode from the room, slamming together the door with unusual force.

When Mrs. Livingstone came in from supper, with a cup of hot tea and a slice of toast for Mabel, she was surprised to find her sobbing like a child. It did not take long for her to learn the cause, and then, as well as she could, she soothed her, telling her not to mind John's freaks--it was his way, and he always had a particular aversion to sick people, never liking to hear them talk of their ailments. This hint was sufficient for Mabel, who ever after strove hard to appear well and cheerful in his presence. But in no way, if he could help it, would he notice her.

Next to Mrs. Livingstone, 'Lena was Mabel's best friend, and when she saw how much her cousin's rudeness and indifference pained her, she determined to talk with him about it, So the first time they were alone, she broached the subject, speaking very kindly of Mabel, and asking if he had any well-grounded reason for his uncivil treatment of her. There was no person in the world who possessed so much influence over John Jr. as did 'Lena, and now, hearing her patiently through, he replied, "I know I'm impolite to Mabel, but hang me if I can help it. She is so flat and silly, and takes every little attention from me as a declaration of love. Still, I don't blame her as much as I do mother, who is putting her up to it, and if she'd only go home and mind her own business, I should like her well enough."

"I don't understand you," said 'Lena, and her cousin continued; "Why, when

Mabel first came here, I do not think she knew what mother was fishing for, so she was not so much at fault, but she does now----"

"Are you sure?" interrupted 'Lena, and John Jr. replied, "She's a confounded fool if she don't. And what provokes me, is to think she'll still keep staying here, when modesty, if nothing else, should prompt her to leave. You wouldn't catch Nellie doing so. Why, she'll hardly come her at all, for fear folks will say she comes to see me, and that's why I like her so well."

"I think you are mistaken with regard to Mabel," said Lena, "for I've no idea she's in love with you a bit more than I am. I dare say she likes you well enough, for there's nothing in you to dislike."

"Thank you," interrupted John Jr., returning the compliment with a kiss, a liberty he often took with her.

"Behave, can't you?" said 'Lena, at the same time continuing--"No, I don't suppose Mabel is dying for you at all. All of us girls like to receive attention from you gentlemen, and she's not an exception. Besides that, you ought to be polite to her, because she's your mother's guest, if for nothing else. I don't ask you to love her," said she, "but I do ask you to treat her well. Kind words cost nothing, and they go far toward making others happy."

"So they do," answered John, upon whom 'Lena's words were having a good effect. "I've nothing under heaven against Mabel Ross, except that mother wants me to marry her; but if you'll warrant me that the young lady herself has no such intentions, why, I'll do my very best."

"I'll warrant you," returned 'Lena, who really had no idea that Mabel cared aught in particular for her cousin, and satisfied with the result of her interview she started to leave the room.

As she reached the door, John Jr. stopped her, saying, "You are sure she don't care for me?"

"Perfectly sure," was 'Lena's answer.

"The plague, she don't," thought John, as the door closed upon 'Lena; and such is human nature, that the young man began to think that if Mabel didn't care for him, he'd see if he couldn't make her, for after all, there was something pleasant in being liked, even by Mabel!

The next day, as the young ladies were sitting together in the parlor, John Jr.

joined them, and after wringing Carrie's nose, pulling 'Lena's and Anna's curls, he suddenly upset Mabel's work-box, at the same time slyly whispering to his cousin, "Ain't I coming round?"

Abrupt as this proceeding, was, it pleased Mabel, who with the utmost good humor, commenced picking up her things, John Jr. assisting her, and managing once to bump his head against hers! After this, affairs at Maple Grove glided on as smoothly as even Mrs. Livingstone could wish. John and Mabel were apparently on the most amicable terms, he deeming 'Lena's approbation a sufficient reward for the many little attentions which he paid to Mabel, and she, knowing nothing of all that had passed, drinking in his every word and look, learning to live upon his smile, and conforming herself, as far as possible, to what she thought would best please him.

Gradually, as she thought it would do, Mrs. Livingstone unfolded to Mabel her own wishes, saying she should be perfectly happy could she only call her "daughter," and hinting that such a thing "by wise management could easily be brought about." With a gush of tears the orphan girl laid her head in Mrs. Livingstone's lap, mentally blessing her as her benefactress, and thanking the Giver of all good for the light and happiness which she saw dawning upon her pathway.

"John is peculiar," said Mrs. Livingstone, "and if he fancied you liked him very much, it might not please him as well as indifference on your part."

So, with this lesson, Mabel, for the first time in her life attempted to act as she did not feel, feigning carelessness or indifference when every pulse of her heart was throbbing with joy at some little attention paid her by John Jr., who could be very agreeable when he chose, and who, observing her apparent indifference, began to think that what 'Lena had said was true, and that Mabel really cared nothing for him. With this impression he exerted himself to be agreeable, wondering how her many good qualities had so long escaped his observation.

"There is more to her than I supposed," said he one day to 'Lena, who was commending him for his improved manner. "Yes, a heap more than I supposed. Why, I really like her!"

And he told the truth, for with his prejudice laid aside, he, as is often the case, began to find virtues in her the existence of which he had never suspected. Frequently, now, he talked, laughed, and rode with her, praising her horsemanship, pointing out some points wherein it might be improved, and never dreaming the while of the deep affection his conduct had awakened in the susceptible girl.

"Oh, I am so happy," said she one day to 'Lena, who was speaking of her improved health. "I never thought it possible for me to be so happy. I dreaded to come here at first, but now I shall never regret it, never."

She was standing before the long mirror in the parlor, adjusting the feathers to her tasteful velvet cap, which, with her neatly fitting riding-dress, became her better than anything else. The excitement of her words sent a deep glow to her cheek, while her large black eyes sparkled with unusual brilliancy. She was going out with John Jr., who, just as she finished speaking, appeared in the doorway, and catching a glimpse of her face, exclaimed in his blunt, jocose way, "Upon my word, Meb, if you keep on, you'll get to be quite decent looking in time."

'Twas the first compliment of the kind he had ever paid her, and questionable as it was, it tended to strengthen her fast forming belief that her affection for him was returned.

"I can't expect him to do anything like other people, he's so odd," thought she, and yet it was this very oddness which charmed her.

At length Nellie, who had returned from Madison, and felt rather lonely, wrote to Mabel, asking her to come home. This plan Mrs. Livingstone opposed, but Mabel was decided, and the week before Christmas was fixed upon for her departure. John Jr., anxious to see Nellie, proposed accompanying her, but when the day came he was suffering from a severe cold, which rendered his stay in the house absolutely necessary. So his mother, who had reasons of her own for doing so, went in his stead. Carrie, who never had any fancy for Mabel, and only endured her because she was rich, was coolly polite, merely offering her hand, and then resumed the novel she was reading, even before Mabel had left. Anna and 'Lena bade her a more affectionate adieu, and then advancing toward John Jr., who, in his dressing-gown and slippers, reclined upon the sofa, she offered him her hand.

As if to atone for his former acts of rudeness, the young man accompanied her to the door, playfully claiming the privilege of taking leave just as his sister and cousin had done.

"It's only me, you know," said he, imprinting upon her forehead a kiss which sent the rich blood to her neck and face.

John Jr. would not have dared to take that liberty with Nellie, while Mabel, simple-hearted, and wholly unused to the world, saw in it a world of meaning, and for a long time after the carriage roiled away from Maple Grove the bright glow on her cheek told of happy thoughts within.

"Did my son say anything definite to you before you left?" asked Mrs. Livingstone, as they came within sight of the city.

"No, madam," answered Mabel, and Mrs. Livingstone continued, "That's strange. He confessed to me that he--ah--he--loved you, and I supposed he intended telling you so; but bashfulness prevented, I dare say!"

Accustomed as she was to equivocation, this down-right falsehood cost Mrs. Livingstone quite an effort, but she fancied the case required it, and after a few twinges, her conscience felt easy, particularly when she saw how much satisfaction her words gave to her companion, to whom the improbability of the affair never occurred. Could she have known how lightly John Jr. treated the matter, laughingly describing his leave-taking to his sisters and 'Lena, and saying, "Meb wasn't the worst girl in the world, after all," she might not have been so easily duped.

But she did not know all this, and thus was the delusion perfect.

CHAPTER XIV.
NELLIE AND MABEL.

Nellie Douglass sat alone in her chamber, which was filled with articles of elegance and luxury, for her father, though far from being wealthy, still loved to surround his only daughter with everything which could increase her comfort. So the best, the fairest, and the most Costly was always for her, his "darling Nellie," as he called her, when with bounding footsteps she flew to greet him on his return at night, ministering to his wants in a thousand ways, and shedding over his home such a halo of sunshine that ofttimes he forgot that he was a lonely widower, while in the features of his precious child he saw again the wife of his bosom, who years before had passed from his side forever.

But not on him were Nellie's thoughts resting, as she sat there alone that afternoon. She was thinking of the past--of John Livingstone, and the many marked attentions, which needed not the expression of words to tell her she was beloved. And freely did her heart respond. That John Jr. was not perfect, she knew, but he was noble and generous, and so easily influenced by those he loved, that she knew it would be an easy task to soften down some of the rougher shades of his character. Three times during her absence had he called, expressing so much disappointment, that with woman's ready instinct she more than half divined his intentions, and regretted that she was gone. But Mabel was coming to-day, and he was to accompany her, for so had 'Lena written, and Nellie's cheeks glowed and her heart beat high, as she thought of what might occur. She knew well that in point of wealth she was not his equal, for though mingling with the first in the city, her father was poor--but one of John Jr.'s nature would never take that into consideration. They had known each other from childhood, and he had always evinced for her the same preference which he now manifested. Several weeks had elapsed since she had seen him, and now, rather impatiently, she awaited his arrival,

"If you please, ma'am, Mrs. Livingstone and Miss Mabel are in the parlor," said a servant, suddenly appearing and interrupting her reverie.

"Mrs. Livingstone!" she repeated, as she glanced at herself in a mirror, and rearranged one side of her shining hair, "Mrs. Livingstone!--and so he has not come. I wonder what's the matter!" and with a less joyous face she descended to the back parlor, where, with rich furs wrapped closely about her, as if half frozen, sat Mrs. Livingstone, her quick eye taking an inventory of every article of furniture, and her proud spirit whispering to herself, "Poverty, poverty."

With a cry of joy, Mabel flew to meet Nellie, who, while welcoming her back, congratulated her upon her improved health and looks, saying, "the air of Maple Grove must have agreed with her;" then turning toward Mrs. Livingstone, who saw in her remark other meaning than the one she intended, she asked her to remove her wrappings, apologizing at the same time for the fire being so low.

"Father is absent most of the day," said she; "and as I am much in my chamber, we seldom keep a fire in the front parlor."

"Just as well," answered Mrs. Livingstone, removing her heavy furs. "One fire is cheaper than two, and in these times I suppose it is necessary for some people to economize."

Nellie colored, not so much at the words as at the manner of her visitor. After a moment, Mrs. Livingstone again spoke, looking straight in Nellie's face.

"My son was very anxious to ride over with Mabel, but a bad cold prevented him, so she rather unwillingly took me as a substitute."

Here not only Nellie, but Mabel, also colored, and the latter left the room. When she was gone, Nellie remarked upon the visible improvement in her health.

"Yes," said Mrs. Livingstone, settling herself a little more easily in her chair, "Yes, Mabel isn't the same creature she was when she came to us, but then it's no wonder, for love, you know, will work miracles."

No answer from Nellie, who almost instinctively felt what was coming next.

"Upon my word, Miss Douglass, you've no curiosity whatever. Why don't you ask with whom Mabel is in love?"

"Who is it?" laughingly asked Nellie, nervously playing with the tassel of her blue silk apron.

After a moment, Mrs. Livingstone replied, "It may seem out of place for me to speak of it, but I know you, Miss Douglass, for a girl of excellent sense, and feel sure you will not betray me to either party."

"Certainly not," answered Nellie, rather haughtily, while her tormentor continued: "Well, then, it is my son, and I assure you, both myself and husband are well pleased that it should be so. From the moment I first saw Mabel, I felt for her a motherly affection for which I could not account, and if I were now to select my future daughter-in-law, I should prefer her to all others."

Here ensued a pause which Nellie felt no inclination to break, and again Mrs. Livingstone spoke: "It may be a weakness, but I have always felt anxious that John should make a match every way worthy of him, both as to wealth and station. Indeed, I would hardly be willing for him to marry one whose fortune is less than Mabel's. But I need have no fears, for John has his own views on that subject, and though he may sometimes be attentive to girls far beneath him, he is pretty sure in the end to do as I think best!"

Poor Nellie! How every word sank into her soul, torturing her almost to madness. She did not stop to consider the improbability of what she heard. Naturally impulsive and excitable, she believed it all, for if John Jr. really loved her, as once she had fondly believed, had there not been a thousand opportunities for him to tell her so? At this moment Mabel reentered the parlor, and Nellie, on the plea of seeing to the dinner, left the room, going she scarce knew whither, until she found herself in a little arbor at the foot of the garden, where many and many a time John Jr. had sat with her, and where he would never sit again--so she thought, so she believed--and throwing herself upon one of the seats, she struggled hard to school herself to meet the worst--to conquer the bitter resentment which she felt rising within her toward Mabel, who had supplanted her in the affections of the only one she had ever loved.

Nellie had a noble, generous nature, and after a few moments of calmer reflection, she rose up, strengthened in her purpose of never suffering Mabel to know how deeply she had wronged her. "She is an orphan--a lonely orphan," thought she, "and God forbid that through me one drop of bitterness should mingle in her cup of joy."

With a firm step she walked to the kitchen, gave some additional orders concerning the dinner, and then returned to the parlor, half shuddering when Mabel came near her, and then with a strong effort pressing the little blue-veined hand laid so confidingly upon her own. Dinner being over, Mrs. Livingstone, who had some other calls to make, took her leave, bidding a most affectionate adieu to Mabel, who clung to her as if she had indeed been her mother.

"Good-bye, darling Meb," said she. "I shall come for you to visit us erelong." Turning to Nellie, she said, "Do take care of her health, which you know is now precious to more than one;" then in a whisper she added, "Remember that what I have told you is sacred."

The next moment she was gone, and mechanically, Nellie returned to the parlor, together with Mabel, whose unusual buoyancy of spirits contrasted painfully with the silence and sadness which lay around her heart. That night, Mr. Douglass had some business in the city, and the two girls were left alone. The lamps were unlighted, for the full golden moonlight, which streamed through the window-panes, suited better the mood of Nellie, who leaning upon the arm of the sofa, looked listlessly out upon the deep beauty of the night. Upon a little stool at her feet sat Mabel, her head resting on Nellie's lap, and her hand searching in vain for another, which involuntarily moved farther and farther away, as hers advanced.

At length she spoke: "Nellie, dear Nellie--there is something I want so much to tell you--if you will hear it, and not think me foolish."

With a strong effort, the hand which had crept away under the sofa-cushion, came back from its hiding-place, and rested upon Mabel's brow, while Nellie's voice answered, softly and slow, "What is it, Mabel? I will hear you."

Briefly, then, Mabel told the story of her short life, beginning at the time when a frowning nurse tore her away from her dead mother, chiding her for her tears, and threatening her with punishment if she did not desist. "Since then," said she, "I have been so lonely--how lonely, none but a friendless orphan can know. No one has ever loved me, or if for a time they seemed to, they soon grew weary of me, and left me ten times more wretched than before. I never once dreamed that--that Mr. Livingstone could care aught for one so ugly as I know I am. I thought him better suited for you, Nellie. (How cold your hand is, but don't take it away, for it cools my forehead.")

The icy hand was not withdrawn, and Mabel continued: "Yes, I think him better suited to you, and when his mother told me that he loved me, and that he would, undoubtedly, one day make me his wife, it was almost too much for me to believe, but it makes me so happy--oh, so happy."

"And he--he, too, told you that he loved you?" said Nellie, very low, holding her breath for the answer.

"Oh, no--he *never told me in* words. 'Twas his mother that told me--he only acted!"

"And what did he do?" asked Nellie, smiling in spite of herself, at the simplicity of Mabel, who, without any intention of exaggerating, proceeded to tell what John Jr. had said and done, magnifying every attention, until Nellie, blinded as she was by what his mother had said, was convinced that, at all events, he was not true to herself. To be sure, he had never told her he loved her in words; but in actions he had said it many a time, and if he could do the same with Mabel, he must be false either to one or the other. Always frank and open-hearted herself, Nellie despised anything like deception in others, and the high opinion she had once entertained for John Jr., was now greatly changed.

Still, reason as she would, Nellie could not forget so easily, and the hour of midnight found her restless and wakeful. At length, rising up and leaning upon her elbow, she looked down upon the face of Mabel, who lay sleeping sweetly at her side. Many and bitter were her thoughts, and as she looked upon her rival, marking her plain features and sallow skin, an expression of scorn flitted for an instant across her face.

"And she is preferred to me!" said she. "Well, let it be so, and God grant I may not hate her."

Erelong, better feelings came to her aid, and with her arms wound round Mabel's neck, as if to ask forgiveness for her unkind thoughts, she fell asleep.

CHAPTER XV.
MRS. LIVINGSTONE'S CALLS AND THEIR RESULT.

After leaving Mr. Douglass's, Mrs. Livingstone ordered her coachman to drive her around to the house of Mrs. Atkins, where she was frequently in the habit of stopping, partly as a matter of convenience when visiting in town, and partly to learn the latest news of the day, for Mrs. Atkins was an intolerable gossip. Without belonging exactly to the higher circles, she still managed to keep up a show of intimacy with them, possessing herself with their secrets, and kindly intrusting them to the keeping of this and that "dear friend."

From her, had Mrs. Livingstone learned to a dime the amount of Mr. Douglass' property, and how he was obliged to economize in various ways, in order to keep up the appearance of style. From her, too, had she learned how often her son was in the habit of calling there, and what rumor said concerning those calls, while Mrs. Atkins had learned, in return, that the ambitious lady had other views for John, and that anything which she, Mrs. Atkins, could do to further the plans of her friend, would be gratefully received. On this occasion she was at home, and of course delighted to meet Mrs. Livingstone.

"It is such an age since I've seen you, that I began to fear you were offended at something," said she, as she led the way into a cozy little sitting-room, where a cheerful wood fire was blazing on the nicely painted hearth. "Do sit down and make yourself as comfortable as you can, on such poor accommodations. I have just finished dinner but will order some for you."

"No, no," exclaimed Mrs. Livingstone, "I dined at Mr. Douglass's--thank you."

"Ah, indeed," returned Mrs. Atkins, feeling a good deal relieved, for to tell the truth, her larder, as was often the case, was rather empty. "Dined at Mr. Douglass's! Of course, then, nothing which I could offer you could be acceptable, after one of his sumptuous meals. I suppose Nellie brought out all her mother's old silver, and made quite a display. It's a wonder to me how they hold their heads so high, and folks notice them as they do, for between you and me, I shouldn't be surprised to hear of his failing any minute."

"Is it possible?" said Mrs. Livingstone.

"Why, yes," returned Mrs. Atkins. "There's nothing to prevent it, they say, except a moneyed marriage on the part of Nellie, who seems to be doing her best."

"Has she any particular one in view?" asked Mrs. Livingstone, and Mrs. Atkins, aware of Mrs. Livingstone's aversion to the match, replied, "Why, you know she tried to get your son----"

"But didn't succeed," interrupted Mrs. Livingstone.

"No, didn't succeed. You are right. Well, now it seems she's spreading sail for a Mr. Wilbur, of Madison----"

Mrs. Livingstone's eyes sparkled eagerly, and, not to lose one word, she drew her chair nearer to her friend, who proceeded; "He's a rich bachelor--brother to Mary Wilbur, Nellie's most intimate friend. You've heard of her?"

"Yes, yes," returned Mrs. Livingstone. "Hasn't Nellie been visiting her?"

"Her or her brother," answered Mrs. Atkins. "Mary's health is poor, and you know it's mighty convenient for Nellie to go there, under pretense of staying with her,"

"Exactly," answered Mrs. Livingstone, with a satisfied smile, and another hitch of her chair toward Mrs. Atkins, who, after a moment, continued: "The brother came home with Nellie, stayed over Sunday, rode out with her Monday, indorsed ever so many notes for her father, so I reckon, and then went home. If that don't mean something, then I'm mistaken"--and Mrs. Atkins rang for a glass of wine and a slice of cake.

After an hour's confidential talk, in which Mrs. Livingstone told of Mabel's prospects, and Mrs. Atkins told how folks who were at Mr. Graham's party praised 'Lena Rivers' beauty, and predicted a match between her and Mr. Bellmont, the former rose to go; and calling upon one or two others, and by dint of quizzing and hinting, getting them to say "they shouldn't be surprised if Mr. Wilbur did like Nellie Douglas," she started for home, exulting to think how everything seemed working together for her good, and how, in the denouement, nothing particular could be laid to her charge.

"I told Nellie no falsehood," thought she. "I did not say John loved Mabel; I only said she loved him, leaving all else for her to infer. And it has commenced operating, too. I could see it in the spots on her face and neck, when I was talking. Nellie's a fine girl, though, but too poor for the Livingstones;" and with this conclusion, she told the coachman to drive faster, as she was in a hurry to reach home.

Arrived at Maple Grove, she found the whole family, grandma and all, assembled in the parlor, and with them Durward Bellmont. His arm was thrown carelessly across the back of 'Lena's chair, while he occasionally bent forward to look at a book of prints which she was examining. The sight of him determined her to wait a little ere she retailed her precious bit of gossip to her son. He was Nellie's cousin, and as such, would in all probability repeat to her what he heard. However communicative John Jr. might be in other respects, she knew he would never discuss his heart-troubles with any one, so, upon second thought, she deemed it wiser to wait until they were alone.

Durward and 'Lena, however, needed watching, and by a little maneuvering, she managed to separate them, greatly to the satisfaction of Carrie, who sat upon the sofa, one foot bent under her, and the other impatiently tapping the carpet. From the moment Durward took his seat by her cousin, she had appeared ill at ease, and as he began to understand her better, he readily guessed that her silent mood was owing chiefly to the attentions he paid to 'Lena, and not to a nervous headache, as she said, when her grandmother, inquiring the cause of her silence, remarked, that "she'd been chipper enough until Mr. Bellmont came in."

But he did not care. He admired 'Lena, and John Jr. like, it made but little difference with him who knew it. Carrie's freaks, which he plainly saw, rather amused him than otherwise, but of Mrs. Livingstone he had no suspicion whatever. Consequently, when she sent 'Lena from the room on some trifling errand, herself appropriating the vacated seat, he saw in it no particular design, but in his usual pleasant way commenced talking with Carrie, who brightened up so much that grandma asked "if her headache wasn't e'en-a'most well!"

When 'Lena returned to the parlor, Durward was proposing a surprise visit to Nellie Douglass some time during the holidays. "We'll invite Mr. Everett, and all go down. What do you say, girls?" said he, turning toward Carrie and Anna, but meaning 'Lena quite as much as either of them.

"Capital,' answered Anna, visions of a long ride with Malcolm instantly passing before her mind.

"I should like it very much," said Carrie, visions of a ride with Durward crossing her mind.

"And I too," said 'Lena, laying her hand on John Jr.'s shoulder, as if he would of course be her escort.

Carrie's ill-nature had not all vanished, and now, in a slightly insolent tone, she said, "How do you know you are included?"

'Lena was about to reply, when Durward, a little provoked at Carrie's manner, prevented her by saying "Of course I meant Miss Rivers, and I will now do myself the honor of asking her to ride with me, either on horseback or in a carriage, just as she prefers."

In a very graceful manner 'Lena accepted the invitation saying that "she always preferred riding on horse back, but as the pony which she usually rode had recently been sold, she would be content to go in any other way."

"Fleetfoot sold! what's that for?" asked Anna; and her mother replied, "We've about forty horses on our hands now, and as Fleetfoot was seldom used by any one except 'Lena, your father thought we couldn't afford to keep him."

She did not dare tell the truth of the matter, and say that ever since the morning when 'Lena rode to Woodlawn with Durward, Fleetfoot's fate had been decreed. Repeatedly had she urged the sale upon her husband, who, wearied with her importunity, at last consented, selling him to a neighboring planter, who had taken him away that very day.

"That's smart," said John Jr. looking at his father, who had not spoken. "What is 'Lena going to ride, I should like to know."

'Lena pressed his arm to keep him still, but he would not heed her. "Isn't there plenty of feed for Fleetfoot?"

"Certainly," answered his father, compelled now to speak; "plenty of feed, but Fleetfoot was getting old and sometimes stumbled. Perhaps we'll get 'Lena a better and younger horse."

This was said in a half timid way, which brought the tears to 'Lena's eyes, for at the bottom of it all she saw her aunt, who sat looking into the glowing grate, apparently oblivious to all that was passing around her.

"That reminds me of Christmas gifts," said Durward, anxious to change the conversation. "I wonder how many of us will get one?"

Ere there was any chance for an answer a servant appeared at the door, asking Mrs. Livingstone for some medicine for old Aunt Polly, the superannuated negress, who will be remembered as having nursed Mrs. Nichols during her attack of rheumatism, and for whom grandma had conceived a strong affection. For many days she had been very ill, causing Mrs. Livingstone to wonder "what old niggers wanted to live for, bothering everybody to death."

The large stock of abolitionism which Mrs. Nichols had brought with her from Massachusetts was a little diminished by force of habit, but the root was there still, in all its vigor, and since Aunt Polly's illness she had been revolving in her mind the momentous question, whether she would not be most guilty if Polly were suffered to die in bondage.

"I promised Nancy Scovandyke," said she, "that I'd have some on 'em set free, but I'll be bound if 'taint harder work than I s'posed 'twould be."

Still Aunt Polly's freedom lay warm at grandma's heart and now when she was mentioned together with "Christmas gifts," a bright idea entered her mind,

"John," said she to her son, when Corinda had gone with the medicine, "John, have you ever made me a Christmas present since I've been here?"

"I believe not," was his answer.

"Wall," continued grandma, "bein's the fashion, I want you to give me somethin' this Christmas, will you?"

"Certainly," said he, "what is it?"

Grandma replied that she would rather not tell him then--she would wait until Christmas morning, which came the next Tuesday, and here the conversation ended. Soon after, Durward took his leave, telling 'Lena he should call for her on Thursday.

"That's a plaguy smart feller," said grandma, as the door closed upon him; "and I kinder think he's got a notion after 'Leny."

"Ridiculous!" muttered Mrs. Livingstone, while Carrie added, "Just reverse it, and say she has a notion after him!"

"Shut up your head," growled John Jr. "You are only angry because he asked her to accompany him, instead of yourself. I reckon he knows what he's about."

"I reckon he does, too!" said Mrs. Livingstone, with a peculiar smile, which nettled 'Lena more than any open attack would have done.

With the exception of his mother, John Jr. was the last to leave the parlor, and when all the rest were gone, Mrs. Livingstone seized her opportunity for telling him what she had heard. Taking a light from the table, he was about retiring, when she said, "I learned some news to-day which a little surprised me."

"Got it from Mother Atkins, I suppose," answered John, still advancing toward the door.

"Partly from her, and partly from others," said his mother, adding, as she saw him touch the door-knob, "It's about Nellie Douglass."

This was sufficient to arrest his attention, and turning about, he asked, "What of her?"

"Why, nothing of any great consequence, as I know of," said Mrs. Livingstone, "only people in Frankfort think she's going to be married."

"I think so, too," was John's mental reply, while his verbal one was, "Married! To whom?"

"Did you ever hear her speak of Mary Wilbur?"

"Yes, she's been staying with her ever since Mrs. Graham's party."

"Well, Mary it seems has a brother, a rich old bachelor, who they say is very attentive to Nellie. He came home with her from Madison, staying at her father's the rest of the week, and paying her numberless attentions, which----"

"I don't believe it," interrupted John Jr., striking his fist upon the table, to which he had returned.

"Neither did I, at first," said his mother, "but I heard it in so many places that there must be something in it. And I'm sure it's a good match. He is rich, and willing, they say, to help her father, who is in danger of failing any moment."

Without knowing it, John Jr. was a little inclined to be jealous, particularly of those whom he loved very much, and now suddenly remembering to have heard Nellie speak in high terms of Robert Wilbur, he began to feel uneasy, lest what his mother had said were true. She saw her advantage, and followed it up until, in a fit of anger, he rushed from the room and repaired to his own apartment, where for a time he walked backward and forward, chafing like a caged lion, and wishing all manner of evil upon Nellie, if she were indeed false to him.

He was very excitable, and at last worked himself up to such a pitch, that he determined upon starting at once for Frankfort, to demand of Nellie if what he had heard were true! Upon cooler reflection, however, he concluded not to make a "perfect fool of himself," and plunging into bed, he fell asleep, as what man will not be his trouble what it may.

CHAPTER XVI.
CHRISTMAS GIFTS.

The sunlight of a bright Christmas morning had hardly dawned upon the earth, when from many a planter's home in the sunny south was heard the joyful cry of "Christmas Gift," "Christmas Gift," as the negroes ran over and against each other, hiding ofttimes, until some one came within hailing distance, when their loud "Christmas Gift" would make all echo again. On this occasion, every servant at Maple Grove was remembered, for Anna and 'Lena had worked both early and late in preparing some little present, and feeling amply compensated for their trouble, when they saw how much happiness it gave. Mabel, too, while she stayed, had lent a helping hand, and many a blessing was that morning invoked upon her head from the hearts made glad by her generous gifts. Carrie, when asked to join them, had turned scornfully away, saying "she'd plenty to do, without working for niggers; who could not appreciate it."

So all her leisure hours were spent in embroidering a fine cambric handkerchief, intended as a present for Mrs. Graham, and which with a delicate note was, the evening previous, sent to Woodlawn, with instructions to have it placed next morning on Mrs. Graham's table. Of course Mrs. Graham felt in duty bound to return the compliment, and looking over her old jewelry, she selected a diamond ring which she had formerly worn, but which was now too small for her fat chubby fingers. This was immediately forwarded to Maple Grove, reaching there just as the family were rising from the breakfast-table.

"Oh, isn't it beautiful--splendid--magnificent!" were Carrie's exclamations, while she praised Mrs. Graham's generosity, secretly wondering if "Durward did not have something to do with it."

On this point she was soon set right, for the young man himself erelong appeared, and after bidding them all a "Merry Christmas," presented Anna with a package which, on being opened, proved to be a large and complete copy of Shakspeare, elegantly bound, and bearing upon its heavy golden clasp the words "Anna Livingstone, from Durward,"

"This you will please accept from me," said he. "Mother, I believe, has sent Carrie something, and if 'Lena will step to the door, she will see her gift from father, who hopes it will give her as much pleasure to accept it, as it does him to present it."

"What can it be?" thought Carrie, rising languidly from the sofa, and following 'Lena and her sister to the side door, where stood one of Mr. Graham's servants, holding a beautiful gray pony, all nicely equipped for riding.

Never dreaming that this was intended for 'Lena, Carrie looked vacantly around, saying, "Why, where is it? I don't see anything."

"Here," said Durward, taking the bridle from the negro's hand, and playfully throwing it across 'Lena's neck, "Here it is--this pony, which we call Vesta. Vesta, allow me to introduce you and your new mistress, Miss 'Lena, to each other," and catching her up, as if she had been a feather, he placed her in the saddle. Then, at a peculiar whistle, the well-trained animal started off upon an easy gallop, bearing its burden lightly around the yard, and back again to the piazza.

"Do you like her ?" he asked of 'Lena, extending his arms to lift her down.

For a moment 'Lena could not speak, her heart was so full. But at last, forcing down her emotion, she replied, "Oh, very, very much; but it isn't for me, I know-- there must be some mistake. Mr. Graham never intended it for me."

"Yes, he did," answered Durward. "He has intended it ever since the morning when you and I rode to Woodlawn. A remark which your cousin John made at the table, determined him upon him buying and training a pony for you. So here it is, and as I have done my share toward teaching her, you must grant me the favor of riding her to Frankfort day after to-morrow."

"Thank you, thank you--you and Mr. Graham too--a thousand times," said 'Lena, winding her arms around the neck of the docile animal, who did her best to return the caress, rubbing her face against 'Lena, and evincing her gentleness in various ways.

By this time Mr. Livingstone had joined them, and while he was admiring the pony, Durward said to him, "I am commissioned by my father to tell you that he will defray all the expense of keeping Vesta."

"Don't mention such a thing again," hastily interposed Mr. Livingstone. "I can keep fifty horses, if I choose, and nothing will give me more pleasure than to take care of this one for 'Lena, who deserves it if any one does."

"That's my Christmas gift from you, uncle, isn't it?" asked 'Lena, the tears gushing from her shining, brown eyes. "And now please may I return it?"

"Certainly," said he, and with a nimble spring she caught him around the neck, imprinting upon his lips the first and only kiss she had ever given him; then, amid blushes and tears, which came from a heart full of happiness, she ran away upstairs followed by the envious eyes of Carrie, who repaired to her mother's room, where she stated all that had transpired--"How Mr. Graham had sent 'Lena a gray pony--how she had presumed to accept it--and how, just to show off before Mr. Bellmont, she had wound her arms around its neck, and then actually kissed pa!"

Mrs. Livingstone was equally indignant with her daughter, wondering if Mr. Graham had lost his reason, and reckoning his wife knew nothing about Vesta! But fret as she would, there was no help for it. Vesta belonged to 'Lena--Mr. Livingstone had given orders to have it well-cared for--and worse than all the rest, 'Lena was to accompany Durward to Frankfort. Something must be done to meet the emergency, but what, Mrs. Livingstone didn't exactly know, and finally concluded to wait until she saw Mrs. Graham.

Meantime grandma had claimed from her son her promised Christmas gift, which was nothing less than "the freedom of old Aunt Polly."

"You won't refuse me, John, I know you won't," said she, laying her bony hand on his. "Polly's arnt her freedom forty times over, even s'posin' you'd a right to her in the fust place which I and Nancy Scovandyke both doubt; so now set down like a man, make out her free papers, and let me carry 'em to her right away."

Without a word Mr. Livingstone complied with his mother's request, saying, as he handed her the paper, "It's not so much the fault of the south as of the north that every black under heaven is not free."

Grandma looked aghast. Her son, born, brought up, and baptized in a purely orthodox atmosphere, to hold such treasonable opinions in opposition to everything he'd ever been taught in good old Massachusetts! She was greatly shocked, but thinking she could not do the subject justice, she said, "Wall, wall, it's of no use for you and I to arger the pint, for I don't know nothin' what I want to say, but if Nancy Scovandyke was here, she'd convince you quick, for she's good larnin' as any of the gals nowadays."

So saying, she walked away to Polly's cabin. The old negress was better to-day, and attired in the warm double-gown which Mabel had purchased and 'Lena had made, she sat up in a large, comfortable rocking-chair which John Jr. had given her at the commencement of her illness, saying it was "his Christmas gift in advance." Going straight up to her, grandma laid the paper in her lap, bidding her "read it and thank the Lord."

"Bless missus' dear old heart," said Aunt Polly, "I can't read a word."

"Sure enough," answered Mrs. Nichols, and taking up the paper she read it through, managing to make the old creature comprehend its meaning.

"Praise the Lord! praise Master John, and all the other apostles!" exclaimed Aunt Polly, clasping together her black, wrinkled hands, while tears of joy coursed their way down her cheeks. "The breath of liberty is sweet--sweet as sugar," she continued, drawing long inspirations as if to make up for lost time.

Mrs. Nichols looked on, silently thanking God for having made her an humble instrument in contributing so much to another's happiness.

"Set down," said Aunt Polly, motioning toward a wooden bottomed chair; "set down, and let's us talk over this great meracle, which I've prayed and rastled for mighty nigh a hundred times, without havin' an atom of faith that 'twould ever be."

So Mrs. Nichols sat down, and for nearly an hour the old ladies talked, the one of her newly-found freedom, and the other of her happiness in knowing that "'twasn't for nothin' she was turned out of her old home and brought away over land and sea to Kentucky."

CHAPTER XVII.
FRANKFORT.

Thursday morning came, bright, sunshiny and beautiful, and at about ten o'clock 'Lena, dressed and ready for her ride, came down to the parlor, where she found John Jr. listlessly leaning upon the table with his elbows, and drumming with his fingers.

"Come, cousin," said she, "why are you not ready?"

"Ready for what?" he answered, without raising his head.

"Why, ready for our visit," replied Lena, at the same time advancing nearer, to see what ailed him.

"All the visit I make to-day won't hurt me, I reckon," said he; pushing his hat a little more to one side and looking up at 'Lena, who, in some surprise, asked what he meant.

"I mean what I say," was his ungracious answer; "I've no intention whatever of going to Frankfort."

"Not going?" repeated 'Lena. "Why not? What will Carrie do?"

"Stick herself in with you and Durward, I suppose," said John Jr., just as Carrie entered the room, together with Mr. Bellmont, Malcolm, and Anna.

"Not going?--of course then I must stay at home, too," said Carrie, secretly pleased at her brother's decision.

"Why of course?" asked Durward, who, in the emergency, felt constrained to offer his services to Carrie though he would greatly have preferred 'Lena's company alone. "The road is wide enough for three, and I am fully competent to take charge of two ladies. But why don't you go?" turning to John Jr.

"Because I don't wish to. If it was anywhere in creation but there, I'd go," answered the young man; hastily leaving the room to avoid all further argument.

"He does it just to be hateful and annoy me," said Carrie, trying to pout, but making a failure, for she had in reality much rather go under Durward's escort than her brother's.

The horses were now announced as ready, and in a few moments the little party were on their way, Carrie affecting so much fear of her pony that Durward at last politely offered to lead him a while. This would of course bring him close to her side, and after a little well-feigned hesitation, she replied, "I am sorry to trouble you, but if you would be so kind----"

'Lena saw through the ruse, and patting Vesta gently, rode on in advance, greatly to the satisfaction of Carrie, and greatly to the chagrin of Durward, who replied to his loquacious companion only in monosyllables. Once, indeed, when she said something concerning 'Lena's evident desire to show off her horsemanship, he answered rather coolly, that "he'd yet to discover in Miss Rivers the least propensity for display of any kind."

"You've never lived with her," returned Carrie, and here the conversation concerning 'Lena ceased.

Meantime, Nellie Douglass was engaged in answering a letter that morning received from Mary Wilbur. A few years before, Mary had spent some months in Mr. Douglass's family, conceiving a strong affection for Nellie, whom she always called her sister, and with whom she kept up a regular correspondence. Mary was an orphan, living with her only brother Robert, who was a bachelor of thirty or thirty-five. Once she had ventured to hope that Nellie would indeed be to her a sister, but fate had decreed it otherwise, and her brother was engaged to a lady whom he found a school-girl in Montreal, and who was now at her own home in England. This was well-known to Nellie, but she did not deem it a matter of sufficient importance to discuss, so it was a secret in Frankfort, where Mr. Wilbur's polite attentions to herself was a subject of considerable remark. For a long time Mary had been out of health, and the family physician at last said that nothing could save her except a sea voyage, and as her brother was about going to Europe to consummate his marriage, it was decided that she should accompany him. This she was willing to do, provided Nellie Douglass would go too.

"It would be much pleasanter," she said, "having some female companion besides her attendant, and then, too, Nellie had relatives in England;" so she urged her to accompany them, offering to defray all expenses for the pleasure of her society.

Since Nellie's earliest recollection, her fondest dreams had been of England, her mother's birthplace; and now when so favorable an opportunity for visiting it was presented, she felt strongly tempted to say "Yes." Still, she would give Mary no encouragement until she had seen her father and John Jr., the latter of whom would influence her decision quite as much as the former. But John Jr. no longer loved her--she was sure of that--and with her father's consent she had half determined to go. Still she was undecided, until a letter came from Mary, urging her to make up her mind without delay, as they were to sail the 15th of January.

"Brother is so sensitive concerning his love affairs," wrote Mary, "that whether you conclude to join us or not, you will please say nothing about his intended marriage."

Nellie had seated herself to answer this letter, when a servant came up, saying that "Marster Bellmont, all the Livingstones, and a heap more were downstars, and had sent for her."

She was just writing, "I will go," when this announcement came, and quickly suspending her pen, she thought, "He's come, at last. It may all be a mistake. I'll wait." With a beating heart she descended to the parlor, where she politely greeted Mr. Everett and Durward, and then anxiously glanced around for the missing one. Mabel, who felt a similar disappointment, ventured to inquire for him, in a low tone, whereupon Carrie replied, loudly enough for Nellie to hear, "Oh, pray don't speak of that bear. Why, you don't know how cross he's been ever since--let me see--ever since you came away. He doesn't say a civil word to anybody, and I really wish you'd come back before he kills us all.'

"Did you invite him to come ?" said Nellie.

"To be sure we did," answered Carrie, "and he said, 'anywhere in creation but there.'"

Nellie needed no further confirmation, and after conversing awhile with her guests, she begged leave to be excused for a few moments, while she finished a letter of importance, which must go out in the next mail. Alone in her room, she wavered, but the remembrance of the words, "anywhere in creation but there," decided her, and with a firm hand she wrote to Mary that she would go. When the letter was finished and sent to the office, Nellie returned to her visitors, who began to rally her concerning the important letter which must be answered.

"Now, coz," said Durward, pulling her down upon the sofa by his side, "now, coz, I claim a right to know something about this letter. Was it one of acceptance or rejection?"

"Acceptance, of course," answered Nellie, who, knowing no good reason why her intended tour should be kept a secret, proceeded to speak of it, telling how they were to visit Scotland, France, Switzerland, and Italy, and almost forgetting, in her enthusiasm, how wretched the thought of the journey made her.

"And Miss Wilbur's brother is to be your escort--he is unmarried, I believe?" said Durward, looking steadily upon the carpet.

In a moment Nellie would have told of his engagement, and the object of his going, but she remembered Mary's request in time, and the blush which the almost committed mistake called to her cheek, was construed by all into a confession that there was something between her and Mr. Wilbur.

"That accounts for John's sudden churlishness," thought 'Lena, wondering how Nellie could have deceived him so.

"Oh, I see it all," exclaimed Mabel. "I understand now what has made Nellie so absent-minded and restless these many days. She was making up her mind to become Mrs. Wilbur, while I fancied she was offended with me."

"I don't know what you mean," answered Nellie, without smiling in the least. "Mary Wilbur wishes me to accompany her to Europe, and I intend doing so. Her brother is nothing to me, nor ever will be."

"Quite a probable story," thought Mr. Everett, without forming his reflections into words.

Toward the middle of the afternoon, a violent ringing of the door-bell, and a heavy tramp in the hall, announced some new arrival, and Nellie was about opening the parlor door, when who should appear but John Jr.! From his room he had watched the departure of the party, one moment wishing he was with them, and the next declaring he'd never go to Frankfort again so long as he lived! At length inclination getting the ascendency of his reason, he mounted Firelock, and rushing furiously down the 'pike, never once slackened his speed until the city was in sight.

"I dare say she'll think me a fool," thought he, "tagging her round, but she needn't worry. I only want to show her how little her pranks affect me."

With these thoughts he could not fail to meet Nellie otherwise than coldly, while she received him with equal indifference, calling him Mr. Livingstone, and asking if he were cold, with other questions, such as any polite hostess would ask of her guest. But her accustomed smile and usual frankness of manner were gone, and while John Jr. felt it keenly, he strove under a mask of indifference, to conceal his chagrin. Mabel seemed delighted to see him, and for want of something better to do, he devoted himself to her, calling her Meb, and teasing her about her "Indian locks," as he called her straight, black hair. Could he have seen the bitter tears which Nellie constantly forced back, as she moved carelessly among her guests, far different would have been his conduct. But he only felt that she had been untrue to him, and in his anger he was hardly conscious of what he was doing.

So when Mabel said to him, "Nellie is going to Europe with Mr. Wilbur and Mary," he replied, "Glad of it--hope she'll"--be drowned, he thought--"have a good time," he said--and Nellie, who heard all, never guessed how heavily the blow had fallen, or that the hand so suddenly placed against his heart, was laid there to still the wild throbbing which he feared she might hear.

When next he spoke, his voice was very calm, as he asked when she was going, and how long she intended to be gone. "What! so soon?" said he, when told that she sailed the 15th of January, and other than that, not a word did he say to Nellie concerning her intended visit, until just before they left for home. Then for a moment he stood alone with her in the recess of a window. There was a film upon his eyes as he looked upon her, and thought it might be for the last time. There was anguish, too, in his heart, but it did not mingle in the tones of his voice, which was natural, and, perhaps, indifferent, as he said, "Why do you go to Europe, Nellie?"

Quickly, and with something of her olden look, she glanced up into his face, but his eyes, which would not meet hers, lest they should betray themselves, were resting upon Mabel, who, on a stool across the room, was petting and caressing a kitten. 'Twas enough, and carelessly Nellie answered, "Because I want to; what do you suppose?"

Without seeming to hear her answer, the young man walked away to where Mabel sat, and commenced teasing her and her kitten, while Nellie, maddened with herself, with him, with everybody, precipitately left the room, and going to her chamber hastily, and without a thought as to what she was doing, gathered together every little token which John Jr. had given her, together with his notes and letters, written in his own peculiar and scarcely legible hand. Tying them in a bundle, she wrote with unflinching nerve, "Do thou likewise," and then descending to the hall, laid it upon the hat-stand, managing, as he was leaving, to place it unobserved in his hand. Instinctively he knew what it was, glanced at the three words written thereon, and in a cold, sneering voice, replied, "I will, with pleasure." And thus they parted.

thought as to what she was doing, gathered together every little token which John Jr. had given her, together with his notes and letters, written in his own peculiar and scarcely legible hand. Tying them in a bundle, she wrote with unflinching nerve, "Do thou likewise," and then descending to the hall, laid it upon the hat-stand, managing, as he was leaving, to place it unobserved in his hand. Instinctively he knew what it was, glanced at the three words written thereon, and in a cold, sneering voice, replied, "I will, with pleasure." And thus they parted.

CHAPTER XVIII.
THE DEPARTURE.

John, how would you like to take a trip to New York--the city, I mean?" said Mr. Livingstone, to his son, one morning about two weeks following the events narrated in the last chapter.

"Well enough--why do you ask?" answered John.

"Because," said his father, "I have to-day received a letter which makes it necessary for one of us to be there the 15th, and as you are fond of traveling, I had rather you would go. You had better start immediately--say to-morrow."

John Jr. started from his chair. To-morrow she left her home--the 15th she sailed. He might see her again, though at a distance, for she should never know he followed her! Since that night in Frankfort he had not looked upon her face, but he had kept his promise, returning to her everything--everything except a withered rose-bud, which years before, when but a boy, he had twined among the heavy braids of her hair, and which she had given back to him, playfully fastening it in the button-hole of his roundabout! How well he remembered that day. She was a little romping girl, teasing him unmercifully about his flat feet *and* big hands, chiding him for his negro slang, as she termed his favorite expressions, and with whatever else she did, weaving her image into his heart's best and noblest affections, until he seemed to live only for her, But now 'twas changed--terribly changed. She was no longer "his Nellie," the Nellie of his boyhood's love; and with a muttered curse and a tear, large, round, and hot, such as only John Jr. could shed, he sent her back every memento of the past, all save that rose-bud, with which he could not part, it seemed so like his early hopes--withered and dead.

Nellie was alone, preparing for her journey, when the box containing the treasures was handed her. Again and again she examined to see if there were not one farewell word, but there was nothing save, "Here endeth the first lesson!" followed by two exclamation points, which John Jr. had dashed off at random. Every article seemed familiar to her as she looked them over, and everything was there but one--she missed the rose-bud--and she wondered at the omission for she knew he had it in his possession. He had told her so not three months before. Why, then, did he not return it? Was it a lingering affection for her which prompted the detention? Perhaps so, and down in Nellie's heart was one warm, bright spot, the memory of that bud, which grew green and fresh again, as on the day when first it was torn from its parent stem.

When it was first known at Maple Grove, that Nellie was going to Europe, Mrs. Livingstone, who saw in the future the full consummation of her plans, proposed that Mabel should spend the period of Nellie's absence with her. But to this Mr. Douglass would not consent.

"He could not part with both his daughters," he said, and Mabel decided to remain, stipulating that 'Lena, of whom she was very fond, should pass a portion of the time with her.

"All the time, if she chooses," said Mr. Douglass, who also liked 'Lena, while Nellie, who was present, immediately proposed that she should take music lessons of Monsieur Du Pont, who had recently come to the city, and who was said to be a superior teacher. "She is fond of music," said she, "and has always wanted to learn, but that aunt of hers never seemed willing; and this will be a good opportunity, for she can use my piano all the time if she chooses."

"Capital!" exclaimed Mabel, generously thinking how she would pay the bills, and how much she would assist 'Lena, for Mabel was an excellent musician, singing and playing admirably.

When this plan was proposed to 'Lena, she objected, for two reasons. The first, that she could not leave her grandmother, and second, that much as she desired the lessons, she would not suffer Mabel to pay for them, and she had no means of her own. On the first point she began to waver, when Mrs. Nichols, who was in unusually good health, insisted upon her going.

"It will do you a sight of good," said she, "and there's no kind of use why you should stay hived up with me. I'd as lief be left alone as not, and I shall take comfort thinkin' you're larnin' to play the pianner, for I've allus wondered 'Tildy didn't set you at Car'line's. So, go," the old lady continued, whispering in 'Lena's ear, "Go, and mebby some day you'll be a music teacher, and take care of us both."

Still, 'Lena hesitated at receiving so much from Mabel, who, after a moment's thought, exclaimed, "Why, I can teach you myself! I should love to dearly. It will be something to occupy my mind; and my instructors have frequently said that I was capable of teaching advanced pupils, if I chose. You'll go now, I know"--and Mabel plead her cause so well, that 'Lena finally consented, saying she should come home once a week to see her grandmother.

"A grand arrangement, I must confess," said Carrie, when she heard of it. "I should think she sponged enough from her connections, without living on other folks, and poor ones, too, like Mr. Douglass."

"How ridiculous you talk," said John Jr., who was present. "You'd be perfectly willing to spend a year at Mr. Graham's, or Mr. Douglass's either, if he had a son whom you considered an eligible match. Then as to his being so poor, that's one of Mother Atkins' yarns, and she knows everybody's history, from Noah down to the present day. For 'Lena's sake I am glad to have her go, though heaven knows what I shall do without her."

Mrs. Livingstone, too, was secretly pleased, for she would thus be more out of Durward's way, and the good lady was again becoming somewhat suspicious. So when her husband objected, saying 'Lena could take lessons at home if she liked, she quietly overruled him, giving many good reasons why 'Lena should go, and finally saying that if Mrs. Nichols was very lonely without her, she might spend her evenings in the parlor when there was no company present! So it was decided that 'Lena should go, and highly pleased with the result of their call, Mr. Douglass and Mabel returned to Frankfort.

At length the morning came when Nellie was to start on her journey. Mr. Wilbur had arrived the night before, together with his sister, whose marble cheek and lusterless eye even then foretold the lonely grave which awaited her far away 'neath a foreign sky. Durward and Mr. Douglass accompanied them as far as Cincinnati, where they took the cars for Buffalo. Just before it rolled from the depot, a young man closely muffled, who had been watching our party, sprang into a car just in the rear of the one they had chosen, and taking the first vacant seat, abandoned himself to his own thoughts, which must have been very absorbing, as a violent shake was necessary, ere he heeded the call of "Your ticket, sir."

Onward, onward flew the train, while faster and faster Nellie's tears were dropping. They had gushed forth when she saw the quivering chin and trembling lips of her gray-haired father, as he bade his only child good-bye, and now that he was gone, she wept on, never heeding her young friend, who strove in vain to call her attention to the fast receding hills of Kentucky, which she--Mary--was leaving forever. Other thoughts than those of her father mingled with Nellie's tears, for she could not forget John Jr., nor the hope cherished to the last that he would come to say farewell. But he did not. They had parted in coldness, if not in anger, and she might never see him again.

"Come, cheer up, Miss Douglass; I cannot suffer you to be so sad," said Mr. Wilbur, placing himself by Nellie, and thoughtlessly throwing his arm across the back of the seat, while at the same time he bent playfully forward to peep under her bonnet.

And Nellie did look up, smiling through her tears, but she did not observe the flashing eyes which watched her through the window at the rear of the car. Always restless and impatient of confinement, John Jr. had come out for a moment upon the platform, ostensibly to take the air, but really to see if it were possible to get a glimpse of Nellie. She was sitting not far from the door, and he looked in, just in time to witness Mr. Wilbur's action, which he of course construed just as his jealousy dictated.

"Confounded fool!" thought he. "I wouldn't hug Nellie in the cars in good broad daylight, even if I was married to her!"

And returning to his seat; he wondered which was the silliest, "for Nellie to run off with Mr. Wilbur, or for himself to run after her. Six of one and half a dozen of the other, I reckon," said he; at the same time wrapping himself in his shawl, he feigned sleep at every station, for the sake of retaining his entire seat, and sometimes if the crowd was great, going so far as to snore loudly!

And thus they proceeded onward, Nellie never suspecting the close espionage kept upon her by John Jr., who once in the night, at a crowded depot, passed so closely to her that he felt her warm breath on his cheek. And when, on the morning of the 15th, she sailed, she little thought who it was that followed her down to the water's edge, standing on the last spot where she had stood, and watching with a swelling heart the vessel which bore her away.

"I'm nothing better than a walking dead man, now," said he, as he, retraced his steps back to his hotel. "Nellie's gone, and with her all for which I lived, for she's the only girl except 'Lena who isn't a libel on the sex--or, yes--there's Anna--does as well as she knows how--and there's Mabel, a little simpleton, to be sure, but amiable and good-natured, and on the whole, as smart as they'll average. 'Twas kind in her, anyway, to offer to pay 'Lena's music bills."

And with these reflections, John Jr. sought out the men whom he had come to see, transacted his business, and then started for home, where he found his mother in unusually good spirits. Matters thus far had succeeded even beyond her most sanguine expectations. Nellie was gone to Europe, and the rest she fancied would be easy. 'Lena, too, was gone, but the result of this was not what she had hoped. Durward had been at Maple Grove but once since 'Lena left, while she had heard of his being in Frankfort several times.

"Something must be done"--her favorite expression and in her difficulty she determined to call upon Mrs. Graham, whom she had not seen since Christmas. "It is quite time she knew about the gray pony, as well as other matters," thought she, and ordering the carriage, she set out one morning for Woodlawn, intending to spend the day if she found its mistress amiably disposed, which was not always the case.

CHAPTER XIX.
THE VISIT.

Mrs. Graham reclined upon a softly-cushioned sofa, her tasteful lace morning-cap half falling from her head, and her rich cashmere gown flowing open, so as to reveal the flounced cambric skirt which her sewing-girl had sat up till midnight to finish. A pair of delicate French slippers pinched rather than graced her fat feet, one of which angrily beat the carpet, as if keeping time to its mistress' thoughts. Nervous and uncomfortable was the lady of Woodlawn this morning, for she had just passed through a little conjugal scene with her husband, whom she had called a brute, lamenting the dispensation of Providence which took from her "her beloved Sir Arthur, who always thought whatever she said was right," and ending by throwing herself in the most theatrical manner upon the sofa in the parlor, where, with both her blood and temper at a boiling heat, she lay, when her waiting-maid, but recently purchased, announced the approach of a carriage.

"Mercy," exclaimed the distressed lady, "whose is it? I hope no one will ask for me."

"Reckon how it's Marster Livingstone's carriage, 'case thar's Tom on the box," answered the girl, who had her own private reason for knowing Tom at any distance.

"Mrs. Livingstone, I'll venture to say," groaned Mrs. Graham, burying her lace cap and flaxen hair still farther in the silken cushions. "Just because I stopped there a few days last summer, she thinks she must run here every week; and there's no way of escaping her. Do shut that blind; it lets in so much light. There, would you think I'd been crying?"

"Lor, no," returned the stupid servant, "Lor, no; I should sooner think your eyes and face were swelled with pisen."

"The Lord help me," exclaimed Mrs. Graham, "you don't begin to know as much as poor Charlotte did. She was a jewel, and I don't see anything what she wanted to die for, just as I had got her well trained; but that's all the thanks I ever get for my goodness. Now go quick, and tell her I've got an excruciating headache."

"If you please, miss," said the girl, trying in vain to master the big word, "if you please, give me somethin' shorter, 'case I done forgit that ar, sartin'."

"Fool! Idiot!" exclaimed Mrs. Graham, hurling, for want of something better, one of her satin slippers at the woolly head, which dodged out of the door in time to avoid it.

"Is your mistress at home?" asked Mrs. Livingstone, and Martha, uncertain what answer she was to make, replied, "Yes--no--I dun know, 'case she done driv me out afore I know'd whether she was at home or not."

"Martha, show the lady this way," called out Mrs. Graham, who was listening. "Ah, Mrs. Livingstone, is it you. I'm glad to see you," said she, half rising and shading her swollen eyes with her hand, as if the least effort were painful. "You must excuse my dishabille, for I am suffering from a bad headache, and when Martha said some one had come, I thought at first I could not see them, but you are always welcome. How have you been this long time, and why have you neglected me so, when you know how I must feel the change from Louisville, where I was constantly in society, to this dreary neighborhood?" and the lady lay back upon the sofa, exhausted with and astonished at her own eloquence.

Mrs. Livingstone was quite delighted with her friend's unusual cordiality, and seating herself in the large easy-chair, began to make herself very agreeable, offering to bathe Mrs. Graham's aching head, which kind offer the lady declined, bethinking herself of sundry gray hairs, which a close inspection would single out from among her flaxen tresses.

"Are your family all well?" she asked; to which Mrs. Livingstone replied that they were, at the same time speaking of her extreme loneliness since Mabel left them.

"Ah, you mean the little dark-eyed brunette, whom I saw with you at my party. She was a nice-looking girl--showed that she came of a good family. I think everything of that. I believe I'd rather Durward would marry a poor aristocrat, than a wealthy plebeian--one whose family were low and obscure."

Mrs. Livingstone wondered what she thought of her family, the Livingstones. The Richards' blood she knew was good, but the Nichols' was rather doubtful. Still, she would for once make the best of it, so she hastened to say that few American ladies were so fortunate as Mrs. Graham had been in marrying a noble man. "In this country we have no nobility, you know," said she, "and any one who gets rich and into good society, is classed with the first."

"Yes, I know," returned Mrs. Graham, "but in my mind there's a great difference. Now, Mr. Graham's ancestors boast of the best blood of South Carolina, while my family, everybody knows, was one of the first in Virginia, so if Durward had been Mr. Graham's son instead of Sir Arthur's, I should be just as proud of him, just as particular whom he married."

"Certainly," answered Mrs. Livingstone, a little piqued, for there was something in Mrs. Graham's manner which annoyed her--"certainly--I understand you. I neither married a nobleman, nor one of the best bloods of South Carolina, and still I should not be willing for my son to marry--let me see--well, say 'Lena Rivers."

"'Lena Rivers !" repeated Mrs. Graham--"why, I would not suffer Durward to look at her, if I could help it. She's of a horridly low family on both sides, as I am told."

This was a home thrust which Mrs. Livingstone could not endure quietly, and as she had no wish to defend the royalty of a family which she herself despised, she determined to avenge the insult by making her companion as uncomfortable as possible. So she said, "Perhaps you are not aware that your son's attentions to this same 'Lena Rivers, are becoming somewhat marked."

"No, I was not aware of it," and the greenish-gray eyes fastened inquiringly upon Mrs. Livingstone, who continued: "It is nevertheless true, and as I can appreciate your feelings, I thought it might not be out of place for me to warn you."

"Thank you," returned Mrs. Graham, now raising herself upon her elbow, "Thank you---but do you know anything positive? What has Durward done?"

"'Lena is in Frankfort now, at Mr. Douglass's," answered Mrs. Livingstone, "and your son is in the constant habit of visiting there; besides that, he invited her to ride with him when they all went to Frankfort--'Lena upon the gray pony which your husband gave her as a Christmas present."

Mrs. Livingstone had touched the right spot. 'Twas the first intimation of Vesta which Mrs. Graham had received, and now sitting bolt upright, she demanded what Mrs. Livingstone meant. "My husband give 'Lena Rivers a pony! Harry Graham do such a thing! It can't be possible. There must be some mistake."

"I think not," returned Mrs. Livingstone. "Your son came over with it, saying 'it was a present from his father, who sent it, together with his compliments.'"

Back among her cushions tumbled Mrs. Graham, moaning, groaning, and pronouncing herself wholly heart-broken. "I knew he was bad," said she, "but I never dreamed it had come to this. And I might have known it, too, for from the moment he first saw that girl, he has acted like a crazy creature. Talks about her in his sleep--wants me to adopt her--keeps his eyes on her every minute when he's where she is; and to crown all, without consulting me, his lawful wife, he has made her a present, which must have cost more than a hundred dollars! And she accepted it--the vixen!"

"That's the worst feature in the case," said Mrs. Livingstone. "I have always been suspicious of 'Lena, knowing what her mother was, but I must confess I did not think her quite so presumptuous as to accept so costly a present from a gentleman, and a married one, too. But she has a peculiar way of making them think what she does is right, and neither my husband nor John Jr. can see any impropriety in her keeping Vesta. Carrie wouldn't have done such a thing."

"Indeed she wouldn't. She is too well-bred for that," said Mrs. Graham, who had been completely won by Carrie's soft speeches and fawning manner.

This compliment to her daughter pleased Mrs. Livingstone, who straightway proceeded to build Carrie up still higher, by pulling 'Lena down. Accordingly, every little thing which she could remember, and many which she could not, were told in an aggravated manner, until quite a case was made out, and 'Lena would never have recognized herself in the artful, designing creature which her aunt kindly pictured her to be.

"Of course," said she, "if you ever repeat this, you will not use my name, for as she is my husband's niece it will not look well in me to be proclaiming her vices, except in cases where I think it my duty."

Mrs. Graham was too much absorbed in her own reflections to make a reply, and as Mrs. Livingstone saw that her company was hardly desired, she soon arose to go, asking Mrs. Graham "why she did not oftener visit Maple Grove."

When Mrs. Graham felt uncomfortable, she liked to make others so, too, and to her friend's question she answered, "I may as well be plain as not, and to tell you the truth, I should enjoy visiting you very much, were it not for one thing. That mother of yours----"

"Of my husband's," interrupted Mrs. Livingstone and Mrs. Graham continued just where she left off.

"Annoys me exceedingly, by eternally tracing in me a resemblance to some down-east creature or other--what is her name--Sco--Sco--Scovandyke; yes, that's it--Scovandyke. Of course it's not pleasant for me to be told every time I meet your mother----"

"Mr. Livingstone's mother," again interrupted the lady.

"That I look like some of her acquaintances, for I contend that families of high birth bear with them marks which cannot be mistaken."

"Certainly, certainly," said Mrs. Livingstone, adding, that "she was herself continually annoyed by Mrs. Nichols's vulgarity, but her husband insisted that she should come to the table, so what could she do?"

And mutually troubled, the one about her husband, and the other about her husband's mother, the two amiable ladies parted.

Scarcely was Mrs. Livingstone gone when Mr. Graham entered the room, finding his wife, who had heard his footsteps, in violent hysterics. He had seen her so too often to be alarmed, and was about to pull the bellrope, when she found voice to bid him desist, saying it was himself who was killing her by inches, and that the sooner she was dead, the better she supposed he would like it. "But, for my sake," she added, in a kind of howl, between crying and scolding, "do try to behave yourself during the short time I have to live, and not go to giving away ponies, and mercy knows what."

Now, Mr. Graham was not conscious of having looked at a lady, except through the window, for many days, and when his wife first attacked him, he was at a great loss to understand; but as she proceeded it all became plain, and on the whole, he felt glad that the worst was over. He would not acknowledge, even to himself, that he was afraid of his wife, still he had a little rather she would not always know what he did. He supposed, as a matter of course, that she would, earlier or later, hear of his present to 'Lena, and he well knew that such an event would surely be followed by a storm, but after what had taken place between them that morning, he did not expect so much feeling, for he had thought her wrath nearly expended. But Mrs. Graham was capable of great things--as she proved on this occasion, taunting her husband with his preference for 'Lena, accusing him of loving her better than he did herself, and asking him plainly, if it were not so.

"Say," she continued, stamping her foot (the one without a slipper), "say--I will be answered. Don't you like 'Lena better than you do me?"

Mr. Graham was provoked beyond endurance, and to the twice repeated question, he at length replied, "God knows I've far more reason to love her than I have you." At the same moment he left the room, in time to avoid a sight of the collapsed state into which his horrified wife who did not expect such an answer, had fallen.

"Can I tell her? oh, dare I tell her?" he thought, as he wiped the drops of perspiration from his brow, and groaned in the bitterness of his spirit. Terribly was he expiating his fault, but at last he grew calmer, and cowardice (for he was cowardly, else he had never been what he was) whispered, "Wait yet awhile. Anything for domestic peace."

So the secret was buried still deeper in his bosom, he never thinking how his conduct would in the end injure the young girl, dearer to him far than his own life. While he sat thus alone in his room, and as his wife lay upon her sofa, Durward entered the parlor and began good-humoredly to rally his mother upon her wobegone face, asking what was the matter now.

"Oh, you poor boy, you," she sobbed, "you'll soon have no mother to go to, but you must attribute my death wholly to your stepfather, who alone will be to blame for making you an orphan!"

Durward knew his mother well, and he thought he knew his father too, and while he respected him, he blamed her for the unreasonable whims of which he was becoming weary. He knew there had been a jar in the morning, but he had supposed that settled, and now, when he found his mother ten times worse than ever, he felt half vexed, and said, "Do be a woman mother, and not give way to such fancies. I really wonder father shows as much patience with you as he does, for you make our home very unpleasant; and really," he continued, in a laughing tone, "if this goes on much longer, I shall, in self-defense, get me a wife and horns of my own."

"And if report is true, that wife will be 'Lena Rivers," said Mrs. Graham, in order to try him.

"Very likely--I can't tell what may be," was his answer; to which Mrs. Graham replied, "that it would be extremely pleasant to marry a bride with whom one's father was in love."

"How ridiculous!" Durward exclaimed. "As though my father cared aught for 'Lena, except to admire her for her beauty and agreeable manners."

"But, he's acknowledged it. He's just told me, 'God knew he loved her better than he did me.' What do you think of that?"

"Did Mr. Graham say that?" asked Durward, looking his mother directly in her face.

"Yes he did, not fifteen minutes before you came in, and it's not a secret either. Others know it and talk about it. Think of his giving her that pony."

Durward was taken by surprise. Knowing none of the circumstances, he felt deeply pained at his father's remark. He had always supposed he liked 'Lena, and he was glad of it, too, but to love her more than his own wife, was a different thing, and for the first time in his life Durward distrusted his father. Still, 'Lena was not to blame; there was comfort in that, and that very afternoon found him again at her side, admiring her more and more, and learning each time he saw her to love her better. And she--she dared not confess to herself how dear he was to her--she dared not hope her affection was returned. She could not think of the disappointment the future might bring, so she lived on the present, waiting anxiously for his coming, and striving hard to do the things which she thought would please him best.

True to her promise, Mabel had commenced giving her instructions upon the piano, and they were in the midst of their first lesson, when who should walk in, but Monsieur Du Pont, bowing, and saying "he had been hired by von nice gentleman, to give Mademoiselle Rivers lessons in musique."

'Lena immediately thought of her uncle, who had once proposed her sharing in the instructions of her cousin, but who, as usual, was overruled by his wife.

"'Twas my uncle, was it not?" she asked of Du Pont, who replied, "I promised not to tell. He say, though, he connected with mademoiselle."

And 'Lena, thinking it was of course Mr. Livingstone, who, on his wife's account, wished it a secret, readily consented to receive Du Pont as a teacher in place of Mabel, who still expressed her willingness to assist her whenever it was necessary. Naturally fond of music, 'Lena's improvement was rapid, and when she found how gratified Durward appeared, she redoubled her exertions, practicing always five, and sometimes six hours a day.

CHAPTER XX.
A FATHER'S LOVE.

When it was known at Maple Grove that 'Lena was taking lessons of Du Pont, it was naturally supposed that Mabel, as she had first proposed, paid the bills.

"Mighty kind in her, and no mistake," said John Jr., throwing aside the stump of a cigar which he had been smoking, and thinking to himself that "Mabel was a nice girl, after all."

The next day, finding the time hang heavily upon his hands, he suddenly wondered why he had never thought to call upon 'Lena. "To be sure, I'll feel awfully to go where Nellie used to be, and know she is not there, but it's lonesomer than a graveyard here, and I'm bound to do something."

So saying, he mounted Firelock and started off, followed by no regrets from his mother or sisters, for since Nellie went away he had been intolerably cross and fault-finding. He found a servant in the door, so he was saved the trouble of ringing, and entering unannounced, walked noiselessly to the parlor-door, which was ajar. 'Lena, as usual, sat at the piano, wholly absorbed, while over her bent Mabel, who was assisting her in the lesson, speaking encouragingly, and patiently helping her through all the difficult places. Mabel's health was improved since first we saw her, and though she was still plain--ugly, many would say--there was something pleasing in her face, and in the expression of her black, eyes, which looked down so kindly upon 'Lena. John Jr. noticed it, and never before had Mabel appeared to so good advantage to him as she did at that moment, as he watched her through the open door.

At last the lesson was finished, and rising up, 'Lena said, "I know I should never learn if it were not for you," at the same time winding her arm about Mabel's neck and kissing her glowing cheek.

"Let me have a share of that," exclaimed John Jr., stepping forward and clasping both the girls in his arms ere they were aware of his presence.

With a gay laugh they shook him off, and 'Lena, leading him to the sofa, sat down beside him, asking numerous questions about home and her grandmother. John answered them all, and then, oh how he longed to ask if there had come any tidings of the absent one; but he would not--she had left him of her own accord, and he had sworn never to inquire for her. So he sat gazing dreamily upon her piano, the chair she used to occupy and the books she used to read, until 'Lena, either divining his thoughts, or fancying he would wish to know, said, "We've not heard from Nellie since she left us."

"You didn't expect to, so soon, I suppose," was John's indifferent reply.

"Why, no, not unless they chanced to speak a ship. I wish they'd taken a steamer instead of a sailing vessel," said 'Lena.

"I suppose Mr. Wilbur had an eye upon the long, cosy chats he could have with Nellie, looking out upon the sea," was John's answer, while Mabel quickly rejoined, that "he had chosen a sailing vessel solely on Mary's account."

In the midst of their conversation, the door-bell rang; and a moment after, Durward was ushered into the parlor. "He was in town on business," he said, "and thought he would call."

Scarcely had he taken his seat, when again the door opened, this time admitting Mr. Graham, who was returning from Louisville, and had also found it convenient to call. Involuntarily Durward glanced toward 'Lena, but her face was as calm and unruffled as if the visitor had been her uncle.

"All right there," thought he, and withdrawing his eyes from her, he fixed them upon his father, who he fancied seemed somewhat disconcerted when he saw him there. Mentally blaming himself for the distrust which he felt rising within him, he still determined to watch, and judge for himself how far his mother's suspicions were correct. Taking up a book which lay near, he pretended to be reading, while all the time his thoughts were elsewhere. It was 'Lena's lesson-day, and erelong Du Pont came in, appearing both pleased and surprised when he saw Mr. Graham.

"I hope you don't expect me to expose my ignorance before all these people," said 'Lena, as Du Pont motioned her to the stool.

"Suppose we adjourn to another room," said Mabel, leading the way and followed by John Jr. only.

Durward at first thought of leaving also, and arose to do so, but on observing that his father showed no intention of going, he resumed his seat and book, poring over the latter as intently as if it had not been wrong side up!

"Does monsieur incline to stay," asked Du Pont, as Mr. Graham took his station at the end of the piano.

"Certainly," answered Mr. Graham, "unless Miss Rivers insists upon my leaving, which I am sure she would not do if she knew how much interest I take in her progress."

So, during the entire lesson, Mr. Graham stood there, his eyes fixed upon 'Lena with a look which puzzled Durward, who from behind his book was watching him. Admiration, affection, pity and remorse, all seemed mingled in the expression of his face, and as Durward watched, he felt that there was a something which he could not fathom.

"I never knew he was so fond of music," thought he--"I mean to put him to the test."

Accordingly, when Du Pont was gone, he asked Mabel, who he knew was an excellent pianist, to favor him with one of her very best pieces--"something lively and new which will wake us up," said he.

Mabel would greatly have preferred remaining with John Jr., but she was habitually polite, always playing when invited, and now taking her seat at the piano, she brought out sounds far different from those of a new performer. But Mr. Graham, if he heard it, did not heed it, his eyes and ears being alone for 'Lena. Seating himself near her, he commenced talking to her in an undertone, apparently oblivious to everything else around him, and it was not until Durward twice asked how he liked Mabel's playing, that he heard a note. Then, starting up and going toward the instrument, he said, "Ah, yes, that was a fine march, ('twas the 'Rainbow Schottish,' then new,) please repeat it, or something just like it!"

Durward bit his lip, while Mabel, in perfect good humor, dashed off into a spirited quickstep, receiving but little attention from Mr. Graham, who seemed in a strange mood to-day, scribbling upon a piece of white paper which lay upon the piano, and of which Durward managed to get possession, finding thereon the name,

"Helena Nichols," to which was added that of "Rivers," the Nichols being crossed out. It would seem as if both father and son were determined each to outstay the other, for hour after hour went by and neither spoke of leaving, although John Jr. had been gone some time. At last, as the sun was setting, Durward arose to go, asking if his father contemplated spending the night; "and if so," said he, with a meaning in his manner, "where shall I tell my mother I left you?"

This roused Mr. Graham, who said he was only waiting for his son to start, adding, that "he could not find it in his heart to tear him away from two so agreeable ladies, for he well remembered the weakness of his own youth."

"In your second youth, now, I fancy," thought Durward, watching him as he bade 'Lena and Mabel goodbye, and not failing to see how much longer he held the hand of the former than he did of the latter.

"Does she see as I do, or not?" thought he, as he took the hand his father dropped, and looked earnestly into the clear, brown eyes, which returned his inquiring glance with one open and innocent as a little child.

"All right here," again thought Durward, slightly pressing the soft, warm hand he held in his own, and smiling down upon her when he saw how quickly that pressure brought the tell-tale blood to her cheek.

*   *   *   *   *

"Durward," said Mr. Graham, after they were out of the city, "I have a request to make of you."

"Well."

The answer was very short and it was several minutes ere Mr. Graham again spoke.

"You know your mother as well as I do----"

"Well."

Another silence, and Mr. Graham continued; "You know how groundlessly jealous she is of me--and it may be just as well for her not to know that----"

Here he paused, and Durward finished the sentence for him.

"Just as well for her not to know that you've spent the afternoon with 'Lena

Rivers; is that it?"

"That's it--yes--yes"--answered Mr. Graham, adding, ere Durward had time to utter the angry words which he felt rising within him, "I wish you'd marry 'Lena."

This was so sudden--so different from anything which Durward had expected, that he was taken quite by surprise, and it was some little time ere he answered,

"Perhaps I shall."

"I wish you would," continued Mr. Graham, "I'd willingly give every dollar I'm worth for the privilege of calling her my daughter."

Durward was confounded, and knew not what to think. If his father had an undue regard for 'Lena, why should he wish to see her the wife of another, and that other his son? Was it his better and nobler nature struggling to save her from evil, which prompted the wish? Durward hoped so--he believed so; and the confidence which had so recently been shaken was fully restored, when, by the light of the hall lamp at home, he saw how white and almost ghostly was the face which, ere they entered the drawing-room, turned imploringly upon him, asking him "to be careful."

Mrs. Graham had been in a fit of the sulks ever since the morning of Mrs. Livingstone's call, and now, though she had not seen her husband for several days, she merely held out her hand, turning her head, meantime, and replying to his questions in a low, quiet kind of a much-injured-woman way, as provoking as it was uncalled for.

*   *   *   *   *

"Father's suggestion was a good one," thought Durward, when he had retired to rest. "'Lena is too beautiful to be alone in the world. I will propose to her at once, and she will thus be out of danger."

But what should he do with her? Should he bring her there to Woodlawn, where scarcely a day passed without some domestic storm? No, his home should be full of sunlight, of music and flowers, where no angry word or darkening frown could ever find entrance; and thus dreaming of a blissful future, when 'Lena should be his bride, he fell asleep.

CHAPTER XXI.
JOEL SLOCUM.

In this chapter it may not be out of place to introduce an individual who, though not a very important personage, is still in some degree connected with our story. On the night when Durward and his father were riding home from Frankfort, the family at Maple Grove, with the exception of grandma, were as usual assembled in the parlor. John Jr. had returned, and purposely telling his mother and Carrie whom he had left with 'Lena, had succeeded in putting them both into an uncomfortable humor, the latter secretly lamenting the mistake which she had committed in suffering 'Lena to stay with Mabel. But it could not be remedied now. There was no good reason for calling her home, and the lady broke at least three cambric-needles in her vigorous jerks at the handkerchief she was hemming.

A heavy tread upon the piazza, a loud ring of the bell, and Carrie straightened up, thinking it might possibly be Durward, who had called on his way home, but the voice was strange, and rather impatiently she waited.

"Does Mr. John Livingstone live here?" asked the stranger of the negro who answered the summons.

"Yes, sir," answered the servant, eyeing the new comer askance.

"And is old Miss Nichols and Helleny to hum?"

The negro grinned, answering in the affirmative, and asking the young man to walk in.

"Wall, guess I will," said he, advancing a few steps toward the parlor door. Then suddenly halting, he added, more to himself than to the negro, "Darned if I don't go the hull figger, and send in my card as they do to Boston."

So saying, he drew from his pocket an embossed card, and bending his knee for a table, he wrote with sundry nourishes, "Mr. Joel Slocum, Esq., Slocumville, Massachusetts."

"There, hand that to your boss," said he, "and tell him I'm out in the entry." At the same time he stepped before the hat-stand, rubbing up his oily hair, and thinking "Mr. Joel Slocum would make an impression anywhere."

"Who is it, Ben ?" whispered Carrie.

"Dunno, miss," said the negro, passing the card to his master, and waiting in silence for his orders.

"Mr. Joel Slocum, Esq., Slocumville, Massachusetts," slowly read Mr. Livingstone, wondering where he had heard that name before.

"Who?" simultaneously asked Carrie and Anna, while their mother looked wonderingly up.

Instantly John Jr. remembered 'Lena's love-letter, and anticipating fun, exclaimed, "Show him in, Ben--show him in."

While Ben is showing him in, we will introduce him more fully to our readers, promising that the picture is not overdrawn, but such as we saw it in our native state. Joel belonged to that extreme class of Yankees with which we sometimes, though not often meet. Brought up among the New England mountains, he was almost wholly ignorant of what really belonged to good manners, fancying that he knew everything, and sneering at those of his acquaintance who, being of a more quiet turn of mind, were content to settle down in the home of their fathers, caring little or nothing for the world without. But as for him, "he was bound," he said, "to see the elephant, and if his brothers were green enough to stay tied to their mother's apron strings, they might do it, but he wouldn't. No, sir! he was going to make something of himself."

To effect this, about two years before the time of which we are speaking, he went to Boston to learn the art of daguerreotype-taking, in which he really did seem to excel, returning home with some money, a great deal of vanity, and a strong propensity to boast of what he had seen. Recollections of 'Lena, his early, and, as he sentimentally expressed it, "his undying, all-enduring" love, still haunted him, and at last he determined upon a tour to Kentucky, purchasing for the occasion a rather fantastic suit, consisting of greenish pants, blue coat, red vest, and yellow neck-handkerchief. These he laid carefully by in his trunk until he reached Lexington, where he intended stopping for a time, hanging out a naming sign, which announced his presence and capabilities.

After spending a few days in the city, endeavoring to impress its inhabitants with a sense of his consequence, and mentally styling them all "Know Nothings," be-cause they did not seem to be more affected, he one afternoon donned his best suit, and started for Mr. Livingstone's, thinking he should create a sensation there, for wasn't he as good as anybody? Didn't he learn his trade in Boston, the very center and source of all the isms *of the day, and ought not Mr. Livingstone to feel proud of such a guest, and wouldn't 'Lena stare when she saw him so much improved from what he was when they picked* checkerberries together?

With this comfortable opinion of himself, it is not at all probable that he felt any misgivings when Ben ushered him at once into the presence of Mr. Livingstone's family, who stared at him in unfeigned astonishment. Nothing daunted, he went through with the five changes of a bow, which he had learned at a dancing-school, bringing himself up finally in front of Mr. Livingstone, and exclaiming,

"How-dy-do?--Mr. Livingstone, I 's'pose, it comes more natural to say cousin John, I've heard Miss Nichols and Aunt Nancy talk of you since I was knee high, and seems as how you must be related. How is the old lady, and Helleny, too? I don't see 'em here, though I thought, at fust, this might be her," nodding to Anna.

Mr. Livingstone was confounded, while his wife had strong intentions of ordering the intruder from the room, but John Jr. had no such idea. He liked the fun, and now coming forward, said, "Mr. Slocum, as your card indicates, allow me the pleasure of presenting you to my mother--and sisters," at the same time ringing the bell, he ordered a servant to go for his grandmother.

"Ah, ladies, how-dy-do? Hope you are well till we are better acquainted," said Joel, bowing low, and shaking out the folds of his red silk handkerchief, strongly perfumed with peppermint.

Mrs. Livingstone did not even nod, Carrie but slightly, while Anna said, "Good-evening, Mr. Slocum."

Quickly observing Mrs. Livingstone's silence, Joel turned to John Jr., saying, "Don't believe she heard you--deaf, mebby?"

John Jr. nodded, and at that moment grandma appeared, in a great flurry to know who wanted to see her.

Instantly seizing her hand, Joel exclaimed, "Now Aunt Martha, if this ain't good for sore eyes. How do you do?"

"Pretty well, pretty well," she returned, "but you've got the better of me, for I don't know more'n the dead who you be."

"Now how you talk," said Joel. "If this don't beat all my fust wife's relations. Why, I should have known you if I'd met you in a porridge-pot. But then, I s'pose I've altered for the better since I see you. Don't you remember Joel Slocum, that used to have kind of a snickerin' notion after Helleny?"

"Why-ee, I guess I do," answered grandma, again seizing his hand. "Where did you come from, and why didn't your Aunt Nancy come with you?

"'Tilda, this is Nancy Scovandyke's sister's boy. Caroline and Anny, this is Joel; you've heard tell of him."

"I've been introduced, thank you," said Joel, taking a seat near Carrie, who haughtily gathered up the ample folds of her dress, lest it should be polluted.

"Bashful critter, but she'll get over it by the time she's seen as much of the world as I have," soliloquized Joel; at the same time thinking to make some advances, he hitched a little nearer, and taking hold of a strip of embroidery on which she was engaged, he said, "Now, du tell, if they've got to workin' with floss way down here. Waste of time, I tell 'em, this makin' holes for the sake of sewin' 'em up. But law!" he added, as he saw the deepening scowl on Carrie's face, "wimmin may jest as well by putterin' about that as anything else, for their time ain't nothin' moren' an old settin' hen's."

This speech called forth the first loud roar in which John Jr. had indulged since Nellie went away, and now settling back in his chair, he gave vent to his feelings in peals of laughter, in which Joel also joined, thinking he'd said something smart. When at last he'd finished laughing, he thought again of 'Lena, and turning to Mrs. Livingstone, asked where she was, raising his voice to a high key on account of her supposed deafness.

"Did you speak to me?" asked the lady, with a look which she meant should annihilate him, and in a still louder tone Joel repeated his question, asking Anna, aside, if her mother had ever tried "McAllister's All-Healing Ointment," for her deafness, saying it had "nighly cured his grandmother when she was several years older than Mrs. Livingstone."

"Much obliged for your prescription, which, fortunately, I do not need," said Mrs. Livingstone, angrily, while Joel thought, "how strange it was that deaf people would always hear in the wrong time!"

"Mother don't seem inclined to answer your question concerning 'Lena," said John Jr., "so I will do it for her. She is in Frankfort, taking music lessons. You used to know her, I believe."

"Lud, yes! I chased her once with a streaked snake, and if she didn't put 'er through, then I'm no 'Judge. Takin' music lessons, is she? I'd give a fo' pence to hear her play."

"Are you fond of music?" asked John Jr., in hopes of what followed.

"Wall, I wouldn't wonder much if I was," answered Joel, taking a tuning-fork from his pocket and striking it upon the table. "I've kep' singin' school one term, besides leadin' the Methodis' choir in Slocumville: so I orto know a little somethin' about it."

"Perhaps you play, and if so, we'd like to hear you," continued John Jr., in spite of the deprecating glance cast upon him by Carrie.

"Not such a dreadful sight," answered Joel, sauntering toward the piano and drumming a part of "Auld Lang Syne." "Not such a dreadful sight, but I guess these girls do. Come, girls, play us a jig, won't you?"

"Go, Cad, it won't hurt you," whispered John, but Carrie was immovable, and at last, Anna, who entered more into her brother's spirit, took her seat at the instrument, asking what he would have.

"Oh, give us 'Money Musk,' 'Hail Columby,' 'Old Zip Coon,' or anything to raise a feller's ideas."

Fortunately, Anna's forte lay in playing old music, which she preferred to more modern pieces, and, Joel was soon beating time to the lively strains of "Money Musk."

"Wall, I declare," said he, when it was ended, "I don't see but what you Kentucky gals play most as well as they do to hum. I didn't s'pose many on you ever seen a pianner. Come," turning to Carrie, "less see what you can do. Mebby you'll beat her all holler," and he offered his hand to Carrie, who rather petulantly said she "must be excused."

"Oh, get out," he continued. "You needn't feel so bashful, for I shan't criticise you very hard. I know how to feel fer new beginners."

"Have you been to supper, Mr. Slocum ?" asked Mr. Livingstone, pitying Carrie, and wishing to put an end to the performance.

"No, I hain't, and I'm hungrier than a bear," answered Joel, whereupon Mrs. Nichols, thinking he was her guest, arose, saying she would see that he had some.

When both were gone to the dining-room, Mrs. Livingstone's wrath boiled over.

"That's what comes of harboring your relatives," said she, looking indignantly upon her husband, and adding that she hoped "the insolent fellow did not intend staying all night, for if he did he couldn't."

"Do you propose turning him into the street?" asked Mr. Livingstone, looking up from his paper.

"I don't propose anything, except that he won't stay in my house, and you needn't ask him."

"I hardly think an invitation is necessary, for I presume he expects to stay," returned Mr. Livingstone; while John Jr. rejoined, "Of course he does, and if mother doesn't find him a room, I shall take him in with me, besides going to Frankfort with him to-morrow."

This was enough, for Mrs. Livingstone would do almost anything rather than have her son seen in the city with that specimen. Accordingly, when the hour for retiring arrived, she ordered Corinda to show him into the "east chamber," a room used for her common kind of visitors, but which Joel pronounced "as neat as a fiddle."

The next morning he announced his intention of visiting Frankfort, proposing to grandma that she should accompany him, and she was about making up her mind to do so, when 'Lena and Mabel both appeared in the yard. They had come out for a ride, they said, and finding the morning so fine, had extended their excursion as far as Maple Grove, sending their servant back to tell where they were going. With his usual assurance, Joel advanced toward 'Lena, greeting her tenderly, and whispering in her ear that "he found she was greatly improved as well as himself," while 'Lena wondered in what the improvement consisted. She had formerly known him as a great, overgrown, good-natured boy, and now she saw him a "conceited gawky." Still, her manner was friendly toward him, for he had come from her old home, had breathed the air of her native hills, and she well remembered how, years ago, he had with her planted and watered the flowers which he told her were still growing at her mother's grave.

And yet there was something about her which puzzled Joel, who felt that the difference between them was great. He was disappointed, and the declaration which he had fully intended making was left until another time, when, as he thought, "he shouldn't be so confounded shy of her." His quarters, too, at Maple Grove were not the most pleasant, for no one noticed him except grandma and John Jr., and with the conviction that "the Kentuckians didn't know what politeness meant," he ordered his horse after dinner, and started back to Lexington, inviting all the family to call and "set for their picters," saying that "seein' 'twas them, he'd take 'em for half price."

As he was leaving the piazza, he turned back, and drawing a large, square case from his pocket, passed it to 'Lena, saying it was a daguerreotype of her mountain home, which he had taken on purpose for her, forgetting to give it to her until that minute. The look of joy which lighted up 'Lena's face made Joel almost repent of not having said to her what he intended to, but thinking he would wait till next time, he started off, his heart considerably lightened by her warm thanks for his thoughtfulness.

CHAPTER XXII.
THE DAGUERREOTYPE.

Look, grandmother!--a picture of our old home. Isn't it natural?" exclaimed Lena, as she ran back to the parlor.

Yes, it was natural, and the old lady's tears gushed forth the moment she looked upon it. There was the well, the garden, the gate partially open, the barn in the rear, now half fallen down, the curtain of the west window rolled up as it was wont to be, while on the doorstep, basking in the warm sunshine, lay a cat, which Mrs. Nichols' declared was hers.

"John ought to see this," said she, wiping the tears from her eyes, and turning towards the door, which at that moment opened, admitting her son, together with Mr. Graham, who had accidentally called. "Look here, John," said she, calling him to her side--"Do you remember this?"

The deep flush which mounted to John's brow, showed that he did, and his mother, passing it toward Mr. Graham, continued: "It is our old home in Massachusetts. There's the room where John and Helleny both were born, and where Helleny and her father died. Oh, it seems but yesterday since she died, and they carried her out of this door, and down the road, there--do you see?"

This question, was addressed to Mr. Graham, who, whether he saw or not, made no answer, but walked to the window and looked out, upon the prospect beyond, which for him had no attractions then. The sight of that daguerreotype had stirred up many bitter memories, and for some time he stood gazing vacantly through the window, and thinking--who shall say of what? It would seem that the daguerreotype possessed a strong fascination for him, for after it had been duly examined and laid down, he took it in his hand, inspecting it minutely, asking where it was taken, and if it would be possible to procure a similar one.

"I have a fancy for such scenes," said he, "and would like to have just such a picture. Mr. Slocum is stopping in Lexington, you say. He can take one from this, I suppose. I mean to see him;" and with his usual good-morning, he departed.

Two weeks from this time Durward again went down to Frankfort, determining, if a favorable opportunity presented itself, to offer 'Lena his heart and fortune.

He found her alone, Mabel having gone out to spend the day. For a time they conversed together on indifferent topics, each one of which was entirely foreign from that which lay nearest Durward's heart. At last the conversation turned upon Joel Slocum, of whose visit Durward had heard.

"I really think, 'Lena," said he, laughingly, "that you ought to patronize the poor fellow, who has come all this distance for the sake of seeing you. Suppose you have your daguerreotype taken for me, will you?"

Durward was in earnest, but with a playful shake of her brown curls, 'Lena answered lightly, "Oh, no, no. I have never had my picture taken in my life, and I shan't begin with Joel."

"Never had it taken!" repeated Durward, in some surprise.

"No, never," said 'Lena, and Durward continued drawing her nearer to him, "It is time you had, then. So have it taken for me. I mean what I say," he continued, as he met the glance of her merry eyes. "There is nothing I should prize more than your miniature, except, indeed the original, which you will not refuse me, when I ask it, will you?"

'Lena's mirth was all gone--she knew he was in earnest now. She felt it in the pressure of his arm, which encircled her waist; she saw it in his eye, and heard it in the tones of his voice. But what should she say? Closer he drew her to his side; she felt his breath upon her cheek; and an inaudible answer trembled on her lips, when noiselessly through the door came Mr. Graham, starting when he saw their position, and offering to withdraw if he was intruding. 'Lena was surprised and excited, and springing up, she laid her hand upon his arm as he was about to leave the room, bidding him stay and saying he was always welcome there.

So he stayed, and with the first frown upon his brow which 'Lena had ever seen, Durward left--left without receiving an answer to his question, or even referring to it again, though 'Lena accompanied him to the door, half dreading, yet hoping, he would repeat it. But he did not, and wishing her much pleasure in his father's company, he walked away, writing in his heart bitter things against him, not her. On his way home he fell in with Du Pont, who, Frenchman-like, had taken a little too much wine, and was very talkative.

"Vous just come from Mademoiselle Rivers," said he. "She be von fine girl. What relation be she to Monsieur Graham?"

"None whatever. Why do you ask?"

"Because he pay her musique lessons and----"

Here Du Pont suddenly remembered his promise, so he kept back Mr. Graham's assertion that he was a near relative, adding in its place, that "he thought probable he related; but you no tell," said he, "for Monsieur bid me keep secret and I forgot."

Here, having reached a cross-road, they parted, and again Durward wrote down bitter things against his father, for what could be his object in wishing it kept a secret that he was paying for 'Lena's lessons, or why did he pay for them at all-- and did 'Lena know it? He thought not, and for a time longer was she blameless in his eyes.

On reaching home he found both the parlor and drawing-room deserted, and upon inquiry learned that his mother was in her own room. Something, he could hardly tell what, prompted him to knock for admission, which being granted, he entered, finding her unusually pale, with the trace of tears still upon her cheek. This of itself was so common an occurrence, that he would hardly have observed it had not there been about her a look of unfeigned distress which he had seldom seen before.

"What's the matter, mother?" said he, advancing toward her; "What has happened to trouble you?"

Without any reply, Mrs. Graham placed in his hand a richly-cased daguerreotype, and laying her head upon the table, sobbed aloud. A moment Durward stood transfixed to the spot, for on opening the case, the fair, beautiful face of 'Lena Rivers looked smilingly out upon him!

"Where did you get this, mother?--how came you by it?" he asked, and she answered, that in looking through her husband's private drawer, the key of which she had accidentally found in his vest pocket, she had come upon it, together with a curl of soft chestnut-brown hair which she threw across Durward's finger, and from which he recoiled as from a viper's touch.

For several minutes not a word was spoken by either, and then Mrs. Graham, looking him in the face, said, "You recognize that countenance, of course?"

"I do," he replied, in a voice husky with emotion, for Durward was terribly moved.

Twice had 'Lena asserted that never in her life had her daguerreotype been taken, and yet he held it in his hands; there was no mistaking it--the same broad, open brow--the same full, red lips--the same smile--and more than all, the same clustering ringlets, though arranged a little differently from what she usually wore them, the hair on the picture being combed smoothly over the forehead, while 'Lena's was generally brushed up after the style of the prevailing fashion. Had Durward examined minutely, he might have found other points of difference, but he did not think of that. A look had convinced him that 'twas 'Lena--his 'Lena, he had fondly hoped to call her. But that was over now--she had deceived him--told him a deliberate falsehood--refused him her daguerreotype and given it to his father, whose secrecy concerning it indicated something wrong. His faith was shaken, and yet for the sake of what she had been to him, he would spare her good name. He could not bear to hear the world breathe aught against her, for possibly she might be innocent; but no, there was no mistaking the falsehood, and Durward groaned in bitterness as he handed the picture to his mother, bidding her return it where she found it. Mrs. Graham had never seen her son thus moved, and obeying him, she placed her hand upon his arm, asking, "why he was so affected--what she was to him?"

"Everything, everything," said he, laying his face upon the table. "'Lena Rivers was all the world to me. I loved her as I shall never love again."

And then, without withholding a thing, Durward told his mother all--how he had that very morning gone to Frankfort with the intention of offering 'Lena his hand--how he had partially done so, when they were interrupted by the entrance of a visitor, he did not say whom.

"Thank heaven for your escape. I can bear your father's conduct, if it is the means of saving you from her," exclaimed Mrs. Graham, while her son continued: "And now, mother, I have a request to make of you--a request which you must grant. I have loved 'Lena too well to cease from loving her so soon. And though I can never again think to make her my wife, I will not hear her name lightly spoken by the world, who must never know what we do. Promise me, mother, to keep secret whatever you may know against her."

"Do you think me bereft of my senses," asked Mrs. Graham petulantly, "that I should wish to proclaim my affairs to every one?"

"No, no, mother," he answered, "but you are easily excited, and say things you had better not. Mrs. Livingstone bears 'Lena no good will, you know, and sometimes when she is speaking disparagingly of her, you may be thrown off your guard, and tell what you know. But this must not be. Promise me, mother, will you?"

Durward was very pale, and the drops of sweat stood thickly about his mouth as he asked this of his mother who, mentally congratulating herself upon her son's escape, promised what he asked, at the same time repeating to him all that she heard from Mrs. Livingstone concerning 'Lena, until Durward interrupted her with, "Stop, stop, I've heard enough. Nothing which Mrs. Livingstone could say would have weighed a straw, but the conviction of my own eyes and ears have undeceived me, and henceforth 'Lena and I are as strangers."

Nothing could please Mrs. Graham better, for the idea of her son's marrying a poor, unknown girl, was dreadful, and though she felt indignant toward her husband so peculiar was her nature that she would not have had matters otherwise if she could and when Durward, who disliked scenes, suggested the propriety of her not speaking to his father on the subject at present he assented, saying that it would be more easy for her to refrain, as she was intending to start for Louisville on the morrow.

"I've been contemplating a visit there for some time and before Mr. Graham left home this morning, I had decided to go," said she, at the same time proposing that Durward should accompany her.

To this consented willingly, for in the first shock of his disappointment, a change of place and scene was what he most desired. The hot blood of the south, which burned in his veins, seemed all on fire, and he felt that he could not, for the present, at least be daily associated with his stepfather. An absence of several days, he thought, might have the effect of calming him down. It was accordingly decided that he should on the morrow, start with her for Louisville, to be gone two weeks; and with this understanding they parted, Durward going to his own chamber, there to review the past and strive, if possible, to efface from his heart every memory of

'Lena, whom he had loved so well. But 'twas all in vain; he could not so soon forget her and far into the hours of night he sat alone striving to frame some excuse for her conduct. The fact that his father possessed her daguerreotype might possibly be explained, without throwing censure upon her; but the falsehood--never; and with the firm conviction that she was lost to him forever, he at last retired to rest, just as the clock in the ball below proclaimed the hour of midnight.

Meantime, Mrs. Graham was pondering in her own mind the probable result of a letter which, in the heat of passion, she had that day dispatched to 'Lena, accusing her of "marring the domestic peace of a hitherto happy family," and while she cast some reflections upon her birth, commanding her never, under any circumstances, "to venture into her presence!"

This cruel letter had been sent to the office before Durward's return, and as she well knew how much he would disapprove of it, she resolved not to tell him, secretly hoping 'Lena would keep her own counsel. "Base creature!" said she, "to give my husband her likeness--but he shall never see it again;" and with stealthy step she advanced toward the secret drawer, which she again opened, and taking from it both daguerreotype and ringlet, locked it, replacing the key in the pocket where she found it. Then seizing the long, bright curl, she hurled it into the glowing grate, shuddering as she did so, and trembling, as if she really knew a wrong had been done to the dead.

Opening the case, she looked once more upon the hated features, which now seemed to regard her mournfully, as if reproaching her for what she had done. No part of the dress was visible--nothing except the head and neck, which was uncovered, and over which fell the chestnut curls, whose companion so recently lay seething and scorching on the burning coals.

There was a footstep without--her husband had returned--and quick as thought was the daguerreotype concealed, while Mrs. Graham, forcing down her emotion, took up a book, which she seemed to be intently reading when her husband entered. After addressing to her a few commonplace remarks, all of which she answered civilly, he went to the wardrobe, and on pretense of looking for his knife, which, he said he believed he left in his vest pocket, he took out the key, and then carelessly proceeded to unlock his private drawer, his wife watching him the while, and keenly enjoying his look of consternation when he saw that his treasure was gone. Again and again was his drawer searched, but all to no purpose, and casting an anxious glance toward his wife, whose face, for a wonder, betrayed no secret, he commenced walking the floor in a very perturbed state of mind, his wife exulting in his discomfiture, and thinking herself amply avenged for all that she had endured.

At last he spoke, telling her of a letter which he had that day received from South Carolina, containing the news of the death of a distant relative, who had left him some property. "It is not necessary for me to be there in person," said he, "but still I should like to visit my old home once more. What do you think of it?"

"Go, by all means," said she, glad of anything which would place distance between him and 'Lena. "No one can attend to your business one-half as well as yourself. When will you start if you go?"

"Immediately--before your return from Louisville--unless you wish to accompany me."

"I'm afraid I should be an incumbrance, and would rather not," said she, in a way which puzzled him, causing him to wonder what had come over her.

"You can do as you choose," said he, "but I should be glad of your company."

"No, I thank you," was her laconic reply, as she, in turn, wondered what had come over him.

The next morning the carriage came up to the door to convey Mrs. Graham and Durward to Frankfort. The latter was purposely late, and he did not see his father until he came down, traveling-bag in hand, to enter the carriage. Then Mr. Graham asked, in some surprise, "where he was going?"

"With my mother to Louisville, sir," answered Durward, stiffly. "I am not willing she should travel alone, if you are;" and he sprang into the carriage, ordering the coachman to drive off ere another word could be spoken.

"Gone, when I had nerved myself to tell him everything!--my usual luck!" mused Mr. Graham, as he returned to the house, and sure of no prying eyes, recommenced his search for the daguerreotype, which was nowhere to be found. Could she have found it? Impossible! for it was not in her jealous nature to have held her peace; and again he sought for it, but all to no purpose, and finally thinking he must have taken it with him and lost it, he gave it up, mourning more for the loss of the curl, which could never, never be replaced, while the picture might be found.

"Why do I live so?" thought he, as he nervously paced the room. "My life is one of continual fear and anxiety, but it shall be so no longer. I'll tell her all when she returns. I'll brave the world, dare her displeasure, take 'Lena home, and be a man."

Satisfied with this resolution, and nothing doubting that he should keep it, he started for Versailles, where he had an engagement with a gentleman who transacted business for him in Lexington.

CHAPTER XXIII.
THE LETTER AND ITS EFFECT.

Mabel had gone out, and 'Lena sat alone in the little room adjoining the parlor which Mr. Douglass termed his library, but which Nellie had fitted up for a private sewing-room. It was 'Lena's favorite resort when she wished to be alone, and as Mabel was this morning absent, she had retired thither, not to work, but to think--to recall every word and look of Durward's, to wonder when and how he would repeat the question, the answer to which had been prevented by Mr. Graham.

Many and blissful were her emotions as she sat there, wondering if it were not a bright dream, from which she would too soon awaken, for could it be that one so noble, so good, and so much sought for as Durward Bellmont had chosen her, of all others, to be his bride? Yes, it must be so, for he was not one to say or act what he did not mean; he would come that day and repeat what he had said before; and she blushed as she thought what her answer would be.

There was a knock on the door, and a servant entered, bringing her a letter, which she eagerly seized, thinking it was from him. But 'twas not his writing, though bearing the post-mark of Versailles. Hastily she broke the seal, and glancing at the signature, turned pale, for it was "Lucy Graham," his mother, who had written, but for what, she could not guess. A moment more and she fell back on the sofa, white and rigid as a piece of marble. 'Twas a cruel and insulting letter, containing many dark insinuations, which she, being wholly innocent; could not understand. She knew indeed, that Mr. Graham had presented her with Vesta, but was there anything wrong in that? She did not think so, else she had never taken her. Her uncle, her cousin, and Durward, all three approved of her accepting it, the latter coming with it himself--so it could not be that; and for a long time Lena wept passionately, resolving one moment to answer the letter as it deserved determining, the next, to go herself and see Mrs. Graham face to face; and then concluding to treat it with silent contempt, trusting that Durward would erelong appear and make it all plain between them.

At last, about five o'clock, Mabel returned, bringing the intelligence that Mrs. Graham was in the city, at the Weisiger House, where she was going to remain until the morrow. She had met with an accident, which prevented her arrival in Frankfort until the train which she was desirous of taking had left.

"Is her husband with her?" asked 'Lena, to which Mabel replied, that she understood she was alone.

"Then I'll see her and know what she means," thought 'Lena, trembling, even then, at the idea of venturing into the presence of the cold, haughty woman.

*　　*　　*　　*　　*　　*

Supper was over at the Weisiger House, and in a handsome private parlor Mrs. Graham lay, half asleep, upon the sofa, while in the dressing-room adjoining Durward sat, trying to frame a letter which should tell poor 'Lena that their intimacy was forever at an end. For hours, and until the last gleam of daylight had faded away, he had sat by the window, watching each youthful form which passed up and, down the busy street, hoping to catch a glimpse of her who once had made his world. But his watch was in vain, and now he had sat down to write, throwing aside sheet after sheet, as he thought its beginning too cold, too harsh, or too affectionate. He was about making up his mind not to write at all, but to let matters take their course, when a knock at his mother's door, and the announcement that a lady wished to see her arrested his attention.

"Somebody want to see me? Just show her up," said Mrs. Graham, smoothing down her flaxen hair, and wiping from between her eyes a spot of powder which the opposite mirror revealed.

In a moment the visitor entered--a slight, girlish form, whose features were partially hidden from view by a heavy lace veil, which was thrown over her satin hood. A single glance convinced Mrs. Graham that it was a lady, a well-bred lady, who stood before her, and very politely she bade her be seated.

Rather haughtily the proffered chair was declined, while the veil was thrown aside, disclosing to the astonished gaze of Mrs. Graham the face of 'Lena Rivers, which was unnaturally pale, while her dark eyes grew darker with the intensity of her feelings.

"'Lena Rivers! why came you here?" she asked, while at the mention of that name Durward started to his feet, but quickly resumed his seat, listening with indescribable emotions to the sound of a voice which made every nerve quiver with pain.

"You ask me why I am here, madam," said 'Lena. "I came to seek an explanation from you--to know of what I am accused--to ask why you wrote me that insulting letter--me, an orphan girl, alone and unprotected in the world, and who never knowingly harmed you or yours."

"Never harmed me or mine!" scornfully repeated Mrs. Graham. "Don't add falsehood to your other sins--though, if you'll lie to my son, you of course will to me, his mother."

"Explain yourself, madam, if you please," exclaimed 'Lena, her olden temper beginning to get the advantage of her.

"And what if I do not please?" sneeringly asked Mrs. Graham.

"Then I will compel you to do so, for my good name is all I have, and it shall not be wrested from me without an effort on my part to preserve it," answered 'Lena.

"Perhaps you expect my husband to stand by you and help you. I am sure it would be very ungentlemanly in him to desert you, now," said Mrs. Graham, her manner conveying far more meaning than her words.

'Lena trembled from head to foot, and her voice was hardly distinct as she replied, "Will you explain yourself, or will you not? What have I done, that you should treat me thus?"

"Done? Done enough, I should think! Haven't you whiled him away from me with your artful manners? Has he ever been the same man since he saw you? Hasn't he talked of you in his sleep? made you most valuable presents which a true woman would have refused? and in return, haven't you bestowed upon him your daguerreotype, together with a lock of your hair, on which you no doubt pride yourself, but which to me and my son seem like so many coiling serpents?"

'Lena had sat down. She could stand no longer, and burying her face in her hands, she waited until Mrs. Graham had finished. Then, lifting up her head, she replied in a voice far more husky than the one in which she before had spoken--"You accuse me wrongfully, Mrs. Graham, for as I hope for heaven, I never entertained a feeling for your husband which I would not have done for my own father, and indeed, he has seemed to me more like a parent than a friend----"

"Because you fancied he might some day be one, I dare say," interrupted Mrs. Graham.

'Lena paid no attention to this sarcastic remark, but continued: "I know I accepted Vesta, but I never dreamed it was wrong, and if it was, I will make amends by immediately returning her, for much as I love her, I shall never use her again."

"But the daguerreotype?" interrupted Mrs. Graham, anxious to reach that point. "What have you to say about the daguerreotype? Perhaps you will presume to deny that, too."

Durward had arisen, and now in the doorway watched 'Lena, whose dark brown eyes flashed fire as she answered, "It is false, madam. You know it is false. I never yet have had my picture taken."

"But he has it in his possession; how do you account for that?"

"Again I repeat, that is false!" said 'Lena, while Mrs. Graham, strengthened by the presence of her son, answered, "I can prove it, miss."

"I defy you to do so," said 'Lena, strong in her own innocence.

"Shall I show it to her, Durward," asked Mrs. Graham, and 'Lena, turning suddenly round, became for the first time conscious of his presence.

With a cry of anguish she stretched her arms imploringly toward him, asking him, in piteous tones, to save her from his mother. Durward would almost have laid down his life to prove her innocent, but he felt that could not be. So he made her no reply, and in his eye she read that he, too, was deceived. With a low, wailing moan she again covered her face with her hands, while Mrs. Graham repeated her question, "Shall I show it to her?"

Durward was not aware that she had it in her possession, and he answered, "Why do you ask, when you know you cannot do so?"

Oh, how joyfully 'Lena started up; he did not believe it, after all, and if ever a look was expressive of gratitude, that was which she gave to Durward, who returned her no answering glance, save one of pity; and again that wailing cry smote painfully on his ear. Taking the case from her pocket, Mrs. Graham advanced toward 'Lena, saying, "Here, see for yourself, and then deny it if you can."

But 'Lena had no power to take it. Her faculties seemed benumbed and Durward, who, with folded arms and clouded brow stood leaning against the mantel, construed her hesitation into guilt, which dreaded to be convicted.

"Why don't you take it?" persisted Mrs. Graham. "You defied me to prove it, and here it is. I found it in my husband's private drawer, together with one of those long curls, which last I burned out of my sight."

Durward shuddered, while 'Lena involuntarily thought of the mass of wavy tresses which they had told her clustered around her mother's face, as she lay in her narrow coffin. Why thought she of her mother then? Was it because they were so strangely alike, that any allusion to her own personal appearance always reminded her of her lost parent? Perhaps so. But to return to our story 'Lena would have sworn that the likeness was not hers, and still an undefined dread crept over her, preventing her from moving.

"You seem so unwilling to be convinced, allow me to assist you," said Mrs. Graham, at the same time unclasping the case and holding to view the picture, on which with wondering eyes, 'Lena gazed in astonishment.

"It is I--it is; but oh, heaven, how came he by it?" she gasped, and the next moment she fell fainting at Durward's feet.

In an instant he was bending over her, his mother exclaiming, "Pray, don't touch her--she does it for effect."

But he knew better. He knew there was no feigning the corpse-like pallor of that face, and pushing his mother aside, he took the unconscious girl in his arms, and bearing her to the sofa, laid her gently upon it, removing her hand and smoothing back from her cold brow the thick, clustering curls which his mother had designated as "coiling serpents."

"Do not ring and expose her to the idle gaze of servants," said he, to his mother, who had seized the bell-rope. "Bring some water from your bedroom, and we will take charge of her ourselves."

There was something commanding in the tones of his voice, and Mrs. Graham, now really alarmed at the deathly appearance of 'Lena, hastened to obey. When he was alone, Durward bent down, imprinting upon the white lips a burning kiss--the first he had ever given her. In his heart he believed her unworthy of his love, and yet she had never seemed one-half so dear to him as at that moment, when she lay there before him helpless as an infant, and all unmindful of the caresses which he lavished upon her. "If it were indeed death;" he thought, "and it had come upon her while yet she was innocent, I could have borne it, but now I would I had never seen her;" and the tears which fell like rain upon her cheek, were not unworthy of the strong man who shed them. The cold water with which they profusely bathed her face and neck, restored her, and then Durward, who could bear the scene no longer, glided silently into the next room.

When he was gone, Mrs. Graham, who seemed bent upon tormenting 'Lena, asked "what she thought about it now?"

"Please don't speak to me again, for I am very, very wretched," said 'Lena softly, while Mrs. Graham continued: "Have you nothing to offer in explanation?"

"Nothing, nothing--it is a dark mystery to me, and I wish that I was dead," answered 'Lena, sobbing passionately.

"Better wish to live and repent," said Mrs. Graham, beginning to read her a long sermon on her duty, to which 'Lena paid no attention, and the moment she felt that she could walk, she arose to go.

The moon was shining brightly, and as Mr. Douglass lived not far away, Mrs. Graham did not deem an escort necessary. But Durward thought differently. He could not walk with her side by side, as he had often done before, but he would follow at a distance, to see that no harm came near her. There was no danger of his being discovered, for 'Lena was too much absorbed in her own wretchedness to heed aught about her, and in silence he walked behind her until he saw the door of Mr. Douglass's house close upon her. Then feeling that there was an inseparable barrier between them, he returned to his hotel, where he found his mother exulting over the downfall of one whom, for some reason, she had always disliked.

"Didn't she look confounded, though, when I showed her the picture?" said she; to which Durward replied, by asking "when and why she sent the letter."

"I did it because I was a mind to, and I am not sorry for it, either," was Mrs. Graham's crusty answer, whereupon the conversation was dropped, and as if by a tacit agreement, the subject was not again resumed during their stay in Louisville.

*   *   *   *   *   *

It would be impossible to describe 'Lena's emotion as she returned to the house. Twice in the hall was she obliged to grasp at the banister to keep from falling, and knowing that such excessive agitation would be remarked, she seated herself upon the stairs until she felt composed enough to enter the parlor. Fortunately, Mabel was alone, and so absorbed in the fortunes of "Uncle True and little Gerty," as scarcely to notice 'Lena at all. Once, indeed, as she sat before the grate so motionless and still, Mabel looked up, and observing how white she was, asked what was the matter.

"A bad headache," answered 'Lena, at the same time announcing her intention of retiring.

"Alone in her room, her feelings gave way, and none save those who like her have suffered, can conceive of her anguish, as prostrate upon the floor she lay, her long silken curls falling about her white face, which looked ghastly and haggard by the moonlight that fell softly about her, as if to soothe her woe.

"What is it," she cried aloud--"this dark mystery, which I cannot explain."

The next moment she thought of Mr. Graham. He could explain it--he must explain it. She would go to him the next day, asking him what it meant. She felt sure that he could make it plain, for suspicious as matters looked, she exculpated him from any wrong intention toward her. Still she could not sleep, and when the gray morning light crept in, it found her too much exhausted to rise.

For several days she kept her room, carefully attended by Mabel and her grandmother, who, at the first intimation of her illness, hastened down to nurse her. Every day did 'Lena ask of Mr. Douglass if Mr. Graham had been in the city, saying that the first time he came she wished to see him. Days, however, went by, and nothing was seen or heard from him, until at last John Jr.; who visited her daily, casually informed her that Mr. Graham had been unexpectedly called away to South Carolina. A distant relative of his had died, bequeathing him a large property, which made it necessary for him to go there immediately; so without waiting for the return of his wife, he had started off, leaving Woodlawn alone.

"Gone to South Carolina!" exclaimed 'Lena. "When will he return?"

"Nobody knows. He's away from home more than half the time, just as I should be if Mrs. Graham were my wife," answered John Jr., at the same time playfully re-marking that 'Lena need not look so blank, as it was not Durward who had gone so far.

For an instant 'Lena resolved to tell him everything and ask him what to do, but knowing how impetuous he was when at all excited, she finally decided to keep her own secret, determining, however, to write to Mr. Graham, as soon as she was able. Just before John Jr. left her, she called him to her side, asking him if he would do her the favor of seeing that Vesta was sent back to Woodlawn, as she did not wish for her any longer.

"What the plague is that for--has mother been raising a row?" asked John Jr., and 'Lena replied, "No, no, your mother has nothing to do with it. I only want Vesta taken home. I cannot at present tell you why, but I have a good reason, and some time, perhaps, I'll explain. You'll do it, won't you?"

With the determination of questioning Durward as to what had happened, John Jr. promised, and when Mrs. Graham and her son returned from Louisville, they found Vesta safely stabled with their other horses, while the saddle with its tiny slipper hung upon a beam, and seemingly looked down with reproach upon Durward, who turned away with a bitter pang as he thought of the morning when he first took it to Maple Grove.

The next day was dark and rainy, precluding all outdoor exercise, and weary, sad, and spiritless, Durward repaired to the library, where, for an hour or more, he sat musing dreamily of the past--of the morning, years ago, when first he met the little girl who had since grown so strongly into his love, and over whom so dark a shadow had fallen. A heavy knock at the door, and in a moment John Jr. appeared, with dripping garments and a slightly scowling face. There was a faint resemblance between him and 'Lena, manifest in the soft, curling hair and dark, lustrous eyes. Durward had observed it before--he thought of it now--and glad to see any one who bore the least resemblance to her, he started up, exclaiming, "Why, Living-stone, the very one of all the world I am glad to see."

John made no reply, but shaking the rain-drops from his overcoat, which he carelessly threw upon the floor, he took a chair opposite the grate, and looking

Durward fully in the face, said, "I've come over, Bellmont, to ask you a few plain, unvarnished questions, which I believe you will answer truthfully. Am I right?"

"Certainly, sir--go on," was Durward's reply.

"Well, then, to begin, are you and 'Lena engaged?"

"No, sir."

"Have you been engaged?"

"No, sir."

"Do you ever expect to be engaged?"

"No, sir."

"Have you quarreled?"

"No, sir."

"Do you know why she wished to have Vesta sent home?"

"I suppose I do."

"Will you tell me?"

"No, sir," said Durward, determined, for 'Lena's sake, that no one should wring from him the secret.

John Jr. arose, jammed both hands into his pockets--walked to the window--made faces at the weather--walked back to the grate--made faces at that--kicked it--and then turning to Durward, said, "There's the old Nick to pay, somewhere."

Nothing from Durward, who only felt bound to answer direct questions.

"I tell you, there's the old Nick to pay, somewhere," continued John, raising his voice. "I knew it all the while 'Lena was sick. I read it in her face when I told her Mr. Graham had gone south----"

A faint sickness gathered around Durward's heart, and John Jr. proceeded: "She wouldn't tell me, and I've come to you for information. Will you give it to me?"

"No, sir," said Durward. "The nature of our trouble is known only to ourselves and one other individual, and I shall never divulge the secret."

"Is that other individual my mother?"

"No, sir."

"Is it Cad?"

"No, sir."

"Had they any agency in the matter?"

"None, whatever, that I know of."

"Then I'm on the wrong track, and may as well go home," said John Jr., starting for the door, where he stopped, while he added, "If, Bellmont, I ever do hear of your having misled me in this matter----" He did not finish the sentence in words, but playfully producing a revolver, he departed. The next moment he was dashing across the lawn, the mud flying in every direction, and himself thinking how useless it was to try to unravel a love quarrel.

In the meantime, 'Lena waited impatiently for an answer to the letter which she had sent to Mr. Graham, but day after day glided by, and still no tidings came. At last, as if everything had conspired against her, she heard that he was lying dangerously ill of a fever at Havana, whither he had gone in quest of an individual whose presence was necessary in the settlement of the estate.

The letter which brought this intelligence to Mrs. Graham, also contained a request that she would come to him immediately, and within a few days after its receipt, she started for Cuba, together with Durward, who went without again seeing 'Lena.

They found him better than they expected. The danger was past, but he was still too weak to move himself, and the physician said it would be many weeks ere he was able to travel. This rather pleased Mrs. Graham than otherwise. She was fond of change, and had often desired to visit Havana, so now that she was there, she made the best of it, and for once in her life enacted the part of a faithful, affectionate wife.

Often, during intervals of mental aberration, Mr. Graham spoke of "Helena," imploring her forgiveness for his leaving her so long, and promising to return. Sometimes he spoke of her as being dead, and in piteous accents he would ask of Durward to bring him back his "beautiful 'Lena," who was sleeping far away among the New England mountains.

One day when the servant, as usual, came in with their letters, he brought one directed to Mr. Graham, which had been forwarded from Charleston, and which bore the post-marks of several places, it having been sent hither and thither, ere it reached its place of destination. It was mailed at Frankfort, Kentucky, and in the superscription Durward readily recognized the handwriting of 'Lena.

"Worse and worse," thought he, now fully assured of her worthlessness.

For a moment he felt tempted to break the seal, but from this act he instinctively shrank, thinking that whatever it might contain, it was not for him to read it. But what should he do with it? Must he give it to his mother who already had as much as she could bear? No, 'twas not best for her to know aught about it, and as the surest means of preventing its doing further trouble, he destroyed it--burned it to ashes--repenting the next moment of the deed, wishing he had read it, and feeling not that he had wronged the dead, as his mother did when she burned the chestnut curl, but as if he had done a wrong to 'Lena.

In the course of two months he went back to Woodlawn, leaving his father and mother to travel leisurely from place to place, as the still feeble state of the former would admit. 'Lena, who had returned from Frankfort, trembled lest he should come to Maple Grove, but he seemed equally desirous of avoiding a meeting, and after lingering about Woodlawn for several days, he suddenly departed for Louisville, where, for a time, we leave him, while we follow the fortunes of others connected with our story.

CHAPTER XXIV.
JOHN JR. AND MABEL.

Time and absence had gradually softened John Jr.'s feelings toward Nellie. She was not married to Mr. Wilbur--possibly she never would be--and if on her return to America he found her the same, he would lose no time in seeing her, and, if possible, secure her to himself. Such was the tenor of his thoughts, as on one bright morning in June he took his way to Lexington, whither he was going on business for his father. Before leaving the city, he rode down to the depot, as was his usual custom, reaching there just as the cars bound for Frankfort were rolling away. Upon the platform of the rear car stood an acquaintance of his, who called out, "Halloo, Livingstone, have you heard the news?"

"News, no. What news?" asked John Jr., following after the fast moving train.

"Bob Wilbur and Nellie Douglass are married," screamed the young man, who, having really heard of Mr. Wilbur's marriage, supposed it must of course be with Nellie.

John Jr. had no doubt of it, and for a moment his heart fainted beneath the sudden blow. But he was not one to yield long to despair, and soon recovering from the first shock, he raved in uncontrollable fury, denouncing Nellie as worthless, fickle, and good for nothing, mentally wishing her much joy with her husband, who in the same breath he hoped "would break his confounded neck," and ending his tirade by solemnly vowing to offer himself to the first girl he met, whether black or white!

Full of this resolution he put spurs to Firelock and sped away over the turnpike, looking neither to the right nor the left, lest a chance should offer for the fulfillment of his vow. It was the dusk of evening when he reached home, and giving his horse into the care of a servant, he walked with rapid strides into the parlor, starting back as he saw Mabel Ross, who, for a few days past, had been visiting at

Maple Grove.

"There's no backing out," thought he. "It's my destiny, and I'll meet it like a man. Nellie spited me, and I'll let her know how good it feels."

"Mabel," said he, advancing toward her, "will you marry me? Say yes or no quick."

This was not quite the kind of wooing which Mabel had expected. 'Twas not what she read of in novels, but then it was in keeping with the rest of John Jr.'s conduct, and very frankly and naturally she answered "Yes."

"Very well," said he, beginning to feel better already, and turning to leave the room--"Very well, you fix the day, and arrange it all yourself, only let it be very soon, for now I've made up my mind, I'm in a mighty hurry."

Mabel laughed, and hardly knowing whether he were in earnest or not, asked "if she should speak to the minister, too."

"Yes, no," said he. "Just tell mother, and she'll fix it all right. Will you?"

And he walked away, feeling nothing, thinking nothing, except that he was engaged. Engaged! The very idea seemed to add new dignity to him, while it invested Mabel with a charm she had not hitherto possessed. John Jr. liked everything that belonged to him exclusively, and Mabel now was his--his wife she would be--and when next he met her in the drawing-room, his manner toward her was unusually kind, attracting the attention of his mother, who wondered at the change. One after another the family retired, until there was no one left in the parlor except Mabel and Mrs. Livingstone, who, as her husband chanced to be absent, had invited her young visitor to share her room. When they were alone, Mabel, with many blushes and a few tears, told of all that had occurred, except, indeed, of John's manner of proposing, which she thought best not to confide to a third person.

Eagerly Mrs. Livingstone listened, mentally congratulating herself upon the completion of her plan without her further interference, wondering the while how it had been so suddenly brought about, and half trembling lest it should prove a failure after all. So when Mabel spoke of John Jr.'s wish that the marriage should be consummated immediately, she replied, "Certainly--by all means. There is no necessity for delay. You can marry at once, and get ready afterwards. It is now the last of June. I had thought of going to Saratoga in July, and a bride is just the thing to give eclat to our party."

"But," answered Mabel, who hardly fancied a wedding without all the usual preparations, which she felt she should enjoy so much, "I cannot think of being married until October, when Nellie perhaps will be here."

Nellie's return was what Mrs. Livingstone dreaded, and very ingeniously she set herself at work to put aside Mabel's objections, succeeding so far that the young girl promised compliance with whatever she should think proper. The next morning, as John Jr. was passing through the hall, she called him into her room, delicately broaching the subject of his engagement, saying she knew he could not help loving a girl possessed of so many excellent qualities as Mabel Ross. Very patiently John Jr. heard her until she came to speak of love. Then, in much louder tones than newly engaged men are apt to speak of their betrothed, he exclaimed, "Love! Fudge! If you think I'm marrying Mabel for love, you are greatly mistaken, I like her, but love is out of the question."

"Pray what are you marrying her for? Her property?"

"Property!" repeated John, with a sneer, "I've seen the effect of marrying for property, and I trust I'm not despicable enough to try it for myself. No, madam, I'm not marrying her for money--but to spite Nellie Douglass, if you must know the reason. I've loved her as I shall never again love womankind, but she cheated me. She's married to Robert Wilbur, and now I've too much spirit to have her think I care. If she can marry, so can I--she isn't the only girl in the world--and when I heard what she had done, I vowed I'd offer myself to the first female I saw. As good or bad luck would have it, 'twas Mabel, who you know said yes, of course, for I verily believe she likes me far better than I deserve. What kind of a husband I shall make, the Lord only knows, but I'm in for it. My word is passed, and the sooner you get us tied together the better, but for heaven's sake, don't go to making a great parade. Mabel has no particular home. She's here now, and why not let the ceremony take place here. But fix it to suit yourselves, only don't let me hear you talking about it, for fear I'll get sick of the whole thing."

This was exactly what Mrs. Livingstone desired. She had the day before been to Frankfort herself, learning from Mrs. Atkins of Mr. Wilbur's marriage with the English girl. She knew her son was deceived, and it was highly necessary that he should continue so. She felt sure that neither her daughters, Mabel, nor 'Lena knew of Mr. Wilbur's marriage, and she resolved they should not. It was summer, and as many of their city friends had left Frankfort for places of fashionable resort, they received but few calls; and by keeping them at home until the wedding was over, she trusted that all would be safe in that quarter. Durward, too, was fortunately absent, so she only had to deal with Mabel and John Jr. The first of these she approached very carefully, casually telling her of Mr. Wilbur's marriage, and then hastily adding, "But pray don't speak of it to any one, as there are special reasons why it should not at present be discussed. Sometime I may tell you the reason."

Mabel wondered why so small a matter should be a secret, but Mrs. Livingstone had requested her to keep silence and that was a sufficient reason why she should do so. The next step was to win her consent for the ceremony to take place there, and in the course of three weeks, saying that it was her son's wish. But on this point she found more difficulty than she had anticipated, for Mabel shrank from being married at the house of his father.

"It didn't look right," said she, "and she knew Mr. Douglass would not object to having it there."

Mrs. Livingstone knew so, too, but there was too much danger in such an arrangement, and she replied, "Of course not, if you request it, but will it be quite proper for you to ask him to be at all that trouble when Nellie is gone, and there is no one at home to superintend?"

So after a time Mabel was convinced, thinking, though, how differently everything was turning out from what she expected. Three weeks from that night was fixed upon for the bridal, to which but few were to be invited, for Mrs. Livingstone did not wish to call forth remark.

"Everything should be done quietly and in order," she said, "and then, when autumn came, she would give a splendid party in honor of the bride."

Mr. Douglass, when told of the coming event by Mrs. Livingstone, who would trust no one else, expressed much surprise, saying he greatly preferred that the ceremony should take place at his own house.

"Of course," returned the oily-tongued woman, "of course you had, but even a small wedding party is a vast amount of trouble, and in Nellie's absence you would be disturbed. Were she here I would not say a word, but now I insist upon having it my own way, and indeed, I think my claim upon Mabel is the strongest."

Silenced, but not quite convinced, Mr. Douglass said no more, thinking, meanwhile, that if he only could afford it, Mabel should have a wedding worthy of her. But he could not; he was poor, and hence Mrs. Livingstone's arguments prevailed the more easily. Fortunately for her, John Jr. manifested no inclination to go out at all. A kind of torpor seemed to have settled upon him, and day after day he remained at home, sometimes in a deep study in his own room, and sometimes sitting in the parlor, where his very unlover-like deportment frequently brought tears to Mabel's eyes, while Carrie loudly denounced him as the most clownish fellow she ever saw.

"I hope you'll train him, Mabel," said she, "for he needs it. He ought to have had Nellie Douglass. She's a match for him. Why didn't you have her, John?"

With a face dark as night, he angrily requested Carrie "to mind her own business," saying "he was fully competent to take charge of himself, without the interference of either wife or sister."

"Oh, what if he should look and talk so to me!" thought Mabel, shuddering as a dim foreboding of her sad future came over her.

'Lena who understood John Jr. better than any one else, saw that all was not right. She knew how much he had loved Nellie; she believed he loved her still; and why should he marry another? She could not tell, and as he withheld his confidence from her, appearing unusually moody and cross, she dared not approach him. At last, having an idea of what she wanted, and willing to give her a chance, he one day, when they were alone, abruptly asked her what she thought of his choice.

"If you ask me what I think of Mabel," said she, "I answer that I esteem her very highly, and the more I know her the better I love her. Still, I never thought she would be your wife."

"Ah--indeed!--never thought she would, hey?" answered John, beginning to grow crusty, and elevating his feet to the top of the mantel. "You see now what thought did; but what is your objection to her?"

"Nothing, nothing," returned 'Lena. "Mabel is amiable, gentle, and confiding, and will try to be a good wife."

"What the deuce are you grumbling for, then?" interrupted John Jr. "Do you want me yourself? If you do, just say the word, and it shall be done! I'm bound to be married, and I'd sooner have you than anybody else. Come, what do you say?"

'Lena smiled, while she disclaimed any intention toward her cousin, who, resuming the position which in his excitement he had slightly changed, continued: "I have always dealt fairly with you, 'Lena, and now I tell you truly, I have no particular love for Mabel, although I intend making her my wife, and heartily wish she was so now."

'Lena started, and clasping John's arm, exclaimed, "Marry Mabel and not love her! You cannot be in earnest. You will not do her so great a wrong--you shall not."

"I don't know how you'll help it, unless you meddle with what does not concern you," said John. "I am doing her no wrong, I never told her I loved her--never acted as though I did, and if she is content to have me on such terms, it's nobody's business. She loves me half to death, and if the old adage be true that love begets love, I shall learn to love her, and when I do I'll let you know."

So saying, the young man shook down his pants, which had become disarranged, and walked away, leaving 'Lena to wonder what course she had better pursue. Once she resolved on telling Mabel all that had passed between them, but the next moment convinced her that, as he had said, she would be meddling, so she decided to say nothing, silently hoping that affairs would turn out better than she feared.

It was Mabel's wish that 'Lena and Anna should be her bridesmaids, Durward and Malcolm officiating as groomsmen, and as Mr. Bellmont was away, she wrote to him requesting his attendance, but saying she had not yet mentioned the subject to 'Lena. Painful as was the task of being thus associated with 'Lena, Durward felt that to refuse might occasion much remark, so he wrote to Mabel that "he would comply with her request, provided Miss Rivers were willing."

"Of course she's willing," said Mabel to herself, at the same time running with the letter to 'Lena, who, to her utter astonishment, not only refused outright, but also declined giving any particular reason for her doing so. "Carrie will suit him much better than I," said she, but unfortunately, Carrie, who chanced to be present, half hidden in the recess of a window, indignantly declined "going Jack-at-a-pinch" with any one, so Mabel was obliged to content herself with Anna and Mr. Everett.

But here a new difficulty arose, for Mrs. Livingstone declared that the latter should not be invited, and Anna, in a fit of anger, insisted that if he were not good enough to be present, neither was she, and she should accordingly remain in her own room. Poor Mabel burst into tears, and when, a few moments afterward, John Jr. appeared, asking what ailed her, she hid her face in his bosom and sobbed like a child. Then, frightened at her own temerity, for he gave her no answering caress, she lifted up her head, while with a quizzical expression John Jr. said, "So-ho, Meb, seems to me you've taken to crying on my jacket a little in advance. But what's the matter?"

In a few words Mabel told him how everything went wrong, how neither 'Lena, Carrie, nor Anna would be her bridesmaids, and how Anna wouldn't see her married because Malcolm was not invited.

"I can manage that," said John Jr. "Mr. Everett shall be invited, so just shut up crying, for if there's anything I detest, it's a woman's sniveling;" and he walked off thinking he had begun just as he meant to hold out.

CHAPTER XXV.
THE BRIDAL.

Twas Mabel's wedding night, and in one of the upper rooms of Mr. Livingstone's house she stood awaiting the summons to the parlor. They had arrayed her for the bridal; Mrs. Livingstone, Carrie, 'Lena, Anna, and the seamstress, all had had something to do with her toilet, and now they had left her for a time with him who was so soon to be her husband. She knew--for they had told her--she was looking uncommonly well. Her dress, of pure white satin, was singularly becoming; pearls were interwoven in the heavy braids of her raven hair; the fleecy folds of the rich veil, which fell like a cloud around her, swept the floor. In her eye there was an unusual sparkle and on her cheek an unwonted bloom.

Still Mabel was not happy. There was a heavy pain at her heart--a foreboding of coming evil--and many an anxious glance she cast toward the stern, silent man, who, with careless tread, walked up and down the room, utterly regardless of her presence, and apparently absorbed in bitter reflections. Once only had she ventured to speak, and then, in childlike simplicity, she had asked him "how she looked."

"Well enough," was his answer, as, without raising his eyes, he continued his walk.

The tears gathered in Mabel's eyes--she could not help it; drop after drop they came, falling upon the marble table, until John Jr., who saw more than he pretended, came to her side, asking "why she wept."

Mabel was beginning to be terribly afraid of him, and for a moment she hesitated, but at length, summoning all her courage, she wound her arms about his neck, and in low, earnest tones said, "Tell me truly, do you wish to marry me?"

"And suppose I do not?" he asked, with the same stony composure.

Stepping backward, Mabel stood proudly erect before him, and answered, "Then would I die rather than wed you!"

There was something in her appearance and attitude peculiarly attractive to John Jr. Never in his life had he felt so much interested in her, and drawing her toward him and placing his arm around her, he said, gently, "Be calm, little Meb, you are nervous to-night. Of course I wish you to be my wife, else I had not asked you. Are you satisfied?"

The joyous glance of the dark eyes lifted so confidingly to his, was a sufficient answer, and as if conscious of the injustice he was about to do her, John Jr. bent for an instant over her slight figure, mentally resolving, that so far as in him lay he would be true to his trust. There was a knock at the door, and Mrs. Livingstone herself looked in, pale, anxious, and expectant. Mr. Douglass, who was among the invited guests, had arrived, and must *have an interview with John Jr. ere the ceremony. 'Twas in vain she attempted politely to waive his request. He* would see him, and distracted with fear, she had at last conducted him into the upper hall, and out upon an open veranda, where in the moonlight he awaited the coming of the bridegroom, who, with some curiosity, approached him, asking what he wanted.

"It may seem strange to you," said Mr. Douglass, "that I insist upon seeing you now, when another time might do as well, but I believe in having a fair understanding all round."

"Meddling old rascal!" exclaimed Mrs. Livingstone, who, of course, was within hearing, bending her ears so as not to lose a word.

But in this she was thwarted, for drawing nearer to John Jr., Mr. Douglass said, so low as to prevent her catching anything further, save the sound of his voice:

"I do not accuse you of being at all mercenary, but such things have been, and there has something come to my knowledge to-day, which I deem it my duty to tell you, so that hereafter you can neither blame me nor Mabel."

"What is it?" asked John Jr., and Mr. Douglass replied, "To be brief, then, Mabel's large fortune is, with the exception of a few thousands, of which I have charge, all swept away by the recent failure of the Planters' Bank, in which it was invested. I heard of it this morning, and determined on telling you, knowing that if you loved her for herself, it would make no difference, while if you loved her for her money, it were far better to stop here."

Nothing could have been further from John's thoughts than a desire for Mabel's wealth, which, precious as it seemed in his mother's eyes, was valueless to him, and after a moment's silence, in which he was thinking what a rich disappointment it would be to his mother, who, he knew, prized Mabel only for her money, he exclaimed, "Good, I'm glad of it. I never sought Mabel's hand for what there was in it, and I'm more ready to marry her now than ever. But," he added, as a sudden impulse of good came over him, "She need not know it; it would trouble her uselessly, and for the present we'll keep it from her."

John Jr. had always been a puzzle to Mr. Douglass, who by turns censured and admired him, but now there was but one feeling in his bosom toward him, and that was one of unbounded respect. With a warm pressure of the hand he turned away, thinking, perchance, of his fair young daughter, who, far away o'er the Atlantic waves, little dreamed of the scene on which that summer moon was shining. As the conference ended; Mrs. Livingstone, who had learned nothing, glided, from her hiding-place, eagerly scanning her son's face to see if there was aught to justify her fears. But there was nothing, and with her heart beating at its accustomed pace, she descended the stairs in time to meet Durward, who, having reached Woodlawn that day, had not heard of 'Lena's decision.

"This way, Marster Bellmont--upstars is the gentleman's room," said the servant in attendance, and ascending the stairs, Durward met with Anna, asking her for her cousin.

"In there--go in," said Anna, pointing to a half-open door, and then hurrying away to meet Malcolm, whose coming she had seen from the window.

Hesitatingly, Durward approached the chamber indicated, and as his knock met with no response, he ventured at last to enter unannounced into the presence of 'Lena, whom he had not met since that well-remembered night. Tastefully attired for the wedding in a simple white muslin, she sat upon a little stool with her face buried in the cushions of the sofa. She had heard his voice in the lower hall, and knowing she must soon meet him, she had for a moment abandoned herself to the tumult of bitter thoughts, which came sweeping over her in that trying hour. She was weeping--he knew that by the trembling of her body--and for an instant everything was forgotten.

Advancing softly toward her, he was about to lay his hand upon those clustering curls which fell unheeded around her, when the thought that from among them had been cut the hated tress which his mother had cast into the flames, arrested his hand, and he was himself again. Forcing down his emotion, he said, calmly, "Miss Rivers," and starting quickly to her feet, 'Lena demanded proudly what he would have, and why he was there.

"Pardon me," said he, as he marked her haughty bearing and glanced at her dress, which was hardly in accordance with that of a bridesmaid; "I supposed I was to be groomsman--am I mistaken?"

"So far as I am concerned you are, sir. I knew nothing of Mabel's writing to you, or I should have prevented it, for after what has occurred, you cannot deem me weak enough to lend myself to such an arrangement."

And 'Lena walked out of the room, while Durward looked after her in amazement, one moment admiring her spirit, and the next blaming Mabel for not informing him how matters stood. "But there's no help for it now," thought he, as he descended the stairs and made his way into the parlor, whither 'Lena had preceded him.

And thus ended an interview of which 'Lena had thought so much, hoping and praying that it might result in a reconciliation. But it was all over now--the breach was wider than ever--with half-benumbed faculties she leaned on the window, unconscious of the earnest desire he felt to approach her, for there was about her a strange fascination which it required all his power to resist.

When at last all was in readiness, a messenger was dispatched to John Jr., who, without a word, offered his arm to Mabel, and descending the broad staircase, they stood within the parlor in the spot which had been assigned them. Once during the ceremony he raised his eyes, encountering those of 'Lena, fixed upon him so reproachfully that with a scowl he turned away. Mechanically he went through with his part of the service, betraying no emotion whatever, until the solemn words which made them one were uttered. Then, when it was over--when he was bound to her forever--he seemed suddenly to awake from his apathy and think of what he had done. Crowding around him, they came with words of congratulation--all but 'Lena, who tarried behind, for she had none to give. Wretched as she was herself, she pitied the frail young bride, whose half-joyous, half-timid glances toward the frigid bridegroom, showed that already was she sipping from the bitter cup whose very dregs she was destined to drain.

In the recess of a window near to John Jr., Mr. Douglass and Durward stood, speaking together of Nellie, and though John shrank from the sound of her name, his hearing faculties seemed unusually sharpened, and he lost not a word of what they were saying.

"So Nellie is coming home in the autumn, I am told," said Durward, "and I am glad of it, for I miss her much. But what is it about Mr. Wilbur's marriage. Wasn't it rather unexpected?"

"No, not very. Nellie knew before she went that he was engaged to Miss Allen, but at his sister's request she kept it still. He found her at a boarding-school in Montreal, several years ago."

"Will they remain in Europe?"

"For a time, at least, until Mary is better--but Nellie comes home with some friends from New Haven, whom she met in Paris;" then in a low tone Mr. Douglass added, "I almost dread the effect of this marriage upon her, for I am positive she liked him better than anyone else."

The little white, blue-veined hand which rested on that of John Jr., was suddenly pressed so spasmodically, that Mabel looked up inquiringly in the face which had no thought for her, for Mr. Douglass's words had fallen upon him like a thunderbolt, crushing him to the earth, and for a moment rendering him powerless. Instantly he comprehended it all. He had deceived himself, and by his impetuous haste lost all that he held most dear on earth. There was a cry of faintness, a grasping at empty space to keep from falling, and then forth into the open air they led the half-fainting man, followed by his frightened bride, who tenderly bathed his damp, cold brow, unmindful how he shrank from her, shuddering as he felt the touch of her soft hand, and motioning her aside when she stooped to part from his forehead the heavy locks of his hair.

That night, the pale starlight of another hemisphere kept watch over a gentle girl, who 'neath the blue skies of sunny France, dreamed of her distant home across the ocean wave; of the gray-haired man, who, with every morning light and evening shade, blessed her as his child; of another, whose image was ever present with her, whom from her childhood she had loved, and whom neither time nor distance could efface from her memory.

Later, and the silvery moon looked mournfully down upon the white, haggard face and heavy bloodshot eye of him who counted each long, dreary hour as it passed by, cursing the fate which had made him what he was, and unjustly hardening his heart against his innocent unsuspecting wife.

CHAPTER XXVI
MARRIED LIFE.

For a short time after their marriage, John Jr. treated Mabel with at least a show of attention, but he was not one to act long as he did not feel. Had Nellie been, indeed, the wife of another, he might in time have learned to love Mabel as she deserved, but now her presence only served to remind him of what he had lost, and at last he began to shun her society, never seeming willing to be left with her alone, and either repulsing or treating with indifference the many little acts of kindness which her affectionate nature prompted. To all this Mabel was not blind, and when once she began to suspect her true position, it was easy for her to fancy slights where none were intended.

Thus, ere she had been two months a wife, her life was one of constant unhappiness, and, as a matter of course, her health, which had been much improved, began to fail. Her old racking headaches returned with renewed force, confining her for whole days to her room, where she lay listening in vain for the footsteps which never came, and tended only by 'Lena, who in proportion as the others neglected her, clung to her more and more. The trip to Saratoga was given up, John Jr. in the bitterness of his disappointment bitterly refusing to go, and saying there was nothing sillier than for a newly-married couple to go riding around the country, disgusting sensible people with their fooleries. So with a burst of tears Mabel yielded and her bridal tour extended no further than Frankfort, whither her husband did once accompany her, dining out even then with an old schoolmate whom he chanced to meet, and almost forgetting to call at Mr. Douglass's for Mabel when it was time to return home.

Erelong, too, another source of trouble arose, which shipwrecked entirely the poor bride's happiness. By some means or other it at last came to Mrs. Livingstone's knowledge that Mabel's fortune was not only all gone, but that her son had known it in time to prevent his marrying her. Owing to various losses her own property had for a few years past been gradually diminishing, and when she found that Mabel's fortune, which she leaned upon as an all-powerful prop, was swept away, it was more than she could bear peaceably; and in a fit of disappointed rage she assailed her son, reproaching him with bringing disgrace upon the family by marrying a poor, homely, sickly girl, who would be forever incurring expense without any means of paying it! For once, however, she found her match, for in good round terms John Jr. bade her "go to thunder," his favorite point of destination for his particular friends, at the same time saying, "he didn't care a dime for Mabel's money. It was you," said he, "who kept your eye on that, aiding and abetting the match, and now that you are disappointed, I'm heartily glad of it."

"But who is going to pay for her board," asked Mrs. Livingstone. "You've no means of earning it, and I hope you don't intend to sponge out of me, for I think I've enough paupers on my hands already!"

"Board!" roared John Jr. in a towering passion. "While you thought her rich, you gave no heed to board or anything else; and since she has become poor, I do not think her appetite greatly increased. You taunt me, too, with having no means of earning my own living. Whose fault is it?--tell me that. Haven't you always opposed my having a profession? Didn't you pet *and* baby 'Johnny' when a boy, keeping him always at your apron strings, and now that he's a man, he's not to be turned adrift. No, madam, I shall stay, and Mabel, too, just as long as I please."

Gaining no satisfaction from him, Mrs. Livingstone turned her battery upon poor Mabel, treating her with shameful neglect, intimating that she was in the way; that the house was full, and that she never supposed John was going to settle down at home for her to support; he was big enough to look after himself, and if he chose to marry a wife who had nothing, why let them go to work, as other folks did.

Mabel listened in perfect amazement, never dreaming what was meant, for John Jr. had carefully kept from her a knowledge of her loss, requesting his mother to do the same in such decided terms, that, hint as strongly as she pleased, she dared not tell the whole, for fear of the storm which was sure to follow. All this was not, of course, calculated to add to Mabel's comfort, and day by day she grew more and more unhappy, generously keeping to herself, however, the treatment which she received from Mrs. Livingstone.

"He will only dislike me the more if I complain to him of his mother," thought she, so the secret was kept, though she could not always repress the tears which would start when she thought how wretched she was.

We believe we have said elsewhere, that if there was anything particularly annoying to John Jr., it was a sick or crying woman, and now, when he so often found Mabel indisposed or weeping, he grew more morose and fault-finding, sometimes wantonly accusing her of trying to provoke him, when, in fact, she had used every means in her power to conciliate him. Again, conscience-smitten, he would lay her aching head upon his bosom, and tenderly bathing her throbbing temples, would soothe her into a quiet sleep, from which she always awoke refreshed, and in her heart forgiving him for all he had made her suffer. At such times, John would resolve never again to treat her unkindly, but alas! his resolutions were too easily broken. Had he married Nellie, a more faithful, affectionate husband there could not have been. But now it was different. A withering blight had fallen upon his earthly prospects, and forgetting that he alone was to blame, he unjustly laid the fault upon his innocent wife, who, as far as she was able, loved him as deeply as Nellie herself could have done.

One morning about the first of September, John Jr. received a note, informing him that several of his young associates were going on a three days' hunting excursion, in which they wished him to join. In the large easy-chair, just before him, sat Mabel, her head supported by pillows and saturated with camphor, while around her eyes were the dark rings which usually accompanied her headaches. Involuntarily John Jr. glanced toward her. Had it been Nellie, all the pleasures of the world could not have induced him to leave her, but Mabel was altogether another person, and more for the sake of seeing what she would say, than from any real intention of going, he read the note aloud; then carelessly throwing it aside, he said, "Ah, yes, I'll go. It'll be rare fun camping out these moonlight nights."

Much as she feared him, Mabel could not bear to have him out of her sight, and now, at the first intimation of his leaving her, her lip began to tremble, while tears filled her eyes and dropped upon her cheeks. This was enough, and mentally styling her "a perfect cry baby," he resolved to go at all hazards.

"I don't think you ought to leave Mabel, she feels so badly," said Anna, who was present.

"I want to know if little Anna's got so she can dictate me, too," answered John, imitating her voice, and adding, that "he reckoned Mabel would get over her bad feelings quite as well without him as with him."

More for the sake of opposition than because she really cared, Carrie, too, chimed in, saying that "he was a pretty specimen of a three months' husband," and asking "how he ever expected to answer for all of Mabel's tears and headaches."

"Hang her tears and headaches," said he, beginning to grow angry. "She can get one up to order any time, and for my part, I am getting heartily tired of the sound of aches and pains."

"Please don't talk so," said Mabel, pressing her hands upon her aching head, while 'Lena sternly exclaimed, "Shame on you, John Livingstone. I am surprised at you, for I did suppose you had some little feeling left."

"Miss Rivers can be very eloquent when she chooses, but I am happy to say it is entirely lost on me," said John, leaving the room and shutting the door with a bang, which made every one of Mabel's nerves quiver anew.

"What a perfect brute," said Carrie, while 'Lena and Anna drew nearer to Mabel, the one telling her "she would not care," and the other silently pressing the little hand which instinctively sought hers, as if sure of finding sympathy.

At this moment Mrs. Livingstone came in, and immediately Carrie gave a detailed account of her brother's conduct, at the same time referring her mother for proof to Mabel's red eyes and swollen face.

"I never interfere between husband and wife," said Mrs. Livingstone coolly, "but as a friend, I will give Mabel a bit of advice. Without being at all personal, I would say that few women have beauty enough to afford to impair it by eternally crying, while fewer men have patience enough to bear with a woman who is forever whining and complaining, first of this and then of that. I don't suppose that John is so much worse than other people, and I think he bears up wonderfully, considering his disappointment."

Here the lady flounced out of the room, leaving the girls to stare at each other in silence, wondering what she meant. Since her marriage, Mabel had occupied the parlor chamber, which connected with a cozy little bedroom and dressing-room adjoining. These had at the time been fitted up and furnished in a style which Mrs.

Livingstone thought worthy of Mabel's wealth, but now that she was poor, the case was altered, and she had long contemplated removing her to more inferior quarters. "She wasn't going to give her the very best room in the house. No, indeed, she wasn't--wearing out the carpets, soiling the furniture, and keeping everything topsy-turvy."

She understood John Jr. well enough to know that it would not do to approach him on the subject, so she waited, determining to carry out her plans the very first time he should be absent, thinking when it was once done, he would submit quietly. On hearing that he had gone off on a hunting excursion, she thought, "Now is my time," and summoning to her assistance three or four servants, she removed everything belonging to John Jr. and Mabel, to the small and not remarkably convenient room which the former had occupied previous to his marriage.

"What are you about?" asked Anna, who chanced to pass by and looked in.

"About my business," answered Mrs. Livingstone. I'm not going to have my best things all worn out, and if this was once good enough for John to sleep in, it is now."

"But will Mabel like it?" asked Anna, a little suspicious that her sister-in-law's rights were being infringed.

"Nobody cares whether she is pleased or not," said Mrs. Livingstone. "If she don't like it, all she has to do is to go away."

"Lasted jest about as long as I thought 'twood," said Aunt Milly, when she heard what was going on. "Ile and crab-apple vinegar won't mix, nohow, and if before the year's up old miss don't worry the life out of that poor little sickly critter, that looks now like a picked chicken, my name ain't Milly Livingstone."

The other negroes agreed with her. Constantly associated with the family, they saw things as they were, and while Mrs. Livingstone's conduct was universally condemned, Mabel was a general favorite. After Mrs. Livingstone had left the room, Milly, with one or two others, stole up to reconnoiter.

"Now I 'clar' for't," said Milly, "if here ain't Marster John's bootjack, fish-line, and box of tobacky, right out in far sight, and Miss Mabel comin' in here to sleep. 'Pears like some white folks hain't no idee of what 'longs to good manners. Here, Corind, put the jack in thar, the fish-line thar, the backy thar, and heave that ar other thrash out o'door," pointing to some geological specimens which from time to time John Jr. had gathered, and which his mother had not thought proper to molest.

Corinda obeyed, and then Aunt Milly, who really possessed good taste, began to make some alterations in the arrangement of the furniture, and under her supervision the room began to present a more cheerful and inviting aspect.

"Get out with yer old airthen candlestick," said she, turning up her broad nose at the said article, which stood upon the stand. "What's them tall frosted ones in the parlor chamber for, if 'tain't to use. Go, Corind, and fetch 'em."

But Corinda did not dare, and Aunt Milly went herself, taking the precaution to bring them in the tongs, so that in the denouement she could stoutly deny having even "tached 'em, or even had 'em in her hands!" (So much for a subterfuge, where there is no moral training.)

When Mabel heard of the change, she seemed for a moment stupefied. Had she been consulted, had Mrs. Livingstone frankly stated her reasons for wishing her to take another room, she would have consented willingly, but to be thus summarily removed without a shadow of warning, hardly came up to her ideas of justice. Still, there was no help for it, and that night the bride of three months watered her lone pillow with tears, never once closing her heavy eyelids in sleep until the dim morning light came in through the open window, and the tread of the negroes' feet was heard in the yard below. Then, for many hours, the weary girl slumbered on, unconscious of the ill-natured remarks which her non-appearance was eliciting from Mrs. Livingstone, who said "it was strange what airs some people would put on; perhaps Mistress Mabel fancied her breakfast would be sent to her room, or kept warm for her until such time as she chose to appear, but she'd find herself mistaken, for the servants had enough to do without waiting upon her, and if she couldn't come up to breakfast, why, she must wait until dinner time."

'Lena and Milly, however, thought differently. Softly had the latter stolen up to her cousin's room, gazing pityingly upon the pale, worn face, whose grieved, mournful expression told of sorrow which had come all too soon.

"Let her sleep; it will do her good," said 'Lena, adjusting the bed-clothes, and dropping the curtain so that the sunlight should not disturb her, she left the chamber.

An hour after, on entering the kitchen, she found Aunt Milly preparing a rich cream toast, which, with a cup of fragrant black tea, were to be slyly conveyed to Mabel, who was now awake.

"Reckon thar don't nobody starve as long as this nigger rules the roost," said Milly, wiping one of the silver tea-spoons with a corner of her apron, and then placing it in the cup destined for Mabel, who, not having seen her breakfast prepared, relished it highly, thinking the world was not, after all, so dark and dreary, for there were yet a few left who cared for her.

Her headache of the day before still remained, and 'Lena suggested that she should stay in her room, saying that she would herself see that every necessary attention was paid her. This she could the more readily do, as Mrs. Livingstone had gone to Versailles with her husband. That afternoon, as Mabel lay watching the drifting clouds as they passed and repassed before the window, her ear suddenly caught the sound of horses' feet. Nearer and nearer they came, until with a cry of delight she hid her face in the pillows, weeping for very joy--for John Jr. had come home! She could not be mistaken, and if there was any lingering doubt, it was soon lost in certainty, for she heard his voice in the hall below, his footsteps on the stairs. He was coming, an unusual thing, to see her first.

But how did he know she was there, in his old room? He did not know it; he was only coming to put his rifle in its accustomed place, and on seeing the chamber filled with the various paraphernalia of a woman's toilet, he started, with the exclamation, "What the deuce! I reckon I've got into the wrong pew," and was going away, when Mabel called him back. "Meb, you here?" said he. "You in this little tucked-up hole, that I always thought too small for me and my traps! What does it mean?"

Mabel had carefully studied the tones of her husband's voice, and knowing from the one he now assumed that he was not displeased with her, the sense of injustice done her by his mother burst out, and throwing her arms around his neck, she told him everything connected with her removal, asking what his mother meant by saying, "she should never get anything for their board," and begging him "to take her away where they could live alone and be happy."

Since he had left her, John Jr. had thought a great deal, the result of which was, that he determined on returning home much sooner than he at first intended, promising himself to treat Mabel decently, and if possible win back the respect of

'Lena, which he knew he had lost. To his companions, who urged him to remain, he replied that "he had left his wife sick, and he could not stay longer."

It cost him a great effort to say "my wife," for never before had he so called her, but he felt better the moment he had done so, and bidding his young friends adieu, he started for home with the same impetuous speed which usually characterized his riding. He had fully expected to meet Mabel in the parlor, and was even revolving in his own mind the prospect of kissing her, provided 'Lena were present. "That'll prove to her," thought he, "that I am not the hardened wretch she thinks I am; so I'll do it, if Meb doesn't happen to be all bound up in camphor and aromatic vinegar, which I can't endure, anyway."

Full of this resolution he had hastened home, going first to his old room, where he had come so unexpectedly upon Mabel that for a moment he scarcely knew what to say. By the time, however, that she had finished her story, his mind was pretty well made up.

"And so it's mother's doings, hey?" said he, violently pulling the bell-rope, and then walking up and down the room until Corinda appeared in answer to his summons.

"How many blacks are there in the kitchen?" he asked.

"Six or seven, besides Aunt Polly," answered Corinda.

"Very well. Tell every man of them to come up here, quick."

Full of wonder Corinda departed, carrying the intelligence, and adding that "Marster John looked mighty black in the face", and she reckoned some on 'em would catch it, at the same time, for fear of what might happen, secretly conveying back to the safe the piece of cake which, in her mistress' absence, she had stolen! Aunt Milly's first thought was of the frosted candlesticks, and by way of impressing upon Corinda a sense of what she might expect if in any way she implicated her, she gave her a cuff in advance, bidding her "be keerful how she blabbed", then heading the sable group, she repaired to the chamber, where John Jr. was awaiting them.

Advancing toward them, as they appeared in the doorway, he said, "Take hold here, every one of you, and move these things back where they came from."

"Don't, oh don't," entreated Mabel, but laying his hand over her mouth, John Jr. bade her keep still, at the same time ordering the negroes "to be quick."

At first the younger portion of the blacks stood speechless, but Aunt Milly, comprehending the whole at once, and feeling glad that her mistress had her match in her son, set to work with a right good will, and when about dusk Mrs. Livingstone came home, she was astonished at seeing a light in the parlor chamber, while occasionally she could discern the outline of a form moving before the window. What could it mean? Perhaps they had company, and springing from the carriage she hastened into the house, meeting 'Lena in the hall, and eagerly asking who was in the front chamber.

"I believe," said 'Lena, "that my cousin is not pleased with the change, and has gone back to the front room."

"The impudent thing!" exclaimed Mrs. Livingstone, ignorant of her son's return, and as a matter of course attributing the whole to Mabel.

Darting up the stairs, she advanced toward the chamber and pushing open the door stood face to face with John Jr., who, with hands crammed in his pockets and legs crossed, was leaning against the mantel, waiting and ready for whatever might occur.

"John Livingstone!" she gasped in her surprise.

"That's my name," he returned, quietly enjoying her look of amazement.

"What do you mean?" she continued.

"Mean what I say," was his provoking answer.

"What have you been about?" was her next question, to which he replied, "Your eyesight is not deficient--you can see for yourself."

Gaining no satisfaction from him, Mrs. Livingstone now turned upon Mabel, abusing her until John Jr. sternly commanded her to desist, bidding her "confine her remarks to himself, and let his wife alone, as she was not in the least to blame."

"Your wife!" repeated Mrs. Livingstone--"very affectionate you've grown, all at once. Perhaps you've forgotten that you married her to spite Nellie, who you then believed was the bride of Mr. Wilbur, but you surely remember how you fainted when you accidentally learned your mistake."

A cry from Mabel, who fell back, fainting, among the pillows, prevented Mrs. Livingstone from any further remarks, and satisfied with the result of her visit, she walked away, while John Jr., springing to the bedside, bore his young wife to the open window, hoping the cool night air would revive her. But she lay so pale and motionless in his arms, her head resting so heavily upon his shoulder, that with a terrible foreboding he laid her back upon the bed, and rushing to the door, shouted loudly, "Help--somebody--come quick--Mabel is dead, I know she is."

'Lena heard the cry and hastened to the rescue, starting back when she saw the marble whiteness of Mabel's face.

"I didn't kill her, 'Lena. God knows I didn't. Poor little Meb," said John Jr., quailing beneath 'Lena's rebuking glance, and bending anxiously over the slight form which looked so much like death.

But Mabel was not dead. 'Lena knew it by the faint fluttering of her heart, and an application of the usual remedies sufficed, at last, to restore her to consciousness. With a long-drawn sigh her eyes unclosed, and looking earnestly in 'Lena's face, she said, "Was it a dream, 'Lena? Tell me, was it all a dream?"--then, as she observed her husband, she added, shudderingly, "No, no, not a dream. I remember it all now. And I wish I was dead."

Again 'Lena's rebuking glance went over to John Jr., who, advancing nearer to Mabel, gently laid his hand upon her white brow, saying, softly, "Poor, poor Meb."

There was genuine pity in the tones of his voice, and while the hot tears gushed forth, the sick girl murmured, "Forgive me, John, I couldn't help it. I didn't know it, and now, if you say so, I'll go away, alone--where you'll never see me again."

She comprehended it all. Her mother-in-law had rudely torn away the veil, and she saw why she was there--knew why he had sought her for his wife--understood all his coldness and neglect; but she had no word of reproach for him, her husband, and from the depths of her crushed heart she forgave him, commiserating him as the greater sufferer.

"May be I shall die," she whispered, "and then----"

She did not finish the sentence, neither was it necessary, for John Jr. understood what she meant, and with his conscience smiting him as it did, he felt half inclined to declare, with his usual impulsiveness, that it should never be; but the rash promise was not made, and it was far better that it should not be.

CHAPTER XXVII.
THE SHADOW.

Mabel's nerves had received too great a shock to rally immediately, and as day after day went by, she still kept her room, notwithstanding the very pointed hints of her mother-in-law that "she was making believe for the sake of sympathy." Why didn't she get up and go out doors--anybody would be sick to be flat on their back day in and day out; or did she think she was spiting her by showing what muss she could keep the "best chamber" in if she chose?

This last was undoubtedly the grand secret of Mrs. Livingstone's dissatisfaction. Foiled in her efforts to dislodge them, she would not yield without an attempt at making Mabel, at least, as uncomfortable in mind as possible. Accordingly, almost every day when her son was not present, she conveyed from the room some nice article of furniture, substituting in its place one of inferior quality, which was quite good enough, she thought, for a penniless bride.

"'Pears like ole miss goin' to make a clean finish of her dis time," said Aunt Milly, who watched her mistress' daily depredations. "Ole Sam done got title deed of her, sure enough. Ki! won't she ketch it in t'other world, when he done show her his cloven foot, and won't she holler for old Milly to fotch her a drink of water? not particular then--drink out of the bucket, gourd-shell, or anything; but dis nigger'll 'sign her post in de parlor afore she'll go."

"Why, Milly," said 'Lena, who overheard this colloquy, "don't you know it's wrong to indulge in such wicked thoughts?"

"Bless you, child," returned the old negress, "she 'sarves 'em all for treatin' that poor, dear lamb so. I'd 'nihilate her if I's Miss Mabel."

"No, no, Milly," said Aunt Polly, who was present. "You must heap coals of fire on her head."

"Yes, yes, that's it--she orto have 'em," quickly responded Milly, thinking Polly's method of revenge the very best in the world, provided the coals were "bilin' hot," and with this reflection she started upstairs, with a bowl of nice, warm gruel she had been preparing for the invalid.

Several times each day Grandma Nichols visited Mabel's room, always prescribing some new tea of herbs, whose healing qualities were wonderful, having effected cures in every member of Nancy Scovandyke's family, that lady herself, as a matter of course, being first included. And Aunt Milly, with the faithfulness characteristic of her race, would seek out each new herb, uniting with it her own simple prayer that it might have the desired effect. But all in vain, for every day Mabel became weaker, while her dark eyes grew larger and brighter, anon lighting up with joy as she heard her husband's footsteps in the hall, and again filling with tears as she glanced timidly into his face, and thought of the dread reality.

"Maybe I shall die," was more than once murmured in her sleep, and John Jr., as often as he heard those words, would press her burning hands, and mentally reply, "Poor little Meb."

And all this time no one thought to call a physician, until Mr. Livingstone himself at last suggested it. At first he had felt no interest whatever in his daughter-in-law, but with him force of habit was everything, and when she no longer came among them, he missed her--missed her languid steps upon the stairs and her childish voice in the parlor. At last it one day occurred to him to visit her. She was sleeping when he entered the room, but he could see there had been a fearful change since last he looked upon her, and without a word concerning his intentions, he walked to the kitchen, ordering one of his servants to start forthwith for the physician, whose residence was a few miles distant.

Mrs. Livingstone was in the front parlor when he returned, in company with Doctor Gordon, and immediately her avaricious spirit asked who would pay the bill, and why was he sent for. Mabel did not need him--she was only babyish and spleeny--and so she told the physician, who, however, did not agree with her. He did not say that Mabel would die, but he thought so, for his experienced eye saw in her infallible signs of the disease which had stricken down both her parents, and to which, from her birth, she had been a prey. Mabel guessed as much from his manner, and when again he visited her, she asked him plainly what he thought.

She was young--a bride--surrounded apparently by everything which could make her happy, and the physician hesitated, answering her evasively, until she said, "Do not fear to tell me truly, for I want to die. Oh, I long to die," she continued, passionately clasping her thin white hands together.

"That is an unusual wish in one so young," answered the physician, "but to be plain with you, Mrs. Livingstone, I think consumption too deeply seated to admit of your recovery. You may be better, but never well. Your disease is hereditary, and has been coming on too long."

"It is well," was Mabel's only answer, as she turned wearily upon her side and hid her face in the pillows.

For a long time she lay there, thinking, weeping, and thinking again, of the noisome grave through which she must pass, and from which she instinctively shrank, it was so dark, so cold, and dreary. But Mabel had trusted in One who she knew would go with her down into the lone valley--whose arm she felt would uphold her as she crossed the dark, rolling stream of death; and as if her frail bark were already safely moored upon the shores of the eternal river, she looked back dreamily upon the world she had left, and as she saw what she felt would surely be, she again murmured through her tears, "It is well."

That night, when John Jr. came up to his room, he appeared somewhat moody and cross, barely speaking to Mabel, and then walking up and down the room with the heavy tread which always indicated a storm within. He had that day been to Frankfort, hearing that Nellie was really coming home very soon--very possibly she was now on her way. Of course she would visit Mabel, when she heard she was sick, and of course he must meet her face to face, must stand with her at the bedside of his wife and that wife Mabel. In his heart he did not accuse the latter of feigning her illness, but he wished she would get well faster, so that Nellie need not feel obliged to visit her. She could at least make an effort--a great deal depended upon that--and she had now been confined to her room three or four weeks.

Thus he reflected as he walked, and at last his thoughts formed themselves into words. Stopping short at the foot of the bed, he said abruptly and without looking her in the face, "How do you feel tonight?"

The stifled cough which Mabel tried to suppress because it was offensive to him, brought a scowl to his forehead, and in imagination he anticipated her answer, "I do not think I am any better."

"And I don't believe you try to be," sprang to his lips, but its utterance was prevented by a glance at her face, which by the flickering lamplight looked whiter than ever.

"Nellie is coming home in a few weeks," he said at length, with his usual precipitancy.

'Twas the first time Mabel had heard that name since the night when her mother-in-law had rang it in her ears, and now she started so quickly, that the offending cough could not be forced back, and the coughing fit which followed was so violent that John Jr., as he held the bowl to her quivering lips, saw that what she had raised was streaked with blood. But he was unused to sickness, and he gave it no farther thought, resuming the conversation as soon as she became quiet.

"To be plain, Meb," said he, "I want you to hurry and get well before Nellie comes--for if you are sick she'll feel in duty bound to visit you, and I'd rather face a loaded cannon than her."

Mabel was too much exhausted to answer immediately, and she lay so long with her eyes closed that John Jr., growing impatient, said, "Are you asleep, Meb?"

"No, no," said she, at the same time requesting him to take the vacant chair by her side, as she wished to talk with him.

John Jr. hated to be talked to, particularly by her, for he felt that she had much cause to reproach him; but she did not, and as she proceeded, his heart melted toward her in a manner which he had never thought possible. Very gently she spoke of her approaching end as sure.

"You ask me to make haste and be well," said she, "but it cannot be. I shall never go out into the bright sunshine again, never join you in the parlor below, and before the cold winds of winter are blowing, I shall be dead. I hope I shall live until Nellie comes, for I must see her, I must make it right between her and you. I must tell her to forgive you for marrying me when you loved only her; and she will listen--she won't refuse me, and when I am gone you'll be happy together."

John Jr. did not speak, but the little hand which nervously moved toward him was met more than half-way, and thus strengthened, Mabel continued: "You must sometimes think and speak of Mabel when she is dead. I do not ask you to call me wife. I do not wish it, but you must forget how wretched I have made you, for oh, I did not mean it, and had I sooner known what I do now, I would have died ere I had caused you one pang of sorrow."

Afterward, when it was too late, John Jr. would have given worlds to recall that moment, that he might tell the broken-hearted girl how bitterly he, too, repented of all the wrong he had done her; but he did not say so then--he could only listen, while he mentally resolved that if Mabel were indeed about to die, he would make the remainder of her short life happy, and thus atone, as far as possible, for the past. But alas for John Jr., his resolutions were easily broken, and as days and weeks went by, and there was no perceptible change in her, he grew weary of well-doing, absenting himself whole days from the sick-room, and at night rather unwillingly resuming his post as watcher, for Mabel would have no one else.

Since Mabel's illness he had occupied the little room adjoining hers, and often when in the still night he lay awake, watching the shadow which the lamp cast upon the wall, and thinking of her for whom the light was constantly kept burning, his conscience would smite him terribly, and rising up, he would steal softly to her bedside to see if she were sleeping quietly. But anon he grew weary of this, too; the shadow on the wall troubled him, it kept him awake; it was a continual reproach, and he must be rid of it, somehow. He tried the experiment of closing his door, but Mabel knew the moment he attempted it, and he could not refuse her when she asked him to leave it open.

John Jr. grew restless, fidgety, and nervous. Why need the lamp be kept burning? He could light it when necessary; or why need he sleep there, when some one else would do as well? He thought of 'Lena--she was just the one, and the next day he would speak to her. To his great joy she consented to relieve him awhile, provided Mabel were willing; but she was not, and John Jr. was forced to submit. He was not accustomed to restraint, and every night matters grew worse and worse. The shadow annoyed him exceedingly. If he slept, he dreamed that it kept a glimmering watch over him, and when he awoke, he, in turn, watched over that, until the misty day-light came to dissipate the phantom.

About this time several families from Frankfort started for New Orleans, where they were wont to spend the winter, and irresistibly, John Jr. became possessed of a desire to visit that city, too. Mabel would undoubtedly live until spring, now that the trying part of autumn was past and there could be no harm in his leaving her for awhile, when he so much needed rest. Accordingly, 'Lena was one day surprised by his announcing his intended trip.

"But you cannot be in earnest," she said; "you surely will not leave Mabel now."

"And why not?" he asked. "She doesn't grow any worse, and won't until spring, and this close confinement is absolutely killing me! Why, I've lost six pounds in six months, and you'll see to her, I know you will. You're a good girl, and I like you, if I did get angry with you, weeks ago when I went a hunting."

'Lena knew he ought not to go, and she tried hard to convince him of the fact, telling him how much pleasure she had felt in observing his improved manner toward Mabel, and that he must not spoil it now.

"It's no use talking," said he, "I'm bent on going somewhere. I've tried to be good, I know, but the fact is, I can't stay put. It isn't my nature. I shan't tell Meb till just before I start, for I hate scenes."

"And suppose she dies while you are gone?" asked 'Lena.

John was beginning to grow impatient, for he knew he was wrong, and rather tartly he answered, as he left the room, "Give her a decent burial, and present the bill to mother!"

"The next morning, as 'Lena sat alone with Mabel, John Jr. entered, dressed and ready for his journey. But he found it harder telling his wife than he had anticipated. She looked unusually pale this morning. The sallowness of her complexion was all gone, and on either cheek there burned a round, bright spot. 'Lena had just been arranging her thick, glossy hair, and now, wholly exhausted, she reclined upon her pillows, while her large black eyes, unnaturally bright, sparkled with joy at the sight of her husband. But they quickly filled with tears when told that he was going away, and had come to say good-bye.

"It's only to New Orleans and back," he said, as he saw her changing face. "I shan't be gone long, and 'Lena will take care of you a heap better than I can."

"It isn't that," answered Mabel, wiping her tears away. "Don't go, John. Wait a little while. I'm sure it won't be long."

"You are nervous," said he, playfully lapping her white cheek. "You're not going to die. You'll live to be grandmother yet, who knows? But I must be off or lose the train. Good bye, little Meb," grasping her hand, "Good-bye, 'Lena. I'll bring you both something nice--good-bye."

When she saw that he was going, Mabel asked him to come back to her bedside just for one moment. He could not refuse, and winding her long, emaciated arms around his neck, she whispered, "Kiss me once before you go. I shall never ask it again, and 'twill make me happier when you are gone."

"A dozen times, if you like," said he, giving her the only husband's kiss she had ever received.

For a moment longer she detained him, while she prayed silently for heaven's blessing on his wayward head, and then releasing him, she bade him go. Had he known of all that was to follow, he would not have left her, but he believed as he said, that she would survive the winter, and with one more kiss upon her brow, where the perspiration was standing thickly, he departed. The window of Mabel's room commanded a view of the turnpike, and when the sound of horses' feet was heard on the lawn, she requested 'Lena to lead her to the window, where she stood watching him until a turn in the road hid him from her sight.

"'Tis the last time," said she, "and he will never know how much this parting cost me."

That night, as they were alone in the gathering twilight, Mabel said, "If I die before Nellie comes I want you to tell her how it all happened, and that she must forgive him, for he was not to blame."

"I do not understand you," said 'Lena, and then, in broken sentences, Mabel told what her mother-in-law had said, and how terribly John was deceived. "Of course he couldn't love me after that," said she, "and it's right that I should die. He and Nellie were made for each other, and if the inhabitants of heaven are allowed to watch over those they loved on earth, I will ask to be always near them. You will tell her, won't you?"

'Lena promised, adding that she thought Mabel would see Nellie herself as she was to sail from Liverpool the 20th, and a few days proved her conjecture correct. Entering Mabel's room one morning about a week after John's departure, she brought the glad news that Nellie had returned, and would be with them to-morrow.

The next day Nellie came, but she, too, was changed. The roundness of her form and face was gone; the rose had faded from her cheek, and her footsteps were no longer light and bounding as of old. She knew of John Jr.'s absence or she would not have come, for she could not meet him face to face. She had heard, too, of his treatment of Mabel, and while she felt indignant toward him, she freely forgave his innocent wife, who she felt had been more sinned against than sinning.

With a faint cry Mabel started from her pillow, and burying her face on Nellie's neck, wept like a child. "You do not hate me," she said at last, "or you would not have come so soon."

"Hate you?--no," answered Nellie. "I have no cause for hating you."

"And you will stay with me until I die--until he comes home--and forgive him, too," Mabel continued.

"I can promise the first, but the latter is harder," said Nellie, her cheeks burning with anger as she gazed on the wreck before her.

"But you must, you will," exclaimed Mabel, rapidly telling all she knew; then falling back upon the pillow, she added, "You'll forgive him Nellie?"

As time passed on, Mabel grew weaker and weaker, clinging closer to Nellie as she felt the dark shadow of death creeping gradually over her.

"If he'd only come," she would say, "and I could place your hand in his before I died."

But it was not to be. Day after day John Jr. lingered, dreading to return, for he knew Nellie was there, and he could not meet her, he thought, at the bedside of Mabel. So he tarried until a letter from 'Lena, which said that Mabel would die, decided him, and rather reluctantly he started homeward. Meantime Mabel, who knew nothing of her loss, conceived the generous idea of willing all her possessions to her recreant husband.

"Perhaps he'll think more kindly of me," said she to his father, to whom she first communicated her plan, and Mr. Livingstone felt that he could not undeceive her.

Accordingly, a lawyer was summoned from Frankfort, and the will duly drawn up, signed, sealed, and delivered into the hands of Mr. Livingstone, whose wife, with a mocking laugh, bade him "guard it carefully, it was so valuable."

"It shows her goodness of heart, at least," said he, and possibly Mrs. Livingstone thought so, too, for from that time her manner softened greatly toward her daughter-in-law.

*   *   *   *   *   *

It was midnight at Maple grove. On the table, in its accustomed place, the lamp was burning dimly, casting the shadow upon the wall, whilst over the whole room a darker shadow was brooding. The window was open, and the cool night air came softly in, lifting the masses of raven hair from off the pale brow of the dying. Tenderly above her Nellie and 'Lena were bending. They had watched by her many a night, and now she asked them not to leave her, not to disturb a single one--she would rather die alone.

The sound of horses' hoofs rang out on the still air, but she did not heed it. Nearer and nearer it came, over the lawn, up the graveled walk, through the yard, and Nellie's face blanched to an unnatural whiteness as she thought who that midnight-rider was. Arrived in Frankfort only an hour before, he had hastened forward, impelled by a something he could not resist. From afar he had caught the glimmering light, and he felt he was not too late. He knew how to enter the house, and on through the wide hall and up the broad staircase he came, until he stood in the chamber, where before him another guest had entered, whose name was Death!

Face to face he stood with Nellie Douglass, and between them lay his *wife*--her rival--the white hands folded meekly upon her bosom, and the pale lips just as they had breathed a prayer for him.

"Mabel! She is dead!" was all he uttered, and falling upon his knees, he buried his face in the pillow, while half scornfully, half pityingly, Nellie gazed upon him.

There was much of bitterness in her heart toward him, not for the wrong he had done her, but for the sake of the young girl, now passed forever away. 'Lena felt differently. His silent grief conquered all resentment, and going to his side, she told him how peacefully Mabel had died--how to the last she had loved and remembered him, praying that he might be happy when she was gone,

"Poor little Meb, she deserved a better fate," was all he said, as he continued his kneeling posture, until the family and servants, whom Nellie had summoned, came crowding round, the cries of the latter grating on the ear, and seeming sadly out of place for her whose short life had been so dreary, and who had welcomed death as a release from all her pain.

It was Mrs. Livingstone's wish that Mabel should be arrayed in her bridal robes, but with a shudder at the idle mockery, John Jr. answered, "No," and in a plain white muslin, her shining hair arrayed as she was wont to wear it, they placed her in her coffin, and on a sunny slope where the golden sunlight and the pale moonbeams latest fell, and where in spring the bright green grass and the sweet wild flowers are earliest seen, laid her down to steep.

That night, when all around was still, John Jr. lay musing sadly of the past. His affection for Mabel had been slight and variable, but now that she was gone, he missed her. The large easy-chair, with its cushions and pillows, was empty, and as he thought of the pale, dark face and aching head he had so often seen reclining there, and which he would never see again, he groaned in bitterness of spirit, for well he knew that he had helped to break the heart now lying cold and still beneath the coffin-lid. There was no shadow on the wall, for the lamp had gone out with the young life for whom it had been kept burning, but many a shadow lay dark and heavy across his heart.

With the sun-setting a driving rain had come on, and as the November wind went howling past the window, and the large drops beat against the casement, he thought of the lonesome little grave on which that rain was falling; and shuddering, he hid his face in the pillows, asking to be forgiven, for he knew that all too soon that grave was made, and he had helped to make it. At last, long after the clock had told the hour of midnight, he arose, and lighting the lamp which many a weary night had burned for her, he placed it where the shadow would fall upon the wall as it had done of old. It was no longer a phantom to annoy him, and soothed by its presence, he fell asleep, dreaming that Mabel had come back to bring him her forgiveness, but when he essayed to touch her, she vanished from his sight, and there was nothing left save that shadow on the wall.

CHAPTER XXVIII.
MRS. GRAHAM'S RETURN.

Mr. and Mrs. Graham had returned to Woodlawn, the former remaining but a day and night, and then, without once seeing 'Lena, departing for Europe, where business, either fancied or real, called him. Often, when lying weary and sick in Havana, had he resolved on revealing to his wife the secret which he felt was wearing his life away, but the cowardice of his nature seemed increased by physical weakness, and from time to time was the disclosure postponed, while the chain of evidence was fearfully lengthening around poor 'Lena, to whom Mrs. Graham had transferred the entire weight of her displeasure.

Loving her husband as well as such as she could love, she was ever ready to forgive when she saw any indications of reform on his part, and as during all their journey he had never once given her cause for offense, she began to attribute his former delinquencies wholly to 'Lena; and when he proposed a tour to Europe she readily sanctioned it, hoping that time and absence would remove from his mind all thoughts of the beautiful girl, who she thought was her rival. Still, though she would not confess it, in her heart she did not believe 'Lena guilty except so far as a desire to attract Mr. Graham's attention would make her so.

For this belief she had a good and potent reason. The daguerreotype which had caused so much trouble was still in her possession, guarded carefully from her husband, who never suspecting the truth, supposed he had lost it. Frequently had Mrs. Graham examined the picture, each time discovering some point of difference between it and its supposed original. Still she never for a moment doubted that it was 'Lena, until an event occurred which convinced her of the contrary, leaving her, meantime, more mystified than ever.

On their way home from Havana, Mr. Graham had proposed stopping a day in Cincinnati, taking rooms at the Burnet House, where the first individual whom they saw at the table was our old acquaintance, Joel Slocum. Not finding his business as profitable in Lexington as he could wish, he had recently removed to Cincinnati. Here his aspiring mind had prompted him to board at the Burnet House, until he'd seen the "Ohio elephant," when he intended retiring to one of the cheaper boarding-houses. The moment he saw Mr. Graham, a grin of recognition became visible on his face, bringing to view a row of very long and very yellow teeth, apparently unacquainted with the use of either water or brush.

"Who is that loafer who seems to know you?" asked Mrs. Graham, directing her husband's attention toward Joel.

Mr. Graham replied that "he had once seen him in Lexington, and that he took daguerreotypes."

The moment dinner was over, Joel came forward, going through with one of his wonderful bows, and exclaiming, with his peculiar nasal twang, "Now you don't say this is you. And this is your old woman, I s'pose. Miss Graham, how-dy-du? Darned if you don't look like Aunt Nancy, only she's lean and you are squatty. S'posin' you give me a call and get your picters taken. I didn't get an all-killin' sight of practice in Lexington, for the plaguy greenhorns didn't know enough to patternize me, and 'taint a tarnation sight better here; but you," turning to Mr. Graham, "employed me once, and pretended to be suited."

Mr. Graham turned scarlet, and saying something in an undertone to Joel, gave his wife his arm, leading her to their room, where he made an excuse for leaving her awhile. Looking from the window a moment after, Mrs. Graham saw him walking down the street in close conversation with Joel, who, by the way of showing his importance, lifted his white beaver to almost every man he met. Instantly her curiosity was roused, and when her husband returned, every motion of his was narrowly watched, the espionage resulting in the conviction that there was something in his possession which he did not wish her to see. Once, when she came unexpectedly upon him, he hastily thrust something into his pocket, appearing so much confused that she resolved to ferret out the secret.

Accordingly, that night, when assured by his heavy breathing that he was asleep, she crept softly from his side, and rummaging his pockets, found a daguerreotype, which by the full moonlight she saw was a fac-simile of the one she had in her possession. The arrangement of the hair--everything--was the same, and utterly confounded, she stood gazing first at one and then at the other, wondering what it meant. Could 'Lena be in the city? She thought not, and even if she were, the last daguerreotype was not so much like her, she fancied, as the first. At all events, she did not dare secrete it as she had done its companion, and stealthily returning it to its place, she crept back to bed.

The next night they reached Woodlawn, where they learned that Mabel was buried that day. Of course 'Lena could not have been absent from home. Mrs. Graham felt convinced of that, and gradually the conviction came upon her that another than 'Lena was the original of the daguerreotypes. And yet she was not generous enough to tell Durward so. She knew he was deceived--she wished him to remain so--and to effect it, she refrained from seeking an explanation from her husband, fearing lest 'Lena should be proved innocent. Her husband knew there was a misunderstanding between Durward and 'Lena, and if she were to ask him about the pictures, he would, she thought, at once suspect the cause of that misunderstanding, and as a matter of course, exonerate 'Lena from all blame. The consequence of this she foresaw, and therefore she resolved upon keeping her own counsel, satisfied if in the end she prevented Durward from making 'Lena his wife.

To effect this, she endeavored, during the winter, to keep the matter almost constantly before Durward's mind, frequently referring to 'Lena's agitation when she first learned that Mr. Graham had started for Europe. She had called with her son at Maple Grove on the very day of her husband's departure. 'Lena had not met the lady before, since that night in Frankfort, and now, with the utmost hauteur, she returned her nod, and then, too proud to leave the room, resumed her seat near the window directly opposite the divan on which Durward was seated with Carrie.

She did not know before of Mrs. Graham's return, and when her aunt casually asked, "Did your husband come back with you?" she involuntarily held her breath for the answer, which, when it came, sent the blood in torrents to her face and neck, while her eyes sparkled with joy. She should see him--he would explain everything--and she should be guiltless in Durward's sight. This was the cause of her joy, which was quickly turned into sorrow by Mrs. Graham's adding,

"But he started this morning for Europe, where he will remain three months, and perhaps longer, just according to his business."

The bright flush died away, and was succeeded by paleness, which did not escape the observation or either mother or son, the latter of whom had watched her from the first, noting each change, and interpreting it according to his fears.

"'Lena, 'Lena, how have I been deceived!" was his mental cry as she precipitately left the room, saying to her aunt, who asked what was the matter, that she was faint and dizzy. Death had been but yesterday within their walls, and as if softened by its presence, Mrs. Livingstone actually spoke kindly of her niece, saying, that "constant watching with poor, dear Mabel had impaired her health."

"Perhaps there are other causes which may affect her," returned Mrs. Graham, with a meaning look, which, though lost on Mrs. Livingstone, was noticed by Durward, who soon proposed leaving.

On their way home, his mother asked if he observed 'Lena when Mr. Graham was mentioned.

Without saying that he did, Durward replied, "I noticed your remark to Mrs. Livingstone, and was sorry for it, for I do not wish you to say a word which will throw the least shade of suspicion upon 'Lena. Her reputation as yet is good, and you must not be the first to say aught against it."

"I won't, I won't," answered Mrs. Graham, anxious to conciliate her son, but she found it a harder matter to refrain than she had first supposed.

'Lena was to her a constant eye-sore, and nothing but the presence of Durward prevented her from occasionally giving vent in public to expressions which would have operated unfavorably against the young girl, and when at last circumstances occurred which gave her, as she thought, liberty to free her mind, she was only too willing to do so. Of those circumstances, in which others besides 'Lena were concerned, we will speak in another chapter.

CHAPTER XXIX.
ANNA AND CAPTAIN ATHERTON.

Malcolm Everett's engagement with General Fontaine had expired, and as was his original intention, he started for New York, first seeking an interview with Mr. and Mrs. Livingstone, of whom he asked their daughter Anna in marriage, at the same time announcing the startling fact that they had been engaged for more than a year. "I do not ask you for her now," said he, "for I am not in a situation to support her as I would wish to, but that time will come ere long, I trust, and I can assure you that her happiness shall be the first object of my life."

There was no cringing on the part of Malcolm Everett. He was unused to that, and as an equal meets an equal, he met them, made known his request, and then in silence awaited their answer. Had Mrs. Livingstone been less indignant, there would undoubtedly have ensued a clamorous call for hartshorn and vinaigrette, but as it was, she started up, and confronting the young man, she exclaimed, "How dare you ask such a thing? My *daughter marry* you!"

"And why not, madam?" he answered, coolly, while Mrs. Livingstone continued: "You, a low-born Yankee, who have been, as it were, an hireling. You *presume to ask for* my daughter!"

"I do," he answered calmly, with a quiet smile, ten-fold more tantalizing than harsh words would have been, "I do. Can I have her with your consent?"

"Never, so long as I live. I'd sooner see her dead than wedded to vulgar poverty."

"That is your answer. Very well," said Malcolm, bowing stiffly. "And now I will hear yours," turning to Mr. Livingstone, who replied, that "he would leave the matter entirely with his wife--it was nothing to him--he had nothing personal against Mr. Everett--he rather liked him than otherwise, but he hardly thought Anna suited to him, she had been brought up so differently;" and thus evasively answering, he walked away.

"Cowardly fool!" muttered Mrs. Livingstone, as the door closed upon him. "If I pretended to be a man, I'd be one;" then turning to Malcolm, she said, "Is there anything further you wish to say?"

"Nothing," he replied. "I have honorably asked you for your daughter. You have refused her, and must abide the consequence."

"And pray what may that be?" she asked, and he answered: "She will soon be of an age to act for herself, and though I would far rather take her with your consent, I shall not then hesitate to take her without, if you still persist in opposing her."

"There is the door," said Mrs. Livingstone rising.

"I see it, madam," answered Malcolm, without deigning to move.

"Oblige me by passing out," continued Mrs. Livingstone. "Insolent creature, to stand here threatening to elope with my daughter, who has been destined for another since her infancy."

"But she shall never become the bride of that old man," answered Malcolm. "I know your schemes. I've seen them all along, and I will frustrate them, too."

"You cannot," fiercely answered Mrs. Livingstone. "It shall be ere another year comes round, and when you hear that it is so, know that you hastened it forward;" and the indignant lady, finding that her opponent was not inclined to move, left the room herself, going in quest of Anna, whom she determined to watch for fear of what might happen.

But Anna was nowhere to be found, and in a paroxysm of rage she alarmed the household, instituting a strict search, which resulted in the discovery of Anna beneath the same sycamore where Malcolm had first breathed his vows, and whither she had repaired to await the decision of her parents.

"I expected as much," said she, when told of the result, "but it matters not. I am yours, and I'll never marry another."

The approach of the servants prevented any further conversation, and with a hurried adieu they parted. A few days afterward, as Mrs. Livingstone, sat in her large easy-chair before the glowing grate, Captain Atherton was announced, and shown at once into her room. To do Mrs. Livingstone justice, we must say that she had long debated the propriety of giving Anna, in all the freshness of her girl-hood, to a man old as her father, but any hesitancy she had heretofore felt, had now vanished. The crisis had come, and when the captain, as he had two or three times before done, broached the subject, urging her to a decision, she replied that she was willing, provided Anna's consent could be gained.

"Pho! that's easy enough," said the captain, complacently rubbing together his fat hands and smoothing his colored whiskers--"Bring her in here, and I'll coax her in five minutes."

Anna was sitting with her grandmother and 'Lena, when word came that her mother wished to see her, the servant adding, with a titter, that "Mas'r Atherton thar too."

Instinctively she knew why she was sent for, and turning white as marble, she begged her cousin to go with her. But 'Lena refused, soothing the agitated girl, and begging her to be calm. "You've only to be decided," said she, "and it will soon be over. Captain Atherton, I am sure, will not insist when he sees how repugnant to your feelings it is."

But Anna knew her own weakness--she could never say, in her mother's presence, what she felt--and trembling like an aspen, she descended the stairs, meeting in the lower hall her brother, who asked what was the matter.

"Oh, John, John," she cried, "Captain Atherton is in there with mother, and they have sent for me. What shall I do?"

"Be a woman," answered John Jr. "Tell him no in good broad English, and if the old fellow insists, I'll blow his brains out!"

But the Captain did not insist. He was too cunning for that, and when, with a burst of tears, Anna told him she could not be his wife because she loved another, he said, good-humoredly, "Well, well, never mind spoiling those pretty blue eyes. I'm not such an old savage as you think me. So we'll compromise the matter this way. If you really love Malcolm, why, marry him, and on your bridal day I'll make you a present of a nice little place I have in Frankfort; but if, on the other hand, Malcolm proves untrue, you must promise to have me. Come, that's a fair bargain. What do you say?"

"Malcolm will never prove untrue," answered Anna.

"Of course not," returned the captain. "So you are safe in promising.'

"But what good will it do you?" queried Anna.

"No good, in particular," said the captain. "It's only a whim of mine, to which I thought you might perhaps agree, in consideration of my offer."

"I do--I will," said Anna, thinking the captain not so bad after all.

"There's mischief somewhere, and I advise you to watch," said John Jr., when he learned from Anna the result of the interview.

But week after week glided by. Mrs. Livingstone's persecutions ceased, and she sometimes herself handed to Anna Malcolm's letters, which came regularly, and when about the first of March Captain Atherton himself went off to Washington, Anna gave her fears to the wind, and all the day long went singing about the house, unmindful of the snare laid for her unsuspecting footsteps. At length Malcolm's letters suddenly ceased, and though Anna wrote again and again, there came no answer. Old Caesar, who always carried and brought the mail for Maple Grove, was questioned, but he declared he "done got none from Mas'r Everett," and suspicion in that quarter was lulled. Unfortunately for Anna, both her father and John Jr. were now away, and she had no counselor save 'Lena, who once, on her own responsibility, wrote to Malcolm, but with a like success, and Anna's heart grew weary with hope deferred. Smilingly Mrs. Livingstone looked on, one moment laughing at Anna for what she termed love-sickness, and the next advising her to be a woman, and marry Captain Atherton. "He was not very old--only forty-three--and it was better to be an old man's darling than a young man's slave!"

Thus the days wore on, until one evening just as the family were sitting down to tea they were surprised by a call from the captain, who had returned that afternoon, and who, with the freedom of an old friend, unceremoniously entered the supper-room, appropriating to himself the extra plate which Mrs. Livingstone always had upon the table. Simultaneously with him came Caesar, who having been to the post-office, had just returned, bringing, besides other things, a paper for Carrie, from her old admirer, Tom Lakin, who lived in Rockford, at which place the paper was printed. Several times had Tom remembered Carrie in this way, and now carelessly glancing at the first page, she threw it upon the floor, whence it was taken by Anna, who examined it more minutely glancing, as a matter of course, to the marriage notices.

Meantime the captain, who was sitting by 'Lena, casually remarked, "Oh, I forgot to tell you that I saw Mr. Everett in Washington."

"Mr. Everett--Malcolm Everett?" said 'Lena, quickly.

"Yes, Malcolm Everett," answered the captain.

"He is there spending the honeymoon with his bride!"

'Lena's exclamation of astonishment was prevented by a shriek from Anna, who had that moment read the announcement of Mr. Everett's marriage, which was the first in the list. It was Malcolm H. Everett--there could be no mistake--and when 'Lena reached her cousin's side, she found that she had fainted. All was now in confusion, in the midst of which the Captain took his leave, having first managed to speak a few words in private with Mrs. Livingstone.

"Fortune favors us," was her reply, as she went back to her daughter, whose long, death-like swoon almost wrung from her the secret.

But Anna revived, and with the first indication of returning consciousness, the cold, hard woman stifled all her better feelings, and then tried to think she was acting only for the good of her child. For a long time Anna appeared to be in a kind of benumbed torpor, requesting to be left alone, and shuddering if Mr. Everett's name were mentioned in her presence. It was in vain that 'Lena strove to comfort her, telling her there might be some mistake. Anna refused to listen, angrily bidding 'Lena desist, and saying frequently that she cared but little what became of herself now. A species of recklessness seemed to have taken possession of her, and when her mother one day carelessly remarked that possibly Captain Atherton would claim the fulfillment of her promise, she answered, in the cold, indifferent tone which now marked her manner of speaking, "Let him. I am ready and willing for the sacrifice."

"Are you in earnest?" asked Mrs. Livingstone, eagerly.

"In earnest? Yes--try me and see," was Anna's brief answer, which somewhat puzzled her mother, who would in reality have preferred opposition to this unnatural passiveness.

But anything to gain her purpose, she thought, and drawing Anna closely to her side, she very gently and affectionately told her how happy it would make her could she see her the wife of Captain Atherton, who had loved and waited for her so long, and who would leave no wish, however slight, ungratified. And Anna, with no shadow of emotion on her calm, white face, consented to all that her mother asked, and when next the captain came, she laid her feverish hand in his, and with a strange, wild light beaming from her dark blue eyes, promised to share his fortunes as his wife.

"'Twill be winter and spring," said she, with a bitter, mocking laugh, "'Twill be winter and spring, but it matters not."

Many years before, when a boy of eighteen, Captain Atherton had loved, or fancied he loved, a young girl, whose very name afterward became hateful to him, and now, as he thought of Anna's affection for Malcolm, he likened it to his own boyish fancy, believing she would soon get over it, and thank him for what he had done.

That night Anna saw the moon and stars go down, bending far out from her window, that the damp air might cool her burning brow, and when the morning sun came up the eastern horizon, its first beams fell on the golden curls which streamed across the window-sill, her only pillow the livelong night. On 'Lena's mind a terrible conviction was fastening itself--Anna was crazed. She saw it in the wildness of her eye, in the tones of her voice, and more than all, in the readiness with which she yielded herself to her mother's schemes, "But it shall not be," she thought, "I will save her," and then she knelt before her aunt, imploring her to spare her daughter--not to sacrifice her on the altar of mammon.

But Mrs. Livingstone turned angrily away, telling her to mind her own affairs. Then 'Lena sought her cousin, and winding her arms around her neck, besought of her to resist--to burst the chain which bound her, and be free. But with a shake other head, Anna bade her go away. "Leave me, 'Lena Rivers," she said, "leave me to work out my destiny. It is decreed that I shall be his wife, and I may not struggle against it. Each night I read it in the stars, and the wind, as it sighs through the maple trees, whispers it to my ear."

"Oh, if my aunt could see her now," thought 'Lena but as if her mother's presence had a paralyzing power, Anna, when with her, was quiet, gentle, and silent, and if Mrs. Livingstone sometimes missed her merry laugh and playful ways, she thought the air of dignity which seemed to have taken their place quite an improvement, and far more in keeping with the bride-elect of Captain Atherton.

About this time Mr. Livingstone returned, appearing greatly surprised at the phase which affairs had assumed in his absence, but when 'Lena whispered to him her fears, he smilingly answered, "I reckon you're mistaken. Her mother would have found it out--where is she?"

In her chamber at the old place by the open window they found her, and though she did not as usual spring eagerly forward to meet her father, her greeting was wholly natural; but when Mr. Livingstone, taking her upon his knee, said gently, "They tell me you are to be married soon," the wildness came back to her eye, and 'Lena wondered he could not see it. But he did not, and smoothing her disordered tresses, he said, "Tell me, my daughter, does this marriage please you? Do you enter into it willingly?"

For a moment there was a wavering, and 'Lena held her breath to catch the answer, which came at last, while the eyes shone brighter than ever--"Willing? yes, or I should not do it; no one compels me, else I would resist."

"Woman's nature," said Mr. Livingstone, laughingly, while 'Lena turned away to hide her tears.

Day after day preparations went on, for Mrs. Livingstone would have the ceremony a grand and imposing one. In the neighborhood, the fast approaching event was discussed, some pronouncing it a most fortunate thing for Anna, who could not, of course, expect to make so eligible a match as her more brilliant sister, while others--the sensible portion--wondered, pitied, and blamed, attributing the whole to the ambitious mother, whose agency in her son's marriage was now generally known. At Maple Grove closets, chairs, tables, and sofas were loaded down with finery, and like an automaton, Anna stood up while they fitted to her the rich white satin, scarcely whiter than her own face, and Mrs. Livingstone, when she saw her daughter's indifference, would pinch her bloodless cheeks, wondering how she could care so little for her good fortune.

Unnatural mother!--from the little grave on the sunny slope, now grass-grown and green, came there no warning voice to stay her in her purpose? No; she scarcely thought of Mabel now, and with unflinching determination she kept on her way.

But there was one who, night and day, pondered in her mind the best way of saving Anna from the living death to which she would surely awake, when it was too late. At last she resolved on going herself to Captain Atherton, telling him just how it was, and if there was a spark of generosity in his nature, she thought he would release her cousin. But this plan required much caution, for she would not have her uncle's family know of it, and if she failed, she preferred that it should be kept a secret from the world. There was then no alternative but to go in the night, and alone. She did not now often sit with the family, and she knew they would not miss her. So, one evening when they were as usual assembled in the parlor, she stole softly from the house, and managing to pass the negro quarters unobserved, she went down to the lower stable, where she saddled the pony she was now accustomed to ride, and leading him by a circuitous path out upon the turnpike, mounted and rode away.

The night was moonless, and the starlight obscured by heavy clouds, but the pale face and golden curls of Anna, for whose sake she was there alone, gleamed on her in the darkness, and 'Lena was not afraid. Once--twice--she thought she caught the sound of another horse's hoofs, but when she stopped to listen, all was still, and again she pressed forward, while her pursuer (for 'Lena was followed) kept at a greater distance. Durward had been to Frankfort, and on his way home had stopped at Maple Grove to deliver a package. Stopping only a moment, he reached the turnpike just after 'Lena struck into it. Thinking it was a servant, he was about to pass her, when her horse sheered at something on the road-side, and involuntarily she exclaimed, "Courage, Dido, there's nothing to fear."

Instantly he recognized her voice, and was about to overtake and speak to her, but thinking that her mission was a secret one, or she would not be there alone, he desisted. Still he could not leave her thus. Her safety might be endangered, and reining in his steed, and accommodating his pace to hers, he followed without her knowledge. On she went until she reached the avenue leading to "Sunnyside," as Captain Atherton termed his residence, and there she stopped, going on foot to the house, while, hidden by the deep darkness Durward waited and watched.

Half timidly 'Lena rang the door-bell, dropping her veil over her face that she might not be recognized. "I want to see your master," she said to the woman who answered her ring, and who in some astonishment replied, "Bless you, miss, Mas'r Atherton done gone to Lexington and won't be home till to-morry."

"Gone!" repeated 'Lena in a disappointed tone. "Oh, I'm so sorry."

"Is you the new miss what's comin' here to live?" asked the negro, who was Captain Atherton's house keeper.

Instantly the awkwardness of her position flashed upon 'Lena, but resolving to put a bold face on the matter, she removed her veil, saying, playfully, "You know me now, Aunt Martha."

"In course I do," answered the negro, holding up both hands in amazement, "but what sent you here this dark, unairthly night?"

"Business with your master," and then suddenly remembering that among her own race Aunt Martha was accounted an intolerable gossip, she began to wish she had not come.

But it could not now be helped, and turning away, she walked slowly down the avenue, wondering what the result would be. Again they were in motion, she and Durward, who followed until he saw her safe home, and then, glad that no one had seen her but himself, he retraced his steps, pondering on the mystery which he could not fathom. After 'Lena left Sunnyside, a misty rain came on, and by the time she reached her home, her long riding-dress was wet and drizzled, the feathers on her cap were drooping, and to crown all, as she was crossing the hall with stealthy step, she came suddenly upon her aunt, who, surprised at her appearance, demanded of her where she had been. But 'Lena refused to tell, and in quite a passion Mrs. Livingstone laid the case before her husband.

"Lena had been off that dark, rainy night, riding somewhere with somebody, she wouldn't tell who, but she (Mrs. Livingstone) most knew if was Durward, and something must be done."

Accordingly, next day; when they chanced to be alone, Mr. Livingstone took the opportunity of questioning 'Lena, who dared not disobey him, and with many tears she confessed the whole, saying that "if it were wrong she was very sorry."

"You acted foolishly, to say the least of it," answered her uncle, adding, dryly, that he thought she troubled herself altogether too much about Anna, who seemed happy and contented.

Still he was ill at ease. 'Lena's fears disturbed him, and for many days he watched his daughter narrowly, admitting to himself that there was something strange about her. But possibly all engaged girls acted so; his wife said they did; and hating anything like a scene, he concluded to let matters take their course, half hoping, and half believing, too, that something would occur to prevent the marriage. What it would be, or by what agency it would be brought about, he didn't know, but he resolved to let 'Lena alone, and when his wife insisted upon his "lecturing her soundly for meddling," he refused, venturing even to say, that, "she hadn't meddled."

Meantime a new idea had entered 'Lena's mind. She would write to Mr. Everett. There might yet be some mistake; she had read of such things in stories, and it could do no harm. Gradually as she wrote, hope grew strong within her, and it became impressed upon her that there had been some deep-laid, fiendish plot. If so, she dared not trust her letter with old Caesar, who might be bribed by his mistress. And how to convey it to the office was now the grand difficulty. As if fortune favored her plan, Durward, that very afternoon, called at Maple Grove, being as he said, on his way to Frankfort.

'Lena would have died rather than ask a favor of him for herself, but to save Anna she could do almost any thing. Hastily securing the letter, and throwing on her sun-bonnet, she sauntered down the lawn and out upon the turnpike, where by the gate she awaited his coming.

"'Lena--excuse me--Miss Rivers, is it you?" asked Durward, touching his hat, as in evident confusion she came forward, asking if she could trust him.

"Trust me? Yes, with anything," answered Durward, quickly dismounting, and forgetting everything save the bright, beautiful face which looked up to him so eagerly.

"Then," answered 'Lena, "take this letter and see it deposited safely, will you?"

Glancing at the superscription, Durward felt his face crimson, while he instantly remembered what Mrs. Livingstone had once said concerning 'Lena's attachment to Mr. Everett.

"Sometime, perhaps, I will explain," said 'Lena, observing the expression of his countenance, and then adding, with some bitterness, "I assure you there is no harm in it."

"Of course not," answered Durward, again mounting his horse, and riding away more puzzled than ever, while 'Lena returned to the house, which everywhere gave tokens of the approaching nuptials.

Already had several costly bridal gifts arrived, and among them was a box from the captain, containing a set of diamonds, which Mrs. Livingstone placed in her daughter's waving hair, bidding her mark their effect. But not a muscle of Anna's face changed; nothing moved her; and with the utmost indifference she gazed on the preparations around her. A stranger would have said 'Lena was the bride, for, with flushed cheeks and nervously anxious manner, she watched each sun as it rose and set, wondering what the result would be. Once, when asked whom she would have for her bridesmaid and groomsman, Anna had answered, "Nellie and John!" but that could not be, for the latter had imposed upon himself the penance of waiting a whole year ere he spoke to Nellie of that which lay nearest his heart, and in order the better to keep his vow, he had gone from home, first winning from her the promise that she would not become engaged until his return. And now, when he learned of his sister's request, he refused to come, saying, "if she would make such a consummate fool of herself, he did not wish to see her."

So Carrie and Durward were substituted, and as this arrangement brought the latter occasionally to the house, 'Lena had opportunities of asking him if there had yet come any answer to her letter; and much oftener than he would otherwise have done, Durward went down to Frankfort, for he felt that it was no unimportant matter which thus deeply interested 'Lena. At last, the day before the bridal came, Durward had gone to the city, and in a state of great excitement 'Lena awaited his return, watching with a trembling heart as the sun went down behind the western hills. Slowly the hours dragged on, and many a time she stole out in the deep darkness to listen, but there was nothing to be heard save the distant cry of the night-owl, and she was about retracing her steps for the fifth time, when from behind a clump of rose-bushes started a little dusky form, which whispered softly, "Is you Miss 'Leny?"

Repressing the scream which came near escaping her lips, 'Lena answered, "Yes; what do you want?" while at the same moment she recognized a little hunch back belonging to General Fontaine.

"Marster Everett tell me to fotch you this, and wait for the answer," said the boy, passing her a tiny note.

"Master Everett! Is he here?" she exclaimed, catching the note and re-entering the house, where by the light of the hall lamp she read what he had written.

It was very short, but it told all--how he had written again and again, receiving no answer, and was about coming himself when a severe illness prevented. The marriage, he said, was that of his uncle, for whom he was named, and who had in truth gone on to Washington, the home of his second wife. It closed by asking tier to meet him, with Anna, on one of the arbor bridges at midnight. Hastily tearing a blank leaf from a book which chanced to be lying in the hall, 'Lena wrote, "We will be there," and giving it to the negro, bade him hasten back.

There was no longer need to wait for Durward, who, if he got no letter, was not to call, and trembling in every nerve, 'Lena sought her chamber, there to consider what she was next to do. For some time past Carrie had occupied a separate room from Anna, who, she said disturbed her with her late hours and restless turnings, so 'Lena's part seemed comparatively easy. Waiting until the house was still, she entered Anna's room, finding her, as she had expected, at her old place by the open window, her head resting upon the sill, and when she approached nearer, she saw that she was asleep.

"Let her sleep yet awhile," said she; "it will do her good."

In the room adjoining lay the bridal dress, and 'Lena's first impulse was to trample it under her feet, but passing it with a shudder, she hastily collected whatever she thought Anna would most need. These she placed in a small-sized trunk, and then knowing it was done, she approached her cousin, who seemed to be dreaming, for she murmured the name of "Malcolm."

"He is here, love--he has come to save you," she whispered, while Anna, only partially aroused, gazed at her so vacantly, that 'Lena's heart stood still with fear lest the poor girl's reason were wholly gone. "Anna, Anna," she said, "awake; Malcolm is here--in the garden, where you must meet him--come."

"Malcolm is married," said Anna, in a whisper--married--and my bridal dress is in there, all looped with flowers; would you like to see it?"

"Our Father in heaven help me," cried 'Lena, clasping her hands in anguish, while her tears fell like rain on Anna's upturned face.

This seemed to arouse her, for in a natural tone she asked why 'Lena wept. Again and again 'Lena repeated to her that Malcolm had come--that he was not married--that he had come for her; and as Anna listened, the torpor slowly passed away--the wild light in her eyes grew less bright, for it was quenched by the first tears she had shed since the shadow fell upon her; and when 'Lena produced the note, and she saw it was indeed true, the ice about her heart was melted, and in choking, long-drawn sobs, her pent-up feelings gave way, as she saw the gulf whose verge she had been treading. Crouching at 'Lena's feet, she kissed the very hem of her garments, blessing her as her preserver, and praying heaven to bless her, also.

It was the work of a few moments to array her in her traveling dress, and then very cautiously 'Lena led her down the stairs, and out into the open air.

"If I could see father once," said Anna; but such an act involved too much danger, and with one lingering, tearful look at her old home, she moved away, supported by 'Lena, who rather dragged than led her over the graveled walk.

As they approached the arbor bridge, they saw the glimmering light of a lantern, for the night was intensely dark, and in a moment Anna was clasped in the arms which henceforth were to shelter her from the storms of life. Helpless as an infant she lay, while 'Lena, motioning the negro who was in attendance to follow her, returned to the house for the trunk, which was soon safely deposited in the carriage at the gate.

"Words cannot express what I owe you," said Malcolm, when he gave her his hand at parting, "but of this be assured, so long as I live you have in me a friend and brother." Turning back for a moment, he added, "This flight is, I know, unnecessary, for I could prevent to-morrow's expected event in other ways than this, but revenge is sweet, and I trust I am excusable for taking it in my own way."

Anna could not speak, but the look of deep gratitude which beamed from her eyes was far more eloquent than words. Upon the broad piazza 'Lena stood until the last faint sound of the carriage wheels died away; then, weary and worn, she sought her room, locking 'Anna's door as she passed it, and placing the key in her pocket. Softly she crept to bed by the side of her slumbering grandmother, and with a fervent prayer for the safety of the fugitives, fell asleep.

CHAPTER XXX.
THE RESULT.

The loud ringing of the breakfast-bell aroused 'Lena from her heavy slumber, and with a vague consciousness of what had transpired the night previous, she at first turned wearily upon her pillow, wishing it were not morning; but soon remembering all, she sprang up, and after a hasty toilet, descended to the breakfast-room, where another chair was vacant, another face was missing. Without any suspicion of the truth, Mrs. Livingstone spoke of Anna's absence, saying she presumed the poor girl was tired and sleepy, and this was admitted as an excuse for her tardiness. But when breakfast was over and she still did not appear, Corinda was sent to call her, returning soon with the information that "she'd knocked and knocked, but Miss Anna would not answer, and when she tried the door she found it locked."

Involuntarily Mr. Livingstone glanced at 'Lena; whose face wore a scarlet hue as she hastily quitted the table. With a presentiment of something, he himself started for Anna's room; followed by his wife and Carrie, while 'Lena, half-way up the stairs, listened breathlessly for the result. It was useless knocking for admittance, for there was no one within to bid them enter, and with a powerful effort Mr. Livingstone burst the lock. The window was open, the lamp was still burning, emitting a faint, sickly odor; the bed was undisturbed, the room in confusion, and Anna was gone. Mrs. Livingstone's eye took in all this at a glance, but her husband saw only the latter, and ere he was aware of what he did, a fervent "Thank heaven," escaped him.

"She's gone--run away--dead, maybe," exclaimed Mrs. Livingstone, wringing her hands in unfeigned distress, and instinctively drawing nearer to her husband for comfort.

By this time 'Lena had ventured into the room, and turning toward her, Mr. Livingstone said, very gently, "'Lena, where is our child?"

"In Ohio, I dare say, by this time, as she took the night train at Midway for Cincinnati," said 'Lena, thinking she might as well tell the whole at once.

"In Ohio!" shrieked Mrs. Livingstone, fiercely grasping 'Lena's arm. "What has she gone to Ohio for? Speak, ingrate, for you have done the deed--I am sure of that!"

"It was Mr. Everett's wish to return home that way I believe," coolly answered 'Lena, without quailing in the least from the eyes bent so angrily upon her.

Instantly Mrs. Livingstone's fingers loosened their grasp, while her face grew livid with mingled passion and fear. Her fraud was discovered--her stratagem had failed--and she was foiled in this, her second darling scheme. But she was yet to learn what agency 'Lena had in the matter, and this information her husband obtained for her. There was no anger in the tones of his voice when he asked his niece to explain the mystery, else she might not have answered, for 'Lena could not be driven. Now, however, she felt that he had a right to know, and she told him all she knew; what she had done herself and why she had done it; that General Fontaine, to whom Malcolm had gone in his trouble, had kindly assisted him by lending both servants and carriage; but upon the intercepted letters she could throw no light.

"'Twas a cursed act, and whoever was guilty of it is unworthy the name of either man or woman," said Mr. Livingstone, while his eye rested sternly upon his wife.

She knew that he suspected her, but he had no proof, and resolving to make the best of the matter, she, too, united with him in denouncing the deed, wondering who could have done it, and meanly suggesting Maria Fontaine, a pupil of Mr. Everett's, who had, at one time, felt a slight preference for him. But this did not deceive her husband--neither did it help her at all in the present emergency. The bride was gone, and already she felt the tide of scandal and gossip which she knew would be the theme of the entire neighborhood. Still, if her own shameful act was kept a secret she could bear it, and it must be. No one knew of it except Captain Atherton and Caesar, the former of whom would keep his own counsel, while fear of a passport down the river, the negroes' dread, would prevent the latter from telling.

Accordingly, her chagrin was concealed, and affecting to treat the whole matter as a capital joke, worthy of being immortalized in romance, she returned to her room, and hastily writing a few lines, rang the bell for Caesar who soon appeared, declaring that "as true as he lived and breathed and drew the breath of life, he'd done gin miss every single letter afore handin' 'em to anybody else."

"Shut your mouth and mind you keep it shut, or you'll find yourself in New Orleans," was Mrs. Livingstone's very lady-like response, as she handed him the note, bidding him take it to Captain Atherton.

For some reason or other the captain this morning was exceedingly restless, walking from room to room, watching the clock, then the sun, and finally, in order to pass the time away, trying on his wedding suit, to see how he was going to look! Perfectly satisfied with his appearance, he was in imagination going through the ceremony, and had just inclined his head in token that he would take Anna for his wife, when Mrs. Livingstone's note was handed him. At first he could hardly believe the evidence of his own eyes.

Anna gone!--run away with Mr. Everett! It could not be, and sinking into a chair, he felt, as he afterwards expressed it, "mighty queer and shaky."

But Mrs. Livingstone had advised him to put a bold face on it, and this, upon second thought, he determined to do. Hastily changing his dress, now useless, he mounted his steed, and was soon on his way toward Maple Grove, a new idea dawning upon his mind, and ere his arrival, settling itself into a fixed purpose. From Aunt Martha he had heard of 'Lena's strange visit, and he now remembered the many times she had tried to withdraw him from Anna, appropriating him to herself for hours. The captain's vanity was wonderful. Sunnyside needed a mistress--he needed a wife, 'Lena was poor--perhaps she liked him--and if so there might be a wedding, after all. She was beautiful, and would sustain the honors of his house with a better grace, he verily believed, than Anna! Full of these thoughts, he reached Maple Grove, where he found Durward, to whom Mrs. Livingstone had detailed the whole circumstance, dwelling long upon 'Lena's meddling propensities, and charging the whole affair upon her.

"But she knew what she was about--she had an object in view, undoubtedly," she added, glad of an opportunity to give vent to her feelings against 'Lena.

"Pray, what was her object?" asked Durward, and Mrs. Livingstone replied,

"I told you once that 'Lena was ambitious, and I have every reason to believe she would willingly marry Captain Atherton, notwithstanding he is so much older."

She forgot that there was the same disparity between the captain and Anna as between him and 'Lena, but Durward did not, and with a derisive smile he listened, while she proceeded to give her reasons for thinking that a desire to supplant Anna was the sole object which 'Lena had in view, for what else could have prompted that midnight ride to Sunnyside. Again Durward smiled, but before he could answer, the bride-groom elect stood before them, looking rather crestfallen, but evidently making a great effort to appear as usual.

"And so the bird has flown?" said he, "Well, it takes a Yankee, after all, to manage a case, but how did he find it out?"

Briefly Mrs. Livingstone explained to him Lena's agency in the matter, omitting, this time, to impute to her the same motive which she had done when stating the case to Durward.

"So 'Lena is at the bottom of it?" said he, rubbing his little fat, red hands. "Well, well, where is she? I'd like to see her."

"Corinda, tell 'Lena she is wanted in the parlor," said Mrs. Livingstone, while Durward, not wishing to witness the interview, arose to go, but Mrs. Livingstone urged him so hard to stay, that he at last resumed his seat on the sofa by the side of Carrie.

"Captain Atherton wishes to question you concerning the part you have taken in this elopement," said Mrs. Livingstone, sternly, as 'Lena appeared in the doorway.

"No, I don't," said the captain, gallantly offering 'Lena a chair. "My business with Miss Rivers concerns herself."

"I am here, sir, to answer any proper question," said 'Lena, proudly, at the same time declining the proffered seat.

"There's an air worthy of a queen," thought the captain, and determining to make his business known at once, he arose, and turning toward Mrs. Livingstone, Durward and Carrie, whom he considered his audience, he commenced: "What I am about to say may seem strange, but the fact is, I want a wife. I've lived alone long enough. I waited for Anna eighteen years, and now's she gone. Everything is in readiness for the bridal; the guests are invited; nothing wanting but the bride.

Now if I could find a substitute."

"Not in me," muttered Carrie, drawing nearer to Durward, while with a sarcastic leer the captain continued: "Don't refuse before you are asked, Miss Livingstone. I do not aspire to the honor of your hand, but I do ask Miss Rivers to be my wife-- here before you all. She shall live like a princess--she and her grandmother both. Come, what do you say? Many a poor girl would jump at the chance."

The rich blood which usually dyed 'Lena's cheek was gone, and pale as the marble mantel against which she leaned, she answered, proudly, "I would sooner die than link my destiny with one who could so basely deceive my cousin, making her believe it was her betrothed husband whom he saw in Washington instead of his uncle! Marry you? Never, if I beg my bread from door to door!"

"Noble girl!" came involuntarily from the lips of Durward, who had held his breath for her answer, and who now glanced triumphantly at Mrs. Livingstone, whose surmises were thus proved incorrect.

The captain's self-pride was touched, that a poor, humble girl should refuse him with his half million. A sense of the ridiculous position in which he was placed maddened him, and in a violent rage he replied, "You won't, hey? What under heavens have you hung around me so for, sticking yourself in between me and Anna when you knew you were not wanted?"

"I did it, sir, at Anna's request, to relieve her--and for nothing else."

"And was it at her request that you went alone to Sunnyside on that dark, rainy night?" chimed in Mrs. Livingstone.

"No, madam," said 'Lena, turning toward her aunt. "I had in vain implored of you to save her from a marriage every way irksome to her, when in her right mind, but you would not listen, and I resolved to appeal to the captain's better nature. In this I failed, and then I wrote to Mr. Everett, with the result which you see."

In her first excitement Mrs. Livingstone had forgotten to ask who was the bearer of 'Lena's letter, but remembering it now, she put the question. 'Lena would not implicate Durward without his permission, but while she hesitated, he answered for her, "I carried that letter, Mrs. Livingstone, though I did not then know its nature. Still if I had, I should have done the same, and the event has proved that I was right in so doing."

"Ah, indeed!" said the captain growing more and more nettled and disagreeable. "Ah, indeed! Mr. Bellmont leagued with Miss Rivers against me. Perhaps she would not so bluntly refuse an offer coming from you, but I can tell you it won't sound very well that the Hon. Mrs. Bellmont once rode four miles alone in the night to visit a bachelor. Ha! ha! Miss 'Lena; better have submitted to my terms at once, for don't you see I have you in my power?"

"And if you ever use that power to her disadvantage you answer for it to me; do you understand?" exclaimed Durward, starting up and confronting Captain Atherton, who, the veriest coward in the world, shrank from the flashing of Durward's eye, and meekly answered, "Yes, yes--yes, yes, I won't, I won't. I don't want to fight. I like 'Lena. I don't blame Anna for running away if she didn't want me--but it's left me in a deuced mean scrape, which I wish you'd help me out of."

Durward saw that the captain was in earnest, and taking his proffered hand, promised to render him any assistance in his power, and advising him to be present himself in the evening, as the first meeting with his acquaintances would thus be over. Upon reflection, the captain concluded to follow this advice, and when evening arrived and with it those who had not heard the news, he was in attendance, together with Durward, who managed the whole affair so skillfully that the party passed off quite pleasantly, the disappointed guests playfully condoling with the deserted bridegroom, who received their jokes with a good grace, wishing himself, meantime, anywhere but there.

That night, when the company were gone and all around was silent, Mrs. Livingstone watered her pillow with the first tears she had shed for her youngest born, whom she well knew she had driven from home, and when her husband asked what they should do, she answered with a fresh burst of tears, "Send for Anna to come back."

"And Malcolm, too?" queried Mr. Livingstone, knowing it was useless to send for one without the other.

"Yes, Malcolm too. There's room for both," said the weeping mother, feeling how every hour she should miss the little girl, whose presence had in it so much of sunlight and joy.

But Anna would not return. Away to the northward, in a fairy cottage overhung with the wreathing honeysuckle and the twining grape-vine, where the first summer flowers were blooming and the song-birds were caroling all the day long, her home was henceforth to be, and though the letter which contained her answer to her father's earnest appeal was stained and blotted, it told of perfect happiness with Malcolm, who kissed away her tears as she wrote, "Tell mother I cannot come."

CHAPTER XXXI.
MORE CLOUDS.

Since the morning when Durward had so boldly avowed himself 'Lena's champion, her health and spirits began to improve. That she was not wholly indifferent to him she had every reason to believe, and notwithstanding the strong barrier between them, hope sometimes whispered to her of a future, when all that was now so dark and mysterious should be made plain. But while she was thus securely dreaming, a cloud, darker and deeper than any which had yet overshadowed her, was gathering around her pathway. Gradually had the story of her ride to Captain Atherton's gained circulation, magnifying itself as it went, until at last it was currently reported that at several different times had she been seen riding away from Sunnyside at unseasonable hours of the night, the time varying from nine in the evening to three in the morning according to the exaggerating powers of the informer.

But few believed it, and yet such is human nature, that each and every one repeated it to his or her neighbor, until at last it reached Mrs. Graham, who, forgetting the caution of her son, said, with a very wise look, that "she was not at all surprised--she had from the first suspected 'Lena, and she had the best of reasons for so doing!"

Of course Mrs. Graham's friend was exceedingly anxious to know what she meant, and by dint of quizzing, questioning and promising never to tell, she at last drew out just enough of the story to know that Mr. Graham had a daguerreotype which looked just like 'Lena, and that Mrs. Graham had no doubt whatever that she was in the habit of writing to him. This of course was repeated, notwithstanding the promise of secrecy, and many of the neighbors suddenly remembered some little circumstance trivial in itself, but all going to swell the amount of evidence against poor 'Lena, who, unconscious of the gathering storm, did not for a time observe the sidelong glances cast toward her whenever she appeared in public.

Erelong, however, the cool nods and distant manners of her acquaintances began to attract her attention, causing her to wonder what it all meant. But there was no one of whom she would ask an explanation. John Jr. was gone--Anna was gone--and to crown all, Durward, too, left the neighborhood just as the first breath of scandal was beginning to set the waves of gossip in motion. In his absence, Mrs. Graham felt no restraint, whatever, and all that she knew, together with many things she didn't know, she told, until it became a matter of serious debate whether 'Lena ought not to be cut entirely. Mrs. Graham and her clique decided in the affirmative, and when Mrs. Fontaine, who was a weak woman, wholly governed by public opinion, gave a small party for her daughter Maria, 'Lena was purposely omitted. Hitherto she had been greatly petted and admired by both Maria and her mother, and she felt the slight sensibly, the more so, as Carrie darkly hinted that girls who could not behave themselves must not associate with respectable people. "'Leny not invited!" said Mrs. Nichols, espousing the cause of her granddaughter. "What's to pay, I wonder? Miss Fontaine and the gineral, too, allus appeared to think a sight on her."

"I presume the general does now," answered Mrs. Livingstone, "but it's natural that Mrs. Fontaine should feel particular about the reputation of her daughter's associates."

"And ain't 'Leny's reputation as good as the best on 'em," asked Mrs. Nichols, her shriveled cheeks glowing with insulted pride.

"It's the general opinion that it might be improved," was Mrs. Livingstone's haughty answer, as she left her mother-in-law to her own reflections.

"It'll kill her stone dead," thought Mrs. Nichols, revolving in her own mind the propriety of telling 'Lena what her aunt had said. "It'll kill her stone dead, and I can't tell her. Mebby it'll blow over pretty soon."

That afternoon several ladies, who were in the habit of calling upon 'Lena, came to Maple Grove, but not one asked for her, and with her eyes and ears now sharpened, she fancied that once, as she was passing the parlor door, she heard her own name coupled with that of Mr. Graham. A startling light burst upon her, and staggering to her room, she threw herself, half fainting, upon the bed, where an hour afterwards she was found by Aunt Milly.

The old negress had also heard the story in its most aggravated form, and readily divining the cause of 'Lena's grief, attempted to console her, telling her "not to mind what the good-for-nothin' critters said; they war only mad 'cause she's so much handsomer and trimmer built."

"You know, then," said 'Lena, lifting her head from the pillow. "You know what it is; so tell me, for I shall die if I remain longer in suspense."

"Lor' bless the child," exclaimed old Milly, "to think she's the very last one to know, when it's been common talk more than a month!"

"What's been common talk? What is it?" demanded 'Lena; and old Milly, seating herself upon a trunk, commenced: "Why, honey, hain't you hearn how you done got Mr. Graham's pictur and gin him yourn 'long of one of them curls--how he's writ and you've writ, and how he's gone off to the eends of the airth to get rid on you--and how you try to cotch young Mas'r Durward, who hate the sight on you--how you waylay him one day, settin' on a rock out by the big gate--and how you been seen mighty nigh fifty times comin' home afoot from Captain Atherton's in the night, rainin' thunder and lightnin' hard as it could pour--how after you done got Miss Anna to 'lope, you ax Captain Atherton to have you, and git mad as fury 'cause he 'fuses--and how your mother warn't none too likely, and a heap more that I can't remember--hain't you heard of none on't?"

"None, none," answered 'Lena, while Milly continued, "It's a sin and shame for quality folks that belong to the meetin' to pitch into a poor 'fenseless girl and pick her all to pieces. Reckon they done forgot what our Heabenly Marster told 'em when he lived here in old Kentuck, how they must dig the truck out of thar own eyes afore they go to meddlin' with others; but they never think of him these days, 'cept Sundays, and then as soon as meetin' is out they done git together and talk about you and Mas'r Graham orfully. I hearn 'em last Sunday, I and Miss Fontaine's cook, Cilly, and if they don't quit it, thar's a heap on us goin' to leave the church!"

'Lena smiled in spite of herself, and when Milly, who arose to leave the room, again told her not to care, as all the blacks were for her, she felt that she was not utterly alone in her wretchedness. Still, the sympathy of the colored people alone could not help her, and dally matters grew worse, until at last even Nellie Douglass's faith was shaken, and 'Lena's heart died within her as she saw in her signs of neglect. Never had Mr. Livingstone exchanged a word with her upon the subject, but the reserve with which he treated her plainly indicated that he, too, was prejudiced, while her aunt and Carrie let no opportunity pass of slighting her, the latter invariably leaving the room if she entered it. On one such occasion, in a state bordering almost on distraction 'Lena flew back to her own chamber, where to her great surprise, she found her uncle in close conversation with her grandmother, whose face told the pain his words were inflicting. 'Lena's first impulse was to fall at his feet and implore his protection, but he prevented her by immediately leaving the room.

"Oh, grandmother, grandmother," she cried, "help me, or I shall die."

In her heart Mrs. Nichols believed her guilty, for John had said so--he would not lie; and to 'Lena's touching appeal for sympathy, she replied, as she rocked to and fro, "I wish you had died, 'Leny, years and years ago."

'Twas the last drop in the brimming bucket, and with the wailing cry, "God help me now--no one else can," the heart-broken girl fell fainting to the floor, while in silent agony Mrs. Nichols hung over her, shouting for help.

Both Mrs. Livingstone and Carrie refused to come, but at the first call Aunt Milly hastened to the room. "Poor sheared lamb," said she, gathering back the thick, clustering curls which shaded 'Lena's marble face, "she's innocent as the new-born baby."

"Oh, if I could think so," said grandma; but she could not, and when the soft brown eyes again unclosed, and eagerly sought hers, they read distrust and doubt, and motioning her grandmother away, 'Lena said she would rather be alone.

Many and bitter were the thoughts which crowded upon her as she lay there watching the daylight fade from the distant hills, and musing of the stern realities around her. Gradually her thoughts assumed a definite purpose; she would go away from a place where she was never wanted, and where she now no longer wished to stay. Mr. Everett had promised to be her friend, and to him she would go. At different intervals her uncle and cousin had given her money to the amount of twenty dollars, which was still in her possession, and which she knew would take her far on her road.

With 'Lena to resolve was to do, and that night, when sure her grandmother was asleep, she arose and hurriedly made the needful preparations for her flight.

Unlike most aged people, Mrs. Nichols slept soundly, and 'Lena had no fears of waking her. Very stealthily she moved around the room, placing in a satchel, which she could carry upon her arm, the few things she would need. Then, sitting down by the table, she wrote:

"DEAR GRANDMA: When you read this I shall be gone, for I cannot longer stay where all look upon me as a wretched, guilty thing. I am innocent, grandma, as innocent as my angel mother when they dared to slander her, but you do not believe it, and that is the hardest of all. I could have borne the rest, but when you, too, doubted me, it broke my heart, and now I am going away. Nobody will care-- nobody will miss me but you.

"And now dear, dear grandma, it costs me more pain to write than it will you to read

"'LENA'S LAST GOOD-BYE"

All was at length ready, and then bending gently over the wrinkled face so calmly sleeping, 'Lena gazed through blinding tears upon each lineament, striving to imprint it upon her heart's memory, and wondering if they would ever meet again. The hand which had so often rested caressingly upon her young head, was lying outside the counterpane, and with one burning kiss upon it she turned away, first placing the lamp by the window, where its light, shining upon her from afar, would be the last thing she could see of the home she was leaving.

The road to Midway, the nearest railway station, was well known to her, and without once pausing, lest her courage should fail her, she pressed forward. The distance which she had to travel was about three and a half miles, and as she did not dare trust herself in the highway, she struck into the fields, looking back as long as the glimmering light from the window could be seen, and then when that home star had disappeared from view, silently imploring aid from Him who alone could help her now. She was in time for the cars, and, though the depot agent looked curiously at her slight, shrinking figure, he asked no questions, and when the train moved rapidly away, 'Lena looked out upon the dark, still night, and felt that she was a wanderer in the world.

CHAPTER XXXII.
REACTION.

The light of a dark, cloudy morning shone faintly in at the window of Grandma Nichols's room, and roused her from her slumber. On the pillow beside her rested no youthful head--there was no kind voice bidding her "good-morrow"--no gentle hand ministering to her comfort--for 'Lena was gone, and on the table lay the note, which at first escaped Mrs. Nichols's attention. Thinking her granddaughter had arisen early and gone before her, she attempted to make her own toilet, which was nearly completed, when her eye caught the note. It was directed to her, and with a dim foreboding she: took it up, reading that her child was gone--gone from those who should have sustained her in her hour of trial, but who, instead, turned against her, crushing her down, until in a state of desperation she had fled. It was in vain that the breakfast-bell rang out its loud summons. Grandma did not heed it; and when Corinda came up to seek her, she started back in affright at the scene before her. Mrs. Nichols's cap was not yet on, and her thin gray locks fell around her livid face as she swayed from side to side, moaning at intervals, "God forgive me that I broke her heart."

The sound of the opening door aroused her, and looking up she said, pointing toward the vacant bed, "'Leny's gone; I've killed her."

Corinda waited for no more, but darting through the hall and down the stairs, she rushed into the dining-room, announcing the startling news that "old miss had done murdered Miss 'Lena, and hid her under the bed!"

"What will come next!" exclaimed Mrs. Livingstone, following her husband to his mother's room where a moment sufficed to explain the whole.

'Lena was gone, and the shock had for a time unsettled the poor old lady's reason. The sight of his mother's distress aroused all the better nature of Mr. Livingstone, and tenderly soothing her, he told her that 'Lena should be found--he would go for her himself. Carrie, too, was touched, and with unwonted kindness she gathered up the scattered locks, and tying on the muslin cap, placed her hand for an instant on the wrinkled brow.

"Keep it there; it feels soft, like 'Leny's," said Mrs. Nichols, the tears gushing out at this little act of sympathy.

Meantime, Mr. Livingstone, after a short consultation with his wife, hurried off to the neighbors, none of whom knew aught of the fugitive, and all of whom offered their assistance in searching. Never once did it occur to Mr. Livingstone that she might have taken the cars, for that he knew would need money, and he supposed she had none in her possession. By a strange coincidence, too, the depot agent who sold her the ticket, left the very next morning for Indiana, where he had been intending to go for some time, and where he remained for more than a week, thus preventing the information which he could otherwise have given concerning her flight. Consequently, Mr. Livingstone returned each night, weary and disheartened, to his home, where all the day long his mother moaned and wept, asking for her 'Lena.

At last, as day after day went by and brought no tidings of the wanderer, she ceased to ask for her, but whenever a stranger came to the house, she would whisper softly to them, "'Leny's dead. I killed her; did you know it?" at the same time passing to them the crumpled note, which she ever held in her hand.

'Lena was a general favorite in the neighborhood which had so recently denounced her, and when it became known that she was gone, there came a reaction, and those who had been the most bitter against her now changed their opinion, wondering how they could ever have thought her guilty. The stories concerning her visits to Captain Atherton's were traced back to their source, resulting in exonerating her from all blame, while many things, hitherto kept secret, concerning Anna's engagement, were brought to light, and 'Lena was universally commended for her efforts to save her cousin from a marriage so wholly unnatural. Severely was the captain censured for the part he had taken in deceiving Anna, a part which he frankly confessed, while he openly espoused the cause of the fugitive.

Mrs. Livingstone, on the contrary, was not generous enough to make a like confession. Public suspicion pointed to her as the interceptor of Anna's letters, and though she did not deny it, she wondered what that had to do with 'Lena, at the same time asking "how they expected to clear up the Graham affair."

This was comparatively easy, for in the present state of feeling the neighborhood were willing to overlook many things which had before seemed dark and mysterious, while Mrs. Graham, for some most unaccountable reason, suddenly retracted almost everything she had said, acknowledging that she was too hasty in her conclusions, and evincing for the missing girl a degree of interest perfectly surprising to Mrs. Livingstone, who looked on in utter astonishment, wondering what the end would be. About this time Durward returned, greatly pained at the existing state of things. In Frankfort, where 'Lena's flight was a topic of discussion, he had met with the depot agent, who was on his way home, and who spoke of the young girl whose rather singular manner had attracted his attention. This was undoubtedly 'Lena, and after a few moments' conversation with his mother, Durward announced his intention of going after her, at least as far as Rockford, where he fancied she might have gone.

To his surprise his mother made no objection, but her manner seemed so strange that he at last asked what was the matter.

"Nothing--nothing in particular," said she, "only I've been thinking it all over lately, and I've come to the conclusion that perhaps 'Lena is innocent after all."

Oh, how eagerly Durward caught at her words, interrupting her almost before she had finished speaking, with, "Do you know anything? Have you heard anything?"

She had *heard--she* did know; but ere she could reply, the violent ringing of the door-bell, and the arrival of visitors, prevented her answer. In a perfect fever of excitement Durward glanced at his watch. If he waited long, he would be too late for the cars, and with a hasty adieu he left the parlor, turning back ere he reached the outer door, and telling his mother he must speak with her alone. If Mrs. Graham had at first intended to divulge what she knew, the impulse was now gone, and to her son's urgent request that she should disclose what she knew, she replied, "It isn't much--only your father has another daguerreotype, the counterpart of the first one. He procured it in Cincinnati, and 'Lena I know was not there."

"Is that all?" asked Durward, in a disappointed tone.

"Why no, not exactly. I have examined both pictures closely, and I do not think they resemble 'Lena as much as we at first supposed. Possibly it might have been some one else, her mother, may be," and Mrs. Graham looked earnestly at her son, who rather impatiently answered, "Her mother died years ago."

At the same time he walked away, pondering upon what he had heard, and hoping, half believing, that 'Lena would yet be exonerated from all blame. For a moment Mrs. Graham gazed after him, regretting that she had not told him all, but thinking there was time enough yet, and remembering that her husband had said she might wait until his return, if she chose, she went back to the parlor while Durward kept on his way.

CHAPTER XXXIII.
THE WANDERER.

Fiercely the noontide blaze of a scorching July sun was falling upon the huge walls of the "Laurel Hill Sun," where a group of idlers were lounging on the long, narrow piazza, some niching into still more grotesque carving the rude, unpainted railing, while others, half reclining on one elbow, shaded their eyes with their old slouch hats, as they gazed wistfully toward the long hill, eager to catch the first sight of the daily stage which was momentarily expected.

"Jerry is late, to-day--but it's so plaguy hot he's favorin' his hosses, I guess," said the rosy-faced landlord, with that peculiar intonation which stamped him at once a genuine Yankee.

"A watched pot never biles," muttered one of the loungers, who regularly for fifteen years had been at his post, waiting for the stage, which during all that time had brought him neither letter, message, friend, nor foe.

But force of habit is everything, and after the very wise saying recorded above, he resumed his whittling, never again looking up until the loud blast of the driver's horn was heard on the distant hill-top, where the four weary, jaded horses were now visible. It was the driver's usual custom to blow his horn from the moment he appeared on the hill, until with a grand flourish he reined his panting steeds before the door of the inn. But this time there was one sharp, shrill sound, and then all was still, the omission eliciting several remarks not very complimentary to the weather, which was probably the cause of "Jerry's" unwonted silence. Very slowly the vehicle came on, the horses never leaving a walk, and the idler of fifteen years' standing, who for a time had suspended his whittling, "wondered what was to pay."

A nearer approach revealed three or four male passengers, all occupied with a young lady, who, on the back seat, was carefully supported by one of her companions.

"A sick gal, I guess. Wonder if the disease is catchin'?" said the whittler, standing back several paces and looking over the heads of the others, who crowded forward as the stage came up. The loud greeting of the noisy group was answered by Jerry with a low "sh--sh," as he pointed significantly at the slight form which two of the gentlemen were lifting from the coach, asking at the same time if there were a physician near.

"What's the matter on her? Hain't got the cholery, has she," said the landlord, who, having hallooed to his wife to "fetch up her vittles," now appeared on the piazza ready to welcome his guests.

At the first mention of cholera, the fifteen years' man vamosed, retreating across the road, and seating himself on the fence under the shadow of the locust trees.

"Who is she, Jerry?" asked the younger of the set, gazing curiously upon the white, beautiful face of the stranger, who had been laid upon the lounge in the common sitting-room.

"Lord only knows," said Jerry, wiping the heavy drops of sweat from his good-humored face; "I found her at the hotel in Livony. She came there in the cars, and said she wanted to go over to 'tother railroad. She was so weak that I had to lift her into the stage as I would a baby, and she ain't much heavier. You orto seen how sweet she smiled when she thanked me, and asked me not to drive very fast, it made her head ache so. Zounds, I wouldn't of trotted the horses if I'd never got here. Jest after we started she fainted, and she's been kinder talkin' strange like ever since. Some of the gentlemen thought I'd better leave her back a piece at Brown's tavern, but I wanted to fetch her here, where Aunt Betsy could nuss her up, and then I can kinder tend to her myself, you know."

This last remark called forth no answering joke, for Jerry's companions all knew his kindly nature, and it was no wonder to them that his sympathies were so strongly enlisted for the fair girl thus thrown upon his protection. It was a big, noble heart over which Jerry Langley buttoned his driver's coat, and when the physician who had arrived pronounced the lady too ill to proceed any further, he called aside the fidgety landlord, whose peculiarities he well knew, and bade him "not to fret and stew, for if the gal hadn't money, Jerry Langley was good for a longer time than she would live, poor critter;" and he wiped a tear away, glancing, the while, at the burying-ground which lay just across the garden, and thinking how if she died, her grave should be beneath the wide-spreading oak, where often in the summer nights he sat, counting the head-stones which marked the last resting place of the slumbering host, and wondering if death were, as some had said, a long, eternal sleep.

Aunt Betsey, of whom he had spoken, was the landlady, a little dumpy, pleasant-faced, active woman, equally in her element bending over the steaming grid-iron, or smoothing the pillows of the sick-bed, where her powers of nursing had won golden laurels from Others than Jerry Langley. When the news was brought to the kitchen that among the passengers was a sick girl, who was to be left, her first thought, natural to everybody, was, "What shall I do?" while the second, natural to her, was, "Take care of her, of course."

Accordingly, when the dinner was upon the table, she laid aside her broad check apron, substituting in its place a half-worn silk, for Jerry had reported the invalid to be "every inch a lady;" then smoothing her soft, silvery hair with her fat, rosy hands, she repaired to the sitting-room, where she found the driver watching his charge, from whom he kept the buzzing flies by means of his bandana, which he waved to and fro with untiring patience.

"Handsome as a London doll," was her first exclamation, adding, "but I should think she'd be awful hot with them curls, dangling' in her neck! If she's goin' to be sick they'd better be cut off!"

If there was any one thing for which Aunt Betsey Aldergrass possessed a particular passion, it was for hair-cutting, she being barber general for Laurel Hill, which numbered about thirty houses, store and church inclusive, and now when she saw the shining tresses which lay in such profusion upon the pillow, her fingers tingled to their very tips, while she involuntarily felt for her scissors! Very reverentially, as if it were almost sacrilege, Jerry's broad palm was laid protectingly upon the clustering ringlets, while he said, "No, Aunt Betsey, if she dies for't, you shan't touch one of them; 'twould spile her hair, she looks so pretty."

Slowly the long, fringed lids unclosed, and the brown eyes looked up so gratefully at Jerry, that he beat a precipitate retreat, muttering to himself that "he never could stand the gals, anyway, they made his heart thump so!"

"Am I very sick, and can't I go on?" asked the young lady, attempting to rise, but sinking back from extreme weakness.

"Considerable sick, I guess," answered the landlady, taking from a side cupboard an immense decanter of camphor, and passing it toward the stranger. "Considerable sick, and I wouldn't wonder if you had to lay by a day or so. Will they be consarned about you to home, 'cause if they be, my old man'll write."

"I have no home," was the sad answer, to which Aunt Betsey responded in astonishment, "Hain't no home! Where does your marm live?"

"Mother is dead," said the girl, her tears dropping fast upon the pillow.

Instinctively the landlady drew nearer to her, as she asked, "And your pa--where is he?"

"I never saw him," said the girl, while her interrogator continued: "Never saw your pa, and your marm is dead--poor child, what is your name, and where did you come from?"

For a moment the stranger hesitated, and then thinking it better to tell the truth at once, she replied, "My name is 'Lena. I lived with my uncle a great many miles from here, but I wasn't happy. They did not want me there, and I ran away. I am going to my cousin, but I'd rather not tell where, so you will please not ask me."

There was something in her manner which silenced Aunt Betsey, who, erelong, proposed that she should go upstairs and lie down on a nice little bed, where she would be more quiet. But 'Lena refused, saying she should feel better soon.

"Mebby, then, you'd eat a mouffle or two. We've got some roasted pork, and Hetty'll warm over the gravy;" but 'Lena's stomach rebelled at the very thought, seeing which, the landlady went back to the kitchen, where she soon prepared a bowl of gruel, in spite of the discouraging remarks of her husband, who, being a little after the Old Hunks order, cautioned her "not to fuss too much, as gals that run away warn't apt to be plagued with money"

Fortunately, Aunt Betsey's heart covered a broader sphere, and the moment the stage was gone she closed the door to shut out the dust, dropped the green curtains, and drawing from the spare-room a large, stuffed chair, bade 'Lena "see if she couldn't set up a minit." But this was impossible, and all that long, sultry afternoon she lay upon the lounge, holding her aching head, which seemed well-nigh bursting with its weight of pain and thought. "Was it right for her to run away? Ought she not to have stayed and bravely met the worst? Suppose she were to die there alone, among strangers and without money, for her scanty purse was well-nigh drained." These and similar reflections crowded upon her, until her brain grew wild and dizzy, and when at sunset the physician came again he was surprised to find how much her fever had increased.

"She ought not to lie here," said he, as he saw how the loud shouts of the school-boys made her shudder. "Isn't there some place where she can be more quiet?"

At the head of the stairs was a small room, containing a single bed and a window, which last looked out upon the garden and the graveyard beyond. Its furniture was of the plainest kind, it being reserved for more common travelers, and here the landlord said 'Lena must be taken. His wife would far rather have given her the front chamber, which was large, airy and light, but Uncle Tim Aldergrass said "No," squealing out through his little peaked nose that "'twarn't an atom likely he'd ever more'n half git his pay, anyway, and he warn't a goin' to give up the hull house."

"How much more will it be if she has the best chamber," asked Jerry, pulling at Uncle Tim's coattail and leading him aside. "How much will it be, 'cause if 'taint too much, she shan't stay in that eight by nine pen."

"A dollar a week, and cheap at that," muttered Uncle Tim, while Jerry, going out behind the wood-house, counted over his funds, sighing as he found them quite too small to meet the extra, dollar per week, should she long continue ill.

"If I hadn't of fooled so much away for tobacker and things, I shouldn't be so plaguy poor now," thought he, forgetting the many hearts which his hard-earned gains had made glad, for no one ever appealed in vain for help from Jerry Langley, who represented one class of Yankees, while Timothy Aldergrass represented another.

The next morning just as daylight was beginning to be visible, Jerry knocked softly at Aunt Betsey's door, telling her that for more than an hour he'd heard the young lady takin' on, and he guessed she was worse. Hastily throwing on her loose gown Aunt Betsey repaired to 'Lena's room, where she found her sitting up in the bed, moaning, talking, and whispering, while the wild expression of her eyes betokened a disordered brain.

"The Lord help us! she's crazy as a loon. Run for the doctor, quick!" exclaimed Mrs. Aldergrass, and without boot or shoe, Jerry ran off in his stocking-feet, alarming the physician, who immediately hastened to the inn, pronouncing 'Lena's disease to be brain fever, as he had at first feared.

Rapidly she grew worse, talking of her home, which was sometimes in Kentucky and sometimes in Massachusetts, where she said they had buried her mother. At other times she would ask Aunt Betsey to send for Durward when she was dead, and tell him how innocent she was.

"Didn't I tell you there was something wrong?" Uncle Timothy would squeak. "Nobody knows who we are harborin' nor how much 'twill damage the house."

But as day after day went by, and 'Lena's fever raged more fiercely, even Uncle Tim relented, and when she would beg of them to take her home and bury her by the side of Mabel, where Durward could see her grave, he would sigh, "Poor critter, I wish you was to home," but whether this wish was prompted by a sincere desire to please 'Lena, or from a more selfish motive, we are unable to state. One morning, the fifth of 'Lena's illness, she seemed much worse, talking incessantly and tossing from side to side, her long hair floating in wild disorder over her pillow, or streaming down her shoulders. Hitherto Aunt Betsey had restrained her barberic desire, each day arranging the heavy locks, and tucking them under the muslin cap, where they refused to stay. Once the doctor himself had suggested the propriety of cutting them away, adding, though, that they would wait awhile, as it was a pity to lose them.

"Better be cut off than yanked off," said Aunt Betsey, on the morning when 'Lena in her frenzy would occasionally tear out handfulls of her shining hair and scatter it over the floor.

Satisfied that she was doing right, she carefully approached the bedside, and taking one of the curls in her hand, was about to sever it, when 'Lena, divining her intentions, sprang up, and gathering up her hair, exclaimed, "No, no, not these; take everything else, but leave me my curls. Durward thought they were beautiful, and I cannot lose them."

At the side door below, the noonday stage was unloading its passengers, and as the tones of their voices came in at the open window, 'Lena suddenly grew calmer, and assuming a listening attitude, whispered, "Hark! He's come. Don't you hear him?"

But Aunt Betsey heard nothing, except her husband calling her to come down, and leaving 'Lena, who had almost instantly become quiet, to the care of a neighbor, she started for the kitchen, meeting in the lower hall with Hetty, who was showing one of the passengers to a room where he could wash and refresh himself after his dusty ride. As they passed each other, Hetty asked, "Have you clipped her curls?"

"No," answered Mrs. Aldergrass, "she wouldn't let me touch 'em, for she said that Durward, whom she talks so much about, liked 'em, and they mustn't be cut off."

Instantly the stranger, whose elegant appearance both Hetty and her mistress had been admiring, stopped, and turning to the latter, said, "Of whom are you speaking?"

"Of a young girl that came in the stage, sick, five or six days ago," answered Mrs. Aldergrass.

"What is her name, and where does she live?" continued the stranger.

"She calls herself 'Lena, but the 'tother name I don't know, and I guess she lives in Kentucky or Massachusetts."

The young man waited to hear no more, but mechanically followed Hetty to his room, starting and turning pale as a wild, unnatural laugh fell on his ear.

"It is the young lady, sir," said Hetty, observing his agitated manner. "She raves most all the time, and the doctor says she'll die if she don't stop."

The gentleman nodded, and the next moment he was as he wished to be, alone. He had found her then--his lost 'Lena--sick, perhaps dying, and his heart gave one agonized throb as he thought, "What if she should die? Yet why should I wish her to live?" he asked, "when she is as surely lost to me as if she were indeed resting in her grave!"

And still, reason as he would, a something told him that all would yet be well, else, perhaps, he had never followed her. Believing she would stop at Mr. Everett's, he had come on thus far, finding her where he least expected it, and spite of his fears, there was much of pleasure mingled with his pain as he thought how he would protect and care for her, ministering to her comfort, and softening, as far as possible, the disagreeable things which he saw must necessarily surround her. Money, he knew, would purchase almost everything, and if ever Durward Bellmont felt glad that he was rich, it was when he found 'Lena Rivers sick and alone at the not very comfortable inn of Laurel Hill.

As he was entering the dining-room, he saw Jerry--whose long, lank figure and original manner had afforded him much amusement during his ride--handing a dozen or more oranges to Mrs. Aldergrass, saying, as he did so, "They are for Miss 'Lena. I thought mebby they'd taste good, this hot weather, and I ransacked the hull town to find the nicest and best."

For a moment Durward's cheek flushed at the idea of Lena's being cared for by such as Jerry, but the next instant his heart grew warm toward the uncouth driver who, without any possible motive save the promptings of his own kindly nature, had thus thought of the stranger girl. Erelong the stage was announced as ready and waiting, but to the surprise and regret of his fellow-passengers, who had found him a most agreeable traveling companion, Durward said he was not going any further that day.

"A new streak, ain't it?" asked Jerry, who knew he was booked for the entire route; but the young man made no reply, and the fresh, spirited horses soon bore the lumbering vehicle far out of sight, leaving him to watch the cloud of dust which it carried in its train.

Uncle Timothy was in his element, for it was not often that a guest of Durward's appearance honored his house with more than a passing call, and with the familiarity so common to a country landlord, he slapped him on the shoulder, telling him "there was the tallest kind of fish in the Honeoye," whose waters, through the thick foliage of the trees were just discernible, sparkling and gleaming in the bright sunlight.

"I never fish, thank you, sir," answered Durward, while the good-natured landlord continued: "Now you don't say it! Hunt, then, mebby?"

"Occasionally," said Durward, adding, "But my reason for stopping here is of entirely a different nature. I hear there is with you a sick lady. She is a friend of mine, and I am staying to see that she is well attended to."

"Yes, yes," said Uncle Timothy, suddenly changing his opinion of 'Lena, whose want of money had made him sadly suspicious of her. "Yes, yes, a fine gal; fell into good hands, too, for my old woman is the greatest kind of a nuss. Want to see her, don't you?--the lady I mean."

"Not just yet; I would like a few moments' conversation with your wife first," answered Durward.

Greatly frustrated when she learned that the stylish looking gentleman wished to talk with her, Aunt Betsey rubbed her shining face with flour, and donning another cap, repaired to the sitting-room, where she commenced making excuses about herself, the house, and everything else, saying, "'twant what he was used to, she knew, but she hoped he'd try to put up with it."

As soon as he was able to get in a word, Durward proceeded to ask her every particular concerning 'Lena's illness, and whether she would probably recognize him should he venture into her presence,

"Bless your dear heart, no. She hain't known a soul on us these three days. Sometimes she calls me 'grandmother,' and says when she's dead I'll know she's innocent. 'Pears Like somebody has been slanderin' her, for she begs and pleads with Durward, as she calls him, not to believe it. Ain't you the one she means?"

Durward nodded, and Mrs. Aldergrass continued:

"I thought so, for when the stage driv up she was standin' straight in the bed, ravin' and screechin', but the minit she heard your voice she dropped down, and has been as quiet ever since. Will you go up now?"

Durward signified his willingness, and following his landlady, he soon stood in the close, pent-up room where, in an uneasy slumber, 'Lena lay panting for breath, and at intervals faintly moaning in her sleep. She had fearfully changed since last he saw her, and with a groan, he bent over her, murmuring, "My poor 'Lena," while he gently laid his cool, moist hand upon her burning brow. As if there were something soothing in its touch, she quickly placed her little hot, parched hand on his, whispering, "Keep it there. It will make me well."

For a long time he sat by her, bathing her head and carefully removing from her face and neck the thick curls which Mrs. Aldergrass had thought to cut away. At last she awoke, but Durward shrank almost in fear from the wild, bright eyes which gazed so fixedly upon him, for in them was no ray of reason. She called him "John" blessing him for coming, and saying, "Did you tell Durward. Does he know?"

"I am Durward," said he. "Don't you recognize me? Look again."

"No, no," she answered, with a mocking laugh, which made him shudder, it was so unlike the merry, ringing tones he had once loved to hear. "No, no, you are not Durward. He would not look at me as you do. He thinks me guilty."

It was in vain Durward strove to convince her of his identity. She would only answer with a laugh, which grated so harshly on his ear that he finally desisted, and suffered her to think he was her cousin. The smallness of her chamber troubled him, and when Mrs. Aldergrass came up he asked if there was no other apartment where 'Lena would be more comfortable.

"Of course there is," said Aunt Betsy. "There's the best chamber I was goin' to give to you."

"Never mind me," said he. "Let her have every comfort the house affords, and you shall be amply paid."

Uncle Timothy had now no objection to the offer, and the large, airy room with its snowy, draped bed was soon in readiness for the sufferer, who, in one of her wayward moods, absolutely refused to be moved. It was in vain that Aunt Betsey plead, persuaded, and threatened, and at last in despair Durward was called in to try his powers of persuasion.

"That's something more like it," said 'Lena, and when he urged upon her the necessity of her removal, she asked, "Will you go with me?"

"Certainly," said he.

"And stay with me?"

"Certainly."

"Then I'll go," she continued, stretching her arms toward him as a child toward its mother.

A moment more and she was reclining on the soft downy pillows, the special pride of Mrs. Aldergrass, who bustled in and out, while her husband, ashamed of his stinginess, said "they should of moved her afore, only 'twas a bad sign."

During the remainder of the day she seemed more quiet, talking incessantly, it is true, but never raving if Durward were near. If is strange what power he had over her, a word from him sufficing at any time to subdue her when in her most violent fits of frenzy. For two days and nights he watched by her side, never giving himself a moment's rest, while the neighbors looked on, surmising and commenting as people always will. Every delicacy of the season, however costly, was purchased for her comfort, while each morning the flowers which he knew she loved the best were freshly gathered from the different gardens of Laurel Hill, and in broken pitchers, cracked tumblers, and nicked saucers, adorned the room.

At the close of the third day she fell into a heavy slumber, and Durward, worn out and weary, retired to take the rest he so much needed. For a long time 'Lena slept, watched by the physician, who, knowing that the crisis had arrived, waited anxiously for her waking, which came at last, bringing with it the light of returning reason. Dreamily she gazed about the room, and in a voice no longer strong with the excitement of delirium, asked, "Where am I, and how came I here?"

In a few words the physician explained all that was necessary for her to know, and then going for Mrs. Aldergrass, told her of the favorable change in his patient, adding that a sudden shock might still prove fatal. "Therefore," said he, "though I know not in what relation this Mr. Bellmont stands to her, I think it advisable for her to remain awhile in ignorance of his presence. It is of the utmost consequence that she be kept quiet for a few days, at the end of which time she can see him."

All this Aunt Betsey communicated to Durward, who unwilling to do anything which would endanger 'Lena's safety, kept himself aloof, treading softly and speaking low, for as if her hearing were sharpened by disease she more than once, when he was talking in the hall below, started up, listening eagerly; then, as if satisfied that she had been deceived, she would resume her position, while the flush on her cheek deepened as she thought, "Oh, what if it had indeed been he!"

Nearly all the day long he sat just without the door, holding his breath as he caught the faint tones of her voice, and longing for the hour when he could see her, and obtain, if possible, some clue to the mystery attending her and his father. His mother's words, together with what he had heard 'Lena say in her ravings, had tended to convince him that she, at least, might be innocent, and once assured of this, he felt that he would gladly fold her to his bosom, and cherish her there as the choicest of heaven's blessings. All this time 'Lena had no suspicion of his presence, but she wondered at the many luxuries which surrounded her, and once, when Mrs. Aldergrass offered her some choice wine, she asked who it was that supplied her with so many comforts. Aunt Betsey's, forte did not lay in keeping a secret, and rather evasively she replied, "You mustn't ask me too many questions just yet!"

'Lena's suspicions were at once aroused, and for more than an hour she lay thinking--trying to recall something which seamed to her like a dream. At last calling Aunt Betsey to her, she said, "There was somebody here while I was so sick--somebody besides strangers--somebody that stayed with me all the time--who was it?"

"Nobody, nobody--I mustn't tell," said Mrs. Aldergrass, hurriedly, while 'Lena continued, "Was it Cousin John?"

"No, no; don't guess any more," was Mrs. Aldergrass's reply, and 'Lena, clasping her hands together, exclaimed, "Oh, could it he be?"

The words reached Durward's ear, and nothing but a sense of the harm it might do prevented him from going at once to her bedside. That night, at his earnest request, the physician gave him permission to see her in the morning, and Mrs. Aldergrass was commissioned to prepare her for the interview. 'Lena did not ask who it was; she felt that she knew; and the knowledge that he was there--that he had cared for her--operated upon her like a spell, soothing her into the most refreshing slumber she had experienced for many a weary week. With the sun-rising she was awake, but Mrs. Aldergrass, who came in soon after, told her that the visitor was not to be admitted until about ten, as she would by that time have become more composed, and be the better able to endure the excitement of the interview. A natural delicacy prevented 'Lena from objecting to the delay, and, as calmly as possible, she watched Mrs. Aldergrass while she put the room to rights, and then patiently submitted to the arranging of her curls, which during her illness had become matted and tangled. Before eight everything was in readiness, and soon after, worn out by her own exertions, 'Lena again fell asleep.

"How lovely she looks," thought Mrs. Aldergrass. "He shall just have a peep at her," and stepping to the door she beckoned Durward to her side.

Never before had 'Lena, seemed so beautiful to him, and as he looked upon her, he felt his doubts removing, one by one. She was innocent--it could not be otherwise--and very impatiently he awaited the lapse of the two hours which must pass ere he could see her, face to face. At length, as the surest way of killing time, he started out for a walk in a pleasant wood, which skirted the foot of Laurel Hill.

Here for a time we leave him, while in another chapter we speak of an event which, in the natural order of things, should here be narrated.

CHAPTER XXXIV
'LENA'S FATHER.

Two or three days before the morning of which we have spoken, Uncle Timothy, who like many of his profession had been guilty of a slight infringement of the "Maine" liquor law, had been called to answer for the same at the court then in session in the village of Canandaigua, the terminus of the stage route. Altogether too stingy to pay the coach fare, his own horse had carried him out, going for him on the night preceding Durward's projected meeting with 'Lena. On the afternoon of that day the cars from New York brought up several passengers, who being bound for Buffalo, were obliged to wait some hours for the arrival of the Albany train.

Among those who stopped at the same house with Uncle Timothy, was our old acquaintance, Mr. Graham, who had returned from Europe, and was now homeward bound, firmly fixed in his intention to do right at last. Many and many a time, during his travels had the image of a pale, sad face arisen before him, accusing him of so long neglecting to own his child, for 'Lena was his daughter, and she, who in all her bright beauty had years ago gone down to an early grave, was his wife, the wife of his first, and in bitterness of heart he sometimes thought, of his only love. His childhood's home, which was at the sunny south, was not a happy one, for ere he had learned to lisp his mother's name, she had died, leaving him to the guardianship of his father, who was cold, exacting, and tyrannical, ruling his son with a rod of iron, and by his stern, unbending manner increasing the natural cowardice of his disposition. From his mother Harry had inherited a generous, impulsive nature, frequently leading him into errors which his father condemned with so much severity that he early learned the art of concealment, as far, at least, as his father was concerned.

At the age of eighteen he left home for Yale, where he spent four happy years, for the restraints of college life, though sometimes irksome, were preferable far to the dull monotony of his southern home; and when at last he was graduated, and there was no longer an excuse for tarrying, he lingered by the way, stopping at the then village of Springfield, where, actuated by some sudden freak, he registered himself as Harry Rivers, the latter being his middle name. For doing this he had no particular reason, except that it suited his fancy, and Rivers, he thought, was a better name than Graham. Here he met with Helena Nichols, whose uncommon beauty first attracted his attention, and whose fresh, unstudied manners afterward won his love to such an extent, that in an unguarded moment, and without a thought of the result, he married her, neglecting to tell her his real name before their marriage, because he feared she would cease to respect him if she knew he had deceived her, and then afterward finding it harder than ever to confess his fault.

As time wore on, his father's letters, commanding him to return, grew more and more peremptory, until at last he wrote, "I am sick--dying--and if you do not come, I'll cast you off forever."

Harry knew this was no unmeaning threat, and he now began to reap the fruit of his folly. He could not give up Helena, who daily grew dearer to him, neither could he brave the displeasure of his father by acknowledging his marriage, for disinheritance was sure to follow. In this dilemma he resolved to compromise the matter. He would leave Helena awhile; he would visit his father, and if a favorable opportunity occurred, he would confess all; if not, he would return to his wife and do the best he could. But she must be provided for during his absence, and to effect this, he wrote to his father, saying he stood greatly in need of five hundred dollars, and that immediately on its receipt he would start for home. Inconsistent as it seemed with his general character, the elder Mr. Graham was generous with his money, lavishing upon his son all that he asked for, and the money was accordingly sent without a moment's hesitation.

And now Harry's besetting sin, secrecy, came again in action, and instead of manfully telling Helena the truth, he left her privately, stealing away at night, and quieting his conscience by promising himself to reveal all in a letter, which was actually written, but as at the time of its arrival Helena was at home, and the post-master knew of no such person, it was at last sent to Washington with thousands of its companions. The reader already knows how 'Lena's young mother watched for her recreant husband's coming until life and hope died out together, and it is only necessary to repeat that part of the story which relates to Harry, who on his return home found his father much worse than he expected. At his bedside, ministering to his wants, was a young, dashing widow, who prided herself upon being Lady Bellmont. On his death-bed her father had committed her to the guardianship of Mr. Graham, who, strictly honorable in all his dealings, had held his trust until the time of her marriage with a young Englishman.

Unfortunately, as it proved for Harry, and fortunately for Sir Arthur, who had nothing in common with his wife, the latter died within two years after his marriage, leaving his widow and infant son again to the care of Mr. Graham, with whom Lady Bellmont, as she was pleased to call herself, lived at intervals, swaying him whichever way she listed, and influencing him as he had never been influenced before. The secret of this was, that the old man had his eye upon her vast possessions, which he destined for his son, who, ignorant of the honor intended him, had presumed to marry according to the promptings of his heart.

Scarcely was the first greeting over, ere his father at once made known his plans, to which Harry listened with mingled pain and amazement. "Lucy--Lady Bellmont!" said he, "why, she's a mother--a widow--beside being ten years my senior."

"Three years," interrupted his father. "She is twenty-five, you twenty-two, and then as to her being a widow and a mother, the immensity of her wealth atones for that. She is much sought after, but I think she prefers you. She will make you a good wife, and I am resolved to see the union consummated ere I die."

"Never sir, never," answered Harry, in a more decided manner than he had before assumed toward his father. "It is utterly impossible."

Mr. Graham was too much exhausted to urge the matter at that time, but he continued at intervals to harass Harry, until the very sight of Lucy Bellmont became hateful to him. It was not so, however, with the son, the Durward of our story. He was a fine little fellow, whom every one loved, and for hours would Harry amuse himself with him, while his thoughts were with his own wife and child, the latter of whom was to be so strangely connected with the fortunes of the boy at his side. For weeks his father lingered, each day seeming an age to Harry, who, though he did not wish to hasten his father's death, still longed to be away. Twice had he written without obtaining an answer, and he was about making up his mind to start, at all events, when his father suddenly died, leaving him the sole heir of all his princely fortune, and with his latest breath enjoining it upon him to marry Lucy Bellmont, who, after the funeral was over, adverted to it, saying, in her softest tones, "I hope you don't feel obliged to fulfill your father's request."

"Of course not," was Harry's short answer, as he went on with his preparations for his journey, anticipating the happiness he should experience in making Helena the mistress of his luxurious home.

But alas for human hopes. The very morning on which he was intending to start, he was seized with a fever, which kept him confined to his bed until the spring was far advanced. Sooner than he was able he started for Springfield in quest of Helena, learning from the woman whom he had left in charge, that she was dead, and her baby too! The shock was too much for him in his weak state, and for two weeks he was again confined to a sick-bed, sincerely mourning the untimely end of one whom he had truly loved, and whose death his own foolish conduct had hastened.

Soon after their marriage her portrait had been taken by the best artist in the town, and this he determined to procure as a memento of the few happy days he had spent with Helena. But the cottage where he left her was now occupied by strangers, and after many inquiries, he learned that the portrait, together with some of the furniture, had been sold to pay the rent, which became due soon after his departure. His next thought was to visit her parents, but from this his natural timidity shrank. They would reproach him, he thought, with the death of their daughter, whom he had so deeply wronged, and not possessing sufficient courage to meet them face to face, he again started for home, bearing a sad heart, which scarcely again felt a thrill of joy until the morning when he first met with 'Lena, whose exact resemblance to her mother so startled him as to arouse the jealousy of his wife.

It would be both needless and tiresome to enumerate the many ways and means by which Lucy Bellmont sought to ensnare him. Suffice it to say, that she at last succeeded, and he married her, finding in the companionship of her son more real pleasure than he ever experienced in her society. After a time Mrs. Graham, growing weary of Charleston, where her haughty, overbearing manner made her unpopular, besought her husband to remove, which he finally did, going to Louisville, where he remained until the time of his removal to Woodlawn. Fully believing what the old nurse had told him of the death of his wife and child, he had no idea of the existence of the latter, though often in the stillness of night the remembrance of the little girl whom Durward had pointed out to him in the cars, arose before him, haunting him with visions of the past, but it was not until he met her at Maple Grove that he entertained a thought of her being his daughter.

From that time his whole being seemed changed, for there was now an object for which to live. Carefully had he guarded from his wife a knowledge of his first marriage, for he dreaded her sneering reproaches, and he could not hear his beloved Helena's name breathed lightly by one so greatly her inferior. When he saw 'Lena, however, his first impulse was to clasp her in his arms and compel his wife to own her, but day after day went by, and he still delayed, hoping for a more favorable opportunity, which never came. Had he found her in less favorable circumstances, he might have done differently, but seeing only the brightest side of her life, he believed her comparatively happy. She was well educated, accomplished, and beautiful, and so he waited, secure in the fact that he was near to see that no harm should befall her. Once it occurred to him that possibly he might die suddenly, thus leaving his relationship to her a secret forever, and acting upon this thought, he immediately made his will, bequeathing all to 'Lena, whom he acknowledged to be his daughter, adding an explanation of the whole affair, together with a most touching letter to his child, who would never see it until he was dead.

This done, he felt greatly relieved, and each day found some good excuse for still keeping it from his wife, who worried him incessantly concerning his evident preference for 'Lena. Many and many a time he resolved to tell her all, but as often postponed the matter, until, with the broad Atlantic between them, he ventured to write what he could not tell her verbally and, strange to say, the effect upon his wife was far different from what he had expected. She did not faint, for there was no one by to see her, neither did she rave, for there was no one to hear her, but with her usual inconsistency, she blamed her husband for not telling her before. Then came other thoughts of a different nature. She *had helped to impair 'Lena's reputation, and if disgrace attached to her, it would also fall upon her own family. Consequently, as we have seen, she set herself at work to atone, as far as possible, for her conduct. Her husband had given her permission to wait, if she chose, until his return, ere she made the affair public, and as she dreaded the remarks it would necessarily call forth, she resolved to do so. He had advised her to tell 'Lena, but she was gone--no one knew whither, and nervously she waited for some tidings of the wanderer. She was willing to receive 'Lena, but not the grandmother,* she was voted an intolerable nuisance, who should never darken the doors of Woodlawn--never!

Meantime, Mr. Graham had again crossed the ocean, landing in New York, from whence he started for home, meeting, as we have seen, with a detention in Canandaigua, where he accidentally fell in with Uncle Timothy, who, being minus quite a little sum of money on account of his transgression, was lamenting his ill fortune to one of his acquaintances, and threatening to give up tavern keeping if the Maine law wasn't repealed.

"Here," said he, "it has cost me up'ards of fifty dollars, and I'll bet I hain't sold mor'n a barrel, besides what wine that Kentucky chap has bought for his gal, and I suppose they call that nothin', bein' it's for sickness. Why, good Lord, the hull on't was for medicine, or chimistry, or mechanics!"

This reminded his friend to inquire after the sick lady, whose name he did not remember.

"It's 'Lena," answered Uncle Timothy, "'Lena Rivers that dandified chap calls her, and it's plaguy curis to me what she's a runnin' away for, and he a streakin' it through the country arter her; there's mischief summers, so I tell 'em, but that's no consarn of mine so long as he pays down regular."

Mr. Graham's curiosity was instantly aroused, and the moment he could speak to Uncle Timothy alone, he asked what he meant by the sick lady.

In his own peculiar dialect, Uncle Timothy told all he knew, adding, "A relation of yourn, mebby?"

"Yes, yes," said Mr. Graham. "Is it far to Laurel Hill?"

"Better'n a dozen miles! Was you goin' out there?"

Mr. Graham replied in the affirmative, at the same time asking if he could procure a horse and carriage there.

Uncle Timothy never let an opportunity pass for turning a penny, and now nudging Mr. Graham with his elbow, he said, "Them liv'ry scamps'll charge you tew dollars, at the lowest calkerlation. I'm going right out, and will take you for six shillin'. What do you think?"

Mr. Graham's thoughts were not very complimentary to the shrewd Yankee, but keeping his opinion to himself, he replied that he would go, suggesting that they should start immediately.

"In less than five minits. You jest set down while I go to the store arter some jimcracks for the old woman," said Uncle Timothy, starting up the street, which was the last Mr. Graham saw of him for three long hours.

At the end of that time, the little man came stubbing down the walk, making many apologies, and saying "he got so engaged about the darned 'liquor law,' and the putty-heads that made it, that he'd no idee 'twas so late."

On their way home he still continued to discourse on his favorite topic, lamenting that he had voted for the present governor, announcing his intention of "jinin' the Hindews *the fust time they met at Suckerport," a village at the foot of Honeoye lake, and stopping every man whom he knew to belong to that order, to ask if they took a* fee, and if "there was any bedivelment of gridirons *and* goats, such as the Masons and Odd Fellers had!" Being repeatedly assured that the fee was only a dollar, and that the initiatory process was not very painful, he concluded "to go it, provided they'd promise to run him for constable. Office is the hull any of the scallywags jine 'em for, and I may as well go in for a sheer," said he, thinking if he could not have the privilege of selling liquor, he would at least secure the right of arresting those who drank it!

In this way his progress homeward was not very rapid, and the clock had struck ten long ere they reached the inn, which they found still and dark, save the light which was kept burning in 'Lena's room.

"That's her chamber--the young gal's--where you see the candle," said Uncle Timothy, as they drew up before the huge walls of the tavern. "I guess you won't want to disturb her to-night."

"Certainly not," answered Mr. Graham, adding, as he felt a twinge of his inveterate habit of secrecy, "If you'd just as lief, you need not speak of me to the young gentleman; I wish to take him by surprise"--meaning Durward.

There was no particular necessity for this caution, for Uncle Timothy was too much absorbed in his loss to think of anything else, and when his wife asked "who it was that he lighted up to bed," he replied, "A chap that wanted to come out this way, and so rid with me."

Mr. Graham was very tired, and now scarcely had his head pressed the pillow ere he was asleep, dreaming of 'Lena, whose presence was to shed such a halo of sunlight over his hitherto cheerless home. The ringing of the bell next morning failed to arouse him, but when Mrs. Aldergrass, noticing his absence from the table, inquired for him, Uncle Timothy answered, "Never mind, let him sleep--tuckered out, mebby--and you know we allus have a sixpence more for an extra meal!"

About eight Mr. Graham arose, and after a more than usually careful toilet, he sat down to collect his scattered thoughts, for now that the interview was so near, his ideas seemed suddenly to forsake him. From the window he saw Durward depart for his walk, watching him until he disappeared in the dim shadow of the woods.

"I will wait until his return, and let him tell her," thought he, but when a half hour or more went by and Durward did not come, he concluded to go down and ask to see her by himself.

In order to do this, it was necessary for him to pass 'Lena's room, the door of which was ajar. She was awake, and hearing his step, thought it was Mrs. Aldergrass, and called to her. A thrill of exquisite delight ran through his frame at the sound of her voice, and for an instant he debated the propriety of going to her at once. A second call decided him, and in a moment he was at her bedside, clasping her in his arms, and exclaiming, "My precious 'Lena! My daughter! Has nothing ever told you that I am your father, the husband of your angel mother, who lives again in her child-- my child--my 'Lena?"

For a moment 'Lena's brain grew dizzy, and she had well-nigh fainted, when the sound of Mr. Graham's voice brought her back to consciousness. Pressing his lips to her white brow, he said, "Speak to me my daughter. Say that you receive me as your father for such I am."

With lightning rapidity 'Lena's thoughts traversed the past, whose dark mystery was now made plain, and as the thought that it might be so--that it was so-- flashed upon her, she clasped her hands together, exclaiming, "My father! Is it true? You are not deceiving me?"

"Deceive you, darling?--no," said he. "I am your father, and Helena Nichols was my wife."

"Why then did you leave her? Why have you so long left me unacknowledged?" asked 'Lena.

Mr. Graham groaned bitterly. The hardest part was yet to come, but he met it manfully, telling her the whole story, sparing not himself in the least, and ending by asking if, after all this, she could forgive and love him as her father.

Raising herself in bed, 'Lena wound her arms around his neck, and laying her face against his, wept like a little child. He felt that he was sufficiently answered, and holding her closer to his bosom, he pushed back the clustering curls, kissing her again and again, while he said aloud, "I have your answer, dearest one; we will never be parted again."

So absorbed was he in his newly-recovered treasure, that he did not observe the fiery eye, the glittering teeth, and clenched first of Durward Bellmont, who had returned from his walk, and who, in coming up to his, room, had recognized the tones of his father's voice. Recoiling backward a step or two, he was just in time to see 'Lena as she threw herself into Mr. Graham's, arms--in time to hear the tender words of endearment lavished upon her by his father. Staggering backward, he caught at the banister to keep from falling, while a moan of anguish came from his ashen lips. Alone in his room, he grew calmer, though his heart still quivered with unutterable agony as he strode up and down the room, exclaiming, as he had once done before, "I would far rather see her dead than thus--my lost, lost 'Lena!"

Then, in the deep bitterness of his spirit, he cursed his father, whom he believed to be far more guilty than she. "I cannot meet him," thought he; "there is murder at my heart, and I must away ere he knows of my presence."

Suiting the action to the word, he hastened down the stairs, glancing back once, and seeing 'Lena reclining upon his father's arm, while her eyes were raised to his with a sweet, confiding smile, which told of perfect happiness.

"Thank God that I am unarmed, else he could not live," thought he, hurrying into the bar-room, where he placed in Uncle Timothy's hands double the sum due for himself and 'Lena, and then, without a word of explanation, he walked away.

He was a good pedestrian, and preferring solitude in his present state of feeling, he determined to go on foot to Canandaigua, a distance of little more than a dozen miles. Meantime, Mr. Graham was learning from 'Lena the cause of her being there, and though she, as far as possible, softened the fact of his having been accessory to her misfortunes, he felt it none the less keenly, and would frequently interrupt her with the exclamation that it was the result of his cowardice--his despicable habit of secrecy. When she spoke of the curl which his wife had burned, he seemed deeply affected, groaning aloud as he hid his face in his hands,

"And she found it--she burned it," said he; "and it was all I had left of my Helena. I cut it from her head on the morning of my departure, when she lay sleeping, little dreaming of my cruel desertion. But," he added, "I can bear it better now that I have you, her living image, for what she was when last I saw her, you are now."

Their conversation then turned upon Durward, and with the tact he so well knew how to employ, Mr. Graham drew from his blushing daughter a confession of the love she bore him.

"He is worthy of you," said he, while 'Lena, without seeming to heed the remark, said, "I have not seen him yet, but I am expecting him every moment, for he was to visit me this morning."

At this juncture Mrs. Aldergrass, who had been at one of her neighbors', came in, appearing greatly surprised at the sight of the stranger, whom 'Lena quietly introduced as "her father," while Mr. Graham colored painfully as Mrs. Aldergrass, curtsying very low, hoped Mr. Rivers was well!

"Let it go so," whispered 'Lena, as she saw her father about to speak.

Mr. Graham complied, and then observing how anxiously his daughter's eyes sought the doorway, whenever a footstep was heard, he asked Mrs. Aldergrass for Mr. Bellmont, saying they would like to see him, if he had returned.

Quickly going downstairs, Mrs. Aldergrass soon came back, announcing that "he'd paid his bill and gone off."

"Gone!" said Mr. Graham. "There must be some mistake. I will go down and inquire."

With his hand in his pocket grasping the purse containing the gold, Uncle Timothy told all he knew, adding, that "'twan't noways likely but he'd come back agin, for he'd left things in his room to the vally of five or six dollars."

Upon reflection, Mr. Graham concluded so, too, and returning to 'Lena, he sat by her all day, soothing her with assurances that Durward would surely come back, as there was no possible reason for his leaving them so abruptly. As the day wore away and the night came on he seemed less sure, while even Uncle Timothy began to fidget, and when in the evening a young pettifogger, who had recently hung out his shingle on Laurel Hill, came in, he asked him, in a low tone, "if, under the present governor, they hung folks on circumstantial evidence alone."

"Unquestionably, for that is sometimes the best kind of evidence," answered the sprig of the law, taking out some little ivory tablets and making a charge against Uncle Timothy for professional advice!

"But if one of my boarders, who has lots of money, goes off in broad daylight and is never heard of agin, would that be any sign he was murdered--by the landlord?" continued Uncle Timothy, beginning to think there might be a worse law than the Maine liquor law.

"That depends upon the previous character of the landlord," answered the lawyer, making another entry, while Uncle Timothy, brightening up, exclaimed, "I shall stand the racket, then, for my character is tip-top."

In the morning Mr. Graham announced his intention of going in quest of Durward, and with a magnanimity quite praiseworthy, Uncle Timothy offered his hoss *and wagon "for nothin', provided Mr. Graham would leave his watch as a guaranty against* his runnin' off!"

Just as Mr. Graham was about to start, a horseman rode up, saying he had come from Canandaigua at the request of a Mr. Bellmont, who wished him to bring letters for Mr. Graham and Miss Rivers.

"And where is Mr. Bellmont?" asked Mr. Graham, to which the man replied, that he took the six o'clock train the night before, saying, further, that his manner was so strange as to induce a suspicion of insanity on the part of those who saw him.

Taking the package, Mr. Graham repaired to 'Lena's room, giving her her letter, and then reading his, which was full of bitterness, denouncing him as a villain and cautioning him, as he valued his life, never again to cross the track of his outraged step-son.

"You have robbed me," he wrote, "of all I hold most dear, and while I do not censure her the less, I blame you the more, for you are older in experience, older in years, and ten-fold older in sin, and I know you must have used every art your foul nature could suggest, ere you won my lost 'Lena from the path of rectitude."

In the utmost astonishment Mr. Graham looked up at 'Lena, who had fainted.

It was long ere she returned to consciousness, and then her fainting fit was followed by another more severe, if possible, than the first, while in speechless agony Mr. Graham hung over her.

"I killed the mother, and now I am killing the child," thought he.

But at last 'Lena seemed better, and taking from the pillow the crumpled note, she passed it toward her father, bidding him read it. It was as follows;

"MY LOST 'LENA: By this title it seems appropriate for me to call you, for you are more surely lost to me than you would be were this summer sun shining upon your grave. And, 'Lena, believe me when I say I would rather, far rather, see you dead than the guilty thing you are, for then your memory would be to me as a holy, blessed influence, leading me on to a better world, where I could hope to greet you as my spirit bride. But now, alas! how dark the cloud which shrouds you from my sight.

"Oh, 'Lena, 'Lena, how could you deceive me thus, when I thought you so pure and innocent, when even now, I would willingly lay down my life could that save you from ruin.

"Do you ask what I mean? I have only to refer you to what this morning took place between you and the vile man I once called father, and whom I believed to be the soul of truth and honor. With a heart full of tenderness toward you, I was hastening to your side, when a scene met my view which stilled the beatings of my pulse and curdled the very blood in my veins, I saw you throw your arms around his **neck--the husband of** my **mother. I saw you lay your head upon his bosom. I heard him as he called you** dearest, and said you would never be parted again!

"You know all that has passed heretofore, and can you wonder that my worst fears are now confirmed? God knows how I struggled against those doubts, which were nearly removed, when, by the evidence of my own eyesight, uncertainty was made sure.

"And now, my once loved, but erring 'Lena, farewell. I am going away--whither, I know not, care not, so that I never hear your name coupled with disgrace. Another reason why I go, is that the hot blood of the south burns too fiercely in my veins to suffer me to meet your destroyer and not raise my hand against him. When this reaches you, I shall be far away. But what matters it to you? And yet, 'Lena, there will come a time when you'll remember one who, had you remained true to yourself, would have devoted his life to make you happy, for I know I am not indifferent to you. I have lead it in your speaking eye, and in the childlike confidence with which you would yield to me when no one else could control your wild ravings.

"But enough of this. Time hastens, and I must say farewell--farewell forever--my lost, lost 'Lena!

"DURWARD."

Gradually as Mr. Graham read, he felt a glow of indignation at Durward's hastiness. "Rash boy! he might at least have spoken with me," said he, as he finished the letter, but 'Lena would hear no word of censure against him. She did not blame him. She saw it all, understood it all, and as she recalled the contents of his letter, her own heart sadly echoed, "lost forever."

As well as he was able, Mr. Graham tried to comfort her, but in spite of his endeavors, there was still at her heart the same dull, heavy pain, and most anxiously Mr. Graham watched her, waiting impatiently for the time when she would be able to start for home, as he hoped a change of place and scene would do much toward restoring both her health and spirits. Soon after his arrival at Laurel Hill, Mr. Graham had written to Mr. Livingstone, telling him what he had before told his wife, and adding, "Of course, my daughter's home will in future be with me, at Woodlawn, where I shall be happy to see yourself and family at any time."

This part of the letter he showed to 'Lena, who, after reading it, seemed for a long time absorbed in thought.

"What is it, darling? Of what are you thinking?" Mr. Graham asked, at length, and 'Lena, taking the hand which he had laid gently upon her forehead, replied, "I am thinking of poor grandmother. She is not happy, now, at Maple Grove. She will be more unhappy should I leave her, and if you please, I would rather stay there with her. I can see you every day."

"Do you suppose me cruel enough to separate you from your grandmother?" interrupted Mr. Graham. "No, no, I am not quite so bad as that. Woodlawn is large--there are rooms enough--and grandma shall have her choice, provided it is a reasonable one."

"And your wife--Mrs. Graham? What will she say?" timidly inquired 'Lena, involuntarily shrinking from the very thought of coming in contact with the little lady who had so recently come up before her in the new and formidable aspect of stepmother!

Mr. Graham did not know himself what she would say, neither did he care. The fault of his youth once confessed, he felt himself a new man, able to cope with almost anything, and if in the future his wife objected to what he knew to be right, it would do her no good, for henceforth he was to rule his own house. Some such thoughts passed through his mind, but it would not be proper, he knew, to express himself thus to 'Lena, so he laughingly replied, "Oh, we'll fix that, easily enough."

At the time he wrote to Mr. Livingstone, he had also sent a letter to his wife, announcing his safe return from Europe, and saying that he should be at home as soon as 'Lena's health would admit of her traveling. Not wishing to alarm her unnecessarily, he merely said of Durward, that he had found him at Laurel Hill. To this letter Mrs. Graham replied immediately, and with a far better grace than her husband had expected. Very frankly she confessed the unkind part she had acted toward 'Lena, and while she said she was sorry, she also spoke of the reaction which had taken place in the minds of Lena's friends, who, she said, would gladly welcome her back,

The continued absence of Durward was now the only drawback to 'Lena's happiness, and with a comparatively light heart, she began to anticipate her journey home. Most liberally did Mr. Graham pay for both himself and 'Lena, and Uncle Timothy, as he counted the shining coin, dropping it upon the table to make sure it was not bogus, felt quite reconciled to his recent loss of fifty dollars. Jerry, the driver, was also generously rewarded for his kindness to the stranger-girl, and just before he left, Mr. Graham offered to make him his chief overseer, if he would accompany him to Kentucky.

"You are just the man I want," said he, "and I know you'll like it. What do you say?"

For the sake of occasionally seeing 'Lena, whom he considered as something more than mortal, Jerry would gladly have gone, but he was a staunch abolitionist, dyed in the wool, and scratching his head, he replied, "I'm obleeged to you, but I b'lieve I'd rather drive hosses *than* niggers!"

"Mebby you could run one on 'em off, and so make a little sumthin'," slyly whispered Uncle Timothy, his eyes always on the main chance, but it was no part of Jerry's creed to make anything, and as 'Lena at that moment appeared, he beat a precipitate retreat, going out behind the church, where he watched the departure of his southern friends, saying afterward, to Mrs. Aldergrass, who chided him for his conduct, that "he never could bid nobody good-bye, he was so darned tender-hearted!"

CHAPTER XXXV.
EXCITEMENT AT MAPLE GROVE.

Lena been gone four weeks and father never stirred a peg after her! That is smart, I must say. Why didn't you let me know it before!" exclaimed John Jr., as he one morning unexpectedly made his appearance at Maple grove. During his absence Carrie had been his only correspondent, and for some reason or other she delayed telling him of 'Lena's flight until quite recently. Instantly forgetting his resolution of not returning for a year, he came home with headlong haste, determining to start immediately after his cousin.

"I reckon if you knew all that has been said about her, you wouldn't feel quite so anxious to get her back," said Carrie. "For my part, I feel quite relieved at her absence."

"Shut up your head," roared John 'Jr. "'Lena is no more guilty than you. By George, I most cried when I heard how nobly she worked to save Anna from old Baldhead. And this is her reward! Gracious Peter! I sometimes wish there wasn't a woman in the world!"

"If they'd all marry you, there wouldn't be long!" retorted Carrie.

"You've said it now, haven't you?" answered John Jr., while his father suggested that they stop quarreling, adding, as an apology for his own neglect, that Durward had gone after 'Lena, who was probably at Mr. Everett's, and that he himself had advertised in all the principal papers.

"Just like Bellmont! He's a fine fellow and deserves 'Lena, if anybody does," exclaimed John Jr., while Carrie chimed in, "Pshaw! I've no idea he's gone for her. Why, they've hardly spoken for several months, and besides that, Mrs. Graham will never suffer him to marry one of so low origin."

"The deary me!" said John Jr., mimicking his sister's manner, "how much lower is her origin than yours?"

Carrie's reply was prevented by the appearance of her grandmother, who, hearing that John Jr. was there, had hobbled in to see him. Perfectly rational on all other subjects, Mrs. Nichols still persisted in saying of 'Lena, that she had killed her, and now, when her first greeting with John Jr. was over, she whispered in his ear, "Have they told you 'Lena was dead? She is--I killed her--it says so here," and she handed him the almost worn-out note which she constantly carried with her. Rough as he seemed at times, there was in John Jr.'s nature many a tender spot, and when he saw the look of childish imbecility on his grandmother's face, he pressed his strong arm around her, and a tear actually dropped upon her gray hair as he told her 'Lena was not dead--he was going to find her and bring her home. At that moment old Caesar, who had been to the post-office, returned, bringing Mr. Graham's letter, which had just arrived.

"That's Mr. Graham's handwriting," said Carrie; glancing at the superscription. "Perhaps he knows something of 'Lena!" and she looked meaningly at her mother, who, with a peculiar twist of her mouth, replied, "Very likely."

"You are right. He does know something of her," said Mr. Livingstone, as he finished reading the letter. "She is with him at a little village called Laurel Hill, somewhere in New York."

"There! I told you so. Poor Mrs. Graham. It will kill her. I must go and see her immediately," exclaimed Mrs. Livingstone, settling herself back quite composedly in her chair, while Carrie, turning to her brother, asked "what he thought of 'Lena now."

"Just what I always did," he replied. "There's fraud somewhere. Will you let me see that, sir?" advancing toward his father, who, placing the letter in his hand, walked to the window to hide the varied emotions of his face.

Rapidly John Jr. perused it, comprehending the whole then, when it was finished, he seized his hat, and throwing it up in the air, shouted, "Hurrah! Hurrah for Miss 'Lena Rivers Graham, daughter of the Honorable Harry Rivers Graham. I was never so glad in my life. Hurrah!" and again the hat went up, upsetting in its descent a costly vase, the fragments of which followed in the direction of the hat, as the young man capered about the room, perfectly insane with joy.

"Is the boy crazy?" asked Mrs. Livingstone, catching him by the coat as he passed her, while Carrie attempted to snatch the letter from his hand.

"Crazy?--yes," said he. "Who do you think 'Lena's father is? No less a person than Mr. Graham himself. Now taunt her again, Cad, with her low origin, if you like. She isn't coming here to live any more. She's going to Woodlawn. She'll marry Durward, while you'll be a cross, dried-up old maid, eh, Cad?" and he chucked her under the chin, while she began to cry, bidding him let her alone.

"What do you mean?" interposed Mrs. Livingstone, trembling lest it might be true.

"I will read the letter and you can judge for yourself," replied John.

Both Carrie and her mother were too much astonished to utter a syllable, while, in their hearts, each hoped it would prove untrue. Bending forward, grandma had listened eagerly, her dim eye lighting up as she occasionally caught the meaning of what she heard; but she could not understand it at once, and turning to her son, she said, "What is it, John? what does it mean?"

As well as they could, Mr. Livingstone and John Jr. explained it to her, and when at length she comprehended it, in her own peculiar way she exclaimed, "Thank God that 'Leny is a lady, at last--as good as the biggest on 'em. Oh, I wish Helleny had lived to know who her husband was. Poor critter! Mebby he'll give me money to go back and see the old place, once more, afore I die."

"If he don't I will," said Mr. Livingstone, upon which his wife, who had not spoken before, wondered "where he'd get it."

By this time Carrie had comforted herself with the assurance that as 'Lena was now Durward's sister, he would not, of course, marry her, and determining to make the best of it, she replied to her brother, who rallied her on her crestfallen looks, that he was greatly mistaken, for "she was as pleased as any one at 'Lena's good fortune, but it did not follow that she must make a fool of herself, as some others did."

The closing part of this remark was lost on John Jr., who had left the room. In the first excitement, he had thought "how glad Nellie will be," and acting, as he generally did, upon impulse, he now ordered his horse, and dashing off at full speed, as usual, surprised Nellie, first, with his sudden appearance, second, with his announcement of 'Lena's parentage, and third, by an offer of himself!

"It's your destiny," said he, "and it's of no use to resist. What did poor little

Meb die for, if it wasn't to make room for you. So you may as well say yes first as last. I'm odd, I know, but you can fix me over. I'll do exactly what you wish me to. Say yes, Nellie, won't you ?"

And Nellie did say yes, wondering, the while, it ever before woman had such wooing. We think not, for never was there another John Jr.

"I have had happiness enough for one day," said he, kissing her blushing cheek and hurrying away.

As if every hitherto neglected duty were now suddenly remembered, he went straight from Mr. Douglass's to the marble factory, where he ordered a costly stone for the little grave on the sunny slope, as yet unmarked save by the tall grass and rank weeds which grew above it.

"What inscription will you have?" asked the engraver. John Jr. thought for a moment, and then replied; "Simply 'Mabel.' Nothing more or less; that tells the whole story," and involuntarily murmuring to himself, "Poor little Meb, I wish she knew how happy I am," he started for home, where he was somewhat surprised to find Mrs. Graham.

She had also received a letter from her husband, and deeming secrecy no longer advisable, had come over to Maple Grove, where, to her great satisfaction, she found that the news had preceded her. Feeling sure that Mrs. Graham must feel greatly annoyed, both Carrie and her mother began, at first, to act the part of consolers, telling her it might not be true, after all, for perhaps it was a ruse of Mr. Graham's to cover some deep-laid, scheme. But for once in her life Mrs. Graham did well, and to their astonishment, replied, "Oh, I hope not, for you do not know how I long for the society of a daughter, and as Mr. Graham's child I shall gladly welcome 'Lena home, trying, if possible, to overlook the vulgarity of her family friends!"

Though wincing terribly, neither Mrs. Livingstone nor her daughter were to be outgeneraled. If Mrs. Graham could so soon change her tactics, so could they, and for the next half hour they lauded 'Lena to the skies. They had always liked her--particularly Mrs. Livingstone--who said, "If allowed to speak my mind, Mrs. Graham, I must say that I have felt a good deal pained by those reports which you put in circulation."

"I put reports in circulation!" retorted Mrs. Graham. "What do you mean? It was yourself, madam, as I can prove by the whole neighborhood!"

The war of words was growing sharper and more personal, when John Jr.'s appearance put an end to it, and the two ladies, thinking they might as well be friends as enemies, introduced another topic of conversation, soon after which Mrs. Graham took her leave. Pausing in the doorway, she said, "Would it afford you any gratification to be at Woodlawn when 'Lena arrives?"

Knowing that, under the circumstances, it would look better, Mrs. Livingstone said "yes," while Carrie, thinking Durward would be there, made a similar reply, saying "she was exceedingly anxious to see her cousin."

"Very well. I will let you know when I expect her," said Mrs. Graham, curtsying herself from the room.

"Spell Toady, Cad," whispered John Jr., and with more than her usual quickness, Carrie replied, by doing as he desired.

"That'll do," said he, as he walked off to the back yard, where he found the younger portion of the blacks engaged in a rather novel employment for them.

The news of 'Lena's good fortune had reached the kitchen, causing much excitement, for she was a favorite there.

"'Clar for't," said Aunt Milly, "we orto have a bonfire. It won't hurt nothin' on the brick pavement."

Accordingly, as it was now dark, the children were set at work gathering blocks, chips, sticks, dried twigs, and leaves, and by the time John Jr. appeared, they had collected quite a pile. Not knowing how he would like it, they all took to their heels, except Thomas Jefferson, who, having some of his mother's spirit, stood his ground, replying, when asked what they were about, that they were "gwine to celebrate Miss 'Lena." Taking in the whole fun at once, John Jr. called out, "Good! come back here, you scapegraces."

Scarcely had he uttered these words, when from behind the lye-leach, the smoke-house and the trees, emerged the little darkies, their eyes and ivories shining with the expected frolic. Taught by John Jr., they hurrahed at the top of their voices when the flames burst up, and one little fellow, not yet able to talk plain, made his bare, shining legs fly like drumsticks as he shouted, "Huyah for Miss 'Leny Yivers Gayum----"

"Bellmont, too, say," whispered John Jr., as he saw Carrie on the back piazza.

"Bellmont, too, say," yelled the youngster, leaping so high as to lose his balance.

Rolling over the green-sward like a ball, he landed at the feet of Carrie, who, spurning him as she would a toad, went back to the parlor, where for more than an hour she cried from pure vexation.

CHAPTER XXXVI.
ARRIVAL AT WOODLAWN.

It was a warm September night at Woodlawn. The windows were open, and through the richly-wrought curtains the balmy air of evening was stealing, mingling its delicious perfume of flowers without with the odor of those which drooped from the many costly vases which adorned the handsome parlors. Lamps were burning, casting a mellow light over the gorgeous furniture, while in robes of snowy white the mistress of the mansion flitted from room to room, a little nervous, a little fidgety, and, without meaning to be so, a little cross. For more than two hours she had waited for her husband, delaying the supper, which the cook, quite as anxious as herself, pronounced spoiled by the delay.

According to promise the party from Maple Grove had arrived, with the exception of John Jr., who had generously remained with his grandmother, she having been purposely omitted in the invitation. From the first, Mrs. Graham had decided that Mrs. Nichols should never live at Woodlawn, and she thought it proper to have it understood at once. Accordingly, as she was conducting Mrs. Livingstone and Carrie to 'Lena's room, she casually remarked, "I've made no provision for Mrs. Nichols, except as an occasional visitor, for of course she will remain with her son. She is undoubtedly much attached to your family, and will be happier there!"

"This 'Lena's!" interrupted Carrie, ere her mother had time to reply. "It's the very best chamber in the house--Brussels carpets, marble and rosewood furniture, damask curtains. Why, she'll hardly know how to act," she continued, half unconsciously, as she gazed around the elegant apartment, which, with one of her unaccountable freaks, Mrs. Graham had fitted up with the utmost taste.

"Yes, this is Lena's," said Mrs. Graham, complacently. "Will it compare at all with her chamber at Maple Grove? I do not wish it to seem inferior!"

Carrie bit her lip, while her mother very coolly replied, "Ye-es, on the whole quite as good, perhaps better, as some of the furniture is new!"

"Have I told you," continued Mrs. Graham, bent on tormenting them,--"have I told you that we are to spend the winter in New Orleans, where 'Lena will of course be the reigning belle? You ought to be there, dear," laying her hand on Carrie's shoulder. "It would be so gratifying to you to witness the sensation she will create!"

"Spiteful old thing--she tries to insult us," thought Carrie, her heart swelling with bitterness toward the ever-hated 'Lena, whose future life seemed so bright and joyous.

The sound of wheels was now heard, and the ladies reached the lower hall just as the carriage, which had been sent to the station at Midway, drove up at a side door. Carrie's first thought was for Durward, and shading her eyes with her hand, she looked anxiously out. But only Mr. Graham alighted, gently lifting out his daughter, who was still an invalid.

"Mighty careful of her," thought Mrs. Livingstone, as in his arms he bore her up the marble steps.

Depositing her in their midst, and placing his arm around her, he said, turning to his wife, "Lucy, this is my daughter. Will you receive and love her as such, for my sake?"

In a moment 'Lena's soft, white hand lay in the fat, chubby one of Mrs. Graham, who kissed her pale cheek, calling her "'Lena," and saying "she was welcome to Woodlawn."

Mrs. Livingstone and Carrie now pressed forward, overwhelming her with caresses, telling her how badly they had felt at her absence, chiding her for running away, calling her a naughty puss, and perfectly bewildering her with their new mode of conduct. Mr. Livingstone's turn came next, but he neither kissed nor caressed her, for that was not in keeping with his nature, but very, very tenderly he looked into her eyes, as he said, "You know, 'Lena, that I am glad--most glad for you."

Unostentatious as was this greeting, 'Lena felt that there was more sincerity in it than all that had gone before, and the tears gushed forth involuntarily. Mentally styling her, the one "a baby," and the other "a fool," Mrs. Livingstone and Carrie returned to the parlor, while Mrs. Graham, calling a servant, bade her show 'Lena to her room.

"Hadn't you better go up and assist your cousin," whispered Mrs. Livingstone to Carrie, who forthwith departed, knocking at the door, an act of politeness she had never before thought it necessary to offer 'Lena. But she was an heiress, now, fully, yes, more than equal, and that made a vast difference.

"I came to see if I could render you any service," she said in answer to 'Lena's look of inquiry.

"No I thank you," returned 'Lena, beginning to get an inkling of the truth. "You know I'm accustomed to waiting upon myself, and if I want anything, Drusa can assist me. I've only to change my soiled dress and smooth my hair," she continued, as she shook out her long and now rather rough tresses.

"What handsome hair you've got," said Carrie, taking one of the curls in her hand. "I'd forgotten it was so beautiful. Hasn't it improved during your absence?"

"A course of fever is not usually very beneficial to one's hair, I believe," answered 'Lena, as she proceeded to brush and arrange her wavy locks, which really had lost some of their luster.

Foiled in her attempt at toadyism, Carrie took another tack. Looking 'Lena in the face, she said, ^What is it? I can't make it out, but--but somehow you've changed, you don't look so--so----"

"So well you would say, I suppose," returned 'Lena, laughingly, "I've grown thin, but I hope to improve by and by."

Drusa glanced at the two girls as they stood side by side, and her large eyes sparkled as she thought her young mistress "a heap the best lookin' now ."

By this time Carrie had thought to ask for Durward. Instantly 'Lena turned whiter, if possible, than she was before, and in an unsteady voice she replied, that "she did not know."

"Not know!" repeated Carrie, her own countenance brightening visibly. "Haven't you seen him? Wasn't he at that funny, out-of-the-way place, where you were?"

"Yes, but he left before I saw him," returned 'Lena, her manner plainly indicating that there was something wrong.

Carrie's spirits rose. There was a chance for her, and on their way downstairs she laughed and chatted so familiarly, that 'Lena wondered if it could be the same haughty girl who had seldom spoken to her except to repulse or command her. The supper-bell rang just as they reached the parlor, and Mr. Graham, taking 'Lena on his arm, led the way to the dining-room, where the entire silver tea-set had been brought out, in honor of the occasion.

"Hasn't 'Lena changed, mother?" said Carrie, feeling hateful, and knowing no better way of showing it "Hasn't her sickness changed her?"

"It has made her grow old; that's all the difference I perceive," returned Mrs. Livingstone, satisfied that she'd said the thing which she knew would most annoy herself.

"How old are you, dear?" asked Mrs. Graham, leaning across the table.

"Eighteen," was 'Lena's answer, to which Mrs. Graham replied, "I thought so. Three years younger than Carrie, I believe."

"Two, only two," interrupted Mrs. Livingstone, while Carrie exclaimed, "Horrors! How old do you take me to be?"

Adroitly changing the conversation, Mrs. Graham made no reply, and soon after they rose from the table. Scarcely had they returned to the parlor, when John Jr. was announced. "He had," he said, "got his grandmother to sleep and put her to bed, and now he had come to pay his respects to Miss Graham!"

Catching her in his arms, he exclaimed, "Little girl! I'm as much delighted with your good fortune as I should b had it happened to myself. But where is Bellmont?" he continued, looking about the room.

Mr. Graham replied she that was was not there.

"Not here?" repeated John Jr. "What have you done with him, 'Lena?"

Lifting her eyes, full of tears, to her cousin's face, 'Lena said, softly, "Please don't talk about it now."

"There's something wrong," thought John Jr. "I'll bet I'll have to shoot that dog yet."

'Lena longed to pour out her troubles to some one, and knowing she could confide in John Jr., she soon found an opportunity of whispering to him, "Come tomorrow, and I will tell you all about it."

Between ten and eleven the company departed, Mrs. Livingstone and Carrie taking a most affectionate leave of 'Lena, urging her not to fail of coming over the next day, as they should be expecting her. The ludicrous expression of John Jr.'s face was a sufficient interpretation of his thoughts, as whispering aside to 'Lena, he said, "I can't do it justice if I try!"

The next morning Mr. Graham got out his carriage to carry 'Lena to Maple Grove, asking his wife to accompany them. But she excused herself, on the plea of a headache, and they set off without her. The meeting between 'Lena and her grandmother was affecting, and Carrie, in order to sustain the character she had assumed, walked to the window, to hide her emotions, probably--at least John Jr. thought so, for with the utmost gravity he passed her his silk pocket handkerchief! When the first transports of her interview with 'Lena were over, Mrs. Nichols fastened herself upon Mr. Graham, while John Jr. invited 'Lena to the garden, where he claimed from her the promised story, which she told him unreservedly.

"Oh, that's nothing, compared with my experience," said John Jr., plucking at the rich, purple grapes which hung in heavy clusters above his head. "That's easily settled. I'll go after Durward myself, and bring him back, either dead or alive--the latter if possible, the former if necessary. So cheer up. I've faith to believe that you and Durward will be married about the same time that Nellie and I are. We are engaged--did I tell you?"

Involuntarily 'Lena's eyes wandered in the direction of the sunny slope and the little grave, as yet but nine months made.

"I know what you think," said John Jr. rather testily, "but hang me if I can help it. Meb was never intended for me, except by mother. I suppose there is in the world somebody for whom she was made, but it wasn't I, and that's the reason she died. I am sorry as anybody, and every night in my life I think of poor Meb, who loved me so well, and who met with so poor a return. I've bought her some gravestones, though," he continued, as if that were an ample atonement for the past.

While they were thus occupied, Mr. Graham was discussing with Mrs. Nichols the propriety of her removing to Woodlawn.

"I shan't live long to trouble anybody," said she when asked if she would like to go, "and I'm nothin' without 'Leny."

So it was arranged that she should go with him, and when 'Lena returned to the house, she found her grandmother in her chamber, packing up, preparatory to her departure.

"We'll have to come agin," said she, "for I've as much as two loads."

"Don't take them," interposed 'Lena. "You won't need them, and nothing will harm them here."

After a little, grandma was persuaded, and her last charge to Mrs. Livingstone and Carrie was, "that they keep the dum niggers from her things."

Habit with Mrs. Nichols was everything. She had lived at Maple Grove for years, and every niche and corner of her room she understood. She knew the blacks and they knew her, and ere she was half-way to Woodlawn, she began to wish she had not started. Politely, but coldly, Mrs. Graham received her, saying "I thought, perhaps, you would return with them to spend the day!" laying great emphasis on the last words, as if that, of course, was to be the limit of her visit Grandma understood it, and it strengthened her resolution of not remaining long.

"Miss Graham don't want to be pestered with me," said she to 'Lena, the first time they were alone, "and I don't mean that she shall be. 'Tilda is used to me, and she don't mind it now, so I shall go back afore long. You can come to see me every day, and once in a while I'll come here."

That afternoon a heavy rain came on, and Mrs. Graham remarked to Mrs. Nichols that "she hoped she was not homesick, as there was every probability of her being obliged to stay over night!" adding, by way of comfort, that "she was going to Frankfort the next day to make purchases for 'Lena, and would take her home."

Accordingly, the next morning Mrs. Livingstone was not very agreeably surprised by the return of her mother-in-law, who, Mrs. Graham said, "was so homesick they couldn't keep her."

That night when Mrs. Graham, who was naturally generous, returned from the city, she left at Maple Grove a large bundle for grandma, consisting of dresses, aprons, caps, and the like, which she had purchased as a sort or peace-offering, or reward, rather, for her having decamped so quietly from Woodlawn. But the poor old lady did not live to wear them. Both her mind and body were greatly impaired, and for two or three years she had been failing gradually. There was no particular disease, but a general breaking up of the springs of life, and a few weeks after 'Lena's arrival at Woodlawn,, they made another grave on the sunny slope, and Mabel no longer slept alone.

CHAPTER XXXVII.
DURWARD.

From place to place and from scene to scene Durward had hurried, caring nothing except to forget, if possible, the past, and knowing not where he was going, until he at last found himself in Richmond, Virginia. This was his mother's birthplace, and as several of her more distant relatives were still living here, he determined to stop for awhile, hoping that new objects and new scenes would have some power to rouse him from the lethargy into which he had fallen. Constantly in terror lest he should hear of 'Lena's disgrace, which he felt sure would be published to the world, he had, since his departure from Laurel Hill, resolutely refrained from looking in a newspaper, until one morning some weeks after his arrival at Richmond.

Entering a reading-room, he caught up the Cincinnati Gazette, and after assuring himself by a hasty glance that it did not contain what he so much dreaded to see, he sat down to read it, paying no attention to the date, which was three or four weeks back. Accidentally he cast his eye over the list of arrivals at the Burnet House, seeing among them the names of "Mr. H. R. Graham, and Miss L. R. Graham, Woodford county, Kentucky!"

"Audacious! How dare they be so bold!" he exclaimed, springing to his feet and tearing the paper in fragments, which he scattered upon the floor.

"Considerable kind of uppish, 'pears to me," said a strange voice, having in its tone the nasal twang peculiar to a certain class of Yankees.

Looking up, Durward saw before him a young man in whose style of dress and freckled face we at once recognize Joel Slocum. Wearying of Cincinnati, as he had before done with Lexington, he had traveled at last to Virginia. Remembering to have heard that his grandmother's aunt had married, died, and left a daughter in Richmond, he determined, if possible, to find some trace of her. Accordingly, he had come on to that city, making it the theater of his daguerrean operations. These alone not being sufficient to support him, he had latterly turned his attention to literary pursuits, being at present engaged in manufacturing a book after the Sam Slick order, which, to use his own expression, "he expected would have a thunderin' sale."

In order to sustain the new character which he had assumed, he came every day to the reading-room, tumbling over books and papers, generally carrying one of the former in his hand, affecting an utter disregard of his personal appearance, daubing his fingers with ink, wiping them on the pocket of his coat, and doing numerous other things which he fancied would stamp him a distinguished person.

On the morning of which we have spoken, Joel's attention was attracted toward Durward, whose daguerreotype he had seen at Maple Grove, and though he did not recognize the original, he fancied he might have met him before, and was about making his acquaintance, when Durward's action drew from him the remark we have mentioned. Thinking him to be some impertinent fellow, Durward paid him no attention, and was about leaving, when, hitching his chair a little nearer, Joel said, "Be you from Virginny?"

"No."

"From York state?"

"No."

"From Pennsylvany?"

"No."

"Mebby, then, you are from Kentucky?"

No answer.

"Be you from Kentucky?"

"Yes."

"Do you know Mr. Graham's folks?"

"Yes," said Durward, trembling lest the next should be something concerning his stepfather--but it was not.

Settling himself a little further back in the chair, Joel continued: "Wall, I calkerlate that I'm some relation to Miss Graham. Be you 'quainted with her?"

Durward knew that a relationship with Mrs. Graham also implied a relationship with himself, and feeling a little curious as well as somewhat amused, he replied, "Related to Mrs. Graham! Pray how?"

"Why, you see," said Joel, "that my grandmarm's aunt--she was younger than grandmarm, and was her aunt tew. Wall, she went off to Virginia to teach music, and so married a nabob--know what that is, I s'pose; she had one gal and died, and this gal was never heard from until I took it into my head to look her up, and I've found out that she was Lucy Temple. She married an Englishman, first--then a man from South Carolina, who is now livin' in Kentucky, between Versailles and Frankfort."

"What was your grandmother's aunt's name?" asked Durward.

"Susan Howard," returned Joel. "The Howards were a stuck-up set, grandmarm and all--not a bit like t'other side of the family. My mother's name was Scovandyke----"

"And yours?" interrupted Durward.

"Is Joel Slocum, of Slocumville, Massachusetts, at your service," said the young man, rising up and going through a most wonderful bow, which he always used on great occasions.

In a moment Durward knew who he was, and greatly amused, he said, "Can you tell me, Mr. Slocum, what relation this Lucy Temple, your great-great-aunt's daughter, would be to you?"

"My third cousin, of course," answered Joel. "I figgered that out with a slate and pencil."

"And her son, if she had one?"

"Would be my fourth cousin; no great connection, to be sure--but enough to brag on, if they happened to be smart!"

"Supposing I tell you what I am Lucy Temple's son?" said Durward, to which Joel, not the least suspicious, replied, "Wall, s'posin' you du, 'twon't make it so."

"But I am, really and truly," continued Durward. "Her first husband was a Bellmont, and I am Durward Bellmont, your fourth cousin, it seems."

"Jehosiphat! If this ain't curis," exclaimed Joel, grasping Durward's hand. "How do you du, and how is your marm. And do you know Helleny Rivers?"

Durward's brow darkened as he replied in the affirmative, while Joel continued: "We are from the same town, and used to think a sight of each other, but when

I seen her in Kentucky, I thought she'd got to be mighty toppin'. Mebby, though, 'twas only my notion."

Durward did not answer, and after a little his companion said, "I suppose you know I sometimes take pictures for a livin'. I'm goin' to my office now, and if you'll come with me I'll take yourn for nothin', bein' you're related."

Mechanically, and because he had nothing else to do, Durward followed the young man to his "office," which was a dingy, cheerless apartment in the fourth story of a crazy old building. On the table in the center of the room were several likenesses, which he carelessly examined. Coming at last to a larger and richer case, he opened it, but instantly it dropped from his hand, while an exclamation of surprise escaped his lips.

"What's the row, old feller," asked Joel, coming forward and picking up the picture which Durward had recognized as 'Lena Rivers.

"How came you by it?" said Durward eagerly, and with a knowing wink, Joel replied, "I know, and that's enough."

"But I must know, too. It is of the utmost importance that I know," said Durward, and after a moment's reflection, Joel answered "Wall, I don't s'pose it'll do any hurt if I tell you. When I was a boy I had a hankerin' for 'Leny, and I didn't get over it after I was grown, either, so a year or two ago I thought I'd go to Kentuck and see her. Knowin' how tickled she and Mrs. Nichols would be with a picter of their old home in the mountains, I took it for 'em and started. In Albany I went to see a family that used to live in Slocumville. The woman was a gal with 'Leny's mother, and thought a sight of her. Wall, in the chamber where they put me to sleep, was an old portrait, which looked so much like 'Leny that in the mornin' I asked whose it was, and if you b'lieve me, 'twas 'Leny's mother! You know she married, or thought she married, a southern rascal, who got her portrait taken and then run off, and the picter, which in its day was an expensive one, was sold to pay up. A few years afterward, Miss Rice, the woman I was tellin' you about, came acrost it, and bought it for a little or nothin' to remember Helleny Nichols by. Thinks to me, nothin' can please 'Leny better than a daguerreotype of her mother, so I out with my apparatus and took it. But when I come to see that they were as nigh alike as two peas, I hated to give it up, for I thought it would be almost as good as lookin' at 'Leny. So I kept it myself, but I don't want her to know it, for she'd be mad."

"Did you ever take a copy of this for any one?" asked Durward, a faint light beginning to dawn upon him.

"What a feller to hang on," answered Joel, "but bein' I've started, I'll go it and tell the hull. One morning when I was in Lexington, a gentleman came in, calling himself Mr. Graham, and saying he wanted a copy of an old mountain house which he had seen at Mr. Livingstone's. Whilst I was gettin' it ready, he happened to come acrost this one, and what is the queerest of all, he like to fainted away. I had to throw water in his face and everything. Bimeby he cum to, and says he, 'Where did you get that?' I told him all about it, and then, layin' his head on the table, he groaned orfully, wipin' off the thumpinest great drops of sweat and kissin' the picter as if he was crazy.

"'Mebby you knew Helleny Nichols?' says I.

"'Knew her, yes,' says he, jumpin' up and walkin' the room as fast.

"All to once he grew calm, just as though nothin' had happened, and says he, 'I must have that or one jest like it.'

"At first I hesitated, for I felt kinder mean always about keepin' it, and I didn't want 'Leny to know I'd got it. I told him so, and he said nobody but himself should ever see it. So I took a smaller one, leavin' off the lower part of the body, as the dress is old-fashioned, you see. He was as tickled as a boy with a new top, and actually forgot to take the other one of the mountain house. Some months after, I came across him in Cincinnati. His wife was with him, and I thought then that she looked like Aunt Nancy. Wall, he went with me to my office, and said he wanted another daguerreotype, as he'd lost the first one. Now I'm, pretty good at figgerin', and I've thought that matter over until I've come to this conclusion--that man--was--'Lena's father--the husband or something of Helleny Nichols! But what ails you? Are you faintin', too," he exclaimed, as he saw the death-like whiteness which had settled upon Durward's face and around his mouth.

"Tell me more, everything you know," gasped Durward.

"I have told you all I know for certain," said Joel. "The rest is only guess-work, but it looks plaguy reasonable. 'Leny's father, I've heard was from South Car'lina----"

"So was Mr. Graham," said Durward, more to himself than to Joel, who continued, "And he's your step-father, ain't he--the husband of Lucy Temple, my cousin?"

Durward nodded, and as a customer just then came in, he arose to go, telling Joel he would see him again. Alone in his room, he sat down to think of the strange story he had heard. Gradually as he thought, his mind went back to the time when Mr. Graham first came home from Springfield. He was a little boy, then, five or six years of age, but he now remembered many things calculated to prove what he scarcely yet dared to hope. He recalled Mr. Graham's preparations to return, when he was taken suddenly ill. He knew that immediately atter his recovery he had gone northward. He remembered how sad he had seemed after his return, neglecting to play with him as had been his wont, and when to this he added Joel's story, together with the singularity of his father's conduct towards 'Lena, he could not fail to be convinced.

"She is innocent, thank heaven! I see it all now. Fool that I was to be so hasty," he exclaimed, his whole being seemed to undergo a sudden change as the joyous conviction flashed upon him.

In his excitement he forgot his promise of again seeing Joel Slocum, and ere the sun-setting he was far on his road home. Occasionally he felt a lingering doubt, as he wondered what possible motive his father could have had for concealment, but these wore away as the distance between himself and Kentucky diminished. As the train paused at one of the stations, he was greatly surprised at seeing John Jr. among the crowd gathered at the depot.

"Livingstone, Livingstone, how came you here?" shouted Durward, leaning from the open window.

The cars were already in motion, but at the risk of his life John Jr. bounded upon the platform, and was soon seated by the side of Durward.

"You are a great one, ain't you?" said he. "Here I've been looking for you all over Christendom, to tell you the news. You've got a new sister. Did you know it?"

"'Lena! Is it true? Is it 'Lena?" said Durward, and John replied by relating the particulars as far as he knew them, and ending by asking Durward if "he didn't think he was sold!"

"Don't talk," answered Durward. "I want to think, for I was never so happy in my life."

"Nor I either," returned John Jr. "So if you please you needn't speak to me, as I wish to think, too."

But John Jr. could not long keep still, he must tell his companion of his engagement with Nellie--and he did, falling asleep soon after, and leaving Durward to his own reflections.

CHAPTER XXXVIII.
CONCLUSION.

We hope the reader does not expect us to describe the meeting between Durward and 'Lena, for we have not the least, or, at the most, only a faint idea of what took place. We only know that it occurred in the summer-house at the foot of the garden, whither 'Lena had fled at the first intimation of his arrival, and that on her return to the house, after an interview of two whole hours, there were on her cheeks traces of tears, which the expression of her face said were not tears of grief.

"How do you like my daughter?" asked Mr. Graham, mischievously, at the same time laying his arm proudly about her neck.

"So well that I have asked her to become my wife, and she has promised to do so, provided we obtain your consent," answered Durward, himself throwing an arm around the blushing girl, who tried to escape, but he would not let her, holding her fast until his father's answer was given.

Then turning to Mrs. Graham, he said, "Now, mother, we will hear you."

Kind and affectionate as she tried to be toward 'Lena, Mrs. Graham had not yet fully conquered her olden prejudice, and had the matter been left wholly with herself, she would, perhaps, have chosen for her son a bride in whose veins no plebeian blood was flowing; but she well knew that her objections would have no weight, and she answered, that "she should not oppose him."

"Then it is settled," said he, "and four weeks from to-night I shall claim 'Lena for my own."

"No, not so soon after grandma's death," 'Lena said, and Durward replied:

"If grandma could speak, she would tell you not to wait!" but 'Lena was decided, and the most she would promise was, that in the spring she would think about it!

"Six months," said Durward, "I'll never wait so long!" but he forbore pressing her further on the subject, knowing that he should have her in the house with him, which would in a great measure relieve the tedium of waiting.

During the autumn, his devotion to 'Lena furnished Carrie with a subject for many ill-natured remarks concerning newly-engaged people.

"I declare," said she, one evening after the departure of Durward, 'Lena, and Nellie, who had been spending the day at Maple Grove, "I'm perfectly disgusted, and if this is a specimen, I hope I shall never be engaged."

"Don't give yourself a moment's uneasiness," retorted John Jr., "I've not the least idea that such a calamity will ever befall you, and years hence my grandchildren will read on some gravestone, 'Sacred to the memory of Miss Caroline Livingstone, aged 70. In single blessedness she lived--and in the same did die!'"

"You think you are cunning, don't you," returned Carrie, more angry than she was willing to admit.

She had received the news of Durward's engagement much better than could have been expected, and after a little she took to quoting and cousining 'Lena, while John Jr. seldom let an opportunity pass of hinting at the very recent date Of her admiration for Miss Graham.

Almost every day for several weeks after Durward's return, he looked for a visit from Joel Slocum, who did not make his appearance until some time toward the last of November. Then he came, claiming, and proving, his relationship with Mrs. Graham, who was terribly annoyed, and who, it was rumored, hired him to leave!

During the winter, nothing of importance occurred, if we except the fact that a part of Mabel's fortune, which was supposed to have been lost, was found to be good, and that John Jr. one day unexpectedly found himself to be the lawful heir of fifty thousand dollars. Upon Mrs. Livingstone this circumstance produced a rather novel effect, renewing, in its original force, all her old affection for Mabel, who was now "our dear little Meb." Many were the comparisons drawn between Mrs. John Jr. No. 1, and Mrs. John Jr. No. 2, that was to be, the former being pronounced far more lady-like and accomplished than the latter, who, during her frequent visits at Maple Grove, continually startled her mother-in-law elect by her loud, ringing laugh, for Nellie was very happy. Her influence, too, over John Jr. became ere long, perceptible in his quiet, gentle manner, and his abstinence from the rude speeches which heretofore had seemed a part of his nature.

Mrs. Graham had proposed spending the winter in New Orleans, but to this Durward objected. He wanted 'Lena all to himself, he said, and as she seemed perfectly satisfied to remain where she was, the project was given up, Mrs. Graham contenting herself with anticipating the splendid entertainment she would give at the wedding, which was to take place about the last of March. Toward the first of January the preparations began, and if Carrie had never before felt a pang of envy, she did now, when she saw the elegant trousseau which Mr. Graham ordered for his daughter. But all such feelings must be concealed, and almost every day she rode over to Woodlawn, admiring this, going into ecstasies over that, and patronizingly giving her advice on all subjects, while all the time her heart was swelling with bitter disappointment. Having always felt so sure of securing Durward, she had invariably treated other gentlemen with such cool indifference that she was a favorite with but few, and as she considered these few her inferiors, she had more than once feared lest John Jr.'s prediction concerning the lettering on her tombstone should prove true!

"Anything but that," said she, dashing away her tears, as she thought how 'Lena had supplanted her in the affections of the only person she could ever love,

"Old Marster Atherton done want to see you in the parlor," said Corinda, putting her head in at the door.

Since his unfortunate affair with Anna, the captain had avoided Maple Grove, but feeling lonely at Sunnyside, he had come over this morning to call. Finding Mrs. Livingstone absent, he had asked for Carrie, who was so unusually gracious that he wondered he had never before discovered how greatly superior to her sister she was! All his favorite pieces were sung to him, and then, with the patience of a martyr, the young lady seated herself at the backgammon board, playing game after game, until she could scarcely tell her men from his. On his way home the captain fell into a curious train of reflections, while Carrie, when asked by Corinda, if "old marster was done gone," sharply reprimanded the girl, telling her "it was very impolite to call anybody old, particularly one so young as Captain Atherton!"

The next day the captain came again, and the next, and the next, until at last his former intimacy at Maple Grove seemed to be re-established. And all this time no one had an inkling of the true state of things, not even John Jr., who never dreamed it possible for his haughty sister, to grace Sunnyside as its mistress. "But stranger things than that had happened and were happening every day," Carrie reasoned, as she sat alone in her room, revolving the propriety of answering "Yes" to a note which the captain had that morning placed in her hand at parting. She looked at herself in the mirror. Her face was very fair, and as yet untouched by a single mark or line. She thought of him, bald, wrinkled, fat *and* forty-six!

"I'll never do it," she exclaimed. "Better live single all my days."

At this moment, the carriage of Mrs. Graham drew up, and from it alighted 'Lena, richly clad. The sight of her produced a reaction, and Carrie thought again. Captain Atherton was generous to a fault. He was able and willing to grant her slightest wish, and as his wife, she could compete with, if not outdo, 'Lena in the splendor of her surroundings. The pen was resumed, and Carrie wrote the words which sealed her destiny for life. This done, nothing could move her, and though her father entreated, her mother scolded, and John Jr. swore, it made no difference. "She was old enough to choose for herself," she said, "and she had done so."

When Mrs. Livingstone became convinced that her daughter was in earnest, she gave up the contest, taking sides with her. Like Durward, Captain Atherton was in a hurry, and it was decided that the wedding should take place a week before the time appointed for that of her cousin. Determining not to be outdone by Mrs. Graham, Mrs. Livingstone launched forth on a large scale, and there commenced between the two houses a species of rivalry extremely amusing to a looker on. Did Mrs. Graham purchase for 'Lena a costly silk, Mrs. Livingstone forthwith secured a piece of similar quality, but different pattern, for Carrie. Did Mrs. Graham order forty dollars' worth of confectionery, Mrs. Livingstone immediately increased her order to fifty dollars. And when it was known that Mrs. Graham had engaged a Louisville French cook at two dollars per day, Mrs. Livingstone sent to Cincinnati, offering three for one!

Carrie had decided upon a tour to Europe, and the captain had given his consent, when it was reported that Durward and 'Lena were also intending to sail for Liverpool. In this dilemma there was no alternative save a trip to California or the Sandwich Islands! The former was chosen, Captain Atherton offering to defray Mrs. Livingstone's expenses if she would accompany them. This plan Carrie warmly seconded, for she knew her mother's presence would greatly relieve her from the society of her husband, which was not as agreeable to her as it ought to have been. But Mr. Livingstone refused to let his wife go, unless Anna came home and stayed with him while she was gone.

He accordingly wrote to Anna, inviting her and Malcolm to be present at Carrie's wedding, purposely omitting the name of the bridegroom; and three days before the appointed time they came. It was dark when they arrived, and as they were not expected that night, they entered the house before any one was aware of their presence. John Jr. chanced to be in the hall, and the moment he saw Anna, he caught her in his arms, shouting so uproariously that his father and mother at once hastened to the spot.

"Will you forgive me, father?" Anna said, and Mr. Livingstone replied by clasping her to his bosom, while he extended his hand to Malcolm.

"Where's Carrie?" Anna said, and John Jr. replied, "In the parlor, with her future spouse. Shall I introduce you?"

So saying, he dragged her into the parlor, where she then recoiled in terror as she saw Captain Atherton.

"Oh, Carrie!" she exclaimed. "It cannot be----that I see you again!" she added, as she met her sister's warning look.

Another moment and they were in each other's arms weeping bitterly, the one that her sister should thus throw herself away, and the other, because she was wretched. It was but for an instant, however, and then Carrie was herself again. Playfully presenting Anna to the Captain, she said, "Ain't I good to take up with what you left!"

But no one smiled at this joke--the captain, least of all, and as Carrie glanced from him to Malcolm, she felt that her sister had made a happy choice. The next day 'Lena came, overjoyed to meet Anna, who more than any one else, rejoiced in her good fortune.

"You deserve it all," she said, when they were alone, "and if Carrie had one tithe of your happiness in store I should be satisfied."

But Carrie asked for no sympathy. "It was no one's business whom she married," she said; and so one pleasant night in the early spring, they decked her in her bridal robes, and then, white, cold, and feelingless as a marble statue, she laid her hand in Captain Atherton's, and took upon her the vows which made her his forever. A few days after the ceremony, Carrie began to urge their immediate departure for California.

"There was no need of further delay," she said. "No one cared to see 'Lena married. Weddings were stupid things, anyway, and her mother could just as well go one time as another."

At first Mrs. Livingstone hesitated, but when Carrie burst into a passionate fit of weeping, declaring "she'd kill herself if she had to stay much longer at Sunnyside and be petted by that old fool," she consented, and one week from the day of the marriage they started. In Carrie's eyes there was already a look of weary sadness, which said that the bitter tears were constantly welling up, while on her brow a shadow was resting, as if Sunnyside were a greater burden than she could bear. Alas, for a union without love! It seldom fails to end in misery, and thus poor Carrie found it. Her husband was proud of her, and, had she permitted, would have loved her after his fashion, but his affectionate advances were invariably repulsed, until at last he treated her with a cold politeness, far more endurable than his fawning attentions had been. She was welcome to go her own way, and he went his, each having in San Francisco their own suite of rooms, and setting up, as it were, a separate establishment. In this way they got on quite comfortably for a few weeks, at the end of which time Carrie took it into her capricious head to return to Maple Grove. She would never go back to Sunnyside, she said. And without a word of opposition the captain paid his bills, and started for Kentucky, where he left his wife at Maple Grove, she giving as a reason that "ma could not spare her yet."

Far different from this were the future prospects of Durward and 'Lena, who with perfect love in their hearts were married, a week after the departure of Captain Atherton for California. Very proudly Durward looked down upon her as he placed the first husband's kiss on her brow, and in the soft brown eyes, brimming with tears, which she raised to his face, there was a world of tenderness, telling that theirs was a union of hearts as well as hands.

The next night a small party assembled at the house of Mr. Douglass, in Frankfort, where Nellie was transformed into Nellie Livingstone. Perhaps it was the remembrance of the young girl to whom his vows had once before been plighted, that made John Jr. appear for a time as if he were in a dream. But the moment they rallied him upon the strangeness of his manner, he brightened up, saying that he was trying to get used to thinking that Nellie was really his. It had been decided that he should accompany Durward and 'Lena to Europe, and a day or two after his marriage he asked Mr. Everett to go too. Anna's eyes fairly danced with joy, as she awaited Malcolm's reply. But much as he would like to go, he could not afford it, and so he frankly said, kissing away the big tear which rolled down Anna's cheek.

With a smile John Jr. placed a sealed package in his sister's hand, saying to Malcolm, "I have anticipated this and provided for it. I suppose you are aware that Mabel willed me all her property, which contrary to our expectations, has proved to be considerable. I know I do not deserve a cent of it, but as she had no nearer relative than Mr. Douglass, I have concluded to use it for the comfort of his daughter and for the good of others. I want you and Anna to join us, and I've given her such a sum as will bear your expenses, and leave you more than you can earn dickering at law for three or four years. So, puss," turning to Anna, "it's all settled. Now hurrah for the sunny skies of France and Italy, I've talked with father about it, and he's willing to stay alone for the sake of having you go. Oh, don't thank me," he continued, as he saw them about to speak. "It's poor little Meb to whom you are indebted. She loved Anna, and would willingly have her money used for this purpose."

After a little reflection Malcolm concluded to accept John's offer, and a happier party never stepped on board a steamer than that which, on the 15th of April, sailed for Europe, which they reached in safety, being at the last accounts in Paris, where they were enjoying themselves immensely.

A few words more, and our story is told. Just as Mr. Livingstone was getting tolerably well suited with his bachelor life, he was one morning surprised by the return of his wife and daughter, the latter of whom, as we have before stated, took up her abode at Maple Grove. Almost every day the old captain rides over to see her, but he generally carries back a longer face than he brings. The bald spot on his head is growing larger, and to her dismay Carrie has discovered a "crow track" in the corner of her eye. Frequently, after a war of words with her mother, she announces her intention of returning to Sunnyside, but a sight of the captain is sufficient to banish all such thoughts. And thus she lives, that most wretched of all beings, an unloving and unloved wife.

During the absence of their children, Mr. and Mrs. Graham remain at Woodlawn, which, as it is the property of Durward, will be his own and 'Lena's home.

Jerry Langley has changed his occupation of driver for that of a brakeman on the railroad between Canandaigua and Niagara Falls.

In conclusion we will say of our old friend, Uncle Timothy, that he joined "the Hindews" as proposed, was nominated for constable, and, sure of success, bought an old gig for the better transportation of himself over the town. But alas for human hopes--if funded upon politics--the whole American ticket was defeated at Laurel Hill, since which time he has gone over to the Republicans, to whom he has sworn eternal allegiance.

www.bookjungle.com *email: sales@bookjungle.com fax: 630-214-0564 mail: Book Jungle PO Box 2226 Champaign, IL 61825*

The Codes Of Hammurabi And Moses
W. W. Davies

The discovery of the Hammurabi Code is one of the greatest achievements of archaeology, and is of paramount interest, not only to the student of the Bible, but also to all those interested in ancient history...

Religion ISBN: *1-59462-338-4*

Pages:132
MSRP $12.95

QTY

The Theory of Moral Sentiments
Adam Smith

This work from 1749. contains original theories of conscience amd moral judgment and it is the foundation for systemof morals.

Philosophy ISBN: *1-59462-777-0*

Pages:536
MSRP $19.95

QTY

Jessica's First Prayer
Hesba Stretton

In a screened and secluded corner of one of the many railway-bridges which span the streets of London there could be seen a few years ago, from five o'clock every morning until half past eight, a tidily set-out coffee-stall, consisting of a trestle and board, upon which stood two large tin cans, with a small fire of charcoal burning under each so as to keep the coffee boiling during the early hours of the morning when the work-people were thronging into the city on their way to their daily toil...

Pages:84

Childrens ISBN: *1-59462-373-2*

MSRP $9.95

QTY

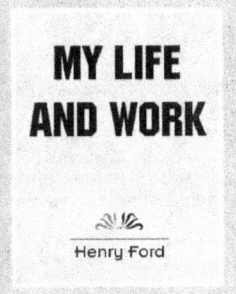

My Life and Work
Henry Ford

Henry Ford revolutionized the world with his implementation of mass production for the Model T automobile. Gain valuable business insight into his life and work with his own auto-biography... "We have only started on our development of our country we have not as yet, with all our talk of wonderful progress, done more than scratch the surface. The progress has been wonderful enough but..."

Pages:300

Biographies/ ISBN: *1-59462-198-5*

MSRP $21.95

QTY

The Art of Cross-Examination
Francis Wellman

QTY

I presume it is the experience of every author, after his first book is published upon an important subject, to be almost overwhelmed with a wealth of ideas and illustrations which could readily have been included in his book, and which to his own mind, at least, seem to make a second edition inevitable. Such certainly was the case with me; and when the first edition had reached its sixth impression in five months, I rejoiced to learn that it seemed to my publishers that the book had met with a sufficiently favorable reception to justify a second and considerably enlarged edition. ..

Reference   **ISBN:** *1-59462-647-2*

Pages:412

MSRP $19.95

On the Duty of Civil Disobedience
Henry David Thoreau

QTY

Thoreau wrote his famous essay, On the Duty of Civil Disobedience, as a protest against an unjust but popular war and the immoral but popular institution of slave-owning. He did more than write—he declined to pay his taxes, and was hauled off to gaol in consequence. Who can say how much this refusal of his hastened the end of the war and of slavery ?

Law   **ISBN:** *1-59462-747-9*

Pages:48

MSRP $7.45

Dream Psychology Psychoanalysis for Beginners
Sigmund Freud

QTY

Sigmund Freud, born Sigismund Schlomo Freud (May 6, 1856 - September 23, 1939), was a Jewish-Austrian neurologist and psychiatrist who co-founded the psychoanalytic school of psychology. Freud is best known for his theories of the unconscious mind, especially involving the mechanism of repression; his redefinition of sexual desire as mobile and directed towards a wide variety of objects; and his therapeutic techniques, especially his understanding of transference in the therapeutic relationship and the presumed value of dreams as sources of insight into unconscious desires.

Pages:196

Psychology   **ISBN:** *1-59462-905-6*

MSRP $15.45

The Miracle of Right Thought
Orison Swett Marden

QTY

Believe with all of your heart that you will do what you were made to do. When the mind has once formed the habit of holding cheerful, happy, prosperous pictures, it will not be easy to form the opposite habit. It does not matter how improbable or how far away this realization may see, or how dark the prospects may be, if we visualize them as best we can, as vividly as possible, hold tenaciously to them and vigorously struggle to attain them, they will gradually become actualized, realized in the life. But a desire, a longing without endeavor, a yearning abandoned or held indifferently will vanish without realization.

Pages:360

Self Help   **ISBN:** *1-59462-644-8*

MSRP $25.45

www.bookjungle.com *email: sales@bookjungle.com fax: 630-214-0564 mail: Book Jungle PO Box 2226 Champaign, IL 61825*

QTY

The Rosicrucian Cosmo-Conception Mystic Christianity *by **Max Heindel*** ISBN: *1-59462-188-8* **$38.95**
The Rosicrucian Cosmo-conception is not dogmatic, neither does it appeal to any other authority than the reason of the student. It is: not controversial, but is: sent forth in the, hope that it may help to clear... New Age/Religion Pages 646

Abandonment To Divine Providence *by Jean-Pierre de Caussade* ISBN: *1-59462-228-0* **$25.95**
"The Rev. Jean Pierre de Caussade was one of the most remarkable spiritual writers of the Society of Jesus in France in the 18th Century. His death took place at Toulouse in 1751. His works have gone through many editions and have been republished... Inspirational/Religion Pages 400

Mental Chemistry *by **Charles Haanel*** ISBN: *1-59462-192-6* **$23.95**
Mental Chemistry allows the change of material conditions by combining and appropriately utilizing the power of the mind. Much like applied chemistry creates something new and unique out of careful combinations of chemicals the mastery of mental chemistry... New Age Pages 354

The Letters of Robert Browning and Elizabeth Barret Barrett 1845-1846 vol II ISBN: *1-59462-193-4* **$35.95**
*by **Robert Browning** and **Elizabeth Barrett*** Biographies Pages 596

Gleanings In Genesis (volume I) *by **Arthur W. Pink*** ISBN: *1-59462-130-6* **$27.45**
Appropriately has Genesis been termed "the seed plot of the Bible" for in it we have, in germ form, almost all of the great doctrines which are afterwards fully developed in the books of Scripture which follow... Religion/Inspirational Pages 420

The Master Key *by **L. W. de Laurence*** ISBN: *1-59462-001-6* **$30.95**
In no branch of human knowledge has there been a more lively increase of the spirit of research during the past few years than in the study of Psychology, Concentration and Mental Discipline. The requests for authentic lessons in Thought Control, Mental Discipline and... New Age/Business Pages 422

The Lesser Key Of Solomon Goetia *by **L. W. de Laurence*** ISBN: *1-59462-092-X* **$9.95**
This translation of the first book of the "Lernegton" which is now for the first time made accessible to students of Talismanic Magic was done, after careful collation and edition, from numerous Ancient Manuscripts in Hebrew, Latin, and French... New Age/Occult Pages 92

Rubaiyat Of Omar Khayyam *by **Edward Fitzgerald*** ISBN:*1-59462-332-5* **$13.95**
Edward Fitzgerald, whom the world has already learned, in spite of his own efforts to remain within the shadow of anonymity, to look upon as one of the rarest poets of the century, was born at Bredfield, in Suffolk, on the 31st of March, 1809. He was the third son of John Purcell... Music Pages 172

Ancient Law *by **Henry Maine*** ISBN: *1-59462-128-4* **$29.95**
The chief object of the following pages is to indicate some of the earliest ideas of mankind, as they are reflected in Ancient Law, and to point out the relation of those ideas to modern thought. Religion/History Pages 452

Far-Away Stories *by **William J. Locke*** ISBN: *1-59462-129-2* **$19.45**
"Good wine needs no bush, but a collection of mixed vintages does. And this book is just such a collection. Some of the stories I do not want to remain buried for ever in the museum files of dead magazine-numbers an author's not unpardonable vanity..." Fiction Pages 272

Life of David Crockett *by **David Crockett*** ISBN: *1-59462-250-7* **$27.45**
"Colonel David Crockett was one of the most remarkable men of the times in which he lived. Born in humble life, but gifted with a strong will, an indomitable courage, and unremitting perseverance... Biographies/New Age Pages 424

Lip-Reading *by **Edward Nitchie*** ISBN: *1-59462-206-X* **$25.95**
Edward B. Nitchie, founder of the New York School for the Hard of Hearing, now the Nitchie School of Lip-Reading, Inc, wrote "LIP-READING Principles and Practice". The development and perfecting of this meritorious work on lip-reading was an undertaking... How-to Pages 400

A Handbook of Suggestive Therapeutics, Applied Hypnotism, Psychic Science ISBN: *1-59462-214-0* **$24.95**
*by **Henry Munro*** Health/New Age/Health/Self-help Pages 376

A Doll's House: and Two Other Plays *by **Henrik Ibsen*** ISBN: *1-59462-112-8* **$19.95**
Henrik Ibsen created this classic when in revolutionary 1848 Rome. Introducing some striking concepts in playwriting for the realist genre, this play has been studied the world over. Fiction/Classics/Plays 308

The Light of Asia *by **sir Edwin Arnold*** ISBN: *1-59462-204-3* **$13.95**
In this poetic masterpiece, Edwin Arnold describes the life and teachings of Buddha. The man who was to become known as Buddha to the world was born as Prince Gautama of India but he rejected the worldly riches and abandoned the reigns of power when... Religion/History/Biographies Pages 170

The Complete Works of Guy de Maupassant *by **Guy de Maupassant*** ISBN: *1-59462-157-8* **$16.95**
"For days and days, nights and nights, I had dreamed of that first kiss which was to consecrate our engagement, and I knew not on what spot I should put my lips..." Fiction/Classics Pages 240

The Art of Cross-Examination *by **Francis L. Wellman*** ISBN: *1-59462-309-0* **$26.95**
Written by a renowned trial lawyer, Wellman imparts his experience and uses case studies to explain how to use psychology to extract desired information through questioning. How-to/Science/Reference Pages 408

Answered or Unanswered? *by **Louisa Vaughan*** ISBN: *1-59462-248-5* **$10.95**
Miracles of Faith in China Religion Pages 112

The Edinburgh Lectures on Mental Science (1909) *by **Thomas*** ISBN: *1-59462-008-3* **$11.95**
This book contains the substance of a course of lectures recently given by the writer in the Queen Street Hall, Edinburgh. Its purpose is to indicate the Natural Principles governing the relation between Mental Action and Material Conditions... New Age/Psychology Pages 148

Ayesha *by **H. Rider Haggard*** ISBN: *1-59462-301-5* **$24.95**
Verily and indeed it is the unexpected that happens! Probably if there was one person upon the earth from whom the Editor of this, and of a certain previous history, did not expect to hear again... Classics Pages 380

Ayala's Angel *by **Anthony Trollope*** ISBN: *1-59462-352-X* **$29.95**
The two girls were both pretty, but Lucy who was twenty-one who supposed to be simple and comparatively unattractive, whereas Ayala was credited, as her Bombwhat romantic name might show, with poetic charm and a taste for romance. Ayala when her father died was nineteen... Fiction Pages 484

The American Commonwealth *by **James Bryce*** ISBN: *1-59462-286-8* **$34.45**
An interpretation of American democratic political theory. It examines political mechanics and society from the perspective of Scotsman James Bryce Politics Pages 572

Stories of the Pilgrims *by **Margaret P. Pumphrey*** ISBN: *1-59462-116-0* **$17.95**
This book explores pilgrims religious oppression in England as well as their escape to Holland and eventual crossing to America on the Mayflower, and their early days in New England... History Pages 268

www.bookjungle.com *email: sales@bookjungle.com fax: 630-214-0564 mail: Book Jungle PO Box 2226 Champaign, IL 61825*

QTY

The Fasting Cure *by Sinclair Upton*　　　　　　　　　ISBN: *1-59462-222-1*　**$13.95**
In the Cosmopolitan Magazine for May, 1910, and in the Contemporary Review (London) for April, 1910, I published an article dealing with my experiences in fasting. I have written a great many magazine articles, but never one which attracted so much attention... New Age/Self Help/Health Pages 164

Hebrew Astrology *by Sepharial*　　　　　　　　　　ISBN: *1-59462-308-2*　**$13.45**
In these days of advanced thinking it is a matter of common observation that we have left many of the old landmarks behind and that we are now pressing forward to greater heights and to a wider horizon than that which represented the mind-content of our progenitors... Astrology Pages 144

Thought Vibration or The Law of Attraction in the Thought World　　ISBN: *1-59462-127-6*　**$12.95**
by William Walker Atkinson　　　　　　　　　　　　　　　　Psychology/Religion Pages 144

Optimism *by Helen Keller*　　　　　　　　　　　　ISBN: *1-59462-108-X*　**$15.95**
Helen Keller was blind, deaf, and mute since 19 months old, yet famously learned how to overcome these handicaps, communicate with the world, and spread her lectures promoting optimism. An inspiring read for everyone... Biographies/Inspirational Pages 84

Sara Crewe *by Frances Burnett*　　　　　　　　　　ISBN: *1-59462-360-0*　**$9.45**
In the first place, Miss Minchin lived in London. Her home was a large, dull, tall one, in a large, dull square, where all the houses were alike, and all the sparrows were alike, and where all the door-knockers made the same heavy sound... Childrens/Classic Pages 88

The Autobiography of Benjamin Franklin *by Benjamin Franklin*　　ISBN: *1-59462-135-7*　**$24.95**
The Autobiography of Benjamin Franklin has probably been more extensively read than any other American historical work, and no other book of its kind has had such ups and downs of fortune. Franklin lived for many years in England, where he was agent... Biographies/History Pages 332

Name	
Email	
Telephone	
Address	
City, State ZIP	

☐ **Credit Card**　　　　　☐ **Check / Money Order**

Credit Card Number	
Expiration Date	
Signature	

Please Mail to:　Book Jungle
　　　　　　　　　PO Box 2226
　　　　　　　　　Champaign, IL 61825
or Fax to:　　　630-214-0564

ORDERING INFORMATION

web: *www.bookjungle.com*
email: *sales@bookjungle.com*
fax: *630-214-0564*
mail: *Book Jungle PO Box 2226 Champaign, IL 61825*
or PayPal *to sales@bookjungle.com*

Please contact us for bulk discounts

DIRECT-ORDER TERMS

**20% Discount if You Order
Two or More Books**
Free Domestic Shipping!
Accepted: Master Card, Visa,
Discover, American Express